Violet

Book One of

tara vanflower

VIOLENT VIOLET

ISBN: 0615870619
ISBN-13: 978-0615870618 (Lycium Music)

Suggested music accompaniment:

Lycia – Ionia, Estrella, a Day in the Stark Corner, Quiet Moments
Mike VanPortfleet – Beyond the Horizon Line
Tara Vanflower – my little fire~filled heart
Stone Breath – The Silver Skein Unwound, Lanterna Lucis Viriditatis
Faith and the Muse – Annwyn, Beneath the Waves, Vera Causa
Secondary Nerve
World of Skin
Swans – Filth, Soundtracks for the Blind
Death in June – Nada!
Current 93 – Swastikas for Noddy
Nitzer Ebb – Showtime
Exploited – Let's Start a War
The Cure – Disintegration, Pornography, The Top
Bauhaus – The Sky's Gone Out
Dark Muse - Beyond the Silver Wheel
Type O Negative – October Rust
Throbbing Gristle – Hamburger Lady
Moth Masque
Queen Adreena – Taxidermy
Arcana – Dark Age of Reason
Siouxsie & the Banshees - Join Hands, Juju
Ministry - The Mind is a Terrible Thing to Taste
Jane's Addiction - Nothing's Shocking
Godflesh – Streetcleaner
Black Mare
Sailors with Wax Wings
The Soft Moon
She Wants Revenge – She Wants Revenge
Dirge

VIOLENT VIOLET

To the characters who come to me in the sideways realm.

VIOLENT VIOLET

**For God has not given us a spirit of fear,
but of power, and of love and of a sound mind.**

2 Timothy 1:7 (NKJV)

VIOLENT VIOLET

1. WALKING BY BARKING DOGS

She felt so alive in the darkness. Her skin almost tingled in the atmosphere, her brain sharp and focused, her body moving symbiotically with the night sky. The moon always looked like it was following her, like a shadow, or a dog trailing just behind, or a warm beacon calling her ahead. The vibrations in her body were kinetic, a thrumming, some electricity that sparked and fired as she fluidly moved through the night. It was always this way, always had been this way. And tonight it was so dark, a comforting blanket of solitude she never felt any other time.

Grey smoky clouds swirled in the starless black sky covering the face of the moon, like billowing dark incense, rising upward to carry prayers to saints that wouldn't hear, or didn't care to listen. The night was thick and dead silent beneath the cover of lush humidity. Her footsteps falling quietly on the pavement, grinding pebbles between the rubber of her boot and the moist blacktop. The noise sounded obnoxiously loud in the stillness, an intrusion on the night, so she tried to move more deftly and succeeded. There was nothing awake, nothing stirring, just the way she liked it. When she was alone in the dark she could be herself. The Violet she showed no one, at least not anymore.

It had been essential that she get out of her house before she broke down for the umpteenth time today. There was no way she could have stood any more compassion. Flowers were still arriving at the house daily, cards, phone calls, neighbors stopping by with plates of food that would go uneaten. But the worst was the looks of pity on everyone's face. Kindness, tiptoeing, and the babying… Oh, the babying, as though she were frail and incapable of taking care of herself. She was used to disdain, even semi-revulsion, but kindness? Pity? No, she could not take another moment of it. And despite the best efforts of those closest to her to remain "normal", the sympathy she was being shown by her best friends was just too much to bear. These were not your sunshine and teddy bear people. They were bitter, sarcastic smartasses, just like her. So, the stark change was unsettling and annoying. Thus, here she was, walking at night again.

Her hands felt hot in the satin lined pockets of her leather jacket. There was no reason to be wearing this at the end of summer, but she was doing it anyway. She had to look cool. She twiddled a warm dime between her index finger and thumb. The tops of her thighs were moist beneath the black leggings, making the skin feel faintly tender from the friction of the tight fabric. Her nose was stuffed slightly due to allergies, which was annoying the crap out of her. Being a mouth breather wasn't attractive by any stretch of the imagination. She stopped walking and reached into her bag and pulled out the cherry lip balm she had bought at the drugstore several hours earlier. The sweet gloss slid over her lips smoothly as she picked up her pace again.

Headlights approached, drawing closer, like some invading beast there in the darkness, eyes glowing, throat grumbling in warning. She stepped behind a hedge of thick bushes and crouched down in hiding. The last thing she needed was some late night perv or truck full of rednecks asking her if she *needed a ride*, or worse, though there wasn't honestly much chance of anything happening in this small town. It still paid to be cautious. She listened as the vehicle came closer. The motor was running roughly and she could hear the muffled rock music amplified by the soundproofing of the low-lying clouds and the stillness of night.

She picked a mud-covered blue jay feather up from the dew soaked grass. Everything was coated in mud these days. It had been raining on and off as the season was changing. Smoothing the feather with her fingers, she ran them backwards against the feather separating each soft little plume. The feather was pretty, so she smoothed it together again and tucked it behind her ear. Unexpectedly she heard the stifled ring of her cell phone from inside her bag. It jolted her back to the present, bringing her shields firmly back into place.

"Damn it!" she cursed, grabbing her chest and falling back onto the cold, wet ground. "I hate this fucking thing!" she said, reaching into her bag.

"What, Amber?" she growled quietly in agitation, and wiped the mud from the seat of her pants.

"Hey! Where are you? Um, why are you whispering?" her friend mumbled back, not taking a breath between words.

"I'm hiding behind a bush right now. Why the hell are you whispering?" Violet's voice was thick with aggravation.

"Oh, I don't know why I'm whispering," Amber laughed in her regular animated voice. "Um, but is there a reason you're hiding behind a bush?"

"Well, duh, of course! There's a car driving by."

"And you're hiding because...?" Amber asked, enunciating each syllable.

The thing about Amber was that she was used to Violet's moods, so she never took offense to them. In fact, she never even seemed to notice them, which either made her the most patient girl in the world, or the biggest doormat. It was neither, in truth, because Amber could be a bitch herself. She simply knew Violet. They were like sisters, so both of them tolerated the crap that only family would ever tolerate. It was a good thing, but also a bad thing, because it meant Violet often took her frustrations out on Amber when no one else was around. And lately there had been a lot of frustrations.

"Because I don't want them to see me," Violet responded, confused as to why her friend couldn't just magically read her mind.

"Oh, okay, that makes sense," Amber answered back with a mocking sarcasm. "When are you coming home? We rented some movies earlier and just ordered a pizza. Oh, and the lovely and effervescent Mark just got here. He's irritated already and obnoxious per usual."

Yes, trying to be normal. Movies, pizza, and friends. *And disgruntled boyfriends.* She closed her eyes and exhaled.

"Don't wait on me, I'm gonna be awhile. Tell Mark I'll be back when I'm back." All the sass had finally gone out of her voice and had returned to the usual listless drone it had carried recently.

Violet talked to everyone like they were on her last nerve.

11

Everyone, including her parents, which cut her to the core when she thought about it. She talked down to the whole world as though she were the Queen of England. Well, if the Queen had a sailor's vocabulary. Things hadn't always been this way, she'd just learned that being nice made you a victim, or more times than not, the monster. This was a lesson she'd learned in the seventh grade while defending a chronic victim from a chronic bully and had somehow ended up the bad guy because of a colossal misunderstanding. So right then she had shut down and become the bitter, jaded girl she was now. Of course, she wasn't always a bitch, but there was always an edge to her that put most people off. Or made her seem even cooler, depending on the crowd.

"Well, be careful. Don't be out too long. I hate babysitting your stupid boyfriend."

"I am being careful, hence the bush hiding, my dear." She laughed, trying to give Amber some reassurance. Then she grew quiet for a moment, thinking about her boyfriend. "And Mark needs a beating. I'm so tired of his fucking possessiveness. He wasn't like this before."

"Who are you kidding, Violet? He's been this way since day one." Amber laughed into the phone, not realizing just how tired Violet really was of all his shenanigans. That was the problem with always being disgruntled and sarcastic. No one took her seriously when it actually mattered.

The car had passed while they had been talking. She waited until she heard it fade into the distance, then stood up and resumed her stealthy pace.

"Okay, I'm gonna go now. You know I hate this thing. You just about scared me to death when you called."

"Sorry. I know how hard it is for you living in this modern age," Amber teased.

"Yeah, well, screw this modern age. I'm not that big a fan of this modern age." There was venom in her voice that went far beyond any annoyance she could have been feeling over a cellphone. There was a whole lot of frustration boiling under the surface of her skin and running over any time there was a reason.

"Alright, well, see you in a little bit then?"

"In a little bit." She hung up.

Violet shook her head in exasperation and shoved the phone back down in her bag. The worry in Amber's voice was glaringly apparent. That was the exact reason she had needed to get out of the house so badly.

She also needed to remember to put her damn cellphone on vibrate so it didn't scare the hell out of her when it went off. It always made her jump when it rang, and she always forgot to put it on vibrate, because once she was off the phone she was happy to be done with it. Not to mention that with her luck she just knew that the moment she finally got around to putting it on vibrate she'd miss something important.

She made her way to her old elementary school. There is something very scary about a school at night. The building that was filled with laughter and boisterous children during the day was painfully silent and forlorn at night. *It's like watching a mourner waiting for the dead to come back.* Morbid thought, that.

The black windows looked so malevolent with the faint red glow of the emergency exit lights drifting through some of them. The swings sat perfectly still in the darkness. Nothing moved around her, not a sound, a creak, or shuffle. Even the trees were still, not so much as a whisper of wind through the paling leaves. It was unsettling. What about feeling this kind of fear gave her some sick comfort? Why did she always seem to seek out this feeling? She had been scared her whole life. Always.

She walked towards the swings, pushing the anxiety away, and leaned back into one. The flexible rubber seat felt cold against her body, but became more pliable when it warmed to her. The galvanized chains were thick and slightly rough where whatever machine that fabricated them had cut the links apart. She remembered having bloody pinch marks from this very swing when she had been a student here. Her mind briefly caught a snapshot of the memory. Slowly she twisted back and forth, dragging her feet in the gravel. The sound seemed so loud, cutting through the oppressive silence. Her arms and legs began to pump back and forth, forcing her higher and higher. She was swinging very quickly now, faster and higher, faster and higher. The cool air felt good, almost wet, against her cheeks. A slight smile spread across her glossed lips.

Higher and higher, faster and faster. The air grew stronger, pushing her hair away from her face, trailing behind her like a glistening mane. And then forward, haloing her head, reaching forward like spiraling tentacles and sticking to her lush lips. Then the chain buckled and jumped. This startled her, nearly causing her to release her grip, which would have thrown her to the ground. But she gripped tighter and continued pumping her arms and legs. Then the swing jumped again, causing the chain to pinch her, sending a sharp, searing pain through her index finger. She threw her feet down into the gravel, forcing the swing to stop, a cloud of dust billowing around her boots. Her eyebrows knit together as she frowned and placed the bleeding finger between her teeth and sucked the drop of blood that welled up. The skin throbbed as she squeezed it, trying to diminish the pain. She sat very still in the swing for several minutes, then got up and started walking again. Apparently the swing had remembered how good her flesh tasted, or just flat out didn't like her sitting on it.

Walking alone at night, past houses filled with sleeping people, made her remember just how alone she was. There was no family left, no one to go to for a cry or a hug. She had not been a particularly loving daughter those last few years, and now it was too late to change any of it. She just hoped her parents knew how much she did love them. It was the reason she had been so snotty to them, she had known they would take it. Why did she feel the need to abuse those she loved? It was not something she had ever put much thought behind, and didn't plan to now either. It was what it was, but why? She was alone now, and always would be. It was true she had her friends, but what did they know about marriage, having babies, or paying taxes, or any of that kind of life crap? Now she was alone on this walk through life. Completely and utterly.

She remembered the last thing her mom had said to her as they had walked out the door. *"We'll be back at nine tonight. Order some pizza if you want, there's money on the table."*

That was it. Nothing profound. Nothing meaningful. Back at nine, pizza, table, and that was that. They were gone.

She lied to me. Violet frowned and stuffed her hands into her pockets dropping her gaze to the ground to watch her boots scuffle

14

along in the dark.

The way she had been living was catching up with her. She felt dirty, tired, and ashamed of her actions a good portion of the time. She felt like she needed to be bathed in bleach and scrubbed with a wire brush, especially after he touched her. Maybe that's why she built up the walls around herself? *Who cares! It doesn't matter!*

Tears fell from her swollen eyes, making stinging trails down her raw cheeks. She had been crying without knowing it for nearly an hour now. Her pace quickened, she walked faster, trying to propel herself home more quickly. She needed to be home right now for some reason, had to get home. She felt as though she was running from something hidden in the darkness, something that never seemed to be far away. Always unseen, but always there just the same. At least at home she could escape to the somewhat loving arms of her boyfriend, even if he had no idea how to comfort her. Or even cared to know how to comfort her.

Small whimpers escaped and she tried forcing them back down her clenched throat. She hated the way her face contorted when she cried, all scrunched and twisted like an aching Charlie horse. *I should be tough! I need to get over this!* Her hand covered her mouth, trying again to force the sounds to be silent, trying to restrain her emotions within her throat where they came from. Deep into her stomach where they could fester in snarling knots as she put a happy face on for her friends.

Like she ever wore a happy face. More like a cynical face. But at least it was a distraction from her personal tragedy.

One hand pressed on top of the other as if the first hand needed the support of the second in order to carry out the task.

"Stop it!" she growled behind the wall of fingers and clenched teeth. "Stop it! Stop it, now!"

Suddenly an eruption of noise came piercing through the night, stopping her abruptly in her tracks and pulling her out of her own mire of emotion. Sucking in a deep breath and holding it as her eyes scanned the darkness, her staccato breaths sucked in quickly silencing her whimpering. Alert, hair on end, she felt something out there in all that blackness.

Dogs. Three dogs. Three large dogs. They barked from behind the fenced yard. They rushed the barrier towards her growling and snapping their glowing white teeth. They looked like Cerberus as they stood side by side, a three-headed beast, grimacing, yowling, and snarling. They would tear her flesh off had they not been trapped behind the metal fence.

No, something else. Yes, there was something else out there thickening the air with gloom, the dogs were looking past her. Her teeth clenched as she turned to peer back into the darkness behind her, eyes wide and searching frantically.

Persephone running from Hades.

Again with the mythic imagery, it filled her head as though she were watching it on television.

Running past the fence, the dogs followed along beside her, snarling, barking, and growling every inch of the yard. They were fading in the distance, though every bit as loud in her ears as if they were right beside her still. Her legs furiously ran toward her house—why had she walked so damn far tonight? Why had she taken a different route from her usual one around the block?

The whimpers choked in her throat again, running as fast as she could from *something*. The dogs. The night. That pain that sat deep in her stomach? The tears and sobs now escaped in a torrent as she continued to run and then suddenly she stopped. Her lungs were swelling in her chest, gasping for air as she sucked in gulps of it, trying to catch her breath as she wiped her eyes. She looked out into the dark again, trying to pull herself together.

"You okay?" the voice asked calmly, the deep resonance a feeling more than a sound.

Silence fell over her, frozen, breath sucked in and waiting. The tall figure cloaked in darkness, haloed by streetlight, stood perfectly still in front of her on the sidewalk. She tried to see his face, tried to read who he was.

"You okay?" he asked again, coming closer to her. She backed away as he reached his hand out towards her. "Has someone hurt you?"

Her breath still had not expelled, her eyes were wide and cautious.

"I'm not going to hurt you," he said calmly, walking closer. He was only two or three feet away now.

She could barely see his face, dark eyes beneath a prominent

16

brow, angular cheekbones, and smooth full lips attempting to smile at her reassuringly. The way the street light landed on his face hid his expression, showing only the hard planes but little else. His eyes were hidden, and thus he was unreadable to her and looked all the more menacing.

"You probably shouldn't be walking the streets alone at night." His voice was low and rumbly, but soft, somehow comforting, despite his dark appearance.

He towered over her, his face finally visible due to proximity. It looked hard, but also non-threatening, at least not threatening to her. His hair was thick and very long, pulled back tight at the nape of his neck, and trailing down his back. He was dressed all in black, jeans and tee shirt stretched tight over a well-muscled body. He was lean, unbelievably large. He had to be seven feet tall, and she should definitely be running away now. There was absolutely no way she could protect herself from him if he meant her harm.

But there was something about his mannerisms, the way his eyes looked, the way his body was relaxed, that, unbelievably, told her there was no reason to run.

She stepped forward to gaze up at him trying to ascertain who he was. He stood there perfectly still studying her expression with a look of amused perplexity. His dark, smiling eyes made her smile in response. She felt at ease with him somehow, comfortable, but also terrified. Something far beyond what her brain understood kept here standing with him instead of forcing herself to run away. It was chemical, somehow elemental.

"I was just running from dogs," she stuttered and sniffed as she wiped her hand across her face, clearing the tears from her wet cheeks and lifting her head in mock conceit. Her voice betrayed her actions, and she knew it, but she had some pride, right?

"Dogs, huh? Could be running from worse things, I guess," he said, handing her a napkin from his pocket.

A shaking hand took the napkin he offered cautiously, and then wiped her face. "Thanks," she said, motioning with the napkin and pushing it into her pocket, then started walking again.

"You shouldn't be out here at night," he warned again as he began following her.

"Yeah, I know," she said quietly, dismissively, as she quickened her steps.

"Bad things happen to girls at night," he said, catching up to her with one long stride and leaning forward to catch her attention.

"Yeah, I know," she answered, more vexed, her face pointed towards the ground at her boots that were scuffling along the wet street.

"My name is Roman," he stated, stopping and placing his hand against her arm to get her to stop walking.

She turned towards him, craning her neck to look up at him. "Roman?" she accused.

"Yeah, like Roman god," he said, grinning while extending his hand towards hers to shake. "What's your name?"

She put her hand in his. The size difference was comical. His fingers were long and slender, his skin warm and rough, the grip powerful.

"Violet." She smiled nervously, shaking his hand and then taking her hand back. She shoved it into her pocket, tucked her chin in, and started walking again. "Like Violent." She smiled at her own joke.

"Violent, where are you going?" he asked, resuming his position beside her.

"I was going home, but I'm not going there now because I don't want you to know where I live."

"I am not going to hurt you. I just have this thing about girls being out alone at night by themselves, call me a sexist."

"Yeah, well, people didn't think Dahmer would hurt them either, you sexist," she said, trying not to crack a smile. .

"Good point, so where are you going?" he asked again.

"I'm going to circle around this neighborhood until you get bored and leave," she said matter of factly, as she looked over at him. She tried not to laugh. It was funny to her that anyone would allow her to be this rude without telling her to fuck off, but she was used to saying whatever she wanted, to whomever she wanted.

"Well, I hope you have comfortable shoes on then." He smirked, looking back at her. "So, what are you doing out so late?"

"Um, *walking*." Violet rolled her eyes.

"Yes, you shouldn't do that by yourself at night." His

demeanor was so casual, despite the cavernous tone of voice and threatening appearance.

"Yes, we already established that, remember?" she said, looking over at him again. She couldn't look for more than a few seconds at a time. Making eye contact with strangers wasn't her strong suit. Especially not with strangers this peculiar.

"Why were you crying?" he asked, his expression sober. "I know you aren't that afraid of dogs."

"How would you know that? Maybe I was mauled as a child?"

"I don't believe that to be true. I don't see any disfigurement. Besides, they're in a fenced yard. I walk by those dogs every day. So, why were you crying?"

She looked down at the pavement, not really wanting to take herself back to that place. And how the hell had she not seen him before if he walked by those dogs every day? This was a small town. There was no way she wouldn't know if he had moved in. He wasn't exactly inconspicuous. In fact, he was quite the opposite for a number of reasons, not the least of which being how stunning he was.

"Alright, you don't have to tell me."

She giggled to herself

He looked at her quizzically, oblivious to the reason his comment would be so funny.

"Sorry for being so vague," she said, looking over at him, flattening her expression.

"You on the run from the law?" he said and laughed.

"Yep, that's it, I'm a fugitive. Please don't turn me in."

"I won't...unless you're pulling a *Dahmer* or something. Oh wait; this was part of your evil plan, wasn't it? You pull your scared little girl routine to lure me back to your house so you can eat me. I figured you out."

"You got me. I'm all about luring huge men back to my house and cooking them alive." She turned and looked up at him. "You would make a rather large meal."

"Sounds like a good time."

He laughed and then she cringed, realizing how that might have sounded if he had the same pervy sense of humor as her.

She didn't say anything, just kept walking. They continued for several blocks, neither of them saying a word. It was comforting having him near. It was nice hearing the sound of someone else breathing, walking, feet shuffling on pavement. Lord knows Mark would never walk with her. She stopped and turned towards him, then looked up at him and back towards her house.

"I'm home," she said, opening the gate to her backyard.

"You said you weren't going to come back here."

"Yeah, well, I say a lot of things I don't mean." She bit her bottom lip and walked into her yard. "You coming?" she offered, looking back at him.

"Nah, I better get home. Besides, I don't feel like being cooked alive tonight." He pushed the gate closed.

She turned and walked back towards him, "Seriously, you can come in. My friends are still up. I won't kill you, I promise."

"Yes, but, you say a lot of things you don't mean," he repeated with a grin and a wink. "I'm gonna go home. It's pretty late."

"Okay, suit yourself." She shrugged her shoulders and started to walk back up the sidewalk towards the backdoor.

"Just answer one question for me, Violet."

It was the first time he had spoken her name. It sounded somehow intimate hearing it on his tongue. She turned and looked back at him.

"What were you crying about?"

She looked down at the pavement running her foot over the sidewalk, creating a soft grating sound and a trail of tiny bubbles as she contemplated whether or not she wanted to reveal herself to this stranger. The emotions roiled inside, as if any movement or care to acknowledge them would bring them erupting to the surface again. She walked back towards him, not saying anything. The porch light behind her flipped on and the curtains were rustling as someone looked out the window. Roman looked away from her ever so briefly, then returned his gaze.

"My parents died a few weeks ago," she said, looking into his dark eyes and pausing briefly. Their eyes locked, conveying unspoken emotion, and then she backed up towards her house, not waiting for a reaction. She did not want pity. He reached out and grabbed the feather from her hair, gesturing with it, and putting it in his pocket.

20

"You know, you really shouldn't be out walking by yourself late at night, Roman." She smiled sadly as the door opened, and a large guy walked out onto the pathway. He glowered at her and then Roman.

"Violet, where the fuck you been?" the guy said, pulling her into the house with his large meaty hand.

She thought maybe the stranger was about to protest, but he hesitated and did nothing. The door closed, and the light shut off. He stood there for several moments, staring at the house, listening to the gurgling murmur of an argument inside, and the loud music, and sound of people partying. The curtain of the door was pulled back slightly, and he saw her face peering out at him. Her eyes were huge and glistening with unshed tears. She looked so sad standing there, desolate, needing something he couldn't discern or understand. She stared for several moments and waved her hand at him , then went back into the house.

"Who was that?" Mark asked, grabbing her arm and shoving her against the kitchen counter.

"I don't know, some guy named Roman. I was being chased by dogs and he scared them away."

"Right, dogs, because that makes total sense," he said, letting go of her and walking back into the living room.

"Déjà vu," Violet muttered under her breath. Her arm was throbbing where his fingers had been clenching it so tightly. She rubbed the spot, trying to get the blood circulating.

"What?" he asked, turning back around with a scowl on his face.

"Nothing."

Amber walked past him and looked at Violet sympathetically. "What was that all about?" she asked, pulling out a seat at the table and sitting down.

"Nothing, this guy walked me home," Violet said, sitting down at the table.

"Who was it?"

"This guy, Roman, I met him while I was walking. I've never seen him before."

"So, let me guess, Mark's mad because you talked to another male?"

"Yep. This is getting old, Amber."

"You should dump his ass. Why put up with all that crap? You know later he'll come around all apologetic like always. Just tell him to fuck off. You've been putting up with this for too long. There are plenty of other guys out there who'd die to go out with you. And life is far too short to waste being miserable."

Life is too short. God how she knew that. "I really should break up with him. Things haven't been good for a long time. I'm not sure they've ever been good. I've bent over backwards for him since the beginning. It's so not like me."

She stood up and walked up to her bedroom. She turned the small lamp on that sat on her dresser and threw herself down on the bed. Her legs dangled over the end as she lay face down on the cool cotton quilt. She lay there quietly for several minutes, then rolled over onto her back feeling numb, dead inside. *This is how life is supposed to be?*

She stared at the band posters hanging on her ceiling, each face more beguiling than the next. If only she could escape from here, find one of these bands, go off with them, and have no responsibilities. Nothing but travel, rock-n-roll, and Prince Charming in leather and eyeliner. She grinned to herself realizing how old that would get quickly. In reality, she just wanted to fuck one of them and get the hell away from her troubles.

"How crass," she said aloud.

She sat up, unlaced her boots, and tossed them across the room onto the ever-increasing pile of laundry and shoes. She leaned back in the bed and bent her knees, letting her toes curl over the edge of the mattress. She wanted to take these posters down, wanted to take all the memories of who she'd been these last few years, throw them into a box, and forget them. She closed her eyes, listening to her friends downstairs laughing and having a good time, and wished she could be that carefree again, but she doubted she would ever be capable of returning to that state. It had been a long time since she had been able to be like them for a variety of reasons, not the least of which was her controlling boyfriend whom she was growing to despise every day. Even though her parents had just died, Mark hadn't even been able to keep from abusing her for more than three days in a row. True, he had never hit her, but his constant barrage of criticisms and jealousy based tirades were enough to make her cower like a dog most of the time. Besides that, he did shove her around and squeeze on her.

This wasn't right. She was not the kind of person who allowed herself to be demeaned or mistreated. She had never been that kind of person. And now here she was doing just that, being that weak, pathetic girl who let herself be victimized. There was no love left for him anymore. It was more like an obligation now, or an old stupid habit that she knew she needed to quit. Like the dog that got used to being beaten, but still allowed itself to be petted. She had liked him in the beginning, and loved that he had made her feel completely protected. Now she was tired of feeling like property. Then of course he would come around all hugging and kissing and sweet and cuddly like a big old puppy dog making her feel like she was being selfish for feeling the way she felt. Therefore, she went through another day of it with him. It was a cycle she needed to end, but didn't know how to.

"Hey," he said opening the door and looking in on her, "sorry for flipping out."

And so it began again.

He sat down beside her and gently pushed the hair away from her face, running his fingers over her skin soothingly. She stiffened momentarily, just like that beaten dog. Then she felt guilty for doing it, and afraid he'd notice, so she relaxed and closed her eyes, remembering the face of the man who had saved her from three barking dogs.

2. PENT UP ENERGY

"If Gwen even looks at me tonight, I'm going to pound her face in," Violet said, leaning back into the seat and putting the seat belt on as she looked over at Amber and grinned.

"Yeah, beat her ass. I can't stand that cunt," Amber said, goading her friend.

"What's your beef with her? She's never done anything to either of you." Steve leaned forward, resting his arms on the seats.

He was a husky man, not very tall and a little plain to look at. They had been friends with him for several years. They had met him through Randy, who had been in a band with him and another guy named Mosley. Amber and Violet had met them at a party one night, and had become friends immediately. Violet felt weird hanging around Steve at times. There always seemed to be some awkward tension in the way he looked at her, and it made her uncomfortable. But most of the time they got along really well, having an affinity for watching stupid cartoons, eating wings, and listening to cheesy eighties metal.

"I just can't stand her, I don't know why. Just looking at her pisses me off. It's like she tries too hard or something," Violet seethed.

"It's because she thinks she's so cute. She's always acting all weird to get attention. It's annoying." Amber added.

"Yeah, maybe that's it. I don't care why I don't like her, I just don't and she needs to avoid me." Violet sneered, as she put the disc in the stereo and aggressively loud music blasted out of the speakers.

"Now you're just trying to get yourself angry." Amber laughed, referencing her music selection.

"No harm in a little anger. It's good for ye old blood."

"Remember that time she had that fake nose ring when we saw

24

her at that show?" Amber asked.

"Oh, man, that was so funny. It's like, why bother? Either get your nose pierced or don't, but don't wear a fake one, you fucking idiot." Violet laughed.

"She's such a fucking poser," Amber added.

"Don't forget to pick Mose up," Steve said, settling back in the seat.

"Mother fucking hell! I'm not a damn taxi service! How is it that I end up carting everyone around ninety percent of the time?" Mosely never had a ride anywhere and she always ended up driving him all over creation. She usually didn't mind so much, but it did get old.

"Cuz people are too lazy to get jobs and buy a car?" Amber quipped, thick with sarcasm.

"Damn, you girls are vicious tonight. I'm avoiding you once we get to The Cage."

They both laughed at him. This was not abnormal behavior or conversation for them, so why he was getting bent out of shape made no sense. There was always the option of not hanging out with them, but, of course, that wouldn't be any fun, now would it?

"I think pretty much everyone should avoid us a good portion of the time." Amber said, and turned the music up louder.

"That's probably wise advice on most days," Violet concurred.

It was a forty-five minute drive to the club. Everywhere was at least a forty-five minute trip around here. They had to drive to a larger neighboring town because theirs was simply too small to support any type of underground scene whatsoever. The same people showed up every night. Violet and her friends pretty much owned this scene. That wasn't really saying much, given the small nature of it. When they made their entrance it was always an event, or maybe more of a spectacle. The girls wanted to be like them, the men wanted to screw them. Either that, or they were despised. The line between either was pretty thin there. It was pathetic and weird. It was too easy to abuse some people, too easy to dismiss others. It made it way too effortless for disgruntled people to take out their frustrations, *and she was disgruntled.* Violet scanned the crowd for Mark and saw him sitting on a bar stool across the room. He looked up at her and raised his hand.

Maybe tonight would be a good night.

She walked across the dance floor, stopping to say hello to the few people she actually liked. There were a couple here and there that piqued her interests, or that she found genuinely nice. She and Amber walked to the end of the bar and ordered a drink, diet soda for Violet, rum and Coke for Amber. Violet could not stand the taste of alcohol. Besides, she wasn't old enough. Amber was served no matter her age. Her large breasts and scantily clad body guaranteed her good service wherever she went.

Liquid, thundering bass pulsed from the lounge in the back of the club. That was where they would spend the bulk of the evening. It was dark and less noisy in that room, mostly "hip" people sitting back there drinking martinis or fake absinthe and smoking clove cigarettes. They got a kick out of the level of pretense present at this club, especially from such a bunch of losers. Industrial techno crap blared on the dance floor. Rivet heads gyrating with their heads down, and martini drinking pseudo-Goths depressing it up in the lounge out back. It was all too funny. Yet, here they were, night after night, making the scene. So what did that say about them? It had been Amber's coercing with the owner and DJ that had allowed a theme night like this to begin with. Sometimes a person just has to take matters into their own hands. And who could resist Amber? Not many.

Violet felt confident tonight, as confident as she ever felt, anyway. Her hair was in two thick, messy braids that hung down her back to her waist. She wore a black baby tee that she had hand sewn with thick green thread, and had painted a green number eleven on the chest. What was the reason for the eleven? There was none, she just liked it. She wore a very short leather pleated skirt, and knee high black leather boots with green stripes painted down the sides. Her nails were stained with black and red paint from the remodeling she had done on her bedroom wall earlier. Her eyes were heavily lined in green with black eye shadow. Yes, the theme was black and green; it was a tribute, of sorts, to a favorite band of hers.

Amber started to follow Violet over to where Mark and Randy sat at the other end of the bar, but stopped to talk to an ex-boyfriend she hadn't seen in several months. Her angular red bob looked vibrant, almost neon, against the white t-shirt and white leather pants she was wearing. She looked like some hot android from a sci-fi movie.

"Hey," Violet said, wrapping her arms around Mark's neck from behind. She kissed his ear absently and squeezed herself between his and Randy's seats.

"Oh, you're gonna be nice tonight?" Mark said, backing away from her playfully.

"I'm always nice to you, fucker." Violet scowled, pinching his arm as hard as she could. He barely flinched, though she wished she'd hurt him. It would likely take a cattle prod to evoke any pain reaction from her pit bull.

"Where've you been?" Mark said, kissing her quickly. His lips felt soft and warm against her mouth.

"I had to go pick up Mosley, and of course he needed to stop five million places. Were you aware that I'm his personal driver and errand runner?" She glowered as she said it, "Sorry it took so long. I should have thought to leave earlier."

"It's no big deal," he said, taking a swig from his nearly empty beer. "Just wondered what was taking so long."

It wasn't a big deal? Since when? It wasn't abnormal for him to flip out on her for being three minutes late somewhere. It had caused her to make the conscious effort to always be ten minutes ahead at all times. Today was an exception to her usual strict rule.

"Why the hell is Amber talking to that dork?" Randy asked, staring at his girlfriend.

"Cuz it's polite?" Violet said, pinching Randy's arm.

"Polite, like you're ever polite. Who cares about being polite?"

"I'm polite, you ass," she said, frowning at him.

"Yeah, okay, you're the shining example of politeness." He shook his head, stood up, and walked towards his girlfriend.

Violet sat in his chair and watched the scene unfold. She wondered if there would be a fight, or if Randy would be calm tonight. You never could tell with him. Most of the time he was an easygoing guy, but on occasion he could be provoked to violence, mostly egged on by Mark. Violet liked to call him randy Randy. She was a dork that way.

The aforementioned was a very good-looking guy. Violet had

harbored a crush for him when they'd first met. He was well-built, above average height, and very charismatic. Randy had a short black Mohawk, a personal predilection of Violet's, and that coupled with his crooked nose made him look far more intimidating than he was. Amber had fallen for him immediately, and had left her boyfriend of the time for him, whom she was now speaking with, much to Randy's chagrin.

Randy walked up behind Amber and put his hand around her waist, snuggling his face against her neck. Violet laughed to herself. Claiming his territory, she thought. Amber turned and kissed his cheek and said goodbye to the ex and the two walked back towards Violet and Mark.

"Let's go to the lounge. I've got gifts," Mark said, standing up and grabbing Violet's forearm. She obediently followed, smiling at a few friends along the way

"Hamburger Lady," Amber sang out loudly as they entered the lounge area. Thank goodness for experimental music.

It was overly dark in there tonight. There was strawberry scented fog wafting down from the smoke machines mounted in the corners of the room. The mixture of that and cigarette smoke could be a bit suffocating at times. This was one of those bars that had not submitted to the No Smoking laws and knew they would not until they had to by force. Who would tell on them? Violet wished someone would, because she hated cigarette smoke.

They slid into a booth near the back corner of the room. Mark handed them each two hits of acid. Violet dutifully placed them on her tongue, as did the others. She stared around the room, watching the crowd. It was one of her favorite pastimes. She liked going to malls, or parks, anywhere there were people to sit and watch. It was fascinating to her. There was a beautiful blonde girl sitting across the room with a guy she had met once. *Where?* Yes, the Italian, Dani. He had been nice at that party. Foggy memories swirled, she shook her head. Back to the blonde. The girl was tall and very delicate looking. Her hair was long and looked like corn silk. Violet watched as she took long, slow sips of her drink and smiled shyly at the young punk boy she was sitting with. She wondered if this girl had any idea how beautiful she was? She doubted it, based on her body language.

After some unknown amount of time went by, everything seeming too slow, Violet shook herself from her self-induced trance, having not heard a word that had been spoken at her own table. She looked at the fluorescent painted stars and planets on the black walls. They seemed to swirl before her eyes and pulse to the rhythm of the lush ambient music that now played. There was no way the acid had kicked in this quickly, but something was making her feel off. Low blood sugar? Crippling depression? Had she finally lost it? That almost made her smile for some reason.

"I don't think I'll be able to drive home," Violet said quietly.

The other three laughed.

Steve joined the booth. They all talked about nonsensical things as Violet's ears didn't seem to function on their level anymore. Something was affecting her strongly. Maybe the drug, and it made her wonder why sometimes when she did LSD nothing much happened and other times it was so powerful it felt like it would last forever. She hated chemistry.

"It's the rat poison," she said softly.

Mark looked at her lifting an eyebrow and grinning at her. "Yep, it's the rat poison," he said, teasing her.

She smiled and rested her head on his shoulder, leaning into him heavily and licked his neck. His skin was salty and hot. She liked the way his thick artery felt beneath her tongue, throbbing lazily, keeping time with the slow, haunting music. She could hear his blood wooshing beneath his skin, flowing under her tongue. Her teeth tingled, wanting to bite into him. Instead she flattened her tongue against his skin and licked him again. Even though he was a dick, he tasted good. *His dick tastes good.* Violet laughed inside her head.

"Here comes Gwen, Violet," Amber said, grabbing her friend's hand and shaking her gently.

"Oh, man, don't start, girls," Steve said, scooting over and letting the girl in the booth.

"Hi, guys," Gwen said, with great excitement.

"Hello," Amber said, with mock enthusiasm.

The conversation picked up as none of the men had any problems with the skank. Violet figured they were too driven by

29

their sex organs to see her for the idiot she was. Violet sat perfectly still, leaning into Mark and staring blankly at Gwen's mouth, not really seeing her or hearing anything. Finally, Gwen grew annoyed by her staring and asked her what she was looking at. Violet didn't answer, as she was quite mystified by the distorted vision she was experiencing.

"Let it go, Gwen," Steve cautioned her, grabbing her arm and leaning her back into the black vinyl bench.

Amber looked at Violet and back at Gwen, wondering how long it was going to take Violet to say something. She wasn't ordinarily one to mince words or waste a golden opportunity to assault someone verbally. Violet sat quietly, continuing to stare at the girl's gaping maw.

It was as if Violet was transfixed by the girl's face. She couldn't make sense of what she was saying, like she was watching Mexican TV or something. Gwen jabbered something about a party, then something about biscuits and gravy? What the fuck was she talking about? Her rubbery, glossy lips looked like two thick night crawlers. Violet was scared of worms, so she couldn't take her eyes off it.

Finally, after several minutes, Violet lifted her head and looked Gwen directly in the eyes. "Do you ever shut your mouth?" Violet asked calmly, unemotionally. The tone of her voice surprised even her. Ordinarily she was much more animated.

"Excuse me?" Gwen said, leaning towards Violet.

"I asked you if you ever shut your fucking mouth? You have been talking nonstop since you sat down. I am wondering why you never stop talking? Do you breathe? Do you swallow? Do you even think about what you're saying? Do you really think what you say is that interesting? Because it's not, it's really, really not very interesting. *So, I'm curious, do you ever shut your mouth?*"

"Why do you hate me? What have I ever done to you?" Gwen's voice was shrill, in that raspy way. It was the the husky voice of a cheerleader that had cheered for one too many games.

What she had said reminded Violet of being on the playground when she was little, and hearing this girl Susan begging this other girl Katey to be her friend. The memory made her sad. Susan had

30

been standing there crying in her hand me down clothes that were too big, with her dirty little chubby face, and Katey had just stood there with her perfect blonde braids and pretty blue dress, looking so superior. Violet felt like puking from guilt.

Gwen asked again.

Was Violet really going to be this mean to her? Gwen was obviously pathetic. Why did she care whether Violet liked her anyway? She had never been nice to her. Ever. So why did Gwen care if she liked her or not? That infuriated Violet. Gwen should despise her, not sit there begging to impress her.

She sat quietly for far too long. It had to be unnerving to Gwen wondering when it was going to come and how bad Violet's tongue-lashing would be. Her friends were eager, all except Steve, who looked like he would kill Violet. She knew he just wanted a chance to sleep with Gwen later, and figured that if she was too mean to her Gwen would take off and his chances would be slim to none. His chances were already slim to none, the delusional idiot. The girl, apparently, had some standards. He had been trying to bed her for months with not so much as a hint of success.

"Do you really want to know why I don't like you?" Violet asked her finally.

Something broke in Gwen's face. Anger turned to absolute fear. Gwen did not want to be humiliated in front of the "cool people". Violet read all of that as plain as day on her face. All she wanted was to fit in with Violet and her friends, and Violet wouldn't give that to her. Why? Jealousy, more than likely. It pissed her off that Gwen was happy. She walked around without a care in the world. Men wanted her because she was perky, and easy, and had big tits. Gwen had a lot of friends; she fit into many different groups of people, due in part to her fakeness. So, why did it matter to Gwen if she and her friends thought she was cool?

Violet scoffed, contempt and disgust dripping off her tongue, "Because I can give you a list of reasons if you'd like. So, tell me, do you *really* want to know why I dislike you?"

Violet could see the tears building in Gwen's eyes, though she was doubtful anyone else noticed. They were too focused on their shark of a friend doing what she did best; eviscerating people.

"Fuck you! You're such a bitch!" Gwen shrieked, and flew

31

from the booth, running from the lounge as quickly as her legs would take her.

"So I've been told," Violet said.

Everyone laughed, except Steve, who was scowling at Violet in disgust. He pulled himself from the seat and followed after Gwen.

"That's my little monster," Mark said, wrapping his arm around her and squeezing. His hot mouth placed a kiss to the top of her head.

Violet felt sick again. She put her head back down on the cool table, pretending she was too stoned to be aware of anything. She shut out her own emotions. She would not grieve for what she'd just done to Gwen. Violet had been just like her, more times than she cared to remember, and had just done it to Gwen despite that fact. Screw it. She was a hateful bitch. Gwen had gotten off relatively easy. Violet closed her eyes and hid the darkness that had crept into them.

"I hafta pee, come with me," Amber said, pulling one of Violet's braids.

She lifted her head and watched as Randy scooted to let Amber out. Violet noticed that someone had sat down on the other side of her, blocking her in the booth. How had she not noticed that before? Was she really so self-absorbed? Or had the acid fucked her up that bad? It was Mosely, no wonder she hadn't noticed him. He was always very quiet and slippery.

She looked at him now, the darkness of his skin and eyes looking like motor oil as the lights reflected on him. His hair looked like snakes undulating as she turned her head towards him. She recoiled and slipped off the seat crawling out beneath the booth. When she straightened herself up she realized how dizzy her head felt. Her stomach growled, starved, ached. "I feel really funny," Violet said, leaning into Amber.

"You look like you feel really funny. Mine's barely working."

"I just feel really out of it. My stomach's doing that weird burning thing too."

"Did you eat anything today?" Amber asked, stopping to adjust the hold her friend had on her arm.

"I ate an apple this morning."

"Man, no wonder your stomach is burning. You're hungry,

32

fucktard."

"Fucktard. I freaking love that word."

They got to the bathroom and there was a line. Violet leaned against the carpeted wall where she would wait for Amber.

"You have to start eating," Amber said, holding the back of her hand to Violet's forehead to check for a fever, just in case she was sick and not just tripping balls and hungry. Violet shrugged her shoulders. It was Amber's turn to go pee.

Violet looked around. A couple people nodded at her, tried to make conversation, but she was incapable of responding. How was she so out of it? She had only taken two stupid hits of acid. Maybe since her emotions were so raw, and her insides were in such turmoil, the drug was hitting her harder than usual?

She saw Mark coming toward her, breaking through the crowd because he was bigger than everyone else. He was built like a tank, tattooed all over with his stupid Nazi bullshit tattoos. She hated that crap, and hated that side of him. She didn't think he really even believed his own shit. He thought it was cool. *Yeah, killing Jews is real cool, fucking moron.* Violet refused to talk to him about his "beliefs", and every time he started one of his rants, that he had no doubt heard from his loser-ass father, she always found a way to distract him so he'd shut up. Like most men, he could be easily distracted with sex. It beat listening to his absurd blathering. She told herself there was no way he really believed that shit. Violet knew deep down inside that if she truly knew who he was down in his core she would hate him. She never allowed herself to look that far down inside of him. He was her boyfriend, she could not allow herself to hate him, so she never looked too deeply. It was easier that way. She hid herself from him, and he hid himself from her. Or she just didn't look.

Though she had to admit, he looked hot as he came towards her with his shaved head and his shirt pulled so tight over his thick muscles. His looks were his only saving grace. Mark was good looking for his type. His body was solid muscle, somewhat tall, his face angular and chiseled. It's what saved him, because it surely wasn't his winning personality. Violet felt her body humming now, warming even more.

His knee parted her legs, pinning her to the wall. His hot mouth

33

was soft and wet as it roved over her neck. The sensation of the warmth of his body and the cool saliva was exhilarating. Violet knew what he wanted, and in that moment it didn't matter to her that they were in public where others could see.

She kissed him back, her hands wrapping as much as they could around the bulk of his arms. She loved his muscles. She wanted to bite into him. His tongue pulled her thoughts back. She loved his tongue right then, velvet soft, lush as it slid over hers. He pulled away, biting her chin and then returning to her mouth. She licked his lips, slipping her fingers around his neck, cradling his heavy skull. Her eyes cracked open.

Roman.

He was there, across the room. The rush of adrenalin from seeing him stopped her. She let go of Mark and pushed her head back against the wall. He kissed her again and she squirmed.

"What?" he said, his mouth smothering hers.

She ineffectively pushed him back, placing her palms against his heavy chest.

"What the fuck?" he asked with a sneer.

"Not in public," she said dismissively.

Roman caught her eye and Violet looked away. He was talking to a friend of hers, Heather. She was a cute girl, very sweet. Violet felt the pit of her stomach drop.

"You're the fucking moodiest bitch. Don't wait up for me," he said, shoving his way back toward the direction he'd come previously.

"Damn. That took forever," Amber said, as she walked up to Violet and followed her gaze towards Mark who was shoving his way through the crowd.

"Yeah, it seemed to," Violet said, watching the throng part and close up again. "I think I'm going to go outside. It's too loud in here for me right now."

"You want me to come?"

"Nah, I'm just going to sit in the car. I feel really crappy. I hate this feeling."

"Well, we can leave if you want," Amber said sincerely.

"No, it's alright. I'm just gonna sit outside."

She walked towards the door passing several people she felt

obliged to say hello to. She hated the way she felt right now. This had been happening more and more frequently. It used to be fun taking this drug and now it was just semi-amusing at times, but generally just made her nauseous and overly moody. It had been a long time since it had been fun.

The night air felt cool as it settled on her skin. It had been very hot in the club. Her flesh felt wet and slimy to her. She opened the door of her car and fell into it. She rolled the window down, leaned back into the seat, and closed her eyes. The chilly breeze felt good on her damp skin. She seemed to hear everything, all the various night sounds, separating them in her mind between natural and unnatural. She stopped to think about how mad Mark had been with her, and admitted to herself she didn't care anymore.

He was overly temperamental and it was getting beyond old. At times she felt like some sort of trophy, or a prize-winning cow he took out to the county fair. He was always criticizing her, every aspect of her body. Her breasts weren't large enough, her waist not thin enough, her thighs too fat. She weighed 95 pounds now and he still always found something to be critical of when it came to her body. It was no wonder she always forgot to eat.

"Who cares?" she said aloud.

"Hey," his voice beckoned from outside, "you alright?"

She opened her eyes, jerked her head up off the seat, and clutched her chest. "Oh my God, you scared me!" she said, reaching out the window and slapping him.

"Sorry," he grinned, "I was just leaving and heard you talking to yourself as I walked by. You don't look so good."

"Yeah, well, neither do you," she said, looking down at her hands that sat heavily in her lap, feeling shame over her appearance. She already felt disgusting if she dropped her guise of arrogance for more than a second, it did not help when people pointed it out, though she ought to be used to that by now.

"I didn't mean it like that, Violet."

She looked up at him, leaning her head out the window and resting it against the door. The light behind him made it difficult for her to see his face. "You look good. I was mistaken," she said, closing her eyes with a faint smile on her face.

He smiled in return. "You aren't driving are you?"

"Well, not currently, no."

He smirked and squatted down so that he was eye level with her. "What are you doing out here?"

"I feel bad. It's hot in there. I want to go home. I hate fighting. Need any more reasons?" She smiled at him faintly.

"Nah, that's pretty much the same reason I'm leaving. Is there someone else that can drive you? You seem sort of out of it."

"Yeah, well, I am feeling rather out of it. You know I'm tired of living like this. I'm tired of doing things I regret," she said, eyes closed, and not even fully aware that she had said those words aloud.

"So, stop," he said, pushing the hair out of her face.

She cracked her eyes slightly open. His face was kind. It didn't seem as though he was trying to get something from her, unlike a good portion of the people around her.

"I wish things were that simple," she said, closing her eyes again. She liked the way his fingertips felt on her sensitive skin. She thought to herself how easy it would be to leave with him, to go away and not see Mark again.

"Things are that simple," he said, standing up. *She looks like a sickly cat curled up...fragile...*

"Roman?" she said, placing her hand palm up on the edge of the door, inviting him to take it.

"Yes?" he answered gently.

"Thanks for walking with me the other night. I appreciated that more than you know." She pulled her hand back in the car embarrassed by the lack of response from him. She wasn't used to being rejected.

"No problem."

"Sit with me in my car." She opened her eyes wide, seeming to become more awake.

He hesitated for a moment, walked around to the passenger side, and waited for her to unlock the door. This was her mother's car. A blue Malibu she had bought only a few months before she'd passed away. Violet was able to pay the car in full with the inheritance her grandparents had left her. The seats were soft steel grey. She loved the way it felt against her bare skin. She leaned over and unlocked the door. He pulled it open and slid into the car.

36

His long legs were cramped and bent, and he looked rather silly all hunched up as if he was riding in a kiddy car at the fair.

"You can put the seat back." She laughed at him.

"Thanks," he said, reaching beneath the seat for the lever.

"So, you were talking to Heather?" she asked, leaning her head to the side and facing him.

"Heather? Yeah I guess. The red haired girl?"

"That would be her," she winked. "So, are you like, looking around for a girlfriend or something? Oh, wait, of course you already have one, I'm sure."

The question seemed to make him uncomfortable. She noticed him look to the floor briefly then back. His face was flawless. Even under the effect of the drug she saw no imperfections in his skin, teeth, hair, nothing. She watched as his face changed with each expression, the muscle and bone moving smoothly beneath the surface of his skin. The way his soft pink tongue curled when he spoke, the pouted lips pursing, and relaxing, his easy smile, it was all transfixing. The fluid movements and beauty of his features were hypnotizing to her.

"I just met her tonight, Violet. I wouldn't have even remembered her name had you not brought it up." He spoke slowly and deliberately. She doubted he ever wasted a word

"Hmm," she said, nodding her head, "so, I guess she wasn't up to par then?" Violet's eyes were slits as she surveyed his reaction.

"I didn't say that, but no, I'm not really interested." He wondered exactly what game she was playing.

"There aren't very many to choose from around here, Roman. They're all kind of idiotic, that is, if you're looking," she said, not taking her eyes away from his. She was trying to read him, just as he looked like he was trying to read her.

"Well, good thing I'm not choosey then. Besides, she was young."

"She's only a few months younger than me."

"Then I guess you're young too."

"And you're so old," she said, smacking his leg and closing her eyes again.

They sat quietly for several minutes. She had her head tilted back against the seat and she could almost feel him watching her.

37

She took slow, deep breaths that seemed drawn from deep within her body like the breaths of sleep. She felt her cheeks flush, and she ached from inner pain.

"So, I assume that was your boyfriend?" he asked casually, breaking the silence.

She jumped, slightly startled by his voice and turned to look at him. She locked eyes with him for several seconds and looked away. "Yep, that's Mark. He's overly affectionate in public," she shrugged, feeling embarrassed by her previous displays of affection.

"Not necessarily," he said, rearranging his legs and looking down at the floor.

"Yes, *necessarily*, I'm not property." She was annoyed by Roman's comment.

"Well, you would know better than I in regards to him. I just meant that sort of behavior isn't necessarily inappropriate if the attention is wanted."

"Hmm, interesting," she said, looking at him again with a skeptical grin on her face.

"What?"

"Nothing," she sighed, closing her eyes. She wished he'd been the one she'd been making out with inside. She felt that he probably wouldn't have minded considering what he'd just said, well, if they were together. "I see things in my head when my eyes are closed." The subject change was abrupt.

"Like what?" he answered, unfazed by the turn.

"Like scary faces. Weird stuff, almost as if I am watching a dream, or a movie, or something. I don't like it, it's too realistic."

"So, stop closing your eyes."

"I have to sleep sometime, right?"

"Do you have trouble sleeping?"

"Not as a rule, but sometimes I have these dreams. Usually they're worse with the drugs, ya know?"

"So, don't take drugs."

"Yeah, good point. I think I already mentioned something about that earlier. You know, *regretting things*? But sometimes they're really peaceful too, the dreams, I mean."

"Does he really treat you as his property?"

"I am his property. He checks me over like I'm some sort of horse he's trying to sell."

"That's an odd analogy."

"I guess it is," she laughed. "Well, I'm surprised he doesn't show people my teeth and tell them how many 'hands tall' I am. Not to mention sex. It's like I'm on call or something." She suddenly turned and looked at him, her eyes very large. "Well, you don't need to know all that." Her face turned a darker shade of pink as she sank into the seat.

"No, not really," he said, and looked out the window.

A tear slid from the outside corner of her eye and down her cheek to her neck. If her eyes were merely watering, a single drop would not have enough volume to trail so far. She was crying, she was incredibly controlled, but crying. She should be alone in her grief, not sitting with some stranger like him... but then again, she wanted him next to her. Her voice was a whisper that caught in her clenched throat. "I'm so sick of this life."

"Then change it," Roman said .

She said nothing back.

Violet felt herself begin to drift off... she felt like a tiny little animal on the island that was a car seat, frail, and somehow, only briefly, being watched over.

***

Violet pulled herself up the stairs, dragging her heavy feet up each maroon carpeted step. She flipped the light on in her room and threw her bag down on the floor in front of the closet. Her stomach felt like it was poisoned. A burning acid feeling twisted inside in steady, painful waves. She pulled her shirt off and tossed it onto the overflowing hamper, then unzipped the skirt and let it fall to the floor. She sat down on her bed, unlaced the boots, and kicked them off, falling back onto the bed and wrapping herself in the thick quilt.

"You all right?" Amber asked, poking her head in the door.

"Sleep."

"Night." Amber flipped her light off and pulled the door shut.

She was tired of people having to ask her if she was all right. No one had ever really cared before, and it peeved her that anyone did now just because her parents were dead. She let her eyes stay closed for once. It had been difficult to do that lately. Her head was swirling with images. Some of them frightening, some peaceful. She rolled over, turned her bedside lamp on, and then quickly drifted off to sleep.

***

Hot breath on her face, the smell of sweat and alcohol, she woke up dizzy and confused. His mouth covered hers before she had a chance to figure out what was happening, and she squirmed against him. His weight was too much for her to lift.

"Wake up," he whispered in her ear, his tongue tracing her artery.

"Mark, I'm tired, let me sleep," she said, pushing her hands against his solid chest without any impact on him. He kissed her again, his hands roving all over her body; he knew she would give in eventually.

She struggled to keep sleeping, then found herself falling under his spell again.

***

The moss felt cool and soothing beneath her bare legs. This was one of her favorite spots here in this dream, encircled by green velvet grass and soft pink clover. The night sky vibrated with the stars' song to her. Like tiny silver bells, they tinkled in her ears whispering tales of places long dead or hidden only here. This place that had always been.

She felt the Presence again. Somewhere in the woods, or across the stream, someone sat watching her. Always here, ever

40

present.

There was never any fear. Only peace and beauty. Did others come here besides the two of them? She had never seen anyone else.

She stood and walked down into the warm water. Catfish swirled at her feet and kissed her legs as they nibbled her. Their long whiskers tickled her skin sending little electric shocks along her flesh that followed up her spine to the top of her head. She sat down on the flat rock at the bank and dipped her hands into the black water. The moon sparkled across the rippling surface making long thin silvery threads of light, dancing like ribbon through black skies.

She bathed for him.

Her hands smoothed the surface of her skin. She glistened beneath the starlight, drops of water like diamond chips trailing along her glistening body. The warmth of the water and air softened her. She pushed her face down into the water and opened her eyes. Shimmering rocks glistened, gold glittered. She took in a deep breath of water and exhaled through her nose as the warm water expelled. She loved this dream world. So real. Hers. His, whoever he was.

She pulled her head back and stared into the dark forest. Water dripped from her face and trailed over her breasts and stomach. His black shadow stood hovering, majestic. He was white as the moon standing there amongst the black trees, his mouth slightly open, teeth gleaming.

She stood up and walked towards him. He waited motionless for her to come into the woods...to finally touch her.

This was the first time.

***

Light filtered through the thin gray drapes. She lay there with her eyes open for several moments, thinking about the dream she just had. It was easy to remember the feel of his eyes on her body, caressing in a way hands could not. Even his scent still hung in the

41

air around her, her fingers still felt velvety as they retained the memory of his hair and lips. Mark snored softy, forcing the detachment she loathed. Aggravated, she sighed and looked over at him sleeping there beside her. Taking her gaze back to the ceiling, she thought back to what Roman had told her the night before. *So change.* She took in a deep breath, exhaling slowly, and pulled herself out of bed and grabbed some clean underwear, a t-shirt, and a pair of old blue jeans from her dresser. The bathroom was directly across the hall. Amber had already left for work, her pajamas sat on the edge of the bathtub. Violet picked them up, folded them, and set them on the vanity.

She looked at herself in the mirror. Her eyes were smudged with makeup and the whites were red. Her hair was in thick knots where the braids had started to come apart and she looked like she'd been dragged behind a truck. Somehow, she had managed to get bruises on her arms last night. Mark was not known for his tenderness. She scowled at herself in the mirror; her naked body looked thin and weak. She had never looked this bad before. There was a stark contrast between her appearance and the yellow rosebud wallpaper and cheery white linens. Her mother had been a sunshiny person. Violet had been a sunshiny person up until three years ago.

The faucet in the bathtub ran as she waited for the water to get hot. She pulled the knob up and the spray was a shock to her system momentarily giving her a jolt of shivers. She stood beneath the stream letting it soak her hair and skin. The flower scented soap felt velvety as it bubbled in her hands. Her skin felt raw as she scrubbed her face. She rubbed harder and harder trying to wash the disgust she had for herself away. Tears mixed with the soap and water, how had she gotten here?

She wondered how her mother might feel about her now. Would she understand why she was doing the things she was doing? Would her mother still have loved her if she had known the things Violet had done even while she was alive? Her mother had been the closest thing to a saint she had ever known. She had loved Violet despite her smart mouth and disgruntled attitude, and had even taken in all her friends and fed them and had always been a second mom to them. How had Violet repaid her kindness? By shutting her out and withdrawing from her, that must have wounded her deeply. It wounded Violet now thinking about it.

Her mother still loved her, she knew it, but that knowledge did not ease her guilt or disgust for herself.

The hot water felt like it was scalding her skin, but she liked the feeling. She lathered her hair in rich smelling shampoo, and scratched her scalp with her short fingernails. It felt good to be clean. She stepped out of the shower and stood in front of the mirror, her skin glowing all shiny and pink. She picked up the wide toothed comb, and began combing the knots and braids from her hair. This was the first time she had actually combed her hair in a week, as she generally preferred it messy. She stared into her own eyes. This was the closest she had looked to the real Violet in years now. Her skin was clean and glowing, her hair straight and smooth. She stared at herself for a long moment, convincing herself she needed to be this person again. She needed to stop all the bullshit. Then she saw the ring of bruises on her arms again. Her eyes welled with tears, her stomach clenched, she swallowed her emotions. If she let them up now she would have a colossal meltdown. She couldn't afford it right now. So, she took three deep breaths… exhaled forcefully… and only then finally braided her hair neatly, having successfully redirected her energy. She gave herself a look of resolve and went back to her room.

So change! So change! So change!

She had stuffed her emotions down, wiped the tears from her face, and now she was going to clean up her life. Mark was turned towards the wall sound asleep. She scowled at him. She hated him now. Seeing the bruises and remembering what Roman had said forced a resolve in her. She looked around her messed up room and started cleaning. There was nothing quiet about her work as she shoved papers in her garbage bin, ripping posters off the walls, and making piles of laundry to be washed.

It was about time she got mad about this shit. Seriously, he bruised her arms, ugly colors already forming. And it wasn't as if it had never happened before. One time when he was angry with her he had kissed her so hard it had split her lip open, and when she had reacted negatively to it he had kissed her harder and laughed. It didn't sound like much, but it was as though he got off on hurting her. Of course he did, dominating others made him feel good about himself because otherwise he would realize what piece of shit he was.

Violet threw one of her boots into the closet, making a loud bang. That woke Mark up.

"What's going on?" he grumbled, looking over his shoulder at her.

She was fuming at this point. "Nothing," she growled continuing to stuff papers into the garbage can. Did she really need notebooks from the seventh grade? Oh, and look at that, a B- on her vocabulary quiz. That was pertinent information that ought to be passed down from generation to generation.

"Will you keep it down?" he said, rolling back over.

"No!" she shouted, stuffing another handful into the trash.

"What is your problem?" he asked, sitting up and slamming his fist into the bed.

"You! You're my problem!" She continued her forceful cleaning.

"What the fuck is going on?" He seemed legitimately confused. It must have been a bit disconcerting being woke from sleep that way.

"Mark, I'm sick of this. I can't do it anymore."

"Do what?" he asked, clearly not grasping what was happening.

"You! I can't do this with you anymore. Where did these come from, Mark?" She held her arms out like she was on the cross, displaying the lovely blue-black bands around each bicep.

That did it. He was way beyond confusion and straight into livid.

"Fuck you, you stupid bitch. You weren't complaining last night." He came to the edge of the bed, slamming his feet on the floor. His face was red with anger. He grabbed Violet's wrist and yanked her towards him. His hand was a clamp from which she would not be able to free herself.

"I shouldn't have to complain, Mark. You should just know not to hurt me." Her eyes were filling with tears she couldn't stop. They spilled over and down her cheeks before she could possibly stop it from happening.

"Oh, yeah, I'm the big bad abusive boyfriend now, right?"

His grip tightened on her wrist, she could feel her own fingers swell with blood from the pressure. He could crush her if he wanted. She tried pulling her arm back with all her might and could not get him to budge. He let go of her wrist, shoving her as he did so, and she flew across the room, landing on the pile of trash she'd had been collecting.

He looked down at her. Violet saw a flash of shock on his face for having thrown her so forcefully, but it evaporated so quickly it barely registered. He stood up, and she didn't know what he was going to do. He looked poised to fight or run and she didn't know which. She scooted away from him in the pile of junk, papers crinkling as she moved. The look on her face must have scared him, because he sat back down on the bed and just looked at her with this sort of stunned, yet blank, expression. Violet did not move or breathe, only sat there waiting for his reaction.

"What do you want from me?" he asked, voice wavering and unsure.

It really seemed like he was stunned by his own actions against her. It was surreal, because it wasn't as though he had never shoved her around before. Violet could not remember it ever being quite like this time though. Usually it was in the heat of the moment, and they were both shoving and yelling at each other. This was strange.

"I want you to leave and not come back," she said, surprising even herself. She had wanted to say that to him so many times, but never found the courage to do it. She meant it, and it was what she wanted, but she was surprised how much it hurt to say it.

He didn't move for a long time, he just stared at her. Emotions were warring all over his face. One second he looked stunned, the next afraid, angry, grief stricken, bewildered, and back to angry. His face always settled on angry.

"You are the most insane fucking bitch I have ever known." His voice was a seething growl as he grabbed his boots and shoved his feet down into them. He stood up, towering over her, glowering down at her. He was so angry, but she knew there was more behind the rage because she had seen it. She knew that he was angry now to save his own pride. He was not going to allow her to hurt him like everyone else had always hurt him. They both

45

came from the same kind of rejection in their pasts. That did not give either one of them a license to be assholes now. His eyes were so dark, so black and void, just like shark eyes.

Violet instinctively pulled her knees into her chest and wrapped her naked arms around them. She felt so vulnerable on the floor with him standing over her. More emotions splayed across his face and she knew he had to feel guilty. She could see it. Violet felt bad, and in that moment, she wanted to take every word back. He looked sad, bereft, and she knew she had wounded him deeply. As big of an ass as he was, she thought he did love her in some way, he was just incapable of doing it right. Or at least with her he was incapable. Roman's words echoed again in her head, and she knew what the right thing was for herself.

"Don't come back," she said again, more quietly. She didn't mean it to sound so hurtful; she just did not know what else to say. She just could not do this anymore. They would just continuously hurt one another until there wasn't anything left unless she pulled the plug now.

His face filled with blood. She watched as his fingers clenched tighter until they were white knuckled, the tension traveling up his arm until he was one solid mass of hardened muscle. It was terrifying. She remembered the show she had watched where crocodiles would do that. The lactic acid would build up in their system until they could do nothing with all that pent up tension but strike.

"Fuck you, you stupid whore," he spat, picking his jacket up off the floor and slamming it into the wall as he stormed out.

She was numb. Completely and utterly. She curled up right where she was, hugging her own body and staring off at nothing. She was vaguely aware that Steve was standing at the door asking her what was going on, but didn't answer him. She just closed her eyes in response and blocked out the world for as long as she could manage.

She woke several hours later in the same position she had fallen asleep. For a moment, she didn't remember what had happened or how she'd had gotten to the position on the floor. She sat up and looked around the room. It was in complete disarray. Every time she did a room overhaul, it always looked far worse before it go better. You have to stir things up in order to fix them. *That applies to most things in life*, she thought.

She pulled herself up off the floor and crammed the pile of stuff she had been laying on into the garbage can. The thing was overflowing and it would be a waste to continue stuffing more into it. She should have walked downstairs and got some garbage bags, but she didn't feel like it.

It was around one in the afternoon. She decided she would shower again and then go for a walk. Ignoring the ringing of her cellphone, she sifted through her dresser for panties, socks, and a bra. The stuff she had put on earlier was all crumpled from sleeping on the floor. She needed to change. She wanted to erase what had happened.

She walked across the hall and took a long, hot shower. It felt good, like her insides needed the warmth. She got out, put the underwear on, and then re-braided her hair. She brushed her teeth and smoothed sweet smelling lotion all over her body. It felt good to be clean.

Violet looked at herself too long in the mirror, spotted the bruises, and then noticed the dead look in her eyes. She felt sick all over. It wasn't a physical sickness, but a feeling of nothingness, of death and dying, and utter loneliness. She couldn't allow herself to cry anymore. It was unacceptable. She just had to change, to make things better. It was up to her now. She didn't have a mom and dad to run to anymore. It was all up to her. All alone.

She stood up straight and pointed at herself in the mirror, scolding the dead-eyed girl who looked back. "Stop it." She scowled at herself and went back to her bedroom.

She looked in her closet for something to put on that was comfortable. Everything looked too contrived to her today. She needed something simple and noticed the denim that was hanging way off to the side. Overalls, perfect.

She put on a black tank top and the overalls, which hung loosely, then rifled through the top drawer of her dresser for black socks. She dug through the closet for her low top Converse All-Stars that she hadn't worn for three years. She had begged her mom for these shoes for months before her birthday, and had been shocked when she had actually received them. Her family didn't have money for expensive shoes, and these were expensive for them. She smiled as she laced them up, then grabbed an armful of laundry to take down and wash. Steve was sitting at the kitchen table eating a bowl of cereal. The phone was ringing again, this time it was the one hanging on the wall.

"You gonna get that?" he asked, looking up at her with an odd expression on his face she could only surmise was confusion.

"Nope," she said, shoving the clothes down into the washer.

The "laundry room" was in a closet off the kitchen. Her dad had put the plumbing in the basement shortly before the accident, and had never had a chance to move the appliances down there.

"Well, I'm not answering it again. Mark's been calling here all day. What the fuck happened this morning?"

"I broke up with him," Violet said casually, closing the lid and cranking the knob to turn on the machine.

Steve stopped chewing briefly, stunned by the announcement. He was used to Mark and Violet having brawls, but they never broke up over them.

"So, what? You're just not going to ever talk to him again?"

"Not any time soon," she said, shrugging her shoulders.

"He sounded really upset on the phone," Steve said, filling his mouth with another spoonful.

"Yeah, I imagine," she said, reaching into the cupboard for a mug and a teabag. Her mom had always made her amaretto tea when she didn't feel good, and she didn't feel good. She filled the mug with water and placed the teabag into it.

"You should talk to him," Steve said again.

That was enough. Who the fuck was Steve to tell her who she should talk to anyway? Violet turned around, full mug in hand, and glowered at him.

"What? I'm just saying… He sounded really upset."

She slammed the mug down on the counter, water slopping over, and stalked towards him. He backed away from her like she was going to punch him, which actually wouldn't be too out of the ordinary. She was a physical person.

"Do you care that I was upset when he was doing this to me?" she seethed, pointing at one of the black and blue bands decorating

48

her bicep. "Or this?" she asked, pointing at the other arm. "No, didn't think so. So, shut the fuck up and quit acting like Mark's little fucking lap dog."

"Violet..." He was trailing behind her but she didn't care what he had to say. She knew that he would feel awful that Mark had done that to her, but she didn't care. Fuck them both.

Violet went upstairs, grabbed her bag and keys, stormed back downstairs, and slammed the door behind her while telling Steve to go fuck himself. She had to admit the look on his face was humorous. A lovely amalgam of fear, shame, and pity. It felt gratifying making him feel so bad.

It took her a good half of a mile before her heart slowed down and her pace eased off the near jog she had been trekking. She shouldn't have yelled at Steve like that. He would have had no way of knowing Mark had hurt her that way. Violet never told anyone how rough Mark had been with her, and yesterday was the first time he had really left any marks on her like that. At least ones that couldn't be played off as nothing. It was apparent by the darkness of the bruises, and the fact that they were clearly fingers marks, that it had been more than just a little playful rough sex. She must have been totally out of it not to notice while they were doing it.

She felt her gut clench again and exhaled forcefully, reaching into her bag for her stupid cellphone. She dialed the house number. It rang twice and Steve picked it up

"What?" he asked, clearly perturbed.

"Hey," she said sheepishly.

"What do you want?" he asked, less angry.

"Um, I'm sorry. I shouldn't have snapped at you. I'm just really frustrated, ya know?"

She stopped walking and looked around. It was a beautiful day. The sun was warm and soft, birds were singing, and the sky had those big fluffy white clouds. The humming whir of a lawnmower off in the distance somewhere was comforting in its familiarity. And she was finally free.

"So, I'm sorry for yelling at you. I just guess I wasn't up for hearing anyone defend him, okay?"

"Violet, I had no idea he did that to you. I never would've told

49

you to call him. He had no right to touch you like that."

Steve's voice was sincerely remorseful and indignant at Mark's brutish behavior. She knew that Mark was his best friend, and she also knew that Steve never saw the worst in pretty much anyone, especially not his best friend. Therefore, she had to let him off the hook. She wasn't going to be angry with him for something he had nothing to do with in the first place. Besides, it's not as if she would not have done the same thing if it were Amber and Randy who had ended their relationship.

"I know, Steve. No worries, okay? I'm not mad at you or anything and I am sorry I yelled like that. So, we good?"

"Of course," he said laughing, "I just wish I had known he was hurting you so I could've..."

"What? What could you have done? It's Mark. No one can do anything to him."

"Yeah," he paused, thinking over what she had just said.

There wasn't anyone who ever challenged Mark but her, his little ninety-five pound girlfriend. And what good did that ever do?

"Well, me and Randy could've done something."

Violet appreciated the gesture but knew the futility of it after the fact. Besides, it wasn't like she had known she even needed rescuing last night. All he had done was hold her down too tightly.

"Thanks, Steve. I'm gonna go. I just wanted to apologize."

"Nothing to apologize for," he said with a casual tone.

"Thanks," she said, resuming her walk. "Later."

The short jaunt that was only supposed to blow off steam turned into a two-hour tour of her town, complete with botanical garden sign reading at the trail down by the river. She finally decided she should go home and face the mountain of debris in her bedroom.

***

The phone rang incessantly. Violet had been successfully ignoring it for the last three hours, until Amber picked it up, having just walked in from work.

"Violet, it's for you," she said, setting the phone down and placing a bag of groceries on the table.

Violet reluctantly came downstairs toward the phone looking over at Amber and rolling her eyes. There was no doubt who it was on the other end of that receiver.

"Yes?" she said stoically.

"I've been trying to call you all day. Where the hell have you been?" Mark's voice was angry, but had a slight sense of panic to it.

"I asked you not to call," she said, looking at Amber whose eyebrows rose in disbelief.

"What is going on with you? Everything was great last night and now this?"

Everything was great? Wow, he was blind, stupid, and completely delusional. "Mark, I just can't take this anymore. You're constantly yelling at me and making me feel like I'm a piece of trash. I'm tired of it. I'm not your property. You don't own me. I'm tired of finding bruises on my body. I'm tired of having to walk on eggshells with you. I'm tired of seeing your fucking face. And if you ever step foot on my property again I will fucking kill you. Goodbye." She hung the phone up feeling rather proud of herself for being firm and not the least bit wishy-washy.

"Good for you," Amber said as she put a bag of apples in the refrigerator. "It's about time you kicked his ass out of your life."

"Yeah, good for me, now I just hope he really goes away, though that doesn't seem very likely."

"You know it's bad when even clueless Randy, who never has a bad thing to say about a friend, says you should break up with him."

"What? When did Randy say that?"

"Last night after he left you at the club. It wasn't a mystery how messed up you were, Violet. Randy just thought it was kind of jacked up that he left you there to drive yourself home, just so he could go out and get more fucked up. Plus Randy's heard Mark's tirades as often as the rest of us have. Randy may be out to lunch about a lot of things, but he's not the kind of guy who thinks the way Mark treats you is okay."

"Well, Randy can kick his ass then if Mark ever shows up."

51

Amber laughed and tossed an old moldy loaf of bread into the trash. "Well, I don't know if Randy would go that far, they are friends. Um, not to mention the fact that Mark would kill him," she said with a chuckle and looked up from the groceries. "You did the right thing, Violet."

"Everyone's so damn afraid of Mark. I wish someone would kick his ass already. That's part of his problem, no one's ever kicked his ass. I meant it when I said I'd kill him. I don't know how the fuck I'd do it, but I'll find a way."

"I just bought some new Ginsus last week. If they can cut through a tin can they can cut through his fat neck." Amber and Violet both laughed at that.

3. COFFEE CLOUDS

She was enjoying the weather. It wouldn't be warm like this much longer. The September sun felt good on her skin. There was a nice breeze rustling through the trees that made them sing. She loved the sound of moving leaves. Her head felt sort of cold from having wet hair and she wished she had put on a long sleeved shirt. She forgot about the fact that her bruises would be so visible to everyone.

Violet walked down to the convenience store with the sole purpose of getting a candy bar and a cup of coffee. She hadn't eaten anything since the sandwich she'd had at noon the day prior. When she walked in, she noticed this kid Chad she had gone to school with. He said hello and she nodded back without making eye contact for too long because it was apparent he wanted to talk to her. It wasn't that she had anything against him necessarily, but what could she have to say to him? They had not been friends since the seventh grade. A lot of people had quit being her friend when she discovered punk music and shaved all of her hair off. Then later when she had started wearing short skirts and corsets that made her breasts look huge they all sort of changed their minds about her, assuming she must be slutty, she was sure. Whatever. There was nothing they needed to discuss with each other, and certainly nothing as inane as casual conversation.

She grabbed the largest cup they had and filled it with hazelnut coffee. She picked up five packets of sugar, dumped them in, and then stirred in some flavored cream until the coffee was barely even brown.

"Want some coffee with that?" Roman's voice was so deep it rumbled in her chest.

"Hey!" She smiled, setting the coffee down and grabbing his arm instinctively. Her heart swelled with excitement seeing him there, like an old friend.

"I like a lot of cream and sugar too," he said, and winked "How are you? You look good," he said, stirring in some sugar.

"Oh, thanks. I'm doing alright, I guess." She looked at him sheepishly and grabbed a napkin to wipe the cream from her fingers.

After he finished stirring his drink and putting a lid on it, they walked up to the counter, Violet snagging a King Size Snicker along the way.

"Breakfast of champions." she said, waving the candy bar at him.

"Breakfast?" he asked, setting his coffee down on the counter It was late afternoon. "Two coffees and a breakfast bar," he said to the cashier as he reached for his wallet.

"Thanks." She smiled, picking up the drink and taking a small sip. She winced as the beverage burned her tongue.

"Be careful, didn't you read the cup?" he smiled, making reference to the 'hot beverage' warning on the side.

"So funny" she said, and rolled her eyes.

They walked outside to his car and leaned against it. It was some kind of classic muscle car she knew her dad would droo over. It was a beautiful black thing with shiny chrome.

"This is your car?" she asked in awe, running her hand over the smooth paint.

"Yeah," he said dismissively, and turned his attention back to her, "did you walk here?"

"Yeah, I only live about a mile away. Well, I guess you know that already," she smiled, taking another sip of her coffee "Where've you been? I haven't seen you around much."

"It's only been a couple days," he said, looking at her with apparent confusion. "I've been around. I haven't seen you either so where have *you* been?"

"Around," she smiled. "After seeing you two days in a row naturally assumed you were a regular."

"Shouldn't assume, sweetie."

They looked at each other for several moments and then she go nervous and looked away.

"So, do you want a ride or what?" he asked, walking to the

driver's side door.

"Yes," she said, coyly walking to the passenger side.

Roman reached over to unlock her door. "I don't know why I lock it when the windows are down." He grinned and started the car.

"Force of habit," she said, buckling herself in and nestling down into the soft leather. The seat felt so smooth as she ran her hands over it. She wondered how he could afford this car. Had he rebuilt it himself or bought it in this condition?

"This was a gift from my parents," he said, as though he could tell by her expression she was wondering. "It was my first car."

"Wow, it's beautiful," she said, running her hand over the dash. She wasn't ordinarily impressed with things like this, but maybe it was because she had never known anyone who owned such a nice car.

"It's nice enough," he said, casually shrugging his shoulders and backing out. "So, where do you want to go?"

"I don't know, just drive around, I guess." She smiled, taking another sip of the coffee, wondering why he seemed so dismissive about the car, almost like it meant nothing to him. Anyone she knew would want to brag about such a thing.

He took a big gulp of his coffee and pulled out of the driveway. She watched him periodically as he drove. His eyes were focused; his hands at two and ten, she had never seen anyone actually drive correctly.

"So, what kind of car is this?" she asked, trying to make conversation.

"It's a '66 Chevelle SS," he said casually.

"I'm sure that's something really impressive, but I don't know anything about cars. I know it's pretty." She laughed and ran her hand over the leather.

"It gets me around."

They drove around the neighborhood, and then off on several of the country roads surrounding the small town. It felt so good to have the cool, crisp air in her face and hair. The sun felt so soft and warm. She looked over at him. His long black hair looked like a horse's mane swishing in the wind.

"You'll have to remind me where you live," he said, looking

over at her. "Oh, yeah, back that way," she said, pointing to the right.

He followed her directions, pulled into her driveway, and turned the car off. He took another drink of his coffee, which was now nearly cold. She turned in her seat towards him and started to speak but hesitated.

"What?" he asked, looking at her with curiosity.

"Nothing, well... I just wanted to thank you," she said, her cheeks flushing.

"Not a problem, it wasn't far," he said, taking another drink.

"No, goof, well, thanks for the ride and the coffee too, but what I meant was for that night you talked to me. You seem to come to my rescue a lot. I mean, for only knowing you for like two days or whatever."

"Rescue? I don't remember rescuing you from anything."

"Well, you did, and I took your advice."

"My advice on what?" he said, furrowing his brow.

"I broke up with Mark," she said, a bright smile spreading across her face.

"Mark?"

"Yeah, my asshole boyfriend, Mark."

"I don't recall telling you to break up with your asshole boyfriend Mark."

Violet laughed in return. "Well, you did, you just didn't realize it."

"Oh, okay," he said, clearly confused. "Well, that's good. But I didn't really tell you to do that, did I?"

"You did, you just didn't realize it," she repeated. She smiled at him. A big warm smile. "What are you doing tonight?" she asked, her eyes bright with enthusiasm.

"Nothing that I know of."

"Do you want to come over? I'll make you dinner or something. I mean, I'm making dinner tonight," she said, her cheeks starting to turn red again.

"Okay, sure," he said, looking down at his cold coffee.

"I mean, you don't have to, I just feel like I owe you."

"First of all, you don't owe me anything. Even if I had saved you from something, I wouldn't have done it to gain a reward

Secondly, I don't want to be a bother to you. I'm sure you've got better, more productive, things to be doing than feeding me."

"It's not a bother, Roman." She smiled, reaching over and pinching his arm and letting her hand linger long enough to get embarrassed.

He was looking at her and it seemed as though he was considering something deeply, or that somehow this situation was a unique one for him, which puzzled her.

His eyes settled on her face, and she could feel her cheeks turning bright red. He didn't say anything, he just stared, and she didn't know what to say. She saw his eyes flick down to each of her arms and she really wished then that she had worn long sleeves. The bruises were embarrassing and she hoped he wouldn't say anything about it. The bruises, or how she got them, were not something she wanted to talk about. She did not want to explain how she was the kind of stupid girl who let her boyfriend manhandle her. It was weak and pathetic. She had always been the in-control-of-everything girl never letting anyone walk on her. So, why had she allowed Mark?

"Okay, what time?"

"Um, like, six? But you can come any time you want."

"Six it is then."

She smiled and returned his gaze. This was strange. She didn't know how she felt about this man, but it was pleasant.

"You really look good, well rested." He started his car back up. "I'll bring dessert."

Violet couldn't help the silly grin that kept taking over her face. She stepped out of the car and stood there for a few seconds watching him, and then jogged up to her house and waved goodbye as he drove away. *Well rested?* What kind of weird compliment was that? That was something you say to an old person who is convalescing. The thought made her giggle.

***

Roman looked through the photo album. This was something

he always seemed to find himself doing whenever he was settling into some strange new place. Most of the photos were of people he really didn't even know and had never met and he regretted the fact that he knew very little about them. It was more a case of curiosity than emotion. He focused on the picture of his parents. His mother had been so pretty and so kind. Memories of sitting in her lap while she sang songs to him brought a wave of contentment over him. He had not felt comfort like that since before she got sick. His father had always been a giant to him. He remembered his dad looming over him in his bed at night, his father unaware that he had been awake to see him there. During the day his dad was either sleeping or distant. At night, when his dad didn't know he was awake, he could see the love on his face. It was the only time his dad ever looked vulernable. Roman had tried every night to stay up long enough to hear his dad come in. He had been told he was his father's spitting image. It was hard for him to imagine that. His father had been a mountain.

Roman was aware that he had come to this town for a reason. There was something here for him. He had been sent. His apartment was neat and stark, black leather furniture and white walls. There was nothing out of place and no personal belongings visible besides his weight bench and the towel he left hanging on the bar. He had purchased these things when he came to this town and he'd leave them when it was time to move on. It was humorous that he considered the weight bench a personal item.

The kitchen was spotless, Roman not having cooked since he moved in. There was an old washer and dryer in the kitchen, which he had used. He was semi-obsessive about doing laundry, actually any kind of cleaning, as he couldn't stand clutter of any type. Stark. That was the way he liked things.

The acrid taste of coffee in his mouth was starting to annoy him. He stood up and walked to the refrigerator, opening it up to find something to drink. There was a jug of juice, so he took a big swig from it and screwed the lid back on, then closed the door. He walked to the sink and looked out the window as he rinsed his sticky hands. The leaves were starting to wither a bit. Their lush green was paling. It would be snowing soon enough, though it was still a ways away, but time flies.

He walked back to the bedroom and undressed, folding and placing each article into the hamper. He grabbed a black t-shirt and black jeans from the closet, reached into the chest of drawers, and selected a clean pair of socks, then walked to the bathroom and pulled the blood red towels from the linen closet. This was the only bit of color in his home. Red was the only color he liked besides black. He looked at his body in the mirror. The long jagged wound on his side was healing nicely. The scabbing was nearly all peeled away. It took all his discipline not to pick at it, but he knew it would bleed again, and possibly leave a scar if he did. He thought about where he was going later and had no idea what to make of it all. She was a cute girl, but so young. He did not have the luxury of making strong ties. Who knew when he'd have to leave again? It felt unsettling to him the way things had transpired. My God, her eyes. Maybe they were the only other color besides black like that he liked. Maybe.

Why did he even care? Why was he going over to her house? This was stupid and foolish. He had no attachment to anyone or anything and would never allow himself that weakness. Any weakness would be exploited.

He picked up his comb, removed the knots from his hair, and climbed into the shower, turning the water on. He let the cold water saturate his hair and body, liking the way the freezing water made him feel awake and coherent like nothing else besides a major adrenalin rush ever did. His life was an amalgam of numbness and apathy, so feeling anything at all, even if it was goose bumps, was good. He noticed the waterlogged scab had detached itself from the gash in his side. He slowly peeled it away.

I am healed.

He stood at the sink and brushed his teeth then let his hair down as it snaked down his back. He wrapped the towel around his waist, walked back to his bed, and lay down. *If only I healed as quickly as I kill…*

"Can't forget dessert," he sighed aloud, fighting the inevitable sleep that was coming over him.

***

"Oh man, that looks good, Violet," Steve said, reaching his meaty paw for the lasagna that was sitting on the stove.

"Hands off, jackass." She smiled, slapping him away. "You can wait. Now run along to your room." She scooted him away with her hands.

"Vi, I think he's here," Amber called from the couch in the other room.

"Wait's almost over," Steve mocked, making a face and sticking his tongue out as he jogged into the living room.

She grinned and threw the dishtowel at him then looked up at the clock. "Six o'clock on the dot."

Violet felt a nervous rush as she looked around the kitchen, making sure all the emptied containers and dirty dishes were hidden in their appropriate places. She pulled her hair out of the makeshift ponytail she had twisted it into and jogged for the door. Steve sat down on the lounge chair as Violet and Amber opened the front door. Roman was still making his way up the driveway and looked a bit uncomfortable that he was being watched. He had never felt this embarrassed his entire life, but then he'd never been in a situation like this either. Amber teased Violet, jabbing her in the side and making noises as they watched him walking towards the house. He waved his hand awkwardly at the two giggling girls.

"He's *hot*," Amber said, digging her finger into Violet's side.

"You think?" Violet said casually, tilting her head to the side and eyeing the man up and down.

"Don't be stupid," Amber chided as she opened the door "Hello, Roman," she sang from the house.

Violet just about died. She poked her friend in the back, nearly knocking her off balance onto the porch.

"Hello," he smiled, taking the door handle and handing Violet a box of something. "I told you I'd bring dessert."

"Oh, thanks," she said, standing aside so he could come in. She could feel her face begin to boil.

"Roman, this is Amber and Randy," she mumbled, pointing out her friends, unable to make eye contact with any of them.

"Hello," he said awkwardly.

60

"Come in," Amber offered, shoving Randy so he would sit up to make room on the couch.

"Thanks," he said, taking a seat beside them.

"So, dude, you're new in town, right?" Randy chimed in, breaking the ice.

Amber and Violet darted for the kitchen.

"He is so hot, Violet. You dork, why didn't you tell me?"

"I don't know, I didn't think about him being hot," Violet said, hiding the shy grin from her.

"Yeah right." Amber laughed.

"Shut up! Remember, I just broke up with *my boyfriend.*"

"And?"

"And shut up." She grinned.

"Lord, no wonder Mark was so jealous of the guy."

"What?" Violet asked, scowling at Amber.

Amber looked at Violet with a grimace, wondering if she should've brought up Mark at all. It was hard telling with Violet these days what she would and wouldn't want to discuss. "I honestly don't know how you stood him as long as you did," she said empathetically.

"I was used to it," she said with a shrug as she looked away from her, not wanting to start crying again.

"Yeah," Amber said, and rubbed Violet's arm and gave her a squeeze, then hugged her. Violet let her.

"So, anyway, let's see what he brought." Amber beamed and looked at the box on the counter.

"Okay," Violet said, equally as excited. Mark had never given her any gift besides drugs and a Valentine/birthday Bear once the day after the holiday that her birthday also just happened to fall on. She pulled the pretty ribbon and then opened the box. A beautiful, humongous cheesecake sat there looking so divine with chocolate and raspberries drizzled all over it.

"Uhhhhhhh," Amber and Violet both slobbered in unison.

"A man after my own heart," Amber sighed. "Seriously, Vi, that cheesecake has to be good for at least a blow job, right?"

"Amber!" she screamed and smacked her arm and then laughed nervously. Amber always knew exactly how to embarrass her. "Oh my god! "

"Dude, I'm just saying. It's cheeeeeeesecake. Chocolat cheesecake. Drool."

Violet looked at her with wide, shocked eyes and just shook he head. "Well, then you give him one."

"Can I? I just might have to if it's as good as it looks."

"Raaan-dy," Violet called to the other room as if she was goin to tattle.

They both laughed when he answered, "What?" in return. Th phone rang and Violet looked at Amber.

"Don't answer it," she said. Amber was shaking her head i total agreement before she'd even gotten the whole sentence out.

The sound cut off mid-ring and Violet knew that mean someone else had answered. It wasn't Randy, because he had bee warned about answering the phone.

"Goddamned Steve!" Amber growled, and marched for th living room.

Violet looked at the lasagna again and decided it had set up lon enough. She put Amber's garlic bread in the oven to brown the walked back into the living room to hear Amber yelling at Stev for answering the phone. How embarrassing. Her house was circus. Steven mumbled something to whomever was on th phone and sheepishly hung up.

Violet sat down in the recliner which was opposite of wher Roman was seated. He and Randy had been talking about som sort of sport, probably baseball since it was nearing the end of th season. Or maybe it was football since that was gearing up t start? Regardless, she had no interest. It had been quite awhil since she'd given a shit about sports, since she and her dad had qui watching together. Every game day he had still sat in his chair an had the wings ready, and every time Violet had something mor important to do. A stab of guilt pierced her insides and she felt he eyes welling again. Thankfully, Amber interrupted her thoughts.

"By the way, this is Steve," she said to Roman, gesturin towards Steven who had finally hung up the phone.

"Nice to meet you," Roman said, standing up and extending hi hand.

"Yeah," Steve said, taking it reluctantly.

Amber and Violet shared a look that Violet knew Roman caugh

because he looked at her and smiled.

"Did you put the bread in?" Amber asked, trying to ease the tension.

"Yep," Violet answered, and smiled at her.

"Good."

Steve slumped on the other side of Randy close enough for Violet to haul off and punch him if she so chose. It could have happened if he opened his mouth and said one more thing to piss her off. Lucky for him he kept it shut.

"So, when can we eat?" Randy asked, patting his stomach instinctively.

Violet had never known another single human being who could put away food at the rate he could. It was a mystery how Randy was so fit because he pretty much ate nothing but junk from sun up to sun down and he drank vast amounts of beer. However, he wasn't fat at all. Lucky bastard. In fact, he was quite lean and lanky.

"I guess we can eat now," Violet said, and shrugged her shoulders.

"Excellent," Randy said, leaping from the couch and heading for the kitchen before the rest of them even stirred.

Violet was rather shocked that Steve sat at the table. Honestly, she didn't really want him there after all the shit he'd said to her that morning. True, she had apologized to him after yelling that morning, but what he'd said still stung. Why was he glaring at her across the table now? The facts had not changed about Mark and her relationship, so what had been said on the phone to change Steve's demeanor?

Amber helped Violet dish out the bread and lasagna. She sat down opposite Roman once everyone had a full plate. It felt really awkward eating in front of him. No one was really talking. He had to have been feeling weird himself. Randy wasn't talking because he was so focused on eating. Steve was chowing down in silence as well. Amber took a big gulp of red wine to wash down the bite of lasagna she had been chewing.

They all looked around the table nervously. "What gives? Talk already," she said, shifting in her seat.

"Well, uh, thanks for dinner?" he said, grinning at her.

"Not you, moron, they aren't usually this quiet." She kicked him under the table then winced and frowned for having called him a moron and kicking him before having a chance to catch herself. She was used to talking to everyone with that snotty tone. She hoped he realized she called everyone a moron. Well, now, how would he know that?

Roman looked at her funny, then looked over at Amber who returned his gaze with a peculiar expression to match his. "Um, okay, so, I won't talk?" he offered with a crooked grin on his face. He was completely inept in regards to situations like this.

"Shut up. You know what I meant," Violet said, kicking him again and then wincing all over.

He shrugged his shoulders and took a bite of lasagna. This was extremely bizarre. Apparently, he had no clue what he was supposed to do.

"Okay, this conversation is going nowhere fast. Before you humiliate and or maim the man any further, hello, Roman, nice to meet you, where are you from?" Amber smiled, extending her hand to him. "That is how one converses, Violet."

He reached across the table and shook her hand. "I'm from a lot of places," he answered, and took his hand back.

"Okay, vague much?" Amber laughed taking a big bite of pasta.

"I mean, I've lived all over the place," he clarified.

"Like where?" Violet said, intrigued by his answer. She had wanted to get away from this town the whole of her existence, well, at least the whole of her teenage years. So the thought of him experiencing somewhere besides here was very appealing to her.

"I've lived mostly in the Midwest; I was born Nebraska. I've lived in Wisconsin, Minnesota, and Iowa, and had stops in some other areas." He was purposely vague in his answers. He did not think people deserved to be lied to.

"And now you're here, lucky man." Randy smirked, barely taking his eyes away from the plate of food that was quickly diminishing.

"Ever been to California?" Violet asked. She was excited to talk to someone who actually knew something about the world. No one she knew had ever traveled much beyond this state. No one had the money to travel or go on vacations.

"Yes, I've been there a number of times. It's kind of too busy for me, I guess. I'd rather live in a smaller town."

"I can't imagine wanting to live here after going to all those other places," Amber questioned.

"Well, I don't know, quiet is good. You don't get that in New York or Los Angeles."

Violet pondered what he said. The idea of constant action seemed appealing to her now.

"So, why have you traveled so much? Were your parents in the military or something? You lived in New York City too?" Amber asked. Her mind was spinning with questions.

"Something like that. And yes, I've lived there too."

"Okay, enough with the third degree," Violet interjected, scowling at her friends in jest. "You wanna know anything about us? It seems only fair since we're needling you for information."

"I'm not good at the whole 'question and answer' thing. I'll learn what I need to know eventually, right?" He smiled at her again. "This is good, Violet," he said, referring to the lasagna and changing the subject. It was awkward being the center of attention.

Violet smiled, and took a big gulp of water then wiped her mouth. She had barely touched her food and was content to watch her friends enjoy what she had made for them. Ordinarily Amber was the cook, but she had made the decision to make lasagna the moment the thought to invite Roman over had crossed her mind. Lucky for Roman.

"I can't believe how quiet Randy is," Amber joked, looking at her boyfriend. He was well on his way through his second piece of lasagna and his third roll.

"No time to talk. Must eat," he said, sauce slopping.

Everyone laughed self-consciously. It was bizarre feeling nervous in their own home.

"Well, this is nice and uncomfortable," Steve interjected as he stood up, having finished his dinner. "I'm gonna head out. Thanks for dinner, Violet. It was nice meeting you," he said, looking over at Roman and lifting his hand.

"Yeah, nice meeting you," Roman answered.

They waited for him to walk out the back door in the kitchen and then Amber turned to Violet. "No, that wasn't rude at all," she said, rolling her eyes.

"It's okay, it is uncomfortable isn't it? The guy's just being honest," Roman said, drinking the red wine and shrugging his shoulders not taking his eyes away from Violet's gaze.

"There's more to it than that," Amber said, as she wiped her mouth with the napkin.

"Yeah, he acts like a baby any time some potential boyfriend comes around," Randy interjected, not looking up from his plate.

"*Oh my god,*" Violet said, covering her face with her hands and shaking her head.

Amber and Roman started laughing at her overreaction.

"What?" Randy said, looking up.

"Stop while you're ahead, sweetie," Amber said, smoothing her hand over the back of his head.

"What?" he asked again.

"Eat, Randy," Amber laughed, handing him another roll.

"Don't have to ask me twice." He shrugged his shoulders continuing to chomp his way through more. He always ate mass quantities due to his overabundance of expendable energy. The guy had two modes: hyperactive or sound asleep.

"So, anyway, Steve's got jealousy issues. It's not just you. He hated Mark there for awhile too," Amber said, turning her attention back towards Roman.

"Yeah, and he was a little miffed about Randy and Amber too as I recall?" Violet said, leaning forward and looking down at Randy who continued shoveling food in his mouth.

"Well, yeah, there was that too," Amber said, leaning back in her chair.

"That's too bad, and completely unnecessary," Roman said, looking at Violet trying to show her this was no big deal and she shouldn't be embarrassed by Randy's comment.

"So, thanks for the cheesecake, Roman. I think I'm going to have some now," Violet said, standing up and walking over to the counter. "You guys want some too?" Her face was hot with embarrassment and she was desperately trying to change the focus of the conversation.

"Yes," Randy and Amber said simultaneously, then started laughing.

***

"So... I want you to know I haven't been going around calling you a 'potential boyfriend'," she said nervously, scraping her fingernails across the red tablecloth.

"I didn't presume you were," he responded, taking another sip of wine.

"Well, okay then. I just don't want you to get freaked out or something."

"It takes far more than that to freak me out," he said with a smile. It was easy just talking to her alone without the others. He was a lot less uncomfortable.

His whole face seemed to change when he smiled. He went from looking like a stern, mysterious man to cheerful and warm with only a minute change in his mouth. She watched his eyes glisten as the soft radiance of the stained glass lamp that hung over the table caught the iris when he moved. His pupils were large and so black. His eyes were the most beautiful glistening shade of green she had ever seen. His body was slouched down slightly in the chair stretching his long legs out beneath him. She watched the large muscles of his arms flex and relax as he lifted the glass repeatedly to his red mouth.

"Want some more?" she asked, leaning for the open bottle that sat in the center of the table.

"Yes," he answered, lifting the glass towards her. "You aren't having any?" His eyebrow lifted slightly in question.

"Nope, not a fan," she said, filling his glass.

"Interesting," he commented, taking another drink and never taking his eyes from hers.

"How so?" It was hard to imagine what he would find interesting about her not drinking.

She leaned back into the chair, rolling her head to the side. She

67

had these seductive moves down so fully she was not even aware she did them. The soft look in her eyes, the sideways glance, moist open lips.

"I just think it's interesting that you take illegal substances but don't drink."

She shifted her weight in the chair looking back down at the red tablecloth. It was revolting to hear that she "took illegal substances" aloud. He said it without any judgment whatsoever, but it felt like a knife in her gut. It did not feel good to hear those words, knowing how disappointed her mom would be with her if she had known all the things Violet had done. And even under her own roof with mom only a few feet away. She felt disgusting and dirty. Would her mom even love her if she had known all the awful things she had done? The question plagued her on repeat.

How did he even know she took illegal drugs? Well, of course a person would have to be a total brain dead moron not to have guessed at The Cage. She sighed.

"No offense?" he said, leaning forward to get her to look him in the eye again.

"None taken, it's just weird to hear that out loud." She looked up at him with a slightly wounded expression in her eyes. Hearing those words in her mother's kitchen was a bit disconcerting, almost as though her mom was listening and would be disappointed in her. "What can I say? I'm not twenty one yet."

"You know we've all been there?" he asked, taking another sip of the drink.

"Not everyone," she answered, standing up and clearing the plates from the table. Neither of her parents or grandparents had ever been like her.

He stood up and walked to the sink handing her another plate.

"Thanks," she said, taking the dish from his hand and scraping it off into the sink.

She turned the water on, letting the sauce and cheese run down the drain. He put his hand on her shoulder as he stood there watching her clear the plates. It felt intimate, warm, and awkward all at the same time. It seemed as though he felt he shouldn't have said what he had, so now he was comforting her. And he was. He drank the last of the wine from his glass, and then set it down on the counter beside the sink.

"There's more," she said, turning her face up toward him and looking into his eyes warily.

"I'm fine," he said.

He squeezed her shoulder and left the room, thinking she may need a moment to collect herself. She looked flustered. Violet turned to look at him when she was sure he was leaving. This was all so freaking strange. She didn't feel comfortable. She didn't know who she was, who she was supposed to be. She hated the way her life had turned. It went beyond losing her mom and dad. She was tired before that happened. Was there a reason she had allowed Mark to hurt her? Was it because she knew she wasn't living right? Violet hadn't been raised to walk around thinking she was better than everyone else, being mean to people who she didn't have any cause to be mean to, just because she could. To take all kinds of drugs. To be fucked up. Her parents were good people. Her grandparents were good people. Her aunts and uncles and cousins were good people. She was the only rotten one of the bunch.

She felt sick to her stomach again. If she kept her stomach empty, she felt sick a lot less easily. *I should not have eaten that cheesecake.*

She finished the dishes leaving them in the drainer to air dry, took a deep breath, and walked out into the living room. Roman was sitting in the red chair again. Amber and Randy were in their usual place side by side on the couch. Violet sat down next to Amber and scrunched down into the sofa, propping her feet up on the coffee table.

Roman looked around the room. Her house was old, but warm as though it had been loved and cared for by her family. The furniture was well worn and comfortable and none of it matched.

Randy was nice and Roman liked him immediately. There was no pretense to Randy, and Roman found that enjoyable because everyone he knew was a fraud. He also liked the casual and blunt way that Amber expressed herself. Neither of these people were pretentious, and he liked that about them. As Randy spoke, Roman looked around the room intermittently. He noticed the collection of crystal pieces and photographs strewn here and there in mismatched frames on the built in bookshelves surrounding the television. It was then that it dawned on him just how much Violet had lost.

All of these things, everything in this house, had been alive and part of a collective. Now they were relics in a museum. He remembered his own home after his mom died. All of her things were gallery pieces to be looked at but would never be used. Remembering all her things, seeing all of these things, brought back horrible memories. Then he noticed a picture of Violet that made it next to impossible for him to listen to the story Randy was telling.

She must have been five or six in the photo. Her hair was pulled up in uneven pigtails tied with big purple yarn bows. She was wearing a purple dress with yellow and white daisies, and her smile was so wide and her eyes twinkling. He could not look away from it.

He honestly could not remember ever being as happy as she looked in that photo. Ever. When he was very young, his mother saw to it that life was as normal as it could be, but death was still always surrounding them. His mother and father had made a huge mistake bringing him into their world, and he knew his father thought that every time he looked at him. It was the reason his dad had always kept him at arm's length, as Roman did with everyone. Feeling... death... almost cause and effect...

Violet shifted on the couch, drawing his eye. He had tried not to look at her. It would be obvious from the chair he sat in if he did. He wanted to tell her he understood her loss, but did he? Roman had never had what she had with her parents. A real home. Permanence. Stability. He grieved for her looking around her familiar, comfortable home.

Violet looked over at him and smiled. He did not smile in return, just looked at her, wondering what went on behind her eyes. She was strange. No, maybe he was strange and she was perfectly normal? He finally smiled back after several moments and looked back to the television, Randy still rambling about something.

Roman assumed that Randy, Amber, and Steve had all moved in after her parents' death. He wondered how that made her feel, imagining on some level it was a comfort, but also thinking it would be such a radical departure of her life before that she would probably wish she could be alone at times. She did not have the same open and friendly demeanor as Amber and Randy, so he imagined she probably liked having her own space.

The dinner she had made had been good. Comfort food. Probably a family favorite. It reminded him of some of the meals his mom had made when his father would come home from being away for longer than usual. Violet seemed to like the cheesecake he brought, seeing as how it was the only thing she had really eaten. It bothered him that she was so thin. Did her friends notice? Or was it fashionable amongst them to be that thin?

He was acutely aware of her eyes on him. He could feel them like a physical touch. If he concentrated he could hear her breathing, almost feel her heart beat. Their breathing and heart fell into rhythm as he continued watching the television, not hearing a word Randy was saying. He felt languorous, more relaxed than he had felt in a very long time. Then Amber and Violet giggled about something, waking him from the dream-like spell that had come over him.

Their eyes found each other, locked. He didn't want to look away from her. It was as though there was some kind of rope attaching him to her then. Again, their breathing fell into rhythm. If he had been unable to control himself he would've gone to her, pressed his ear against her chest and listened to her heart beat over and over and over. What the hell was happening?

He took a deep breath and cleared his head, feeling as though someone had tried to put some kind of spell on him.

***

She noticed his eyes moving with the images on the screen. She was well aware that he knew she was watching him. He took deep, seemingly bottomless, breaths. His muscular chest rose and fell in such slow, smooth measure. The shirt was tight around his arms and across his chest because of the way he was slouching in

71

the chair, his lower back exposed and visible to her. His legs were long and bent and she noticed the flatness of his stomach even as he slumped in the chair. He tilted his head, resting it on the back of the chair, and looked over at her through half closed lids, squinted by the angle at which his head lay. She didn't take her gaze from his, and they sat there for several more minutes contemplating this moment and the other person with calm, perplexed interest. His mind went over all the different scenarios in which he had arrived in this town, the frantic calls, the hurried move, and now this distraction. There had to be some reason.

He had never made eye contact with anyone for this length of time. It was strange, but not uncomfortable.

"Do you want to go upstairs?" she asked, breaking the silence. Both Randy and Amber looked at Violet with inquiring expressions.

"Sure," he said, leaning forward, pulling his tall body up out of the chair.

Violet stood up quickly and started walking towards the staircase.

"Remember what I said about the cheesecake," Amber called after her.

Violet turned around, bugged her eyes out, and kept walking while Amber laughed. Roman trailed behind her, nodding his head casually at her friends.

Amber threw her legs over Randy's lap. "Have fun, kiddos," she said, looking back at the television.

"Later, dude," Randy said, squeezing Amber's feet.

Roman followed Violet up the stairs. The wood paneling coupled with the low ceiling gave the stairwell a dark cavernous feel. It would be easy to trip and fall down these stairs, or hit his head, which he was nearly doing. He looked at the top of the stairway and saw Violet's head sticking out a doorway on the left hand side of the hall. He unhurriedly walked towards her and stopped in front of the open door.

"What was wrong with the cheesecake?" Roman asked Violet paranoid he had brought something she hated.

"Ugh, nothing. She was being stupid," Violet said, shrugging off the question and rolling her eyes, cheeks turning red. "It's kind of messy," she said, standing aside and letting him enter. She had not finished the overhaul that she had started on again earlier in the day.

He looked around the room and then leaned against the large black dresser. The mirror shook slightly from his weight being pressed against it. This was so different from his bright, orderly apartment. It wasn't bad, it was just different. Her bed was unmade; a hand sewn looking quilt of dark velvets, cotton, wool, and corduroy lay in a clump in the center of the bed, the dark red sheets nearly off. He looked at the black wall behind her bed with the dark red painted spirals and remembered seeing her black and red fingers that night at the club.

She noticed he was looking at her wall. "Those spirals are supposed to catch witches," she said nonchalantly.

"Yes, they are. Is there a major infestation running rampant in Mantua, Ohio?"

"Bitches maybe," she laughed. "Not too sure about witches."

His eyes settled on her again. She liked looking at him and she thought he liked looking at her too. His face was that perfect kind of beautiful that was not in any way feminine. His eyes were so expressive, dark green like emeralds, and set under black eyebrows. His face was cut in hard planes, long perfect nose, wide, lush lips that were tinted red from the wine he had been drinking. She knew that all it would take was for him to move closer to her, to even remotely look like he was going to kiss her, and she would let him. She would let him do anything he wanted to her.

Where is my self respect? Why would I let a stranger touch me? Do I have absolutely zero self-esteem? I just broke up with Mark.

"I like that color," he stated, referring to the dark red sheets that crumpled, half off the bed.

"Yeah, me too."

She looked away from him and let her eyes travel over all the things she needed to either give away, throw away, or put away. There were two stacks of CDs beside her dresser, at least a foot high each, which needed to be sorted. There were all the shoes, the papers, the magazines, the clothes. It stressed her out thinking

73

about it. He looked awkward standing there looking at her and the room. It dawned on her what he might be thinking, of course.

"Don't worry," she said, pulling herself across the bed to rest her back against the wall again, "I'm not going to sully your good virtue."

He chuckled and noticeably relaxed. Violet wasn't used to guys not trying to sully her good virtue, whatever was left of it.

They sat in silence for a long time. She didn't think he was bored because he didn't move around a lot and most people who are bored try to make conversation or they can't sit still. He had not moved since he had finally sat down on the end of her bed and hadn't felt the need to speak.

She reached over to her stereo that sat on the floor beside her bed and put a CD in, turning to look at him. "You like music?"

"I don't listen to it much," he said, crossing one foot over the other, folding his arms across his chest. His muscles looked huge as he stood there.

"You don't listen to music that much?" She grabbed an elastic hair tie and twisted her messy crimped tresses into a knot, securing it with the band. She leaned against the wall and kicked the quilt to the floor.

"No, I've never had the time to bother," he answered, looking around the room and back to her, "but this is nice."

She leaned over to her nightstand and adjusted the bright light to the lowest setting. He uneasily wondered where this was going. She looked down at her hands and he noticed a change in her face. The corners of her mouth were drawn down and she seemed to be trembling.

"Hey, what's going on?" he asked softly, without moving.

"There's just been a lot to deal with this last month," she said, not looking up at him. She did not want to lose it in front of this relative stranger. Something about him made her want him close—she wanted him near when she felt this way—but her nature was to hide her emotions.

"I imagine so, Violet. Having your life turned upside down is never an easy thing to go through."

He turned sideways, resting his bent knee on the bed. The feel of his knee against her leg was comforting. She had kept all these

74

emotions bottled up inside knowing Amber would have helped her through this, but she was apprehensive to talk to her. She felt like Amber knew her too well, and it would have hurt her friend too much, knowing the extent of the sadness and misery she felt.

"Fond Affections" by This Mortal Coil came on, and as the words were sung they sank into Violet, the grief welled up inside of her, and she didn't know if she would be able to hold it down.

"There's no light at the end of it all, let's all sit down and cry..."

The haunted voice of the singer always got her anyway and now the words seemed to have even more punch than before.

Roman had obviously listened to the lyrics himself, and sensed the change in her, because he moved closer. She pulled her knees up and wrapped her arms around them, tucking her face into her chest as tight as she could. She was crying, but she didn't know if he could hear her or not. She had gotten really good at hiding it, as long as her eyes were covered and no one reacted. The moment someone asked if she was okay, she usually crumbled.

He did not say anything, for which she was thankful. Violet sniffled and she knew then that the jig was up. Roman reached out and put his hand on her back. He didn't move, just put his hand on her back. The moment his palm touched her she leaned over against him, as close as she could get, and curled up there like a little dog in his lap.

Her head and upper torso rested against him, her arms still held her knees tight to her chest. She could not pull into herself far enough. She wanted to hide, wanted to make herself small enough to disappear.

His hand was so warm on her skin. He let her cry, never saying anything, which she appreciated. His hand rested right where Mark's had held her down the night before, only his hand was gentle and warm, meant to comfort, not control. She was thankful not to be sobbing audibly, but she was trembling all over and snuffling loudly from time to time. Her body was quaking so violently that she could feel the vibration from it in the mattress. Roman's hand never left her arm, never saying a word.

Violet was so exhausted, so worn out from being tense for so long. She relaxed the hold she had on her knees some and stretched out a little. His jeans were wet with her tears. She wrapped her arms around his waist and hugged him. Finally, his hand moved pushing the loose wet strands of hair that were stuck to her cheek. She snuffled again. It sounded so loud to her. He rubbed her arm and pulled her a little tighter against him but never said a word. She almost started crying harder because he was being so kind.

No man she had ever been with had been kind to her. Violet didn't know what was so wrong with her that made them always want to abuse her. It had to be her, because it had happened in all three of her serious relationships. Roman's gentleness and the respect he showed her by not asking a bunch of questions, interjecting a bunch of opinions, or telling her just to suck it up, meant everything to her.

Violet exhaled and wiped the tears from her face. She felt as though she had been crying for hours, eyes swollen, and face stinging.

"Sorry," she whispered hoarsely.

"You know, it's alright to cry and grieve?"

"Is it?" she asked, looking up at him, a thick veil of tears still covering her eyes. "I'm not so sure it's okay to cry and grieve. I need to get on with life, or whatever." She was obviously repeating something someone had told her, probably in an effort to avoid dealing with her emotions. She looked away from him again, settling back into him.

"No offense, but that's bullshit," he said, his hand tucking her loose braid behind her ear.

Violet's insides were warring. All the bottled up emotions had just overflowed all over this man. Amber would have helped her through all of this, but Violet would have never allowed her to see just how much pain she was feeling.

"You will never get over your parents dying. Sorry, I know that's not what most people tell someone after someone they love dies. They always tell you it will get easier or that things will get better. That's bullshit. The pain will become less immediate over time, but the second you stop and think about them, all the memories and grief will come flooding back. It's never going to go away, and I don't think you want it to."

"I want it to," she said, looking up at him, giant tears falling from her eyes in big silent drops.

"No, you don't, because if it did it would mean you didn't love them, and you know that's not true." He wiped the tears from her face, cupping her cheek. Violet held his hand there, not letting him take it back.

Her eyes closed, allowing the wave of his comfort to roll over her. She had been apprehensive about coming up to her bedroom, thinking he may take it as an advance, or permission to try to fuck her. What she had wanted was a few quiet moments with someone who would allow her to grieve and take down her guard without making her feel guilty. And she had wanted to be comforted. No one gave her solace anymore. She didn't know why she thought he would. But she had, and he did. She let go of his hand and wrapped her arms around his waist again, her face resting against his stomach as he was slouching on the bed. She let out a deep, humid breath, her tears soaking into his shirt.

"I'm sorry," he said, his thumb moving gently over her cheek.

Violet closed her eyes, relishing the comfort.

***

The CD had finished. Violet had cried herself to sleep. Roman sat there looking around the room at all the various stacks and piles. He could see the clothing hanging in her closet haphazardly, mostly black and red and the occasional purple and green. He liked her in denim. It was the least of her disguises.

There was a large photo of her and Amber across the room tacked to the wall. They were sticking their tongues out with wide smiles spread across their faces. She had been a happy person in the not so distant past. He looked down at her. Her hair was soft and shiny and smelled like some sort of flower he could not place. She was so tiny curled up in a little ball against him. Her little toes peeked out beneath the long legs of her pants, little black nails so minuscule they looked almost childlike. Her knees had fallen over and rested against him, her small hands curled in his lap. He wanted to take each little finger and look at them individually. She was a marvel to him. Perfectly made. He leaned his head back against the wall and closed his eyes.

What am I doing here?

***

"Violet, Mark's here," Amber called frantically from the hallway.

Roman and Violet simultaneously jumped, Roman clutching his chest taking a deep breath from the shock. Violet leapt off the bed looking around the room and then to Roman. She felt disoriented having awoken so abruptly. Roman was surprised by the depth of his sleep—even more by his shock. *I should never be that...*

"Violet!" Amber called again, knocking on the door.

Violet walked to the door and opened it. "What?" she asked still dazed.

"Mark's downstairs. Steve brought the asshole back over here with Mose."

"Oh, fuck! I'm so tired of all this drama," Violet said, pacing back to the center of the room. Her makeup was smeared around her eyes from crying, her heart racing.

Roman stood up and walked towards the door. "I'm going to go downstairs," he said, looking back at Violet. "You should go wash your face and wake up a little more," he said, smiling at her.

"Don't go down there!" Violet said, grabbing his thick wrist.

"Why not? We don't have anything to hide. We're just friends," he said casually.

"Randy's trying to get rid of him. Just wait a little bit. I'm so pissed at Steve right now," Amber said, looking at both of them.

Roman had to admit Steve bringing Mark over was a rather fucked up thing to do given the fact that she'd just broken up with him apparently.

Violet was equally as angry, and she didn't want Roman walking into her drama. "Mark will start a fight, Roman. It's what he does."

"With all due respect, ladies, I can take care of myself. It'll be fine." Roman took his wrist back from her, and patted her on the head then walked out of the room and down the stairs. He almost hoped Mark would start a fight with him for the simple fact that he hated people like him and the thought of pounding him with his fists sounded appealing. He knew it was best for Violet for things to remain diplomatic though.

"You better go with him, Amber," Violet begged, rushing across the hall to the bathroom.

Amber looked at her friend with concern, "What happened? Your makeup is all jacked up?"

"Nothing, Amber," Violet reassured. "Go with him, hurry!"

Amber rushed down the stairs catching up with Roman. She didn't know him at all really. Maybe he would be the one to start a fight? He looked like he could be the type.

Violet quickly washed her face with cold water, slowly getting her wits back. She looked in the mirror, quickly making sure her face was clean, and dried herself with the yellow towel on the vanity, then ran downstairs to the living room. Mark was sitting on the couch with his feet on the coffee table, his arms spread across the back. He looked over at her and smiled.

"Hi, Violet," he said calmly, almost triumphantly, looking away from her and back to Steve whom he had been talking to.

Roman was sitting in the red velvet chair. Steve had introduced the two. Randy was sitting on the edge of the couch waiting for the trouble to break out. He wanted to be able to jump up fast if Mark blew his top, which would be likely.

"Why don't you all relax? I just stopped by to say hello, geez." He smiled, looking at Roman for several seconds, then eyeing Violet.

"Don't start!" Amber chided, giving Mark a stern look.

"Don't start what? So, I'm not even welcome here at all? I just wanted to stop by, say hello, maybe talk to Violet for a few minutes, and be on my merry way. We are all friends, right? Is that okay with you, Violet?" He spoke in an overly sweet tone of voice. It was unnerving.

"Come on then," she said, pulling his sleeve. She looked over at Roman and then walked into the kitchen, Mark following behind her.

"So, who's that fag?" Mark asked, referring to Roman.

"Shut up, Mark. What do you want? Tell me and then leave."

"I just wanted to come by and talk to you. You won't eve answer my calls, Violet. I had to do something. I wanted to see i we could work things out, but apparently you're already fuckin someone else." He grabbed her arm and shoved her back into th counter.

"Stop it, Mark. I told you I do not want to see you anymore I'm sorry," she said, rubbing her arm where he had squeezed her She did not want this to get out of hand. No one she had eve known was capable of controlling Mark when he got out o control. She had seen him flip out and smash out windows an break furniture, let alone when he actually fought someone.

"So, you're seriously already over me? You're already fuckin some asshole you don't even know?" He squeezed her again, thi time harder. "Or were you already fucking him and that's why yo wanted me to go away?"

"Stop it!" she begged, trying to get her arm from his grip.

The others could hear them and they all stood up and ran to th kitchen.

"Mark, just leave, man," Randy said cautiously, grabbing hi friend by the shoulder.

"Fuck off," Mark shouted, turning and punching Randy in th face.

Randy grabbed his jaw and leaned against the counter, trying t right himself.

"Come on, man, let's leave," Steve said, as he and Mosle walked towards him.

"Stay out of this." Mark was clenching his fists, focused o Roman who did not say a word, he just stood behind the other casually staring the man down with no facial expression.

"Mark, leave, you fucking asshole!" Amber growled, shovin Mark from behind. She had made her way to Violet who was nov crying and holding her bruised arm.

Roman looked at Violet, he would not allow this man to la another finger on her or any of the others. This wouldn't even be challenge to him.

"Fuck you, Amber, you fucking cunt! I have a right to be here."

"You keep saying that, Mark, but you don't have a right to be here. She doesn't want you here," Amber snarled, putting her arm around Violet.

"Yeah, come on, just leave," Randy said, still holding his jaw. It took all his energy not to go after him after the way he spoke to Amber, but he also knew there was no way he could win a fight with him.

Mark focused on Roman again, who still had not moved. There was a fire flashing in Roman's eyes and Violet watched as he seemed to glow in the darkened room. Power surged from him, filling the room. It was palpable and Mark must have sensed it too, as he turned away and focused back on Violet.

"Stop crying! You're not even hurt. You'll be fucking him ten minutes after I leave, bitch." He turned to face Roman, "You want to fuck her? Take her, you can have the whore." Mark shoved Roman, who did not move at all. It was as if he had shoved a brick wall. They all looked at each other with wide eyes, never having seen anyone who did not crumble when Mark went after them.

Roman backed away from Mark, trying to avoid fighting. Under normal circumstances, Roman would not think twice about it, but he did not want to mess up Violet's house, and did not want to cause her unnecessary stress. He could only imagine how much this was hurting her, and she had enough to deal with already.

Mark looked like he was a full foot shorter than Roman. Mark was muscular and stout, but Roman was just plain huge.

"Come on, mother fucker," Mark barked, shoving Roman again.

"Why don't you just leave?" Roman continued taking the blows. It was difficult not to react.

"Come on, pussy." Mark shoved him; spit flying from his snarling mouth. "You think I'm scared of you, faggot?"

That was it. That was the final thing that triggered Violet to explode. She ran towards Mark, throwing her fists at his back and shrieking like a banshee. It took them all by surprise. It was as though some slumbering demon had awoken inside of her.

"Get off me, you fucking whore," he spat, and turned around, shoving her to the ground and kicking her as hard as he could.

Roman lunged forward, grabbed him by the chest, and shoved

him back onto the ground. He hovered over him, fists clenched in Mark's shirt. "Do not touch them. You want a fight, here I am."

Violet pulled herself up from the floor, stunned by Roman's actions. He had seemed so calm. Steve and Mosley begged Mark to just leave. There was no way Mark stood a chance against Roman, and they knew it. Mosely was backing out of the kitchen and into the living room, not wanting to be involved in the drama. He had always been a loner. Randy and Amber grabbed Violet, heaving her back away from Mark.

Roman pulled Mark to his feet, raising him slightly off the ground and then dropped him. "It's time for you to go. Follow your friends out the front door."

"Come on, faggot!" Mark goaded as a last ditch pathetic attempt to save face.

"Just leave! I don't want you here!" Violet yelled again, her voice cracking and high pitched. She pulled away from Amber and Randy and shoved Mark as she roared. He turned around backhanding her as she fell to the ground stunned.

Roman growled and latched onto Mark's shirt, dragging him towards the living room. "Get the fuck out of her house," he snarled as he shoved him, throwing him to the floor in front of the door, then hovering over him like a predator.

Steven was trying to place himself between Roman and Mark to no avail. Mark stood up; eyes filled with rage and disbelief, and picked up the crystal vase from the end table and threw it at Roman as he charged. Roman looked at the broken vase knowing that it was Violet's mother's, and seething anger erupted inside of him. He met Mark's charge with his fist.

They heard the bones crack as the punch landed on Mark's jaw and he hit the floor. Steven and Mosely were at the door waiting to get their friend. Roman lifted the writhing asshole from the floor, shoving him at the two of them, who nearly fell beneath the weight of him. They looked at Roman wondering if he would attack them as they dragged their bloody friend out the door and across the porch. Mark struggled in their arms trying to get loose while screaming with anger. Roman followed them out onto the lawn, making sure he would be leaving.

"That's enough. Okay, man?" Steve said, looking at Roman

like a dog that was pissing on itself.

Roman waited for them to get Mark loaded into the car and back out of the driveway before he walked back towards the house. The three others stood huddled in the doorway. The neighbor's light had come on and an older woman was standing on her porch.

"Is everything okay, Violet?" she called across the front lawn.

"Yes, Mrs. Stevens," Violet answered in the calmest voice she could muster.

The woman turned away and headed back into her house and so did Violet and Amber. Randy was still holding his jaw.

"I'm really sorry," Roman apologized, walking up to the house and entering cautiously. He doubted any of these people would want him here now. "I had no idea how angry that guy is. I should have listened to you. I'm sorry I didn't take it seriously," he apologized again, and began to pick up the shattered glass from the floor.

"Dude, I wish I had been the one to shut him up." Randy said enthusiastically. "That guy's supposed to be my fucking friend and he belted me in the mouth."

"You alright, Violet?" Amber asked her friend.

"Yes, I think so," she replied, bending over to help pick up the glass.

"Come on," Amber said to Randy, pulling his sleeve and heading upstairs. She knew she needed to let Violet talk to Roman, and besides that, Randy's jaw needed some attention.

"I'm so sorry about this," Roman said, standing up with a handful of glass. "I know this was your mom's."

"It's not your fault, Roman. I'm glad this happened. Maybe he'll finally get the message." She stood up and looked at him wanting him to follow her to the kitchen. "Besides, my mom is probably smiling right now. She hated Mark."

"Still, it's not cool," he said, tossing the glass into the garbage can that she held up to him.

"Roman, I'm glad it happened," she repeated, reaching out to hug him.

He wrapped his arms around her and squeezed. "I wasn't going to stand there and let him hurt you, but I'm sorry it came to that."

"Yeah, me too, though it was quite satisfying when he hit the floor that last time. Seeing the look of shock on his face was awesome."

He could feel her smiling against his chest.

"Plus, you're like a foot and a half taller than him. It was hilarious watching him attack you to no avail." She looked up at him with a glow on her face. "He's not used to being Omega."

He smiled at her warily, shook his head, and then backed away. "Okay, well, I guess it's sort of late. Call me if he comes back or if you need anything."

"How do I call you? I don't have your number, goofus," she said, grabbing the grocery list and pen from the refrigerator. "Write it on here."

"Thanks again for the dinner," he said, walking to the living room.

"Yeah, some dinner." She laughed.

"No, I had a good time," he said with a smile and put his arm around her shoulder. "I enjoy beating the snot out of people."

Violet looked at him sweetly and leaned her head against his chest. "Well, see you again soon," she said reluctantly, not wanting him to go. She pressed herself against him, wrapping her arms around him, and squeezing her eyes shut.

"Yeah, see ya soon," he said, hugging her casually and walking outside.

As he walked across the lawn, got in his car and drove away, she really hoped she would see him again soon. She knew the sadness would hit her again shortly, but for the time being she felt vindicated.

4. SILVER HEARTS

"That was pretty intense last night, eh?" Violet asked Amber, who was getting ready for work again.

"Yeah, kind of cool actually. I mean, Mark getting his ass kicked was cool, not Randy getting punched in the mouth, or you being shoved around."

"Finally someone Mark can't dominate, it was nice to see him put in his place. Roman felt really bad about it, but I was glad, well, apart from Randy getting decked." Violet smiled.

"So, what happened up in your room last night?" Amber asked, nudging her in the arm as she brushed her hair. She looked at her friend with a grin on her face.

"Nothing. I actually fell asleep." Violet laughed, then spit the toothpaste out and rinsed her mouth.

"You fell asleep? Riiight. Come on," Amber said, and rolled her eyes.

"I'm totally serious. I was talking to him about stuff and next thing I know I was sleeping."

"So, that's the story you're going to stick with?"

"That's the story. I swear."

"Okay, I guess." Amber sat the brush down and reached for the perfume in the cabinet.

"Well it's true, I swear."

"Okay, I believe you, sort of." She smirked and picked up her compact, smoothing the translucent powder over her pale skin.

"Sort of?"

"Violet, your makeup was all screwed up; something else must've been going on."

"Yeah, well I'll never tell." Violet smiled nervously, and walked out of the bathroom and back to her own room, shutting the door behind her. It was easier to let Amber think she was screwing

85

Roman than it was to admit she had been crying. She lay back on the bed, replaying the evening before in her head, every single moment, stopping to analyze certain looks, words, and actions. She was glad her relationship with Mark was finally over and that he had had his ass handed to him. Roman had been a good friend to her last night, a confidant, and a protector.

***

She sat up and looked around her room. The piles of stuff lying around everywhere disgusted her, she really needed to finish cleaning her room but instead she dressed and walked downstairs. Steve was sitting at the kitchen table.

"What the fuck are you doing here?" Violet asked him, raising her voice and slamming her hand down on the table.

"I live here," he muttered.

"Oh, my gosh, you have a lot of nerve coming back here after what you did last night, Steve."

"You know what? Last night was not my fault. I went to Mark's and he wanted to come over here and talk to you. He was completely calm and sensible about it and didn't flip out until you started arguing with him. I tried to get him to leave once you got him all fucking freaked out."

"Are you fucking kidding me right now? Yeah, well good job Steven. Awesome effort there trying to get him out of here and for blaming me for his anger issues. Thank you for your support *friend*."

"I didn't know he was going to go ballistic, Violet. I never would have brought him here if I thought he was going to act like he did."

"That's ridiculous. You knew Roman was here and you know how Mark is when other men are around. For fuck's sake. Don't tell me you had *no idea* how he might react."

"I'm sorry. I just thought he had a right to find out what was going on and should be able to talk to you about it, considering you never explained yourself or your actions."

"Well, it's really none of your business, and you should've kept your fucking nose out of it."

Violet grabbed her bag and keys off the chair and walked out the back door. She slung the bag over her shoulder and started walking very quickly, not paying attention to her surroundings whatsoever. The warm morning sun felt good, so she slowed her pace and let her mind stop racing. Last night was good. It happened the way it had for a reason. Maybe the blow up was the only way she could have gotten truly free from Mark. She should have thanked Steve for being such an idiot, even though she knew his motives may or may have not been legit. She reached into her purse, grabbed her phone, and called the house.

"Yeah?" Amber said hurriedly.

"Hey, is Steve there?"

"He's taking a shower, I think. You really pissed him off," Amber said, laughing. "Don't worry, I told him he was a fucking idiot too."

"Well, whatever. I was calling to tell him no big deal for bringing Mark over. I realize now that it didn't matter that he brought that fucker to our house last night, what happened was good regardless."

"Are you turning over some sort of new forgiving leaf? This doesn't sound like you at all."

Violet snickered. "I'm not sure, I was just thinking about it, and decided to let it go. Anyway, the old me was very forgiving, remember?"

"Yeah, I guess so. The *old you*, funny, I don't remember her very well."

"Yeah, I don't remember the old you very well either."

"Well, I'll give the idiot your message."

"Thanks."

"Uh huh, stop by the shop if you're bored later."

"Yeah, I will. I wanna talk about how hot that was when Roman busted Mark's face."

Violet and Amber both laughed the evil laugh girls do.

"Yeah, that was pretty cool. Ugh, I hafta go, man, or I'll be late for work."

"Alright, *man*, talk to you later."

"Oh, by the way, I'm proud of you for using your cell phone." Amber teased, knowing how rarely she ever actually called someone on it.

"Yuck, don't remind me." Violet laughed, and hung up.

She continued walking and decided she would go down to the convenience store for a coffee and something to eat for breakfast. She noticed a wooly bear crawling across the sidewalk, bent over, and scooped the fuzzy caterpillar up in her hand. It rolled up in a ball as she felt the prickly fur of the bug with her index finger. It was so cute. She smiled and set it back in the grass, not wanting it to wander out into the street and then noted that she couldn't stop it from going wherever it wanted to go. God, she literally had zero control of her life, let alone the life of that cute little thing. *What the fuck am I thinking about this shit for?*

The air smelled thickly of fresh cut grass, and she looked at the houses as she walked by them one by one, each of them looking like a gingerbread house. Some were nicely painted, some cracked and not very well taken care of at all. Some lawns very well-manicured, some overgrown with junk in the yard. Each one had a distinct character to it.

At one time, she thought she hated this town. It was small, nothing to do, and inhabited by what she considered closed-minded people. She lived in the good part of town that was populated mostly by young couples who were moving out of the city, and people who had grown up here and never left. Other areas of town were not quite so nice, with low income families who were supported by tax dollars and boasting a half dozen kids and three dogs chained in the yard. Not to mention the beaten up cars and trash. She tended to avoid those areas, not because she was stuck up in any way, but because those folks tended to not like "her kind" coming around. She had been threatened on more than one occasion.

She wasn't sure how she felt about her town anymore. It would be easy for her to move anywhere she wanted now. There was nothing besides Amber, really, keeping her here, and she was pretty confident she could convince her to move with her. But what was really the point of leaving? Everywhere else probably had its own set of problems. She couldn't run from everything and she didn't want to forget her parents. Roman made her realize last night that she didn't want to forget the pain of them not being here either.

She walked into the store, got her usual sickeningly sweet hazelnut coffee, and decided on a candy bar again for breakfast. "Breakfast of champions," she said to the clerk, setting the items on the counter.

"Caffeine and sugar, just the thing to get you started," the man said. He was a nice man, older, with a kind rosy face. She liked him. He had never once made her feel bad about herself by looking at her with hate or disgust in his eyes, like so many other people had. The price of looking different was often harsh treatment, but she didn't really blame people, she knew the risks. She had finally realized that if you want to dress like a character from a comic book, then you had better expect to get harassed.

She paid for her things and gave him the kindest smile she could muster, not really being used to showing kindness to strangers, in order to protect herself. Her defenses were strong due to the last several years. No thanks at all to her nihilistic ex.

She walked outside and took a sip of the coffee very slowly as to avoid scalding her tongue. She remembered the warning on the cup this time and smiled. She sat the cup down on the curb for a moment so that she could unwrap the candy bar, then took a bite and picked up her cup, and began walking again. She walked down a street she rarely walked down, as it was in the opposite direction of her house, but she knew the street well from having driven it her whole life. Walking gave one a completely different perspective, though. Certain details could only be observed on foot.

She continued studying each house, making note of certain homes of people she'd gone to school with. She walked for what seemed like miles, and then realized she was pretty far away from her house. Her coffee was long gone, she would put the empty cup in her bag since she didn't want to be rude and throw it down. She turned around to come back home because she had to pee. She started walking more quickly, hoping she would be able to make it back to the store, at least. That seemed very unlikely.

"What a stupid idea," she said aloud.

She stopped paying attention to anything other than her heavy bladder. Then she looked up, a Chevy SS sat in a driveway. She stopped and looked at the car. It had to be his car. She looked at the house. He lived in a house? It was a large white house that she had never paid any attention to before. The yard was well kept and neat, all the shrubs perfectly trimmed. A large maple tree stood in the center of the yard and shaded the whole area. She felt her bladder twinge again. There was no more holding it. She walked quickly up the cement driveway and to the door on the side of the house and knocked quickly. There was no answer. She knocked again. There was still no answer.

"Hey."

The voice fell down from above. She bent her head back, her eyes squinting from the bright sun, which was reflecting off the white siding. Roman was standing at the top of a set of metal stairs that lead to an apartment.

"They already left for work," he said, smiling down at her.

Violet smiled anxiously and then began dancing around a little.

"You alright?" Roman asked, resting his arms on the railing and leaning over.

"I have to pee *really* badly," Violet said, holding her abdomen.

Roman laughed, then invited her up.

She ran as quickly as she could without peeing her pants. "Thanks and sorry," she said, dancing around again.

"It's back there," he said, pointing to the hallway beyond the living room.

"Thank you," she exhaled, and ran to the bathroom.

It took all her abdominal muscle strength to get her pants down without peeing in them. She sat down and sighed, then looked around the room. It was spotless, stark, and clean. There was nothing sitting out at all except for two red towels, which hung on the towel rack. They appeared to be wet, and the room smelled humid and shampooey. He must have just gotten out of the shower. She had been in such agony that she hadn't even been able to focus on anything but getting to a bathroom to remember if his hair was wet or not. The shower had small white ceramic tile with a thin border of shiny black that continued around the room.

She finished and washed her hands, then dried them on the

damp towels. She was embarrassed to go back into the living room. What must he be thinking? She convinced herself he must be thinking something like she was stalking him, so, she quickly tried to figure out something to tell him, and then gave up, realizing she was taking far too long. She opened the bathroom door, and walked back to the living room feeling awkward and shy. It was a large room, with nothing but a couch, a chair, a coffee table, and some exercise equipment. Roman was sitting on his couch, slouched down with one foot on the coffee table.

"Sorry, I swear I'm not stalking you. I was out walking and I stopped and got coffee and got way too far away from my house and I had to pee really bad and I knew I wouldn't make it back even to the store and I saw your car and I figured I better try and see if this is really your house…"

"It's okay, Violet, glad I could be of service," he spoke very calmly and evenly.

She looked up at him. In her rambling, she had been avoiding eye contact. He was smiling at her. "You must think I'm a nut," she said, smiling back at him.

"Pretty much, but who am I to judge? You can sit down if you want."

"I should probably go. I don't want to bother you." She started walking towards the door.

"Well, you can go if you want, but you're not bothering me."

She stopped and looked at him. He had to be the nicest person she had ever met. She walked over and sat on the chair that was diagonally across from him. The television was playing some game show, and she noticed that he had just taken a shower, because his hair was still wet.

"I like your apartment," she said, sitting back in the chair. The leather was soft and pliable.

"Thank you," he said, not taking his eyes off her.

"It's so clean and nice; you must be horrified by my house."

"No, why would I expect everyone to live like I live? I don't have very many things. It's easy to keep clean when you don't have much."

Violet smiled at him, then stood up and looked around the room, finally walking into the kitchen which was right next to the living room. She could still see him sitting in the living room from where she stood. "I like how everything is black and white," she said, as she looked out the window over the sink.

"You can thank the landlord for that, I guess," he said, watching her. She genuinely amused him.

Violet turned around and looked at him. "Would you have it any other way?" she asked, walking back into the living room.

"I think so," he said, pulling his hair from behind his back.

"Like what would you want?" she asked, walking towards the hallway.

"Red walls, maybe," he said, wondering what she was doing.

"Red is nice," she agreed, turning back around toward him and grinning. "I want to see the rest."

Roman stood up and joined her in the hallway. "Well, you've met the bathroom already," he said, pointing to the room on the right. "That's my bedroom," he continued, pointing to the open door straight ahead. They walked forward a few steps and she walked in. He stood in the doorway watching her. He thought it was funny how she went from nervous to bold in a matter of thirty seconds.

She walked forward, taking in his room. Once again, the room was bare, nothing out, just a chest of drawers and his bed, which had a black cover on it. It was neatly made. She sat down on the foot of the bed and lay back, stretching her arms wide.

"I like your room," she said, propping herself up on her elbow and looking up at him.

He was leaning on the doorframe, which was also painted black. "What's there to like?"

"Nothing, that's what I like about it, there's no clutter to distract you."

"I need distracting sometimes," he said, walking into the room and sitting down on the bed.

She sat up and looked at him. He seemed faintly sad, though he really gave no outward expression of it. It was something she felt more than anything else. A certain sense of dread that nestled somewhere inside him that she doubted he even knew existed—or maybe he did—she didn't know the man. "I've given you enough distractions in the last few days haven't I?"

"Yes, thank you," he said, leaning over and patting her on the head.

"And sorry about last night, that wasn't cool at all. If I had known he was going to show up, I never would have invited you over. It wasn't fair to put you in that situation, and I should've known better anyway."

"It's no big deal; do I look like I'm bothered? Seriously, I'm not the one with the broken jaw." He laughed. "Sorry, that's probably not funny."

"Well, it wasn't really funny at the time it was happening, but I have to say it was quite nice seeing the shock on his face as he hit the floor."

"How about you? Any damage?" he asked, forehead wrinkled with concern.

"Nah, I'm no worse for wear." She shrugged and looked away from him, deciding not to mention all her bruises.

"I do regret your mom's stuff being broken. Which reminds me..." He stood up and opened his closet door. His closet was as clean as the rest of his home. Nothing but black clothing all hung neat and orderly. He reached on the shelf and grabbed a small white box and took something out of it, then placed the box back on the shelf and closed the door. He turned around and sat back down on the bed. "I want you to have this. It's my mom's." He handed her a silver heart necklace.

She held it up and looked at it. The heart was heavy silver and the chain was long and very shiny. She held the heart between her thumb and index finger. It was solid and felt cold against her fingers. "You want me to have this?" she asked, looking up at him.

"Yeah, I mean, you're going through a lot right now, plus I broke something of your mom's, so I figure I should give you something of my mom's to replace it. It's a good reminder anyway. Put it on," he said, and smiled.

She slipped the chain over her head and looked down at the heart that she held lovingly in her hands. "I love this," she smiled, and looked up at him.

"Good, you should have it then," he said, and tapped her nose with his finger. *Moron.*

"But it wasn't you who broke the vase, Roman."

"Not technically, but my presence made things worse."

She looked in his eyes for several moments, then looked down at the heart and smiled to herself. No one usually gave her anything, especially not anything this personal.

"I guess I should go," she said, looking back up at him with reluctance.

"It's up to you," he replied, leaning back onto the bed.

"Well, I don't want to be a pest," she said, leaning back into the bed too.

"You're not a pest," he said with a yawn.

"Tell me if I am, okay?" she said, following his yawn with one of her own.

"I will."

***

He slowly opened his eyes. He was so tired, and felt almost as if he'd been drugged, which was obviously not the case. He never slept that well. He looked up and realized that from the angle the sun was drifting through his shades it was late afternoon. That had been a long nap. He tried to roll over onto his back, but felt resistance. She was there, curled up with her forehead pressed between his shoulder blades. Slowly he turned over, trying not to wake her up.

Her hands were tucked beneath her face, with the silver heart he had given her pressed between her palms. Her hair fell in thick swathes over her neck and shoulders. Gently, he pushed the hair away from her face. She looked so young and little curled up there.

Slowly, he sat up and pulled himself off the bed, trying to be as careful as possible. She must need the sleep. Emotional overload will do that to a person. His excuse was that he'd been out all night and during the day was the normal time he slept. He walked to the kitchen and looked at the round white clock that hung on the wall above the stove. It was two o'clock. They had been sleeping

94

for four hours. He grabbed a glass from the cupboard and filled it with tap water and drank it down, then opened the refrigerator to find nothing but butter, juice, and a loaf of stale bread. He walked to the phone and grabbed the carry out menu that was tucked behind it, and then dialed the number on the front. He ordered a large pizza with pepperoni, mushrooms, and extra cheese, and asked them to deliver soda as well, then he sat down on his couch. The television was still on from the morning, and now some court show was playing. He stared blankly at the television, not hearing much of what was going on, feeling half-asleep. When he noticed something out of his peripheral vision, he looked up to see Violet standing in the hallway watching him. A grin came to his lips, and he sat up straight on the couch.

She came and sat in the chair opposite him, rubbing her eyes and pulling her knees into her chest. "I'm so sleepy," she said with a yawn, as her eyes settled on the TV.

"Me too, I think I could sleep another six hours."

"Sorry I fell asleep. It's sort of rude how I just sort of barged in on you like this today."

"I don't mind. What else would I be doing?"

"What *do* you do?" she asked, looking over at him. He had slouched down on the couch again, half laying down, with one leg on the couch and the other leg bent with his foot on the floor.

"Not much." He smirked at her. "I ordered pizza."

"Cool," she muttered. Her eyes were growing heavy again.

***

She jumped as the knock came. He was standing at the door, holding money out and taking the box in one hand as the young man made it to the top of the stairs. The soda sat on the floor. She walked up behind him and picked the soda up, waiting for him to direct her. She peered around from behind him, and smiled at the pizza deliveryman who smiled back then walked down the stairs. It was someone she had gone to school with.

Roman turned around, bumping into her accidentally and nearly knocking her over.

"Sorry."

"It's okay," she reassured.

He set the pizza down on the coffee table, and walked to the kitchen with her trailing behind him. "You know, I don't even have anything besides paper plates and three or four glasses," he said, turning to look back at her as he reached in the cabinet above the stove.

She realized she wouldn't even be able to reach the shelf where he had the plates. "That's okay. I'd have nothing at all if my parents didn't leave me their things." Violet grinned, feeling nervous.

He looked at her and handed her a glass. It was a heavy glass with diamond shaped ridges along the base. She placed the rim of the glass to her mouth feeling the cool smoothness. He took the bottle of soda from her, twisted the cap off, and began pouring it into her glass as she held it with two hands. It reminded him of his mother pouring him his drinks in just this way.

She took a sip and felt the fizz on the tip of her nose. "My favorite," she said, licking her lips and walking back into the living room.

He poured himself a glass and joined her in the other room. She was sitting on the floor in front of the coffee table, staring at the television.

"Do you think it's weird that I'm here? I mean, I kind of don't know you and I'm sitting here letting you do all this for me. I think that might be weird."

"It's probably weird, but so what," he answered. "What's even weirder is that I don't own any plates." He laughed, and lifted the top of the box. "Help yourself," he said, grabbing a piece of pizza and biting into it.

She felt awkward, yet knew there was no reason to feel awkward. It didn't seem like he minded her being here, but it still felt weird. A very tight knit group of people had surrounded her for several years now, no one new to get to know, and this felt foreign to her. She imagined that at some point there would be some sort of price to pay for this kindness. That maybe he would eventually want her to "pay up." That was the way things worked in the real world, right? Moreover, he was a legitimate man, not some stupid college aged douche. So wouldn't he expect *something*? She could not imagine that he had absolutely no ulterior motive whatsoever. After all, every guy she had ever known had had one agenda or another.

"Eat. You're skin and bones." he said, mocking some grandmother somewhere. He had startled her, and she jumped. "Sorry, didn't mean to scare you."

"I guess I zoned out," she said, turning around to look at him. He was already eating his second slice.

"You do that a lot," he said, looking away from her and back to the television.

"Kind of," she answered, taking the smallest slice of pizza.

"There has to be something better on TV than this," he said, grabbing the remote and running through the channels. He stopped on several things for seconds at a time, then kept flipping. "What do you want to watch?" he asked, continuing to flip.

"I don't know. Whatever you want is fine."

"I know you have an opinion, Violet," he said, setting the remote down on the couch. "So, what is it?"

"Um, I don't know."

"Don't be afraid of me," he said, leaning forward on the couch. "You have no reason to be this passive with me."

She looked into his eyes, seeing the sincerity. Surely she never shied away from voicing her opinion any other time, and she always had one, so she took a deep breath and relaxed. "Okay, let's watch whatever's on channel seventy-four then," she said, taking another slice of pizza.

"That's better." He flipped through the channels until he found the station. "I don't have plates but I damn sure have cable." He laughed.

"Well, duh, TV is important, man."

"I feel very passionate about my relationship with television. It's my only friend," he said, in a very serious tone of voice. The sad thing was that it was true.

She looked at him, and he just smiled at her. "Yeah, I think it's my only friend too." She leaned back into the chair finishing her second slice of pizza. "I knew that boy who delivered this," she said, gesturing at the pizza.

"Seems like a nice young man," he responded, reaching for another slice. "I've seen him almost on a daily basis since I moved here."

"I never spoke to him once in school."

"His fault or yours?"

"Probably mine, I'm sure."

"What a shame."

"I know." She grabbed another slice of pizza.

"I love *Green Acres*"

"Yeah, me too."

They watched the show, laughing and making quips back and forth until the pizza was gone.

"I'm going to buy you stuff tomorrow," she said, standing up "You need stuff."

"Stuff like what?" he said, nestling down into the couch.

"Like dishes and stuff like that. I'll buy it, don't worry."

"Okay," he said nonchalantly, looking back at the television "you can buy me anything you want."

"Really?" she said wit excitement.

"Yeah, buy whatever you want, just nothing pink or purple or girlie."

It was shocking that he was actually going to allow her to spend money on him. She shouldn't be shocked, considering the mooches she had surrounded herself with, but she was shocked he would let her. Of all her friends, Amber was the only one who had never asked her for a single dime, and she appreciated that about her. He didn't seem like the type to let a girl spend money on him but then she didn't really know his type, did she?

"So, maybe I should go home and let you do whatever it is you do?" she asked him.

"It's up to you," he said, looking over at her. "I can drive you home."

"No, I'll walk," she said, taking the glass to the kitchen. She set it in the sink and walked back towards him.

"You sure you want to walk?"

"I'm fine," she said, going to the door and grabbing the handle.

He stood up and walked over to her. "Maybe you should go to

the bathroom before you leave? I don't want you stopping at some strange man's house to go to the bathroom," he teased her.

"Is that what you are? *A strange man*? I'll be fine," she said, picking her bag up from the floor and slinging it over her shoulder.

"I'm a little strange, yes."

"Thanks for the pizza and pop," she said, smiling at him. She reached out to hug him and then felt apprehensive and backed away.

He put his hand on the top of her head and shook her head back and forth gently. "It's no problem, V. I look forward to my new plates tomorrow. Just don't spend too much, okay?"

"I won't," she smiled, and walked out. He watched her until she made it to the end of his driveway and then went back inside.

V. She liked that.

***

A faint knock, it was late afternoon. He put the weights down and walked to the door. She stood there, looking nervously out at the street with her arms full. He opened the door quickly, smiling down at her and putting his hands out to offer help in carrying whatever it was she had in the box.

"I told you I'd buy you stuff." She smiled, handing him a fairly heavy box. "There's more in the car," she said, darting down the stairs towards the blue vehicle.

He sat the box down on the ground and followed her to the car. She was rifling through her trunk and handing bags to him.

"I brought you something to eat," she said, stopping to look at him. "I owed you." She slammed the trunk shut and stood there looking at the dumfounded expression on his face. "Come on," she said, motioning for him to go back to his apartment while she opened the passenger side door and grabbed a bag of fast food. She followed him up the stairs and he set the bags down on the coffee table.

"You went overboard, I think," he said, leaning back into the couch. Why had he encouraged her to do this?

99

"Well, maybe, but who cares?"

Her face was radiant with excitement, her cheeks so red and plump from smiling she looked fevered. Her eyes were wide, wet, and sparkling. He had not experienced this look on her before, and decided he would not wreck this moment for her, because she clearly needed this.

"Okay, so let me show you," she said, grabbing the box first. "Here are the plates. And I don't even care if you never need them; you should just have them because they're awesome." She pulled the lid up, reached in, and pulled out a dark red plate with thinly painted black swirls on the outer rim. "Pretty cool huh?" She smiled ecstatically.

"Those are really cool, Violet. Seriously, I would pick that if I was ever actually going to buy a plate."

"They catch witches," she said, smiling as she ran her finger over one of the black swirls.

"So I see," he smiled, remembering a prior conversation.

"Oh, wait," she said, reaching into a bag, "Food, here." She handed him a wrapped sandwich and fries. "I think there's ketchup and stuff in the bag. You don't have a shirt on," she stammered.

He laughed, and ate a couple fries. God she was so young "Where's your lunch?"

"I ate already."

"No you didn't."

"I ate."

He looked at her with doubt and ate another fry.

"So, I bought some other stuff too. Here," she said, handing him another bag.

He sat the food down on the table and reached into the bag pulling out a set of black sheets and another set of dark red.

"Everyone needs new sheets."

"Thanks, seriously, I never buy this stuff for myself. You know what I mean?"

"I know exactly what you mean. I don't buy them either." She leaned back against the chair with a wide smile spreading across her face. "I like buying stuff for people."

"Thanks," he said, setting the sheets down and picking up his sandwich. "I really appreciate this, though you obviously didn't have to do it." He had never had anyone to buy things for before, but he could imagine the joy it might bring.

"I know, but you've been cool and I wanted to. I got you something else too," she said, leaning forward and reaching into the last bag. She pulled out a chenille blanket. It was dark red, and very soft. "This is for when you just want to lay on the couch and stuff. It's king sized too. You know, because you're king sized."

Roman chuckled and shoved some more fries in his mouth. "Nothing worse than when you have to choose to either cover your shoulders and your feet are hanging out, or cover your feet and your shoulders are out."

"Yeah, I don't usually experience that because I'm short, but, fuck that. It'll be getting cold soon." She smiled, handing him the throw.

"This is the softest thing I've ever felt," he said, rubbing the blanket between his hands.

"Yeah, I have one at home. It's awesome. Don't rub grease on it."

"I'm not." He frowned at her, dropping the blanket. "Thank you." He smiled, and looked into her eyes purposely trying to make her aware that he was sincere.

"You're welcome. I figured since you really can't paint your walls red we may as well add some besides just towels." She leaned over, gathering the empty bags and putting them together, shoving one inside the other.

He watched as she did this. She looked very content. He would not rob her of this for the world.

"Were you busy? I should have called first."

"No, I was just lifting weights, no big deal." He finished the sandwich, then crumpled the wrapper and tossed it in the bags she had sitting by her feet.

She watched as he ate the fries. God, he was huge. She could not remember ever seeing a man as large as him. "You're like a giant," she said, leaning back into the chair.

He laughed out loud. "A giant, yeah, I guess so compared to you."

"Compared to most people you're a giant. Do you have any

family?"

"Not really," he said, his facial expression shifting suddenly.

She could see that this was a sensitive subject. "You exercised, then I fed you crap, not good." Another subject again.

"I eat like this every day. Believe me, if you hadn't brought me this I would have probably gone out for it shortly anyway. Now that I have these fancy plates I guess I'll have to start cooking"

"You have a nice body," she commented nonchalantly.

He nearly choked on what he was eating, having been taken off guard by the comment. "Um, thanks."

"Well, you do, I'm just saying. If I looked that good I'd walk around without a shirt on too."

"What are you talking about? You don't want to look like me."

"Well, no, but I mean if I was as in shape as you."

"Well feel free to walk around without a shirt on anyway. encourage that sort of thing. No, actually don't," he corrected himself, remembering again how young she was, and how it wasn' a good idea to encourage an attachment.

She looked at him quizzically and grinned.

"Besides, like you're out of shape. You walk like a hundred miles a day from what I gather."

"It's not the same though."

"You're insane."

"Pretty much." She smiled as she stood up and grabbed the empty bags. "Where's your trash?"

"Under the sink, take this too." He threw the empty frie container at her. It hit her in the middle of the back.

"Goof," she said, picking it up off the ground.

He grabbed the remote control and started flipping through th channels and stopped on *Gilligan's Island.*

She walked back into the living room. "I love this show."

"Yeah, me too," he said, spreading the blanket over his ches and stomach. "Sit with me." He should not be spending time wit this girl. Nothing good could possibly come from it, but it just fel nice to have a friend, and she was a cute girl. Damn, way t maintain distance.

She awkwardly walked over and sat on the couch beside him He lifted the blanket for her to get under with him. "You're nake under there," she scoffed.

"I don't have cooties."

"You have sweat cooties," she said, wrinkling her nose up.

"I do not. Don't be such a girl." He grabbed her shirt sleeve and tugged on her until she slid next to him letting him cover her.

"It's so soft," he said, sinking deeper into the couch and propping his feet on the table.

"Yeah, I know," she said, snuggling up against him doing the same. "You're like the brother I never had. A really sort of hot brother, which is kinda gross, I guess."

He laughed.

5. THREE STEPS BACK

"Going out will be fun, come on. You have to go," Amber said, finishing the sandwich and walking the empty plate to the sink.

"And suppose Mark's there?" Violet asked.

"Who cares? You are going to have to learn to coexist, don't you think? This is a small town. Besides, it's not like there isn't security there, and a bunch of people are going tonight that we haven't seen in a long time."

"Yeah, I guess. It just seems weird going back there. It almost feels like something's changed."

"Don't be dumb, nothing's changed, you just lost some dead weight. Think about all the other fish in the sea, old, pre-Mark friends included."

"I don't know that I need any other fish. I don't think I'm in the best frame of mind to be worrying about stupid dudes. Men should be the last thing I should be thinking about."

"Violet, I know things have been really tough, all the more reason to go out and do something and have some fun."

"I guess you're right. I just think it's going to be weird. So what *fish* are you referring to anyway?" she said with a smirk.

"I'm sure it will be weird, you dork. You guys were seeing each other for over a year. Jim and Matt are supposed to be there tonight," she said, shifting the direction of the conversation back to the fish.

"Oh really?" Violet raised her eyebrow, letting a sly smile pass her lips as she remembered how hot Jim had been the last time she'd seen him.

"Yes really. Anyway, are you sure you aren't just missing your new boyfriend? Where's he been anyway?"

"He's not my boyfriend. I saw him yesterday morning and we had breakfast," Violet said, giving her friend a dirty look. She and

Roman had been hanging out for a little over a week now. They walked every night, him always seeming to show up right as she was headed up the street from her house. They'd been out all night last night, and had decided to go eat breakfast.

"Well you can't tell me you aren't interested in him in that way."

"Seriously, not really. Okay maybe at first it was sort of like that. I mean, obviously he's fucking hot as hell, but it's just not like that anymore. He's a nice guy, and he makes me feel good about myself. That's all there is to it. He's like a brother or something."

"Well, I find that hard to believe, but whatever floats your boat," Amber said with skepticism. "So, are you going tonight or what?"

"I suppose."

***

They walked through the lobby, stopping to say hello to a few people. Violet peered past her friends, eyeing Jim who sat at the bar with Gwen. She immediately felt herself becoming annoyed. "Stupid bitch. Look at her. She moves in on everyone," she seethed.

Amber laughed and agreed with her friend. "So, go talk to him anyway. Like he's not gonna stop talking to her for you. Come on."

"Hmm, you're right. I mean, *come on!*" Violet laughed and walked towards the two.

Gwen stopped talking, looked up at her, and smiled. "Hi, Violet. How've you been? I haven't seen you in awhile."

Was this girl actually being nice? Or was this some act? Well, she actually always was nice. It was Violet who was the bitch.

"I've been a little under the weather," Violet said, sitting down on the other side of Jim.

"So I heard." Gwen grinned and walked away.

Nope, she wasn't being nice, just patronizing. Violet glared after her and looked at Jim. He was sitting sideways facing her, looking at her intently when her eyes returned to him. His eyes were large, dark, and very expressive. They looked wet and bright in the pulsating lights of the room. His thin, short black mohawk was spiked, and his nose was pierced twice, his pale pink mouth looked soft and moist.

"How've you been?" he asked, and took a drink from the bottle he was nursing. His long, thin neck bent back revealing the milk white skin beneath his chin.

Violet smiled. "I've been better, but whatever."

"Yeah, life sucks, huh? I get that," he said, nodding his head and grinning at her.

Violet ordered a Diet Coke from the bartender. She really didn't know what to say to Jim. They had really only been casual friends, even though at one point they had known each other better than they did now. Mark had seen to that friendship ending.

"So, you and Mark aren't together now?" he asked, looking at her out of the corner of his eye.

"Wow, word travels fast."

"Yeah, Gwen made sure to gloat over that one," he said, with a wry grin letting Violet know he was hip to Gwen's game.

"Ugh, whatever," Violet said, rolling her eyes and taking a sip of her pop. "I haven't seen you in a long time."

"Yeah, it's been awhile. Why do you think most of us stopped coming around this place?" he asked, taking another drink.

"I don't know, why?" Violet questioned. She had known Mark had sent out "stay away from Violet" vibes, but had he actually scared people off?

"Your ex is a little violent," Jim said, motioning to the bartender for another beer. His long, thin arm stretched across the bar and she noticed the vague marks in the crook.

"Yeah, tell me about it," she said, looking down and taking a sip of her drink. She felt semi-nauseas now. Before she had met Mark, this man had been the center of her universe. She had massive crush on him the moment they had met, but he was dating someone at the time, and then just when he was single and they were starting to hang out a little, Mark came along. Now she looked at him and felt sadness and remorse. Maybe if he'd been

106

hanging around her and Amber he wouldn't be shooting up. Maybe her whole life would have been different. Maybe she would have been happier, and had someone to care for her after...

There was no sense going over it. They hadn't hooked up and he was a drug addict. End of story.

"So, I guess you aren't tied down anymore then?" he said, and took another drink.

"Nope, not at the moment," she sighed. "I'm gonna go find Amber," she said, patting his shoulder and getting up and walking away. She really had no interest in getting involved with a junkie no matter how nice or hot. Her life was fucked up enough without adding that level of insanity. And she wasnt equipped to help someone else when she was already feeling lost herself.

Violet walked through the club, stopping to chat with a few of her favorite people. She spoke to two young girls she'd known for only a year, and whom she thought were probably heading down the wrong path quickly, judging by their appearance. They had been so bright eyed and giddy when she'd met them, and for once, that hadn't turned her stomach because it was genuine. Now as she looked at them she could see the dullness in their eyes. The radiant energy they had projected was gone. She had craved their exuberance when she first met them. Both of them had been funny and smart. Now they were jaded just like her. The light was leaving them, and she wondered how this had happened so quickly and where had she been that she hadn't noticed sooner?

Had this happened to her too? Had someone seen her as the wide-eyed child when she first walked through these doors, and then watched as the light slowly faded?

She saw her other friend Matt across the room, his bright red hair bouncing as he danced around from person to person. He was a funny guy. She had been drawn to him immediately. Her heart sped up with excitement see him, and then she remembered how fried he'd been the last time she'd spoken with him. His sentences had barely fit together and the manic words fell from his mouth in nonsensical rants.

She was feeling very out of place, and she wondered what had happened to her in the span of just a few weeks to open her eyes to all this. All these things were nothing to her before; the drug use, the casual sex amongst them all, but now as she looked around she felt a sad disgust. She wanted to be like them and be completely unaware of the debauchery, but something had changed. She could not see all of this as she had before. Her parents' death had woken her up some, but it seemed like time itself had caused some rapid evolution.

She circled around the room and made her way to the lounge where she saw Randy and Amber sitting with Steve. A grimace came to her face at the sight of Steve, even after having forgiven him for his stupidity. He smiled at her and she smiled back dutifully and walked towards them, sliding in beside Randy.

"So?" Amber asked, kicking her friend under the table.

"Not as great as I remember." Violet shrugged, and took another sip of her drink.

Amber looked at her, wanting to talk more but realized the last thing these men probably wanted to hear was girl talk.

"So, what's the deal, Steve? Is Mark going to be here tonight?" Violet asked nonchalantly.

"I'm not sure. He didn't say anything about coming."

"Hmm..." Violet responded as she chewed on the swizzle stick.

Amber looked at her friend now with concern on her face wondering why she was asking about Mark. Did she want to see him? Or did she not want to see him?

Violet took another sip and looked across the room to the other patrons, feeling reminiscent and sad. She had changed dramatically and it was freaking her out. "I'm gonna go dance," she said, pulling herself out of the booth and heading for the other room.

The throbbing industrial beats were overpowering to her tonight. The frenetic pound of the bass was lulling her into some sort of trance. She walked to the center of the floor, head lowered and slowly began rocking her body back and forth to the rhythm. She held the same movement for minutes on end, barely changing her motion. Others around her gyrated to their own beat-possessed spasms as she remained unaware, solely focused on rhythm and her body. The tight black velvet of her dress began feeling very thick and heavy against her moistened skin. The silver heart swung back and forth, lightly hitting her stomach as it jumped around her neck. She kept her eyes closed, blocking out everything but music and rhythm.

"Haven't seen you dance in months." His voice invaded her privacy, shattering whatever illusion of seclusion she had been feeling.

She stopped all movement, forcing her eyes open. Even the dim red light seemed too much to her right now. She stared blankly into his eyes.

"You look pretty." He smiled as he wiped the loose swathe of black hair from across her face.

She started walking away and went towards the bar, taking a seat on a wooden stool, her heart pounding with anger and fear. He followed her. "What do you want, Mark?" she asked, ordering another pop. She had left the other one and was smart enough not to drink something that had been sitting unattended, not to mention it wasn't worth the energy of walking way back there for one fourth of a drink.

"I just want to say hello. I miss you, Vi," he said, sitting beside her. His face was bruised but healing. She could see the cut across his mouth from where Roman had pulverized him.

"Well, I don't miss you," she said, taking a drink and rolling her eyes.

"I know there's no way you don't miss me a little." He grinned, rubbing his hand on her leg for a moment.

She did not react, she just stared at him. Seeing him after the way she'd felt tonight was unsettling.

"A little maybe?" he asked, with a grin.

She couldn't resist his smile, as rare and goofy as it was. She hated that he could do this to her. How many times had she been so angry with him she could kill him, only to be undone with his smile and deep, lulling voice?

"Maybe a little, but so what?" she said, biting the end of the swizzle stick and rolling her eyes again.

"I knew it." He ordered a beer and took a drink of it. "I miss you so much, Violet. I'm so sorry about what happened at your house. I just wanted to talk, and you know how stupid I am. I'm sorry."

"I don't want to talk about this, Mark." She looked into his eyes momentarily, then looked past him to the dance floor. Jim was dancing with Gwen, and she felt that twinge of vague jealousy for a man she didn't even want anymore.

"I just wanted you to know I'm sorry. I wish I could take a lot of things back."

"Please stop talking about this. I am far too depressed to go into all this again, Mark. Let's just say you fucked up and I don't have the capacity to deal with you fucking up anymore. Can we leave it at that? I'm incapable of feeling, and you're incapable of loving. Fair enough? I honestly don't care and don't want to keep rehashing this stuff."

"Wow, *incapable of loving*. You know how to cut me, don't you?" he said, shocked by the bluntness of her statement.

She looked at him. He was obviously bothered by what she'd said. Had he really been so cruel? Maybe she was just completely unable to care about anyone but herself, and that had led to him being so angry and abusive? It's not as if she hadn't felt selfish and demanded *her way* a good portion of the time.

Amber walked up behind Mark, looking at her friend for some sort of sign that she was okay or needed help. Violet smiled at her sadly. "It's alright," she sighed, looking back at Mark.

His eyes were heavy and wet. She knew how to hurt him. She had always known the right words to say to hurt him. "Look, I'm sorry I said that, okay? But I can't just go back and pretend nothing ever happened. I don't think we belong together, Mark."

"Fair enough, I guess," he said, taking another drink from his beer. "Your new boyfriend has a good left hook," he said, rubbing his jaw and changing the subject.

Violet tried not to laugh at him. "Yeah, well, he's not my boyfriend, but it was sort of nice to finally see you put in your place, you brat."

He smiled at her again, knowing he was getting to her. "I'll remember not to piss him off if I see him around. So, what are you depressed about, same old, same old?"

She was shocked by him actually wanting to know how she was feeling. He had never even seemed concerned after her parents had died. He had asked, but she could tell by his tone of voice and body language he'd never wanted a truthful answer.

"I don't know, so much has changed, and I don't know where I fit anymore. Coming back here has made me feel very strange. Seeing people I haven't seen in months and noticing things about them I never bothered to see before has made me feel very strange and awkward."

"You still fit with me," he said, pleading to her with his eyes.

She looked down at her glass and shook her head. "Don't do this again," she said, almost inaudibly.

"Violet, I'm not *doing* anything. I can't live without you. I can't sleep. My heart aches all the time. I have had time to think this time. I'm sorry I wasn't there for you. Violet, your parents died and I expected you to just get on with your life and not look back. How could I be that way? What the fuck is wrong with me? Your friend was right to kick my ass. I treated you like an asshole and I'm sorry. I don't know what more to say to you but I'm sorry."

He stood up and walked away. She watched him walk across the room and lean against the wall, staring blankly into the writhing dancers. He took intermittent sips from his beer and never stopped looking forward.

She felt sadness for him. He had been the only thing she had in her life that mattered to her until recently. She could have caused this. It could have been her fault that he'd reacted to her the way he had. Maybe if she had been more patient and explained how she felt and what she was going through. Maybe if she had told him what she needed from him. If she had done any of those things then maybe he would not have been so angry all the time. She knew how he was, and she pushed his buttons anyway.

She walked across the room to him. He looked down at her confused by her actions. "I'm sorry too. I'm sure this is all my fault."

He wiped the single tear that fell down her cheek, and shook his head and cradled her face in his hand, kissing her gently on the mouth.

It felt good to have his familiar mouth against hers, his warm thick hands on her skin, she wanted this. She yielded to him, kissing him hungrily.

"Let's get out of here," he said quietly against her ear. His

111

voice was brusque and husky against her.

She kissed him again, feeling her will completely disintegrate They walked through the club. She paid no attention to the few people staring at them. They didn't speak much in the car on the way to her home. His hand rubbed her thigh, keeping her from being able to think straight. Of course he knew this, he knew exactly how to keep her from thinking straight.

They made their way to her room. He peeled her dress of quickly as she tore at him. She slipped the silver heart from her neck and let it slide to the floor. They fucked. No thought. No emotion. Just bodies reacting to chemicals. It was nothing but animal instinct.

He fell asleep with his arm wrapped around her. *The Conquering Hero.*

She stared off into the black room until her eyes blurred and she saw geometric patterns of red, yellow, and purple morphing from one to another. She was void of emotion, void of thought. She had fallen again.

So, this was her fate. She would stay in this situation until something permanently stopped her – like death. The depth of depression and defeat she felt was all consuming and inescapable She knew he wasn't sincere. She had heard this speech in its various forms at least a dozen times, but she hadn't cared tonight She knew he did not mean those words, and she had fallen for them again anyway. This time she would not bother trying to escape. She would accept this fate.

She took his thick wrist and removed his arm from around her She sat on the edge of the bed with her head in her hands. No tear would come, no sobbing, she was void of emotion. He rolled over completely unaware of the depth of disgust she felt for herself.

She begged some unnamed force to do something. She begged him to save her or let her die.

She heard Amber and the others stirring downstairs. She stood up, reaching for her discarded dress, pulled it on over her head, and zipped it. She felt the necklace cold against her bare foot. She picked it up, holding it tightly in her hand for a long moment, and then put it around her neck. She quietly opened the door and slipped downstairs. They had ordered pizza and were watching

112

television. Amber looked up as Violet snuck around the corner.

"Hey," Randy said, smiling at her. "Whatcha doin'?" He snickered.

Violet tried to grin and sat in the red velvet chair. "As if you don't know." Her voice was low and dead sounding.

Amber looked at her raising an eyebrow.

"What can I say? I'm a glutton for punishment." Violet reached for the pizza and took a slice. Her brows knotted up with realization. "I haven't eaten today."

Amber shook her head and looked back at the television. "I just hope you know what you're doing, Vi."

"I'm well aware, trust me. I'm sleeping with the devil," she said dejectedly.

***

"Mmm...Good morning," he said, nuzzling against her neck.

Violet tried to muster a smile and leaned her head into him. He wrapped his arms around her and started kissing her neck. She grunted and squirmed against him.

"What's wrong?" he asked.

"Nothing, Mark, just tired," she spoke quietly.

"I would imagine so."

She could feel his smile against her neck. He kissed her again. "Can we do this later?" she asked softly, trying not to anger him. "I'm feeling really weird about all this. Not you, just so much going on lately and I feel confused and a little panicky," she said ,squeezing his arm.

He sat up in the bed and looked down at her. She lay there nearly fully clothed on top of the blankets. "What the fuck? Not this again!" he said, running his hand over his face. "Violet, you're always feeling weird and panicky. What's the problem? I thought everything was okay?"

She rolled over and looked up at him. His eyes had the look they always had when he was filled with rage. "Mark, I'm sorry, this is just a lot to deal with. I'm not trying to be difficult."

"No, of course not, you're never trying to be difficult are you?"

She felt her own anger building but she didn't say anything. She just kept looking him in the eye. "So what you want is for me to put aside my emotions like I did last night for the rest of our lives? What happened to you being sorry for being unsympathetic?" she said, sitting up so that she wouldn't feel so small next to him.

"And what happened to all this being your fault?" he said, standing up and grabbing his pants from the floor.

"That was just me and my *battered woman syndrome* talking"

"Oh, so now you're a battered woman? Give me a fucking break, Violet. Gwen was right, you are a fucking psycho. I should have just stayed with her again last night."

Violet's heart sank, her stomach turning to stone. Every emotion she had been feeling was gone, now buried deep in her stomach and to the back of her mind where she wouldn't feel. She lay back in the bed and pulled the blanket over her shoulders. Hot silent tears fell from her eyes and onto the pillow.

"Thanks for the fuck, whore," he growled, throwing his t-shirt at her and stomping out of the room.

Several minutes had passed before she pulled herself off the bed. She was numb again, finally able to shut down after those last stabbing words he'd spat at her. She stripped her dress off, threw it to the floor, and walked to her closet, grabbing the small wooden box on the top shelf. She pulled out a bottle of sedatives that had been prescribed to her after the accident to help her get through. She took four and swallowed them.

* * *

"Hey, Violet, Roman's here," Steve yelled from downstairs.

She opened her eyes, not responding completely to the words she had heard. Groggily, she looked over at the alarm clock. It was six o'clock in the afternoon. There was a faint knock on the door. She closed her eyes again, unable to respond.

The door creaked open and he peered in. "Sorry to just come

in, Steve told me to come up." He peeked his head in the door.

She lay there naked on the bed, her arm and leg falling off the edge limply. He knew something was wrong with her. He walked in and kneeled down beside her. The heart necklace he had given her was tucked beneath her cheek.

"Hey, wake up," he said gently, brushing the hair out of her face. *She is beautiful,* he noted, not allowing it to register because he was concerned. It was almost a clinical observation. He looked away from her body as he reached behind her for the blanket and covered her, knowing she'd be embarrassed if she woke up and realized he'd seen her naked. She opened her eyes and looked into his. It took her several moments to determine whether or not he was really there or if she was dreaming.

"Violet, what did you take?" he asked, tapping her cheek with his finger. He felt so warm against her cheek. She grumbled something and closed her eyes again.

"Hey, wake up." He picked her up so that she was sitting and he sat beside her and let her lean into him. "Tell me what you took."

"Just some sedatives, no big deal," she muttered.

"How many?" he asked, hoping she was coherent enough to remember.

"Only four, it's no big deal, Roman. Let me sleep." She fell back down on the bed throwing the blanket off her body and kicking it to the end of the bed.

He stood up and walked to her dresser where he saw a bottle of pills. He thought she was safe to sleep this off, but he would stay there until she woke up. He sat down on the floor and leaned against her door at the foot of the bed. *Why the fuck did he even care?*

***

He had dozed off again. An adrenaline rush had awoken him and he instinctively looked up to see if her chest was still rising slowly and rhythmically beneath the thick quilt he had covered her with again. Her face looked perfectly still and peaceful with her hands tucked beneath her cheek like the proverbial sleeping baby angel. *She's no angel.*

Her thin arms looked ghost white against the deep reds and blacks of the blanket. The pointed bone of her hip jutted sharply over her slender waist showing that if she had not been so painfully thin she could be curvaceous. This was not something he should be contemplating.

He picked up a magazine from the floor and began leafing through it. She didn't seem like the type of girl to be reading teen magazines and he wondered what on earth she gleaned from this drivel. Certainly she didn't get makeup tips from here. Nor did she follow any of the "boyfriend etiquette" rules he had glanced over apparently. Still, this made him laugh to think she might actually read this. She wasn't nearly as cool as she wanted everyone to believe.

Where were her friends anyway? Amber did not seem like the type not to notice Violet hadn't left her bedroom in what appeared to be hours.

There must be a reasonable explanation for their absence. He knew from talking to Violet that Steve would certainly not think twice about leaving her in her room to die, but where were the other two? They seemed like good enough friends. He sat the magazine back down and crossed his long legs at the ankle and tucked his hands between his knees and shut his eyes.

What the hell am I doing...

***

Her eyes felt funny, thick with eye makeup and smudged black mascara. She blinked, trying to focus. First one eye cleared then clouded over again and then the other. Her fists swirled over her eyes then she stared at the clock, forcing her vision to react. Nine o'clock. She had succeeded in her task to sleep all day. She rolled onto her back and pulled the blanket down to her waist. It was hot. She had that almost fevered feeling. Maybe she was getting sick.

Then she noticed Mark's t-shirt lying beside her on the bed and remembered the stickiness of his mouth, dried thick spit on her face and neck. Her emotions flooded back. She was not supposed to feel anything. She was supposed to be numb.

Roman opened his eyes and watched her, saying nothing. Violet's face was pressed into the bed as she sobbed gently. Thick black hair hung over her hiding her face from him, and he felt uncomfortable, invasive.... He didn't know what to say, or how to make her aware of his presence, without startling or humiliating her. So he sat quietly and closed his eyes again, deciding it was best just to do nothing.

Violet's cries were humming deep in the back of her throat, low quiet rumbles that sounded like growls, and then she was quiet again.

He heard her sniffle and then she sat up in the bed. He opened his eyes and watched as she wiped her face, smearing the black makeup beneath her eyes even more. Her hair was tangled and sloppy hanging in front of her face. She took the back of her hand and wiped her nose then pushed the hair away from her face. She stopped suddenly, realizing he was there, and said nothing but just stared at him. He didn't react, just looked at her, trying not to convey pity or any other negative emotion.

"Why are you here?" she asked, lifting the quilt to cover her breasts instinctively.

"I stopped by to see you, and Steve told me to come up. You weren't doing very well and I wanted to make sure you were going to be alright."

"Of course I'm going to be alright. Don't be stupid," she said, throwing her legs over the edge of the bed and slamming her feet on the floor.

"I didn't mean to upset you, Violet. I was just worried because you took those pills. I wanted to make sure you were going to wake up."

"Like I don't know how to take sedatives. Fuck! I'm not a moron." She was angry, but mostly embarrassed by him seeing her in this state.

"No, you're not a moron," he said calmly. "I wasn't implying you that were." He realized she was lashing out at him because

117

she wasn't able to lash out at anyone else. Nevertheless, that didn't mean he could help himself from being affected by her words. "But you act like a stupid little girl sometimes."

She looked up at him stunned. Mark had said so many hateful things to her that it had nearly stopped hurting completely. She and Mark always spoke to each other with a lack of respect, so it was normal for them. But those few words of criticism from Roman made her feel so low she wanted to crumble. Mark was never able to get to the core of her like that. And certainly, no one else ever dared to do it either, especially not since her parents had died. There was not anyone left alive capable of hurting her with words. There was honesty to what he said—as though he could see straight through all of her acts—and it was unnerving.

"Stupid little girl," Roman repeated, angry at her for being so arrogant.

"Why are you even here? I don't need a babysitter." That was not what she wanted to say to him. She wanted to say she was sorry for being a bitch and wrap her arms around him. She wanted to thank him for giving a fuck about whether she woke up or not. She wanted him to tell her that he didn't mean what he said, give her a hug, and never let go.

"Apparently, the point of me being here is to watch you cry and feel sorry for yourself." His green eyes bore straight into her, his words cold and dead. He bent his knee and rested his arm on it. It pissed him off that all he'd done was try to be helpful, and she was so ungrateful and dismissive. Hell, he wasn't looking for gratitude, but he sure as fuck hadn't expected her to be so pissed.

She was bewildered. He had been nothing but kind and supportive towards her up until this point. Eyebrows drawn together, she tried to read him. He looked straight into her, never backing down. They were like two wild animals, one stalking the other. But which one of them was the hunter and which was the prey?

"What is it you want from me?" she asked quietly, her voice wavering.

"I don't want anything." His gaze broke for a second and then returned. "I have no idea what I want from you, but here I am again." The coldness in his eyes was different now, something

118

electric and angry flashed there. It really didn't make any sense to him that he was here with her. What was the point? He had never pursued anyone he was not trying to kill the whole of his existence. Why her and why now?

She stood up and walked to the closet, turning around and glaring at him as she reached in and pulled out a t-shirt balling it up in her fist as she stood there defiantly, antagonizing. He watched her as she moved across the floor, completely unfazed by her own nakedness.

"Does it bother you that I'm naked? I couldn't care less if it does."

"Then why do you ask?" he grumbled back.

She glared at him. "Everyone always wants me. Are you going to want to fuck me too?" she said, casually accusing him with an arched eyebrow.

"Darling, I've seen a lot of women naked. You're nothing special."

The condescension in her tone pissed him off but the intonation of his voice remained smooth and nonchalant. He couldn't quite understand where his words and emotions were coming from. He certainly had not come to her house, or sat there so long, to be mean to her. Hurting her wasn't something he intended to do, but somehow the words kept coming. And yes, it did make him uncomfortable that she paraded around naked. He was still a man.

Her heart sank as his words hit. No, there wasn't anything special about her. She had always believed that, but somehow she had managed to convince a whole lot of people otherwise. It hurt hearing the truth from him.

Her eyes left his unable to bear the weight of them anymore. She put on the t-shirt she was holding and then found PJ bottoms, turning away from him, but the weight of his gaze burned straight through her. She turned back, unable to keep from returning his glare with a well honed one of her own She couldn't take her eyes off him again. There was something so odd about his expression and the tone of his voice. He was being completely honest with her, not mean, honest, and it seemed foreign. Everyone in her life, including her best friends, hid their thoughts from her at times in order not to anger or hurt her feelings. He was being honest... and it hurt.

She walked back to the bed and sat down. Her head was still clouded, still exhausted. "So, are you pissed off at me for sleeping with Mark last night or something? I don't get what's going on here."

Roman's eyes widened as he exhaled, incredulous. He certainly had not expected that question. "I didn't know anything about that, Violet. How would I?" He paused for a moment and continued, "It is up to you if you want to continue in a pointless relationship with an abusive asshole. That has nothing to do with me. I just came by to see you and you were fucked up. I was afraid you OD'd so I decided to hang out and make sure you were going to wake up. How does that make me the bad guy here?"

The blood drained from her face. She felt her cheeks turn cold and her eyes felt like two dry heavy orbs too large for their sockets. Her arms wrapped around her knees drawing them up into her chest as she tucked her head into them. Hugging herself, futily trying to keep from crying again. Her toes curled under as she kept her balance on the soft bed trying to make her body as small as possible. She wanted to curl up in a ball so tight she would disappear. He was able to see through all her facades and it was disturbing. No one else ever called her on her bullshit. No one. And he saw straight through all of it. She couldn't fake anything with him. He wasn't impressed with her act. Finally someone saw her for the fraud she had always been.

He was furious with himself for being so emotionally inept. How the hell had he gotten himself into this mess? "Look, I didn't mean to add to your problems and I certainly didn't mean to butt in where I'm not welcome. I'm obviously completely incapable of handling this situation. You're okay so I'll leave now."

He stood up and waited for some type of response. Her little body rocked back and forth, her long hair nearly covering her completely. Seeing her look so small and frail made him want to go to her and comfort her. He had not meant to be such an asshole but she was being ridiculous. He was not the bad guy in this. Except that now he had made her feel completely worthless, just like Mark, and apparently others had always done. *Fuck.*

"I'm gonna go now," he said louder, and reached for the door handle. Anger still seeped into his voice. He was frustrated with himself more than he was frustrated with her at this point.

The soft fabric of her pajamas stifled a sniffle causing him to turn around and look at her again as he pulled the door open. Her tiny hands were clenched together, white knuckles straining.

"I'm sorry for crying," she said without lifting her head. Her voice was muffled and wet sounding.

He stood there for a moment with his hand on the doorknob feeling like a complete asshole. She had just lost her parents and broke up with her boyfriend. Or something, he wasn't sure after the bomb she'd dropped about fucking Mark the night before. Yes, she would be crying a lot. It was normal for people to cry when those things happened to them. He was just a heartless bastard. He hadn't minded her crying at all, but he did mind people feeling sorry for themselves. The problem was he didn't really know how to judge that since he was secluded from humans the vast majority of the time.

"Please don't apologize for crying. I'm an asshole," he said, feeling a bit of pity for himself for being so inept and stupid. His voice was gentle again, not angry.

She looked up at him. His face was kind again, so beautiful. She reached her hand out toward him. He walked over to her, took her hand in his, and squeezed it. She scooted back on the bed, trying to coax him to follow her. She lay back on her pillow and never took her eyes from his.

Roman followed her. For someone so strong he was so weak. He leaned on his elbow and gently wiped the tears and smudged makeup from her eyes, then wiped his wet fingers on her shirt leaving black stains. "You really need to stop crying over stupid boys."

She took her hand and pulled the hair back away from his face studying the dark intensity in his eyes, then rolled over on her side with her back towards him reaching her arm behind and grabbing his wrist. With his arm now pulled around her she closed her eyes.

"We sleep way too much when we're together." She sniffled, settling into the bed.

Roman lay his head down and pulled her back against him. "Yeah, we're good at it though." He brushed her hair out of his face then kissed the back of her head.

6. EVERYTHING IS COMING TO A GRINDING HALT

"Mm...I love coffee," she said, taking a large swallow.

"Sweetheart, that's not coffee, it's dessert." He smiled, and took a sip of his own sugary drink.

"You should talk, doof." She kicked him under the table.

He smiled at her sheepishly and licked the whipped cream from his lip.

They were avoiding the subject of "last night". She could tell that the event was hanging out in the air almost tangibly, neither one of them wanting to revisit it. Violet distracted herself with a smallish blonde girl who walked up to the counter and ordered a drink. She looked so pretty in the fuzzy pale pink sweater and faded jeans. A few months prior even the site of these normal people would have turned her stomach and she wondered about the slow evolution she was going through. She reasoned that it must be her getting older, because it could not be that she was longing for normalcy.

"You know I didn't mean what I said?" he asked, looking up from the paper he was browsing.

"I don't know what you mean," she responded, looking back to him. She noticed the insecure air about him. This was abnormal. He was usually so self-assured.

"Yeah, well, anyway, sorry for being an ass yesterday."

"I was the ass, Roman. You were trying to save me, as usual, and I promise you that you will not have to do that for at least another week. Okay?" She grinned and took a bite of the shortbread cookie she had been savoring since they had sat down. "This is so good," she said and smiled. Another successful subject change.

"So, get another one, or a dozen. You could stand to gain some weight," he said and paused. "That sounded really dickish. I just

123

never see you eat anything." He looked back at the newspaper and continued reading an article on global warming. "I'm not sure I completely buy this. Some of it could just be cyclical weather patterns that have happened throughout the earth's history. What do you think?"

Violet looked up at him having no idea what he was ever talking about since she had no idea what he was reading.

"Global warming?" he clarified, looking back at the paper.

"Oh, I don't know. It seems legit to me?" she said, and shrugged. "Humans suck."

"I'm sure we're not helping matters by any stretch of the imagination," he said, furrowing his brow. "It seems like it could be a combination of things. But what do I know? And yes, I was an ass and I'm sorry."

He looked over the top of the paper briefly, then back down at the article.

She looked at him quizzically and went to buy herself some more cookies. As she walked up to the counter she looked around the place, taking everyone and everything in. An odd feeling that something had changed settled over her skin. Something was different about her, but it wasn't really anything she could put her finger on. There were three people ahead of her in line. A little girl turned and looked up at her and Violet smiled at her awkwardly. The girl studied Violet, her eyes moving from one area of her body to the next. Violet was uncomfortable.

"Stop staring," her mother scolded, yanking the girl's arm. She then turned and smiled at Violet apologetically.

Was she really that odd to look at? She looked down at her body then back at the little girl. It was her turn, so she stepped up to the counter and ordered a cranberry muffin and three more shortbread cookies.

"Sweet tooth today?" the cute alternative boy asked with a sly grin on his face.

Violet shrugged her shoulders, "I guess the waif look is out." She handed the boy money and dropped a couple dollars in the tip jar.

She grabbed the bag of treats and started back towards Roman passing the table the mother and little girl were sitting. The girl was looking at her again. Violet reached into the bag, pulled out a cookie, and handed it to her, watching her eyes light up.

"Enjoy, kitten." Violet smiled and winked.

She sat down with Roman and began eating the muffin. Roman looked up, grinned, and continued reading. "So, I guess I want to tell you what happened yesterday," Violet said, wiping the crumbs that had landed on her black thermal shirt. She looked down and noticed the crumbled muffin remnants on her black corduroy pants as well. She shook her head and wiped herself off. "I didn't really explain what happened."

Roman folded the newspaper and leaned forward. His eyes were intense. "Just so you know, I don't believe I merit any sort of explanation, but if you want to talk, feel free." He leaned back into the tufted leather chair and took another sip of his coffee.

She picked off another piece of the muffin, handed it to him, and started explaining the evening before at the club. "We showed up there and I was reluctant about going, but was sort of a little bit excited too. I knew there was going to be some people I hadn't seen in a long time, some people I was quite fond of before Mark. So I was excited. Then I got there and it just wasn't right. I saw Jim, and he just looked different. There were things about him, stuff I didn't notice about him before. Like he looked pretty sick to me, like strung out or something. I didn't realize what a junkie he was before for some reason, or maybe he hadn't been before? I don't know... And Matt was just Matt, and I noticed how bizarre he really is. And it was all just not right. I felt like something was dead inside me and it was freaking me out. Even people who I saw as being so innocent and naïve looked like they'd aged five years or something. I felt completely out of place. I've been feeling like that a lot since, you know... It just put me in this weird state of mind."

Roman watched her mannerisms as she spoke, the awkward way her eyes darted around the room and back to him every few seconds, and how her hands never stopped fiddling with something. It was interesting watching her movements, and the way she spoke and pronounced words. The Midwestern accent was obvious, though he knew she had no idea she even had one. He could not understand how a person this seemingly intelligent, attractive, and strong could allow herself to be in the situation she was in with her boyfriend. He himself had never allowed any person to control him. He didn't ever allow anyone near enough to get the chance.

"So, I saw Mark and he came over and started talking. I knew he was working me. I knew he was playing me the same way he always plays me. The same words he always says, the same actions. But I didn't care. I wanted things to be normal and familiar and I didn't care how ridiculously stupid I was being. just didn't care about the consequences of my actions. As soon as we got back to my house, it was over, he was asleep, and I was there staring at the ceiling alone again. I realized things would never be normal, not ever again, and I was just defeated. I figured I would just live this existence with him, pointless and without any passion for anything, and that eventually I would learn to be happy, or content to be miserable. I couldn't do it though. couldn't go through with it. I hadn't even tried, and I knew would never be able to go through with it. It was wrong, and knew that he had to go. So I told him to leave, he freaked out again, and I just went completely numb. I couldn't even speak. didn't react at all, and that made him even angrier. After he left, just wanted to sleep. That's why I took those sedatives. I wasn't trying to hurt myself or anything, I just needed to sleep. I needed the dreams to stop so that I could finally sleep peacefully for a few hours."

"Dreams?" Roman asked suddenly.

"Yeah, I've been having weird dreams for weeks now, scary monsters, me fighting them, blah blah blah. Remember, I told you? I just don't sleep well," she said, and paused for a moment, "unless you're around, ironically." She ate the last of the muffin and swallowed some coffee.

Roman drew his hand to his face and scratched his chin. He had no advice to give, no words of wisdom, this certainly wasn't his area of expertise. "Who cares?" he said nonchalantly.

Violet coughed a laugh, nearly choking on her coffee, not expecting his reaction. "What?"

"Who cares? You slept with the guy again. Big deal. Move on. Don't beat yourself up over it. Lots of people have one night stands." He shrugged his shoulders and stood up. "I'm going to go to the restroom," he said, and walked off towards the facilities.

Violet watched him cut through the room, still somewhat stymied by his reaction. He seemed to be the vortex in the room, a black hole that pulled every bit of attention to itself. He was so tall and enigmatic that it seemed to draw every eye to him, and he didn't seem to notice at all. Of course, he had always lived in his skin, so perhaps he no longer noticed the eyes on him.

She had expected some sort of lecture, or a scolding, or some deep talk about how it's important to *do the right thing* and *take care of yourself*—but yeah—fuck Mark. Who cares? She did not need to make this a bigger deal than it was. People really did have one night stands all the time, granted she was not one of them, but why should she care about one night of stupidity anyway? People fucked their exes all the time. It was easy, convenient. Like a dog returning to its own vomit, she thought. *Fuck Mark* and *who cares*. Those were two philosophies she could live by.

She took a bite of a cookie and stared down at the rich dark wood of the table. A smile was trying to force its way across her lips.

"So, tell me about your dreams," he said, sitting back down and reaching over to take her last cookie.

"Hey, I thought you wanted me to get fat?" she pouted.

"I don't remember saying that," he said, taking a bite of the cookie. "But be fat if you want. It doesn't matter to me. I just rarely see you eat. It's disconcerting." He furrowed his brow and then looked her in the eye. "And I'm not trying to demean what you're going through, V, just don't take life so seriously all the time. You made a mistake, move on, and forget about it. God knows I've made enough stupid mistakes." *Getting involved in her life for one.*

Violet titled her head to the side slightly and studied his face. He was right. She needed to not take life so seriously. A blurry figure approached out of her peripheral   The closer it got, the larger it seemed until she finally realized it was coming towards her. She looked away from him momentarily to see who was coming.

"Violet," the girls cooed. They stood there linked arm in arm

dressed nearly identically. Like two dolls they looked; long wav
auburn hair against terribly pale skin. Their lips were glossed ar
shiny, and their eyes were lined in dark pink.

"You two look like twins now," Violet said, smiling at the girl
somewhat shocked by their appearances. "Roman, this is Dory ar
Malinda," she said, looking back to Roman, who was looking wi
a blank expression at the girls.

The two seemed almost like characters from a storybook. Tw
Gothic dolls in vintage black lace and black granny boots.

"Like our hair?" Dory asked, tilting her head towards the oth
girl. They had been blonde and brunette before.

"Yeah, you look really pretty, both of you, it's just shockir
how much you look alike is all," Violet said, nearly dumbfounde
by their transformation. These were the same girls she had ju
spoken to a few nights prior, and had noticed the slight change
their demeanor. Now they were like scary dolls, barely resemblir
their former selves.

"Well, anyway, we wanted to invite you to the party tonig
after the Ox Roast."

"Ox Roast?" Roman asked, looking at Violet and attempting n
to laugh.

"It's a carnival," Violet answered, conveying her lack o
enthusiasm with her eyes.

Roman laughed.

"It's going to be in the woods behind my grandparents' hou:
again like last year. Remember how fun that was?" Malinda sai
smiling from ear to ear.

It had been the girls' first taste of the "cool kids" hanging o
with them. Violet looked back briefly remembering that it ha
been fun. "Yes, it was fun," she said, and smiled, noticing agai
how creepy the two girls looked now. They almost move
identically as they stood side by side like those girls from T/
Shining.

"Well, make sure you come, and tell Amber and Randy too,
Dory said.

"Yeah, I will," Violet assured them with a smile.

"And make sure he comes to," Malinda said, winking at Roma
Roman looked away from Malinda and grinned at Violet. H

128

was semi embarrassed for the girl seeing as how he had no interest in either of the two. He thought of them as children. They were children.

"Well, that will be up to him," Violet answered, kicking him under the table.

"Okay, well, I hope you make it. It won't be the same without you," Dory said, and urged her friend to walk away.

"Bye," they both said in tandem.

"Wow, they're like gothic cyborgs or something," he said, shaking his head.

"If you only knew how happy that comparison would probably make them. It's so weird though, because not too long ago they were these sweet, very naïve young girls, and now they seem really weird." Violet laughed, and drank the final bit of her coffee. "So, you're going to go, right?"

Roman looked at her with a funny look on his face. "To the Ox Roast or the party?" he teased her.

"Uh, *both*?"

"Well, I could go for a candy apple..."

***

"We're not gonna stay that long are we?" Amber asked, and slammed the door to Randy's beater.

Violet looked at Roman and smiled.

"Well, duh, how else are we going to win mirrors with pot leaves on them and glow in the dark velvet posters?" Randy joked, shoving her as they met in front of the car.

"All I care about is cotton candy, a caramel apple, and a corndog." Violet muttered, jogging ahead of them.

Roman lagged behind, noticing how people seemed to turn and look at the three with caution, disgust, or amusement. He could not see what the big deal was himself, but then generally speaking, he didn't judge people. His family had taught him that at least.

For all her coolness, she seemed thrilled to be here. Her eyes were wide and sparkling in the twinkling lights and commotion of the crowd. She seemed vibrant; as she had that day she had brought him all the gifts. She was much more attractive when she smiled like this. It made him content to see her enjoying herself.

She was already in line for the aforementioned corndog when he caught up to her. Amber and Randy were standing aside waiting and scanning the crowd for familiar faces. They assumed none of their friends would be here, but they certainly recognized a lot of people. Roman walked over to her, excusing himself to the woman who stood behind her, who clucked her tongue and scowled. He returned her distaste with a smile he knew made her uncomfortable. Assholes like her weren't used to being called on their behavior, and Roman understood how to disarm them.

"You want one?" she asked with excitement. She hoped he would say yes, because she wanted someone else to enjoy this experience besides just her. This fair had been important to her the whole of her existence. Her parents had always brought her here and it had always been one of the highlights of the year. She remembered how they would bring her and a friend, and buy them both wristbands so that they could ride all the rides they wanted all day long. She used to watch the tractor pulls sitting on her father's lap, covering her ears from the loud noise. And she had always had to have a corndog, cotton candy, and a caramel apple to eat on the ride home. She had not been to this fair the last few years because it was so unfashionable being seen at such a place, not to mention she didn't always like enduring the stares and jeers they sometimes drew out of people simply for existing. She was glad he had wanted a candy apple enough to make her want to come again.

"Of course I want one," he said, smiling at her. "You know you aren't nearly as scary and strange as you want people to believe."

"So you've told me. It's all an act, I know." She smiled and then stepped up to the counter and ordered their food.

They walked over to the fixin's bar and she pulled back the paper wrapper and squirted mustard on the dog, then took a big bite, which brought a smile to her lips. "Just like I remember. should make these at home and eat them every day."

"Nah, it's not the same," he said, already having eaten most of his in one bite.

The lights and all the action felt magical to her. Almost like they had entered some kind of realm outside of the real world. She saw a few people she recognized from school, smiled casually to them, and continued walking. Amber and Randy had long since wandered off, and Roman barely spoke. He was content to watch the crowd and her reaction to the place. They stopped in front of the dunking booth and decided subconsciously to stand and watch for a while. Neither of them spoke, they just watched in interest as the balls were thrown aimlessly and the wet teenagers hurled mocking insults to the throwers, who occasionally made contact with the target, dunking their goading victims.

"Want something to drink?" he asked, finally breaking the spell.

"Uh, yes, I would like something to drink," she said, barely taking her eyes from the spectacle.

"Be right back," he said as he walked away.

She watched him as he walked to the lemonade stand, then she turned around and worked her way through the crowd to the grassy hill that sat parallel to the dunking booth. She made sure to sit in a spot where he would be able to see her. He so noticeably stood out from everyone around him. His height and long black hair were enough to bring notice, the fact that he was muscular and dressed in black from head to toe, and gorgeous by anyone's definition, made him even more obvious.

Though perhaps the harshness of his features, the angular cut of his cheekbones and prominent brow, might not appeal to everyone? His look was distinctive and maybe even intimidating, but of course she liked that. She realized there probably wasn't anywhere he could go that he would not be set apart from the crowd.

He looked really beautiful tonight with his hair pulled back away from his face. It was hanging down his back in a ponytail almost as long as her own hair. He was wearing a long sleeved black t-shirt and black jeans with black leather boots. There was a dark shadow of growth on his face that she found particularly attractive.

She watched as several women checked him out as he walked through the crowd. It was mostly the biker types that looked at

him with lust, which made total sense. It was amusing to her, ar
she wondered if he even noticed. Could he really not notice tha
She imagined what type of woman he would find attractive. Ta
slender, long hair, and long legs. Someone exotic. Violet would l
her complete opposite.

He paid for the drinks and began walking back toward her. Sl
raised her hand so that he would see her, but he already had.

"I hope you like lemonade. I should have asked." He hand
her a drink and then sat down beside her.

"I do," she said, taking a big gulp of the sweet drink. "Mr
more sugar." She grinned licking her lips.

"Yeah, I thought you needed some."

Violet observed him as he scanned the crowd, silently taking
everything he saw. She could tell by the stillness that came ov
him that he was thinking and giving each thing he saw—eac
person—consideration. She wanted to be like him. Roman didn
seem to judge anyone, nor did he seem to try to fit in, she want
to be like that. She wanted to be free of the constraints she place
on herself, the stupid rules she had forced herself to live by the
last few years all to be a part of some moronic clique of peop
who didn't really matter in the grand scheme of things.

And where had they all been for her? They all acted as if sl
walked on water, or at the very least, was the coolest thing sin
sliced bread, so where had they all been when she needed suppor
But she didn't deserve their support, not really. She was mean
half of her friends, so why would they truly care about her?

"There are some interesting people here," he said suddenl
making her jump a little.

"I suppose," she answered, trying to cover her uncool reaction.

"Really, it's interesting to me that all these people have the
own little worlds. I don't know, I am just fascinated by that sort o
thing I guess." He looked at her, his green eyes vibrant as the
collected the colored lights.

"You don't get out much do you?" she asked as a grin peele
across her face.

"No, I guess not," he answered, and looked back towards tl
crowd. "This means a lot to you," he said, knowing.

"Yes," she answered, somewhat surprised by his perceptio

132

"My parents always brought me here."

"I'm glad you came then. You should do more things that make you happy."

She didn't say anything but sat in awe of his words. *You should do more things that make you happy.* Such simple, basic, truthful words. She thought she had been happy these last few years until her parents died. Their death made her realize how pointless her life had been. All she had done was hang out with friends and make the scene, even if it was a little one. Her life still had no point. What the fuck was she going do with the rest of it?

They watched as Amber and Randy approached through the sea of plaid, denim and sun bleached hair. They looked like comic book characters in context to the rest. Randy was gripping a mirror in one hand and Amber's in the other.

"My guess is they want to leave," Violet said despondently.

"I haven't even had a candy apple yet," he joked, and looked at her.

"Momma promises you'll have one before we leave," she smiled.

"So, yep, we're ready to go. Randy just about got his ass kicked by some rednecks," Amber said, short of breath.

"What?" Violet asked, standing up and wiping the grass from her corduroys.

"Yeah, some asshole started saying shit and it pissed me off. So I told him to fuck off and then a bunch of fucking hillbillies started in," Randy said, still full of adrenalin.

Violet felt her stomach knot. She had been enjoying the time with Roman and she wasn't really ready for it to end. "Well, you guys go to the car. We'll catch up. There's apples to buy," Violet said, trying to laugh off what they had told her.

She was disappointed that this evening was ending so abruptly. It would have made her happy to sit with him all night, but it wasn't in the cards. Disappointment should feel like second nature to her, but it still always stung. She should have known better than to try to make this a group effort anyway. This wasn't the sort of thing Amber enjoyed.

"Well don't take too long. That party is probably in full swing," Amber said, grabbing Randy's hand and pulling him

133

toward the parking lot.

Violet looked up at Roman. The disappointment in her eyes was more than obvious. He felt sick for her.

"Sorry."

"No biggie," she said, walking toward where she knew the candy apples would be. Everything was in the same place it had been her entire life. Everything but the people she needed and missed dearly. The lump in her throat was aching, tears threatening to fall. She tried to force herself to be happy, to enjoy this place for what it was, and to stay focused on good things for once. She swallowed down her grief and made a beeline for the candy apples.

Roman knew this was a big deal to her and he wondered why her own friends didn't realize it too. But then he knew they had their own problems to worry about. He reached his hand out towards her and rested it on her shoulder. She appreciated the gesture.

***

"I really don't want to have to pee in the woods," Violet said leaning forward and resting her arms on the back of Amber's seat. Her lips were sticky with sugar from the apple she had been busily munching.

"Yeah, I hate that too, but remember how fun her party was last year?" Amber said, turning towards her friend.

"Yeah, it was pretty fun." Violet sat back in the seat and looked over at Roman who was contentedly eating his apple. His lips were red and glossy from the candy coating and for a brief second he almost looked like he had blood smeared across his mouth. He winked at her and continued eating the apple.

"Dude, remember how fucked up you got last year, Violet. That was so freaking funny when you and Sam started wrestling." Randy laughed, looking over at Amber who was chuckling at the memory herself.

Violet felt her face turn red. Why was she embarrassed for him to hear this? "I wasn't wrestling with him for fun. The guy scares the hell out of me and it was sorta self-defense, Randy."

"Yeah, he's scary. Thank God he likes us." Amber said, looking at her friend for acknowledgment.

"Yep, we're damn lucky he likes us." Violet shook her head.

"So who's Sam?" Roman interjected. He was busy cleaning the remaining candy coating from the wooden stick.

"He's this big scary schizophrenic that hangs around the scene. He is just about as big as you are, and can sort of *go off* from time to time for no reason. He's always been nice to us thankfully," Amber answered.

"It's like being around a wild animal or something. You never know when the guy's gonna snap," Randy said, looking at Roman in the rearview mirror.

"And you were wrestling him?" Roman said, smirking at Violet.

"Well, sort of. It was more like him throwing me around until I finally kneed him in the groin and got away," Violet explained sheepishly.

"Then he just laughed and thought it was cute for some odd reason," Amber said.

"How bizarre," Violet said curiously, and looked out the window thinking back to that evening.

"Very bizarre," Amber and Randy said in tandem.

They all laughed. Violet threw the stick and nibbled apple core out the window. She felt sticky all over and like an asshole for littering. She felt like an asshole ninety-seven percent of the time. Some animal would eat the core, right? She swallowed her guilt and started licking her fingers hoping to get them at least somewhat cleanish.

"I hope ants don't crawl on me," she said quietly, mostly to herself.

"Ants? Somehow I doubt that's going to happen," Roman laughed. "You didn't get your cotton candy." Roman spoke in a hushed tone so that the others didn't hear him. The carnival had obviously meant a lot to her and the fact that her friends hadn't noticed sort of mystified him, but he also didn't want to call attention to it. He assumed it was something she had not shared the relevance of with them, because why else would they be so dismissive?

"Next year," she answered and smiled. She settled back into the seat closing her eyes content to soak up the cool air that was blowing in her face and the lulling rumble of the car. Roman did the same.

***

They could see the bonfire off in the distance. There were several cars parked in the driveway and on the lawn of Malinda's grandmother's house. Randy opened the trunk grabbing the twelve pack of beer he had stashed there before they had even left for the fair. Violet rolled her eyes and started walking toward the field behind the house. Roman and Amber followed. Randy was busy talking to a friend who had just pulled up.

"We should have brought jackets or something," Amber said looking at the three in their thin shirts. She was wearing a concert t-shirt and old jeans.

"There's a fire to keep yourself warm beside," Roman answered.

"Yeah, I guess so. Plus alcohol keeps ya warm, that and wrestling, huh, Violet?"

"Ugh, don't remind me," Violet said with a wry grin.

They walked through the thin tree line and into the open field. The fire was past the field, close to the edge of the woods several hundred yards away. They could already hear the whooping and hollering and could see several people in the distance bouncing about.

"I'm pretty sure Sam's gonna be here," Violet said and shrugged.

"Just knee him in the groin more quickly this time. Don't be afraid to hurt him," Amber giggled demonically.

"Yeah, that's pretty much my plan," Violet said. "So, you think Mark's gonna show up?"

Roman looked over at her, wondering what this might do to her if he did.

"I don't know, he might? We'll just leave if he does, okay?" Amber said, looking at her friend and offering support.

"Yeah, this is gonna be weird anyway. When we saw Dory and Malinda this morning they seemed all weird, Amber. Like they looked like those creepy twins from *The Shining* or something. Didn't they, Roman?"

"Yeah, sort of, they were cute though." Violet rolled her eyes and gave him a dirty look. "What? For creepy little twins they looked cute," he said, shoving her in the arm.

"Ah, you just like them because they were all 'Make sure he comes,'" she said, mocking the girls as she slapped his arm and rolled her eyes again.

"Come now, I'm not *that* easily intrigued," Roman said, with an eye roll of his own.

"Typical man," Amber joked, and jogged ahead of them towards the fire.

Violet looked around the dark field. There was a malevolence that sunk into her skin and settled in her bones. "I'd be creeped out if I had to walk out here by myself," Violet said, walking closer to him. She had always been scared in the woods even in broad daylight. There was something scary and far too isolating about it.

"It is creepy."

"Okay, we've officially exhausted the use of the word creepy for this evening. That's like the thousandth time we've said it." She smiled and looked up at him.

They walked up to the group. There were about fifteen people already there, most of which were already drunk or well on their way. Malinda and Dory came immediately towards them, still looking like evil doll twins. They took Roman by the arm and walked him toward their friends to introduce him. He looked back over his shoulder at Violet, who teased him with a smile and shake of her head and a silent "ha ha".

Amber walked over to Violet. "Ugh, I see what you mean about D & M. What is up with their creepy new look? They seem really different than the last time I spoke to them, and that was only like last week or something."

"I know, they seem like they went from cute, innocent girls to scary devil dolls or something," Violet said, sitting down on a log. The heat of the large fire felt good on her. Her face, chest, and legs were tingling with warmth and her back was still cool from the late summer night. Amber sat down beside her and looked over the group who were sitting and standing around.

"I'm not sure about these people anymore," she said, looking back at Violet.

What do you mean?" Violet asked, curious about the statement.

"I don't know what I mean actually, just seems weirder than usual or something, like we're outgrowing all this."

"I get what you're saying," Violet agreed. She was surprised Amber had been feeling the same way she had been feeling. Amber always seemed to love being in the center of all this, but then she had too, probably even more so. Amber had always been the outgoing one, the one who had been friends with everyone. Violet had been the more reluctant of the two keeping most people at arm's length. That seemed to intrigue the others, naturally. People always want what they can't have, right?

"It's only a matter of time before Sam comes over here cookie." Amber pinched Violet's arm and looked in the lug' direction.

"Yep, I know," Violet sighed.

"Well at least you have Roman to protect you this year, unlike Mark who thought it was funny. Speaking of which, your boyfriend is being monopolized."

"Uh, not my boyfriend," Violet said with venom.

"Yep, so you keep saying," Amber mocked her, and stood up to greet Randy who had finally made his way to them.

Violet watched Roman interact with the others. He was confident and sure of himself. She envied that about him. He knew who he was and had no problem fitting in with anyone, or so it seemed. When he was one on one he sometimes seemed awkward, but not enough for anyone else to notice. Or maybe he was only awkward with her? Things had gotten much more comfortable the more time they spent together. Of course it would, that was normal. She shook her thoughts and looked back at him.

He was surrounded by girls, all of whom looked so insanely

young and tiny standing next to him, and she wondered if she looked that young when she was with him. Maybe he saw her as a child, just as these girls looked to her now. He must think so, he'd told her himself she acted like a stupid little girl. The memory of that evening made her sick to her stomach, suddenly. He'd seen her at one of her lowest points. She must have looked like a strung out teenager to him. She remembered how her face and hair had looked when she'd finally made it to the shower, and how she had even sort of smelled sweaty and gross. But he had never even remotely made mention of her hideous state, to his credit, she supposed.

She was suddenly horrified by the embarrassment of it, and had to look away from him, and back to the fire. Roman had been so kind to her that night, once she had stopped being an asshole to him. It must've been annoying to him to stay there with her, not that he'd shown any annoyance, but how could it have been anything but annoying? She was always breaking down around him, and he'd commented about being sick of her crying. Of course that's how she interpreted what he'd said. He hadn't said that at all, really. Roman was a good person. Far more patient than she could ever hope to be. He never had judged her, only pointed out what he saw. She looked back up at him and noticed that he was now chatting with Sam. And now the group was looking in her direction. She wanted to crawl away and hide under a rock somewhere.

"Huh oh, hope you brought your wrastlin' tights. Looks like the hulk might be coming on over," Amber mused, bending to whisper to Violet.

"Oh man," Violet said, putting her head down and resting it on her lap. Amber patted her friend on the head and Violet could hear Randy snickering in the background.

"Maybe he's forgotten," Amber said, trying to comfort her friend.

Violet looked up at her with a smile on her face. "Yeah, maybe he did. That was a whole year ago, and he was really drunk and stuff too."

"Sweetie, I was just saying that to be nice. There ain't no way he's forgotten." Amber laughed and leaned into her friend with a little shove.

"Dick," Violet said with a scowl, and made a brat face. Sl looked away from her friend and back across the fire to the others

They had turned around and weren't looking at her anymor much to her relief. She hated how Roman looked so comfortab with them, almost as if they were his long lost friends. It was lil he was already better friends with them than she was, of cour that was her fault, though, wasn't it? She had always kept herse at arm's length from all of them. Truly Amber was her only re link to any of them.

She hated herself for how she was, she wanted to be the happ light hearted girl she'd been when she was younger. But she h no idea how to be that person anymore. She had sufficient convinced everyone how tough and icy she was, only it was f from the truth, and not one of these people, besides the three sl came with, knew her to any extent at all. Again, all her fault.

Suddenly she heard the shrill sound of her cell phone fro within her bag and jumped grabbing her chest. "Damnit!" Viol winced, and reached into her bag. She looked at the phone ar didn't recognize the number. "Hello?"

"Well hello, little rabbit," a sultry female voice purred.

"Who is this?" Violet asked, unable to recognize the voice.

"I'm the big bad wolf," the woman said, giggling.

"Who is this, and what the fuck do you want?" Viol demanded.

"I just wanted to hear your voice. Better build your hou: strong, little one." And then the line went dead.

"Who was that?" Amber asked, her eye brows creased wi concern.

"I have no idea at all, some girl," Violet said, looking at tl number again and trying to figure it out.

"I bet it's a wrong number."

"No, it wasn't a wrong number. Whoever it was definite wanted to talk to me." Violet lifted the phone towards her frien "Do you recognize this number?"

Amber squinted in the dim light of the fire and shook her hea no. "I've never seen that number."

"Hmm...Probably someone Mark put up to calling me, c

something stupid like that."

"Well what did she say?"

"She said 'Hello, little rabbit' and then some crap about being the big bad wolf, and building my house strong."

"Wow way to make weird ass lame cross references." Amber said, and rolled her eyes. "Blow it off, Vi. It's probably like you said, Mark screwing around."

"I'm sure you're right," she said, trying to convince herself as she turned the phone off and shoved it back in her bag. Mark had made her jealous in the past with other girls, but he'd never had one threaten her before.

She looked up to watch Roman and the others again. He seemed to be in the center of the Cute Girl Circle. It was like he was the Pied Piper standing there in the midst of all those tiny little girls. Could he be attracted to them? Maybe one of them would be bold enough to actually put some sort of moves on him and he would go right along with it? He was a guy, and guys generally took what they could get, didn't they? It was possible, more than possible really. He had already called them cute. And he was male. And they did seem more than intrigued by him. *And he was male.*

"Stare much?" Amber asked, shoving her friend.

Violet jolted herself away from the trance she'd been in and smiled at Amber. "So, I think at least one of those girls is going to try to fuck him tonight," she predicted casually.

"You kiss your mom with that mouth?" Amber grinned, and then winced realizing what she'd said. "Sorry..." she apologized.

"Don't be so sensitive. You know my mom would have busted my mouth if she heard the way I talk." Violet smiled, remembering her tough little mom.

"Yep, and then she would have told you to march to your room." Amber was relieved to see her friend joking again. She hadn't talked much about her parents in the last few weeks.

"Well anyway, those girls are hot for teacher," Violet reiterated, looking back to the group.

"Well duh. Fucking look at him. I'd be all over him too if I was single. But, does that bother you?"

"I don't think so? I mean, not really, it's not like that with us, I don't think. I mean, I'd know right? Like if he liked me I'd know and I haven't really thought of him like that. It's just more annoying to me or something, like stay away from my brother!"

"Hmm... okay," Amber said skeptically.

"Shut up," Violet snapped, smacking Amber's leg.

"Ouch, I didn't say anything!" Amber pouted, and rubbed her leg where she'd been hit.

"Anyway, he's coming over here, so shut up."

"Good lord, woman," Amber laughed, and stood up to go hunt down Randy who'd last been seen running off into the field sans shirt with his friend on his shoulders. "Gotta go find Randolph before he hurts himself or someone else." She rolled her eyes.

Violet smiled and nodded. Roman was walking towards her. She saw the girls watching him walk away and she immediately recognized their giggle and whispering. She and Amber had been guilty of that girlish behavior too many times to even recount.

He sat down beside her and took a sip of the beer he was drinking. "You cold yet?" he asked, looking at her.

"Nope," she answered not looking away from the girls.

"Strange group of people here," he said, looking across the circle towards the others.

"I don't know how strange they are in all reality, that's just what they want you to think. It's a part of the overall package," she said, holding her hands out and making circular gestures.

"That's part of your overall package too isn't it?" he asked grinning at her.

"I guess so. I'm just more convincing and better at it than them." She smirked at him, but was serious and spoke with condescension towards the others.

"You don't like these people very much do you?"

"Not particularly, but I envy them all to a degree."

"Envy them how?" he asked curiously.

"I envy the fact that they can be content being so completely full of shit. It's all such a fucking act."

"Wow, you are a funny girl," he said, bemused, as he took another swallow of his drink.

"Funny how?" she asked, raising an eyebrow. She was unsure whether he was insulting or complementing her.

142

"It's funny to me that you see straight through all this crap, and yet you're sort of the queen of it all. From what I gather from speaking to them you and Amber are pretty much responsible for creating half these people, and they worship the ground you guys walk on."

"Please don't give me the credit for that," she chuckled. "If I was going to create something it would be much better than this."

"But aren't you friends with these people? Violet, I've seen the way these girls react to you—and Amber—for that matter. They worship you two. Those girls couldn't be any more enamored with you. So, you're telling me you hate them all? I mean, wasn't this a very important part of your world up until very recently?"

"What other options are there around here? I could hang out with white trash hillbillies, or I could take the little lost sheep and form them into something halfway decent. What else is there here in this pathetically small and inward looking town?"

He just smiled and looked at her out of the corner of his eye while taking another swig from the bottle. "You're a funny little girl."

That struck a nerve in her. She hated being called a little girl, at least the way he was saying it. It was dismissive and chiding somehow. "I'm not a little girl," she said, crossing her arms over her chest just like any good little tantrum-having-girl would.

"Okay, no offense, *old lady*," he said, smiling at her.

She couldn't help smiling back. "And besides, no one created Sam. He was always a freak all on his own."

"Speaking of which," he said, leaning forward and resting his arms on his knees and lacing his fingers together, "seems he's pretty interested in wrestling with you again, though not in the classic Greco Roman fashion."

"Sick," she said with a grimace, her face almost as if she'd taken a huge mouthful of spoiled milk.

Roman laughed out loud. "Hey, I'm just saying, expect an offer at some point."

"You're so sick," she said, shaking her head.

"Don't kill the messenger, sweetie."

"Yeah, well, those evil Doublemint twins are totally going to try to jump you too. I recognize that look in their eyes," She said

143

with force, hoping to make him squirm as much as he had her.

"Sweetie, I'm old enough to be their, well, really older brother or something. Not interested."

"Good!" Violet exclaimed.

"Good?" he asked.

"Yes, *good*, cuz they aren't good enough for you," she answered casually, looking at her fingers and examining the peeled green paint.

He cocked his head to the side and looked at her, "I swear you talked about how those two girls were 'so sweet and cute' just like a couple of days ago."

"Yeah, well I changed my mind. Woman's prerogative."

"I'm just a little too old for anyone here, and besides, there' nothing terribly interesting about any of them."

Violet wondered if he included her in his statement. Her sense of paranoia made her sure he must find her terribly dull, or at least immature to some extent.

Amber and Randy came running up behind them through the tall grass. Both were out of breath and laughing hysterically.

"What?" Violet asked, standing up to face the two.

"It was so funny. Randy had John on his shoulders and he tripped and John fell face first into a pile of cow crap." Amber said, barely able to get the whole sentence out.

"Dude, it was hilarious," Randy said, wiping the sweat off his forehead with his t-shirt.

"Where's he now?" Violet laughed.

"He ran up to the house looking for a hose outside. Or he' going home, I'm not sure? Dude, he got a mouthful! It was freaking hilarious." Randy sat down on the log and tried catching his breath.

Roman looked at Violet and shook his head and smiled.

The rest of the group came over to join them. They all sat in the grass around them listening to Randy recount the story in great detail. He was a charismatic speaker, and always knew how to hold a crowd's attention. The others were held rapt by his story. Violet noticed Malinda occasionally watching Roman. She couldn't help the possessiveness she felt towards him, but she found it amusing, still, because she knew how Roman felt

Malinda's pupils were large and black from the dark night and few hits of acid she'd undoubtedly taken earlier in the evening. They were all tripping, all of them, including Randy and Amber. She felt disconnected from this whole scene, as though she was watching from somewhere high above the ground. The sounds of their chattering was fading in and out, words missing from every sentence as her thoughts trailed off somewhere else.

Her eyes now drifted to the woods beyond the field. The trees were like dark spires jutting from the ground, black leaves rustling like paper. She feared what might lurk there. Suddenly she was too terrified to look out there. Her heart raced in her chest, forcing her attention back to the rest of the group who were now talking of past events and people who weren't present.

"You alright?" Roman asked, leaning into her with his heavy shoulder.

"Uh huh," she answered quickly, shaking her head and looping her arm through his. He patted her arm with a concerned look on his face.

"You guys want to drink my blood?" Malinda interjected suddenly. Everyone was startled by the randomness of her question.

Roman looked at Violet with an odd look on his face, almost as if he were ready to laugh out loud by the absurdity of it. Violet shrugged her shoulders and rested her head against him. It felt good to have something solid to hold onto. Malinda was busy rifling through her black fuzzy faux fur backpack. She pulled out a box cutter and held it up with a devilish grin on her face. Violet rolled her eyes and yawned. The others gathered around her in anticipation. Randy and Amber sat quietly observing the scenario. This wasn't anything uncommon to any of them, despite the thrill the young girl seemed to get by being so "shocking". They had exchanged blood numerous times, all in correlation to some random ritual or another they'd read about or just plain made up.

Malinda pushed the blade out and held it to her forearm. Roman seemed anxious. Violet could feel his muscles tense beneath the thin fabric of his shirt. The girl placed the blade to her arm and made a small incision. A small stream of blood began trickling from the wound. Dory's eyes widened with excitement.

145

Malinda lifted her arm towards Roman and Violet, a small pouty smile bruising her white face.

"No thanks," Roman said deeply. The hint of disgust was evident in his tone.

Violet looked at her and smiled briefly. "No thanks."

Malinda seemed hurt by the rejection, then offered her arm to the others almost rebelliously. Dory licked the trail of blood up Malinda's arm and greedily covered the wound with her mouth.

Roman watched as they traded off cutting and drinking from each other. He could sense the fear just beneath the surface in all these people and he wondered why they felt the need to do this. Was it really *that* important to them all to be "cool"? And since when was *this* cool? He looked over at Amber and Randy who didn't seem the slightest bit fazed by what they saw and he knew then that even these three had partaken in this activity at some point. It wasn't as though he was unaware people did this shit, he had just naturally assumed Violet would be above such a thing. Judging by her lack of response to something that should've been repugnant, he guessed not.

Violet's eyes gravitated back up from the ground and toward the wood line. She felt almost as if she had been drugged because of the way the warmth of the crackling fire and the scene around her made her feel disjointed and out of touch. The fear rose in her again as she watched the dark limbs sway against the night sky. Suddenly, she saw a glowing face emerge through the trees. She sucked in air and squeezed Roman's bicep, anchoring herself to him. He looked down at her quickly then his eyes followed hers to the edge of the trees. A man approached through the tall grass. White blonde hair reflected the moonlight as he stealthily made his way towards them. Roman stood up releasing the grip Violet had on him. The others looked up from what they were doing and watched the man approach. Violet didn't recognize him. He was tall and thin, long white blonde hair like silk, and skin so white he glowed there against the fire. His eyes were black and glistening, huge round orbs reflecting the orange yellow glow of the flames. He was dressed in a long black leather coat and tight pants. He looked like the coolest rock star she'd ever seen. And God was he beautiful. Everything on him was perfectly proportioned, perfectly

146

symmetrical.

Amber scooted down to her friend and grabbed onto her arm. Both girls smiled at each other wondering who on earth the god walking toward them was.

"Roman," the man said, his voice silken and thick with an accent. His lips lifted slightly into a smile. His face was sharp and angular, his long thin nose like chiseled stone. He looked like an expertly carved statue.

Roman stepped over the girls and toward the man, extending his hand to shake. "Hello," he said brusquely, with his back towards the others. The man took his hand firmly in return and placed his other hand on Roman's shoulder.

"What have we here? Little vampires?" he asked, looking over Roman's shoulder towards the coven of blood drinkers sprawled about on the ground. A wide smile spread across his face, his eyes seemed too playful and predatory.

Roman turned slightly and smiled at the group and shook his head. "Vampires, Lux, aren't they scary?" Roman chuckled.

"Lord almighty, he's hot," Violet whispered to her friend as she leaned into her.

The man looked at her briefly then looked back at Roman.

"I think that's probably the most beautiful man I've ever seen," Amber whispered to Violet, clutching her arm.

"He's like every daydream I think I've ever had." Violet pinched her, acutely aware she was being every bit as girlie as the others had been with Roman.

"Violet, I'm going to go have a chat with him," Roman said, turning to look at her. He grinned as he noticed that she and Amber were now in the same embrace Dory and Malinda had been in earlier.

"Now, now, don't be rude, Roman. Who are all your friends?" the man asked, stepping around him towards the group. He seemed to be particularly interested in Amber and Violet.

Roman looked down at the ground. He hesitated then stepped forward again. "This is Violet, Amber, and Randy," he said somewhat impatiently. "The *vampires* are Malinda, Dory and Sam. And I can't recall your names?" he said, leaning over towards the other girls and young men. Their mouths were red and wet and shining.

"That's Karen and Peter." Malinda smiled at the two men "And Candy and Rafe"

"Ah, lovely," the man said, looking at Roman and laughing "And who am I, Roman? Aren't you going to introduce me?" he asked, lifting his hands.

"This is Lux, and he's an idiot." Roman grinned, and clapped him on the back.

Violet smiled shyly as the man seemed to look into her. She felt her heart twisting and pounding. She wondered if this was what the girls felt who cried uncontrollably at concerts. She felt as if her heart would burst right in her chest cavity as it pressed into her ribcage swollen with blood and lust. Roman grabbed his leather sleeve and pulled the man away from them. He looked back at Violet shaking his head and smiling at her.

"Holy heck he's hot," Violet said to Amber.

"How did you find me?" Roman asked, looking back at the fire and the young girls staring in their direction.

"You're not difficult to find, Roman," Lux answered, turning also to look at the group from afar. "Hanging with *goths* these days?" he smirked.

"Not by choice," Roman answered, turning to face the man "What's going on?"

"Violet and Amber are quite lovely," he continued, "I could enjoy them both tonight."

"Yeah, I'm sure you could, but what's so important that you came here to track me down?"

"You know they both want me, right?" he smiled, teasing Roman, his eyes gravitating from the girls to him.

"Of course they do, *Prince of Darkness*, mighty Lux of the Underworld, they want you, they all want you. Stop being such a pretentious ass." Roman laughed.

"Okay." Lux smiled devilishly, turning his back to the scene and changing his tone of voice. He had only been kidding with the overt demeanor. "I came to warn you."

***

"Soooo… who was that?" Violet asked, as they walked back towards the car. The others were lagging behind.

"Lux," Roman answered casually.

"Well duh, I know that much, but who is he?" She smacked him with the back of her hand.

"He's an old friend of mine. He's just going through town and he tracked me down to say hello."

"So, he's not going to be sticking around then?"

"No, Violet, he's not. Why?" Roman asked, looking down at her. He could tell she was prying him for information and that she was completely in awe of his friend just like he'd told him she was. He found it humorous and annoying.

"I don't know, I just thought he seemed cool," she said, shrugging her shoulders as if she wasn't dying on the inside to know everything about the man.

"Trust me, sweetheart, you don't want him. He's a lady killer." Roman laughed to himself. Violet looked up at him annoyed by his casual, flippant tone. "Besides, he's much too old for you." He laughed again.

She scowled at him and looked back at the ground.

7. COTTON BLOSSOMS

She had spent the morning gathering the laundry from her room
Three loads had been done so far and that would be all she'd do
today. A girl could only stand to do so much laundry at a time
The laundry basket of wet clothes was heavy as she hoisted it up
and balanced it with her hip and trekked it outside. She grabbed
each piece of clothing and clipped it to the rope line her father had
attached from the house to the tall maple. She squinted as the sun
hit her eyes, sending sharp pain.

The smell of clean laundry made her happy and reminiscent
She was looking forward to climbing into her clean crisp bed
tonight. After finishing hanging the final load she walked over to
the wooden Adirondack chair and sat back into it. She hadn't sat
in the sun in years. The soft warmth felt good to her. It wasn't
exactly "cool" for her type to be all tanned and freckled, so she
hadn't lain in the sun in eons. Then again, she hadn't allowed
herself to do a lot of things because of the uncool factor. How
stupid.

"What're you doing?" Amber asked, cranking the door open
"Why are you being all *Susie Homemaker*?" She walked out
barefoot, still dressed in her cotton pajamas and gripping a hot mug
of ginger tea.

"I just miss that smell. You know, you can't get it any other
way. Mom used to hang clothes all summer," Violet said, placing
her hand above her eyes and staring up at her friend.

"And the sun bathing?"

"It feels good," Violet said with a shrug. "Feel it, Amber."
Amber looked at her funny like she was a pod person. "I think
want to completely overhaul my room soon," she said calmly
looking back out across the yard. The flowers were starting to fade
now and it made her feel sad. Soon enough it would be September

and summer would be over.

"Just let me know if you want help. You know, I should hang our clothes too. That's a good idea." Amber finally agreed, after thinking about it.

"I told you." Violet smiled.

"So, who was that guy last night? Did Roman say much about him?" Amber sat on the ground beside Violet, waiting to hear the scoop with eager anticipation.

"No, he was really evasive about the whole thing. I don't get him. He's got like secret stuff going on or something, I swear."

"Yeah, like what does he do? I mean, he doesn't work or anything right?"

"Not that I'm aware of. I think he's loaded though, that's just my guess."

"Well, he'd have to be not to work, right? Maybe he's a drug dealer? Ooo, or Mafioso. Wouldn't that make sense?" Amber's eyes were wide with the possibilities. "So, he didn't say anything about the guy at all?" Amber asked, taking another drink and leaning against the lawn chair.

"He said he was a lady killer and way too old for me," Violet answered, and shrugged her shoulders in annoyance. "He has this thing about age. Everyone's too young."

Amber looked at her with a curious expression on her face. "I wonder how old he is? The guy didn't look very old to me."

"Me either, but Roman thinks he's too old too. But I can sort of see his point, I guess. Dory and Malinda looked like teenagers standing next to him last night, ya know?"

"Yeah, Roman looks older than us for sure, but I mean, it's not like he can be that much older. Plus too, who fucking cares? You're legal!"

"I have no idea how old he is. I should ask, though it's not like it matters. You're right, I *am* legal, so WTF?"

"Well anyway, that Lux guy was really freaking hot and definitely doesn't look like he's from around here. Well, plus there's the accent. Man..." Amber said, her eyes widening to accentuate her point as she fanned herself dramatically.

"Yeah, I know," Violet said, leaning her head back against the chair and grinning. "Seriously, dude, he was foxy."

"Foxy." Amber laughed and stood up. "I gotta go get ready fo
work."

***

Violet pulled the clothes from the line and carried them upstairs
folding each piece, a feat for her, and placed them in her dresse
and closet. Then she made her bed and looked around the room
pleased by the progress she'd made. She grabbed the half full
garbage bag that had been sitting there since her last tirade and
began stuffing more papers and old magazines into it, and dragged
it out to the garage and put it in the aluminum can. She placed the
lid down on the can carefully, attempting not to rub the meta
together as the sound always made her teeth hurt. Why she hadn'
just gotten a big plastic garbage can already she didn't know
though it was likely due to some bizarre attachment she had to
sentimental objects. But a garbage can? Her parents weren'
going to come back because she held onto this garbage can.

She walked back upstairs, she still had a lot of work to do, but
she'd at least gotten something accomplished today.

She grabbed her black turtleneck sweater and black wool min
skirt and a clean pair of panties and walked across the hall to take a
shower. A cold front had come through the last couple days and i
was cooler out. It already felt like fall. She stripped her clothe
off and stared at herself again like she'd done a few days before
Her face and arms were red from the small amount of sun she'd
gotten this morning. She looked almost healthy from the slightly
pink hue it gave her skin. Her face seemed to glow. She brushed
her hair and stepped into the shower and turned the knobs on
waiting for the water to get hot. She stood beneath the hot wate
and enjoyed the privacy and solitude of the moment. She finished
washing and stepped out of the shower and dried herself off, then
wrapped her hair in the thick cotton towel and applied the sof
moisturizer to her skin. Her mother had bought her this orange
blossom scented lotion for her birthday earlier in the spring, and i
was nearly gone now, which sent a sudden jolt of panic through

152

her and then it left as quickly as it had come. It's only lotion, she told herself. *It's only a garbage can,* her other voice whispered and made her laugh.

She pulled the turtleneck over her head. It felt extra tight on her damp skin. She pulled the sleeves up to her elbows as she was still hot from the shower. The room was steamy. She put the black cotton panties on and zipped the wool skirt then brushed her teeth. Her mouth was stinging from the strong mint of the paste. She looped the towel over the shower rod then combed the knots out of her hair again and pulled it up into a ponytail.

She walked back to her bedroom and grabbed her bag and keys then headed downstairs. Steve was sitting at the kitchen table eating cereal again. She smiled at him.

"Haven't seen you lately, Steven. How've you been?" she asked, taking a bottle of water from the refrigerator.

"I'm okay, same old, same old, ya know?" he answered as milk dribbled down his chin.

"Well, I miss you. I half expected to see you guys last night at Malinda's shindig."

"No, we were partying out at Mark's."

Violet stopped and looked at him, now curiously, "Hey, did Mark have some girl call me last night?"

Steve looked up at her with an almost insulted look on his face. "Not that I'm aware of, Violet. I'm pretty sure he's moved on."

"I wasn't trying to start anything, Steve. I know he's your friend. I just got a weird call last night and I'm trying to figure out where it came from."

"Sorry for jumping on you," he apologized, taking another bite of cereal.

"It's alright. I know it's weird for all of us involved. You do understand why it had to end right?"

"I get it. I just don't want to be put in the middle."

"I totally understand," she said, taking a sip from the water. She wanted to ask him how Mark was doing. She wondered if he was okay. After all, she had loved him and she was pretty certain he'd cared for her as well, however fucked up his methods were, but she decided against asking. "I'm gonna take off now, don't be a stranger okay?"

"Yeah, sure. I'll be around. I'm not going anywhere." H smiled at her which made her feel better about the situation Having him around had been awkward lately.

***

The sky was robin's egg blue and cloudless. The fading leave looked vibrant against the sky. She drove around th neighborhood, wanting to go to Roman's, but she didn't want to b a pest. The man had a life and she really needed to sto monopolizing his time. But what if Lux was at his house? Mayb he'd needed a place to crash while he was in town and was stayin there? She grinned to herself, thinking how nice it might be to a least see that gorgeous creature again, and of course the bonus o being able to see both of them at the same time, now that woul truly be nice.

She drove around the block and pulled up his driveway. Ther was an extra car parked in the street in front of his apartment. Sh smiled and looked at herself in the rearview mirror, making sur she didn't have anything strange going on with her face or hai She wiped the black makeup gunk out of the corner of her eye an stepped out of the car walking up to the house and up the stairs t his door. Knocking gently, she stared at the small diamond shape window waiting to see Roman's familiar face peering out at he No one answered so she knocked again. She looked back at th driveway. His car was here, so she knew he was home. H wouldn't still be sleeping at two o'clock in the afternoon? Sh turned around and saw a flash of blonde hair in the glass Suddenly she felt her heart begin to race, the heat of her cheek flushing red.

"Hello?" a woman asked. Her voice was low and sultry with hint of some accent. She was tall and very shapely with long pal blonde hair. Her eyes were catlike and dark and her expressio was cold and detached.

"Oh, I guess this is a bad time," Violet said, backing away fron the door and starting to walk down the metal staircase. Had sh

154

been more unlucky she would have fallen backwards down the stairs as she wasn't paying attention to her footing--and wouldn't that have been nice—falling and busting her ass and Roman having to help her yet again?

"Are you here to see Roman?" the woman asked from inside the apartment. Her eyes were dark and intense.

Violet turned around and looked at her briefly. The woman was wearing one of Roman's t-shirts and nothing else. Her hair was mussed and it was obvious she'd slept there. "I'll talk to him later," Violet said quickly as she hit the bottom of the stairs and started down the driveway.

"Who should I say stopped by?" the woman asked as a grin snaked across her face.

"Uh, don't worry about it. I'll talk to him later," Violet said, opening the door to her car. She simply couldn't get away fast enough. She threw herself into the seat and fumbled for the keys. She looked up briefly at the woman who was still watching her. Yes, her exact opposite in every way, just as she'd expected.

Violet sped off wanting to get far away from his house before he'd have a chance to see her. She felt stupid and embarrassed, though there really wasn't any reason to feel either of those things. She and Roman were friends. It was normal for a friend to stop by another friend's house. So why did she feel so stupid? Her heart pounded and her thoughts raced. And who was this woman? When had he even picked her up? Roman had been with them last night until very late. He truly did live a secret life. Then she felt herself feeling very angry. How could he be gross enough to pick up some random slut like that? He had to have just picked her up somewhere. Wouldn't he have mentioned it if he'd had a girlfriend? And surely he wouldn't have been spending so much time with her if he'd had a girlfriend. How utterly disgusting and pig-like of him. He was no different than all the other men she'd known. And if he was such a pig then what was so wrong with her that he never even tried to kiss her? Was she that revolting to him?

Then it struck her. *He really truly had no attraction for her at all.* He honestly only viewed her as nothing more than a friend, some helpless little girl he, for some reason, felt the need to take care of. She felt sort of sad, but also kind of relieved, like some

155

weight had been lifted. There it was in black and white. There was nothing between them but friendship.

Then she giggled. How silly of her to get mad considering the main reason for her wanting to go there this afternoon was to see another man.

Who was she to get mad at him?

8. A CHANGE IN PERSONALITY – SORT OF

"So, what'd you do last night?" she giggled.

"Uh, I was with you, remember?" he said, raising an eyebrow.

"Yeah, I remember." She laughed, and tossed an orange at him.

"Okay, did you eat a bunch of sugar or something? You're being a spaz," he asked, watching her skip across the living room towards the stereo. She opened the cabinet and searched through the CDs.

"No, actually I'm starved right now. We should go get something to eat," she said, turning the volume to the stereo up.

Throbbing, heavy bass tones surged from the speakers. Roman was slightly taken aback not expecting the bombastic percussion and low rumbling bass. The music was harsh and heavy and it seemed slightly oxymoronic to him that this tiny little girl should be so enraptured by something this emotionally brutal and assaulting. She rhythmically moved her head to the slow, thunderous beat of the dirge.

She noticed the odd expression he was wearing and it made her laugh. "Why do you hang out with me? It seems like you'd have better things to do, being a grown man and all." She flopped down on the couch and tossed her feet up on the coffee table. He was sitting in the lounge chair beside her and began peeling the orange.

"Good question, sometimes I wonder myself," he said with a smirk, and leaned back into the chair.

"Seriously, obviously there has to be some reason you spend time with me. Is it that I'm some helpless lost kitten you're trying to save? Or what's the deal?"

"Why all the questions?" he asked, a little annoyed by her flippant tone of voice.

She leaned forward and looked him directly in the eye, "I'm curious, Roman. I want to know what you see in me and what you're getting out of our friendship."

"Friendship. Is that a good enough answer?" He put a slice o
orange in his mouth and savored the acidic sweetness of the frui
"I don't have many friends in case you haven't noticed."

"Oh, so if something better comes along you'll be gone?" Sh
teased him, knowing that she was sort of being an ass. Sh
wondered how long he'd allow her to act this way before he tol
her to shut the fuck up.

He tilted his head to the side and placed another piece of orang
in his mouth. She watched as his fingers peeled the orange. Th
fruit looked small in his hands, almost comical. His hair covere
half his face and his eyes were probing and glistering.

"I won't play your game, Violet," he spoke methodically. "I'r
not one of your little moronic minions. If I need to remind yo
why I'm your friend all the time I'd rather not be."

"Okay," she smiled, "but I still think I deserve an answer."

"Maybe some other time when you aren't trying to manipulat
something out of me." Really, he had no idea where her questio
was coming from. What difference did it make why he hung ou
with her? Clearly he wasn't trying to use her for anything, so wha
did it matter?

Randy stumbled down the stairs and stood for a momer
orienting himself to the room and situation. He had just woken u
and was still groggy. "Hey," he whispered, not yet having the fu
strength of his voice.

"Hello," Roman answered, turning to look at the boy.

"That's fucking loud, Violet," Randy said, scratching his bar
stomach. His eyes were still closed and he had pillow creases o
his cheek.

"Yep, thought I'd wake you up before Amber gets home an
yells at you for sleeping all day again." Violet winked at him. Hi
pants were hanging off of him, ready to fall to the ground at an
moment and his lean naked torso would have been far mor
attractive to Violet had it not belonged to her friend.

"Oh fuck," he said, jogging back up the stairs towards th
shower.

"So you want to go eat?" Violet asked, putting her feet bac
down on the ground.

"I could eat," he answered.

"Oh reeeeally?" she asked, raising her eyebrow with a smirk on her face.

He stopped chewing for a brief moment pondering her mood. What the hell was up with that? Was she making some kind of sexual joke? She'd never talked like that to him. What had gotten into her today?

Violet stood up and took the peelings from Roman and ran into the kitchen and threw them away. "Be right back," she called to him as she trotted up the stairs.

His gaze shifted around the room. Everything was still as though her parents lived there. He wondered if she would ever have the strength to finally put her family's things away or if she would always leave them out like a museum to the dead. He looked again at the picture of her in purple, the wide toothless smile and freckle-kissed cheeks; she looked so pretty and happy.

"Okay, I'm ready," she said, jumping off the bottom stair landing with a thud.

Roman stood up and walked towards her. He could almost see the freckle faced girl standing there in front of him. *Why am I friends with her?* What was he getting from this relationship? Friendship? He'd never needed nor desired that. His only friends were his enemies.

***

He watched as she shoveled forkful after forkful of syrup-dripping pancakes into her mouth. It was good to see her eat this way.

"In answer to your question, I'm not sure," he said, as he lifted the hamburger to his mouth and took a big bite.

She looked up at him, her eyes a bit filled with wonder. She had no idea he'd actually bring this subject back up this soon, if ever. "Well that's comforting to know," she said, swallowing her mouthful of food.

"I don't mean that negatively, I just really don't know."

"You have no earthly idea why you would be friends with me?" She was starting to feel insulted now. "And I shouldn't be hurt by that?"

"No, I could give you a list of reasons why anyone should be friends with you. I mean I don't know why *I* am friends with you. I should be concentrating on other things, and yet here I am with you--every day--and it makes no sense to me." He was looking down at his plate, contemplating his words as he spoke them.

She sat her fork down and looked at him. What the hell? What the hell was his deal?

"I have never needed a single person my whole life, and I've been content to live that way. I am confused by the need I have to know how you are at any given moment, and I don't know why I want to see you every day. It's very confusing, and that's not a reflection on you, it's a reflection on the bizarre isolation I've kept myself in for years."

"You're not in love with me, are you?" she asked, the question timid as her nose crinkled as if disgusted by the possibility. She was unsure she should even dare ask, and half embarrassed to find out the inevitable answer, but she needed to know.

"No." A smile came to his lips at her expression. He looked at her briefly, locking eyes with her, and then took a drink of his soda. "I'm not in love with you. That--I think--would make sense to me."

"Okay good, cuz I just made sense of all this today and didn't want some whole other variable factoring into the equation and messing my brain up."

"Figured out what today?"

"Um, nothing, just glad we're on the same page." She smiled and took another bite of pancake. "I'm so full," she said slouching down in the booth.

He looked at her again, wondering how her brain worked. She seemed to speak randomly, sometimes the dots didn't connect in her sentences, and it was confusing and annoying at times. Hard to follow. "So you're into that vampire thing?" He threw that at her from left field.

She furrowed her brow and laughed. "Um, huh?"

"You know, that vampire stuff like last night?"

"Well, I guess. I mean, where do you think those dolts learned it from?" she asked, sliding back up in the seat. "Why?"

"Just wondered what the attraction is."

"I've loved vampires ever since I was little. I had a dream once when I was about six or seven that Dracula was in my bedroom. It was so completely realistic. I was awake, I know I was, and then my mom got up to go to the bathroom, and he sort of just floated out my window. There was a lot of black cloth. I remember a lot of black cloth like capes or something. I can still remember what it felt like. He had a fur collar that brushed against my cheek, his breath was hot on my neck. It was...I don't know..."

"That's bizarre," he said, listening intently, "but what is it about them you like?"

"I guess it's the immortality aspect. The fact they'll never get old, never get sick," she paused and smiled, "well, and most of them are hot, at least in my imagination. Oh, and all the books and movies. Well, not all of them, sometimes they're hideous like Nosferatu."

Roman shook his head and laughed. "Yeah, but they're evil."

"I guess, but in my little universe they aren't evil—just a different species or something. Besides, what's evil? Human beings can be evil. So, who cares?"

"You'd probably care, if you ever came face to face with one," he said, looking up into her eyes again.

"I suppose I would, but I doubt I need to worry about that, now do I?" she asked, cocking her head to the side and crossing her arms over her food-swollen belly.

"Nope, I guess not."

"So, tell me about Lux. That man is beautiful." She grinned and sat up in her seat.

Roman rolled his eyes and leaned back. "You think?" he asked and wiped his mouth with a napkin. He had the cutest, orneriest smile on his face.

"Yes, I do," she answered, lacing her fingers together and resting her chin on her hands.

"Yeah, he thinks so too."

"I'd like to talk to him." She ran her finger through the pancake syrup on her empty plate.

"No, I don't think so, besides, he's gone already I'm sure."

"You can't tell me who I can and can't talk to, dork."

He looked at her for a long moment. He had never dealt with giddy girl before and had no idea how to proceed with th conversation. "Trust me on this one, Violet, you're better off n knowing him."

"So you think." She grinned and put the syrup soaked finger her mouth. The lids of her eyes were half closed as she coy smiled at him.

"Trust me on this, sweetie. I wasn't kidding. He's a tot asshole that makes Mark look like a fluffy kitten."

Violet frowned at that.

***

Her cell phone rang and she reached into her bag and looked the number. It was Amber calling. "Hello?" she asked, lookir over at Roman who was quietly driving, having not spoken muc in the last fifteen minutes. He looked like some famous actor rock star there with his hair blowing in the wind and his leath jacket. Like one of those guys from a movie about vikings or some black metal band. Come to think of it, he looked sort familiar but she couldn't place from what. He definitely didn look like some normal dude from her town.

Roman liked the way the sky looked tonight. Black, no stars, n moon. He would enjoy walking later tonight. His muscles ache from the work out he'd had in the morning though. His legs wei stiff and his muscles were tight and felt swollen like they'd po] That's what happened when he didn't take his training seriously.

He was deep in thought. He'd gotten himself into a strang predicament. There was this connection with Violet, and h purpose for being here, and there seemed to be maybe some vagu connection between the two that he'd been unable to determin thus far. Lux had warned him of this, and yet Lux had n information either. Lux was usually right on though, given hi considerable abilities. But he also couldn't help feeling Lux wa holding something back.

His thoughts drifeted back to the party with her friends. It had been particularly disturbing to him to watch those young girls cutting and bleeding each other. If they only knew the trouble they invited with such actions. Not to mention, glorifying something so heinous was just stupid. And to think Violet had been involved in such behavior turned his stomach. He would never partake for good reason. His thoughts were so far off he barely noticed when Violet spoke to him.

"Roman!" she yelled, slapping his arm.

"What?" he answered nonplussed, turning his head to look at her.

"I've been yelling at you for like twenty minutes!"

"Don't exaggerate, you dork," he said, looking back at the road.

"I'm not. What the heck were you thinking about? You really creeped me out," she said with concern in her eyes.

"Nothing important," he answered, "Sorry. What did you want?"

Violet sat speechless for a few moments and then continued. "That was Amber. She said Lux and some woman are at my house right now and they're looking for you."

Roman turned his head to look at her again. His eyes were dark and intense and had she not known him she would be terrified by the look in his eyes. He seemed very angry.

"How the heck did he know where I live?" she asked.

"It's a small town." Roman pulled on the stearing wheel, quickly turning the car around in the middle of the street and speeding towards her house. "Well, I guess you'll get your chance to talk to Lux," he said through clenched teeth.

Violet was confused by Roman's sudden surge of anger. She had never really seen that emotion in him like this. Annoyed, yes, but never completely angry. And if Lux was his friend, why did he seem to hate him so much?

"What did Amber say is going on?"

"She said they're just sitting there talking and listening to music. Why are you so mad?" She reached her hand over to him and touched his arm to get him to look at her.

"Violet, I told you you'd be better off not knowing Lux, and

163

I'm fucking pissed off he actually went to your house."

Violet pressed herself back into the seat. She was unsure wha was going on with Roman, and why he had such distrust, or hatred or whatever was going on, for this Lux guy.

"He shouldn't be at your house," he added, slamming his palm against the stearing wheel as he shifted gears and sped up.

Violet said nothing, but sat quietly as she watched him. His jaw was clenched, and she could see the muscle twitching beneath the soft white skin of his face. His left foot tapped the floorboard seemingly trying to will the car to go faster.

Then he noticed how quiet she'd grown, uncharacteristically quiet. "I'm sorry for yelling," he said, taking his eyes off the road briefly to look at her. The look of confusion in her eyes pained him. He wanted her to know the truth of the matter, but he would never tell. It would put her in too much danger.

"It's okay," she answered, releasing her tense shoulders and relaxing again. She ws used to dealing with angry men from being around Mark. She just hadn't expected it with Roman. "Is he like drug dealer or something?" she asked with caution.

"Something like that," Roman answered.

Neither of them spoke again until they pulled into her driveway a few minutes later. The car she'd seen earlier at Roman's was parked in the street in front of her house. Roman was generally very polite, and always waited on Violet to go ahead of him, but now he walked quickly to the house, then turned to wait for her to let him inside.

"Go ahead." she nodded.

They walked in and found everyone seated in the living room talking. Music played softly and the lights were all dim. The woman whom Violet had seen earlier in the day was seated in the red velvet lounge, and Lux was stretched across the length of the couch.

Amber turned around in her chair and smiled. "Hi guys."

"Hello." Violet smiled, conveying the message with her eyes that only a true friend would understand. Yes he's here, and yes he's hot. Her heart raced again, her cheeks hot, and she felt mildly dizzy as if she were under some spell.

"Roman, nice to see you again," Lux said with a smile on his face. His voice was so deep and sensual.

The woman looked at him and smiled. Violet looked at her cautiously as the woman nodded her head and stared Violet in the eyes.

"Follow me," Roman said to Lux, walking through the living room and into the kitchen.

Amber looked at Violet, wondering why Roman was acting so strange. Violet shrugged her shoulders and sat down on the edge of the couch.

"Lovely home you have here, dear," Lux said, as he stood and walked into the other room.

No one spoke. They all just looked at each other waiting for someone to say something. Even Randy was speechless for once.

"I didn't mention you stopped by this morning," the woman said, finally breaking the awkward silence. Her accent was vague and unrecognizable to Violet. She was dressed in tight red leather. Sickeningly beautiful. Her limbs were long and thin, and she sat in the chair as Violet would imagine a supermodel would sit. She could be a supermodel. "I didn't want to distract him."

"That's okay," Violet responded, completely aware that she'd made up her mind to dislike this woman from the second she saw her sitting in her red chair looking so damned gorgeous.

***

"Why did you come here?" Roman asked, looking the man in the eye. Lux was nearly his height, but nowhere near his build. Lux was lean, built more like a swimmer, whereas Roman had the shape and size of a football player. A really tall football player.

"Relax, Roman. I have no plans for your little girlfriends." He laughed and sat down at the kitchen table. "Although, I must admit, if they weren't yours I'd consider it."

"What do you want?" Roman asked, walking closer to the man but refusing to partake in the banter.

Lux watched as his finger moved across the tablecloth, slowly making a trail in the nap of the fabric. His long legs bent beneath him as he slouched in the heavy wooden chair. "I like these people, though I can't speak of Violet as I have yet to really talk to her." He grinned, knowing how annoyed Roman must be with him.

"There's no reason for you to talk to any of them," Roman said, pulling a chair out and sitting down. "Why do you have to be such a dick?"

"Oh, come on now, Romeo, what would you do without me?"

"Just get to the point already."

"There's vampires in this here town," Lux said, mocking southern drawl.

"Yes, I am aware," Roman said, waiting for the punch line.

"And your friends are involved somehow." There was no kidding in his tone now.

"How so?" Roman asked, leaning forward, concerned by the prospects.

"Not sure entirely, I just know they're somehow connected. And your lady love is a target--although I'm thinking she won't be an easy target."

"Of course she won't be. I'm protecting her." There was nothing cute or arrogant about the statement, he was simply stating a fact. "Are you staying in town?"

"No, Roman, we're leaving tomorrow. But as always, I'll tell you if I hear anything."

"Ever think about using a phone?" Roman smirked.

"Nah, where's the fun in that?" Lux laughed. "Plus I was curious. You, here. Interesting to say the least."

Roman scowled at the man. "You sent me here."

"Indeed. And what a pretty little thing you've hooked up with."

"Fuck off," Roman growled.

"Touchy. Touchy."

Roman scowled again, looking down at his hands and refusing to contemplate why he was feeling so touchy on the topic. He looked up. "Can I handle this, Lux?" Roman asked with concern. It wasn't like Lux to take such a personal interest in the mission he sent him on. This concerned Roman.

"Yes. My concern is for the girl and her immediate friends. I wish I could tell you more, but I honestly don't know." Lux cocked his head to the side. "I'm offended that you'd think I would harm a hair on their little heads."

"Yeah, cuz you've never harmed a hair on anyone's head, right?"

"I'm *reformed*, you imbecile."

"Okay, whatever," Roman said dismissively, and stood up.

"Well, are you going to let me talk to her? How're we going to *marry and have kids* if you never let us speak?"

Roman shook his head and walked out of the room with Lux trailing behind.

Violet looked up and watched the two enter. Roman looked relaxed now. Concerned, maybe, but relaxed. She was relieved to see his happy green eyes again and not the scary angry ones she saw earlier. Ugh, and Lux. Tight black leather pants, black t-shirt, and that long blonde hair…

"Violet, you know Lux. This is Mylori," Roman said, sitting down on the couch beside her.

"Hello," Violet said softly, smiling at the two, though more at one than the other.

"Nice to meet you again," Lux said, sitting on the arm of the red chair.

Violet smiled at him. She felt awkward sitting here with the two of them looking at her so intently on one side and Roman towering over her on the couch. She continued to watch the two, not breaking eye contact with Lux. He occasionally looked away, as he was conversing with Amber and Randy. The woman never said a word. She just sat politely and occasionally shifted the focus of her attention. Maybe Mylori was Lux's girlfriend? Had they stayed at Roman's last night? Obviously they must have, and she had misunderstood seeing the woman at his apartment?

Violet noticed that Mylori seemed to move in a way that was seductive and deliberate. Every movement was a way to elicit lust. She knew, because she was a master of these moves herself when she chose to be.

And what she wanted right now was to be alone with Lux. Her heart was beating wildly in her chest. She could barely keep from reaching out to him. She wanted to talk to him all alone. She wanted those pale pink lips between her teeth… god, she had a thing for biting.

His eyes flashed with some kind of acknowledgment, and h smiled and stood up. She looked away from him as he looked a her, almost as though he knew what she was thinking.

"Let's go and let these fine people sleep." Lux turned an looked at Mylori.

She stood behind him and started for the door. "It was pleasure meeting you all. Thank you for welcoming us into you home," Mylori said, looking from one person to the next.

They all stood up and followed them out the front door. The stood on the porch which ran the whole length of the house. needed a coat of paint on the floorboards. The furniture was ol and weathered. Violet had enjoyed sitting out here with he mother. Her mom would sing her songs as they rocked in the ol rocking chair watching the birds pick at the seed they'd placed i the glass feeders. This was where she had played house a thousan times with her friends when she was little. This was also the plac she'd kissed Mark for the first time. And now two completel exotic and foreign strangers who exuded otherworldiness wer standing there looking at her with a mix of hunger and curiosity One more hungry looking than the other.

"Come back any time," Amber said, as she reached out to hug the two mysterious people.

"Careful what you wish for," Lux said with a grin, and winke at Roman.

"Really," Roman responded, rolling his eyes.

"Be careful, little Violet," Lux whispered, placing one hand o her arm and lifting her chin with the other before place a delicat kiss her on her mouth. His lips were cool and lush and soft as bab skin.

Violet was startled by his actions but felt her heart begin t pound as her blood seemed to rush to her lips and arm where he' touched her.

He opened his eyes slowly and looked into hers, then stood u and walked away. "You be good, Randy, or I'll come back an steal your woman." he said, not turning around but throwing hi hand up to gesture farewell.

Roman looked at Violet momentarily, then followed the two t

their car.

"Was that really necessary?" Roman asked Lux, and smacked the back of his head.

"Of course it was necessary, it's been awhile since I've gotten any." Lux grinned, and turned around.

"Pig," Mylori said in a bored tone, shaking her head. She stopped and then kissed Roman. "See you soon, love," she said, and opened the car door, sliding in and shutting the door behind her.

Violet cringed when she saw that.

"Violet will help you," Lux said, as he looked intently into Roman's eyes.

"How so?"

"She'll help you, that's how."

"Thanks for the clarification, dick," Roman said, shutting the car door and walking back up to the house. Now he was going to have to clean up the mess Lux left in his wake.

***

"So, you finally got to really meet him, happy?" Roman asked, unlacing his boots and pulling them off. He yanked his socks off and stuffed them down into his boots.

Violet realized she'd never seen his bare feet. She stopped for a moment and looked at them.

"What?"

"Nothing, just never saw your naked feet before." She grinned childishly. "And yes, that was nice." She took her jeans off and tossed them in the hamper. Her mind was still sort of reeling from the kiss he had given her, her head still dizzy almost as though she was a little drunk.

"Want me to take my pants off too?" he said, teasing her.

"If you want to." She shrugged, not getting that he was teasing. She pulled the shirt over her head and it found its way to the hamper too, She then kicked her own socks off.

She pulled her hair back away from her face and braided it then

secured it with a hair band. He was sitting on the edge of the e
of her bed watching her get ready. He lifted his foot and massag
the stiffness out of one arch then the other. It felt good for his f
to actually breathe, having been stuffed in his boots since pret
early in the morning.

"Your feet are nice," she said, looking down at them and ba
up to his eyes.

He furrowed his brow and leaned back against the wall.

"I wasn't being sarcastic," she said, and walked across the ha
to wash her face and brush her teeth.

He could see her from her room. She looked so thin standir
there in her black satin bra and panties. He knew that the men sl
was generally around found this quality extremely attractive, b
he thought she looked *too* thin. It wasn't her natural size. Her ri
were visible and the jutting bones of her hips and shoulders looke
too sharp. She looked very young to him, and he thought mc
men his age would probably want her anyway. If not for
girlfriend, at least for a night. She was beautiful, there was r
doubt about it, but that wasn't why he was here. Why was h
here? It was something he had been confused a out before. B
now he was here to keep her safe.

She spit the toothpaste out and washed her face then walke
back to the room. "You can borrow my toothbrush if you want
she offered and reached into her closet for a t-shirt.

The silver chain he'd given her hung around her neck down t
her navel. She grabbed a pink shirt with a fluffy bear on it ar
pulled it over her head and smoothed it down. She reache
beneath the back of the shirt and unhooked her bra ar
maneuvered it through the sleeve and tossed it on the floor. The
she pulled the chain out from under the shirt and took it off and s
it on her dresser. She looked at it briefly then looked at him.

Now she truly did look sixteen. Her face was so pretty withou
any make up on to hide it. She looked like a child standing there i
the pink shirt and pretty, clean face. It disturbed him that sh
looked so young because it made him feel sick for thinking sh
was beautiful.

"I'm fine," he answered, still watching her. It took him way to
long to answer her about the toothbrush.

"I wonder if he'll come back soon? Where's he from?'

"He's from a lot of places. I think he's staying in Chicago at the moment."

She walked over to the light switch and flipped it off. The soft glowing hoot owl night light by the closet lit the room with a soft glow. She pulled the blankets back and climbed beneath. The coolness of the cotton felt calm and relaxing against her bare legs. He crawled towards her and lay down on his stomach, resting his head on the pillow.

"Come on," she said, trying to lift the blankets beneath him.

He followed her instructions and maneuvered his way beneath the thick blanket and soft, cool sheets. This situation between them was so strange. How he had found himself in her life was a real mind fuck. It was so unlike him to get involved. So beyond out of character.

"Aren't you going to take your pants off? That can't be comfortable." The tone of her voice was scolding and annoyed.

"Wow, aren't you gonna buy me dinner first?" He looked at her out of the corner of his eye and smiled. "I'm fine," he said, continuing to study her.

"Oh please, that cannot be comfortable. Just wear your underwear. I'm not gonna put the moves on you or anything."

"I'm fine," he said, rolling onto his back. "Besides, who says I'm wearing any?"

"Sick," she said, scrunching her nose.

"Thanks, that's a real ego booster." He smirked and looked at her.

She laughed in return and rolled her eyes. "Oh, come on, you don't need any ego boosting. Like you don't know you're hot."

He just looked at her and shook his head then looked back at the ceiling.

She rolled over on her side and faced him. Had she not known he had no attraction for her whatsoever this would be an entirely different situation for her. She would either be trying to put the moves on him, or he would be trying to do it to her. The thought made her giggle.

"What?" he muttered, nearly asleep. He rolled over on his side and faced her. His heavy eyelids opened briefly and he looked at

her face. She had the softest smile there in the darkness. "You'r
thinking about Lux, aren't you?"

She could tell had his eyes been open at that moment he'd b
rolling them. "Something like that." She snickered, and bit he
bottom lip trying not to smile.

"Well, forget about it, okay?"

"Alright," she said, knowing full well it would be replayin
itself over and over in her head until the next time she saw Lux, i
she saw Lux again.

"Violet, your sheets smell like something I remember as
child," he said, his voice a tired grumble. Sleep was taking hir
over quickly.

"I hung them outside today," she answered, as she took in
deep breath and relished the sweet fragrance.

"Mmm... that's the smell," he muttered.

"Night, Roman," she whispered, and shut her eyes enveloped b
actual happiness for the first time in months.

***

He woke with his face against the wall, his moist breat
creating condensation. She had pinned him against it, her forehea
planted between his shoulder blades. This wasn't the first tim
he'd found himself in this position. A sleepy smile spread acros
his face as he slowly moved his legs, trying to rouse her to mov
over. As he arched his back she rolled over, giving him barel
enough space to turn onto his other side. His hip was numb wher
he'd been laying for so long.

It was still dark outside. He loved this time of mornin;
Ordinarily he'd be coming home right about now. His eyes fe
like sandpaper as he opened them to read the clock, it was fou
a.m. He settled back into the sweet smelling pillow and looked ₹
the girl who lay beside him. Her mouth was slightly open and h
could hear the slow, shallow breaths emanating from her. As he
eyes danced beneath her eyelids, her eyelashes kissed her pin
cheeks. He wondered what she was dreaming about. She had sai

172

she'd been having scary dreams, might she be having one now? His tired eyes closed again and he fell quickly to sleep.

***

She walked down the street. The night was perfectly still. No lights in any house, no sound, and no moon. She gripped her purse tightly, ready to use it as a weapon if needed. There was an intangible feeling in the air, something malevolent, ominous, and empty. She walked hurriedly hoping to get home more quickly.

She stood there naked before him. The roundness of her breasts and hips guided his eyes; his eyes were magnets drawing her flesh towards his. He was white and opalescent under the pale moon light. His teeth were silvery slivers that gleamed as he smiled at her, long white hair seemed to spin and coil and grow. She smiled at him, moving her hands across her bare belly. This seemed to arouse him, and he leaned forward, drawing her closer. Her own hair swirled around her small frame in long snaking swathes that moved in airless wind.

She went to her knees in the thick green moss at his feet. Her eyes peered up at him in willing surrender. The moist earth smelled thick and lush as she lay back into it. The velvet carpet felt soft as wet fur against her bare back and legs. He was pleased by her sacrifice. Standing above her, eyes wide, smile expanding; his hair fell in mass toward her, tickling the bareness of her body. He bent over her, kissing her face gently and caressing her skin with his cool hands. His mouth suckled her throat, ripping her open like a nectarine, the red juice flowing from her into his mouth as he swallowed her down. Through dizzy eyes she saw his face, now dark and gray and glowering at her. His mouth was blood red and dripping as he smiled and sunk his teeth into her neck again.

She walked to the back door. It was open so she walked in. There was no sound and all the lights were on. She stepped through the kitchen cautiously knowing that what was around the corner would horrify her. All of them would be dead.

***

Roman jumped and gripped the pillow. His heart wa
pounding, heavy breaths escaping his lips. He sat up and looke
down at the girl. She was okay, safe, and still sleeping in the sam
position they'd fallen asleep. She stirred reaching to wipe th
loose hair from her face and licked her lips. Her head shifted o
the pillow and she settled back into stillness.

He steadied his thoughts, caught his breath, and lay back dowr
The reflection of the streetlights outside dappled her ceilin
catching his eyes and ocking them to it as he contemplated hi
dream. Lux would do this to her if he wasn't here to protect he
from him. But there were others like Lux that he didn't knov
about yet. He had to find out what was going on and stop it. H
would kill this whole town if he had to in order to protect her. Hi
need to protect her was a curious feeling. He had protected other:
of course, but he never cared this much. It had always been mor
about eliminating the threat than protecting someone. Why did h
care so much now? He'd been around other beautiful women. Sh
wasn't extraordinary in that regard. *Wait. He just thought of her a
beautiful. He shouldn't be thinking like this.* She was a jot
Nothing else.

He turned to his side and watched her as she slept, if she onl
knew the danger that surrounded her even now. All it took wa
one moment of weakness on his part. He caressed her cheek wit
the back of his hand. She was so soft. It would be easy to give in.

Her arm fell around his, pulling it to her as if she were grippin,
onto a teddy bear. The soft cotton of her shirt and the warmth o
her skin felt good against his forearm. He could feel her puls
lullingly throbbing against his hand. He closed his eyes and force
himself back to sleep. Being awake now was dangerous.

***

Violet lay awake with her eyes closed for a while. The bed was so warm and comfortable, *she* felt so warm and comfortable. Her eyes slowly opened and focused on Roman. She was surprised to find his palm pressed beneath her cheek, fingers caressing her face even as he slept. His hand was so large and strong and warm. It was heavy, his long fingers thick and calloused, and she loved the way the blue veins rose just beneath the surface of his skin like soft little rivers. She watched his pulse jump in his neck. The rhythm was hypnotic though it frightened her too. It was proof he was human and might die someday. She couldn't bear the thought of that. In such a short time he had become so important to her. He felt like the most important thing right now. She blinked her eyes at the realization and her bottom lip quivered. She couldn't lose anyone else.

His head was turned away from her and she was disappointed that she couldn't study his face as he slept. His long body spanned the entire length of the bed, his feet dangling off the end. She hoped she hadn't hogged the bed as much as she normally did. Mark used to get so mad at her, often shoving her over in her sleep for more room. She couldn't have blamed him for that, really, because she was a bed hog.

Violet hadn't thought about Mark in a few days now and felt almost guilty about that fact. She should probably miss him more than she did, but she'd been fairly distracted. Thank God. But shouldn't she care more? Shouldn't she be sick with the grief of their ended relationship? Instead she was happy. Loved. *Loved?*

She felt Roman's fingers move again against her face. They gently rubbed her cheek, almost as though they knew she needed another distraction. She closed her eyes, enveloped in the softness of the moment, then opened them again to find he was looking at her. A sleepy grin came to his lips that she returned and closed her eyes again. She felt his strong arm snaking beneath her warm body pulling her against him. She rested her head on his shoulder as she wrapped her arm around his strong chest. His warm body was comforting. He tilted his head, resting his face against her flowery smelling hair.

God, what were they doing? This wasn't normal friend

175

behavior.

"Good morning," he whispered.

"Good morning," she said with a smile, a deep exhaling breat and a stretch. "I had the weirdest dream."

"Yeah, me too.".

"Mine was about Lux."

He could feel her face grinning against his chest.

"Yeah, mine too." His stomach lurched and he backed away.

***

"You guys are so kidding yourselves," Amber said, as sh flipped the french toast.

"Huh?" Violet responded, taking a drink of juice.

Roman looked up from the newspaper at Amber. He wa shirtless, having just gotten out of their shower, his wet hair stuc to his back and neck.

"Oh, nothing." Amber grinned at them both, and placed tl food on the table and sat down.

Violet had already finished her breakfast and was lookir through the ads from the newspaper. She glanced up at Roma and back down at the coupons.

"So, did she hog the bed?" Amber asked.

Roman looked up with a cautious grin on his face. Viol looked over at him, eagerly awaiting his answer.

"I decline to comment," he said, looking back down at th paper.

"I figured." Amber laughed. "She usually kicks like a mul too."

"I try really hard not to." Violet pouted.

"It's okay," he said, not looking up. "It is your bed."

"You so do not try, Violet. You splay yourself all over th place without a thought in the world."

"Well, it *is* my bed," she said, parroting Roman and then stoo up. She leaned over and smelled the top of his wet head. Her lip felt the heat radiating from him. "It's nice to smell my shampoo i your hair," she said, and walked back upstairs.

"Um, okay?" Roman said, raising his eyebrow and looking at Amber.

"Oh god," Amber said, rolling her eyes with amusement and snorted. They were as comfortable together as an old married couple. Just because they were in denial didn't mean she was. "Such kidders," Amber said, shaking her head and walking out of the room to give Randy, who was transfixed by the morning cartoons, his breakfast.

Roman finished reading the article and then walked upstairs to her room. Violet was seated on the floor rummaging through her jewelry box and separating things she wore from things she'd give away. He sat down at the foot of her bed and leaned against the wall. He looked at Violet awkwardly for a moment, and then looked across the room at her closet wondering how on earth she fit so much stuff into such a small space.

Violet looked up at him and noted how awkward he looked. "What?" she asked, grinning at him. He wasn't acting like his usual confident self and it cracked her up.

"You think we're kidding ourselves about something?" he asked, looking down at her.

That definitely wasn't what she had expected him to say. She was silent for several moments and then resumed her chore. "Nah, remember, I'm *too young for you*. And besides, me and Lux are going to get married and have at least fifteen kids," she joked, and looked back up at him. This subject was way too awkward not to joke her way out of it. The truth was that despite the fact that she tried to convince herself otherwise, it was hard not being attracted to him. And the fact that she wanted to be with him 24/7 hadn't gone unnoticed by her either.

He leaned forward so she'd look at him and raised his eyebrows. "Oh really?"

"Yep, he didn't tell you?"

"Not in those words, no."

"Huh, I'm surprised. He's going to ask you to be the best man."

Not in those words? So had Lux said something about her otherwise?

"And you think you're too young for me? If you only knew."

177

Roman laughed and shook his head.

"Actually, you think I'm too young for you. I never said a wo
about that. And what the heck do you mean anyway?" she aske
sitting up and resting her elbows on the edge of the bed looking
at him intently.

"It's just funny."

"Funny how?" she asked, looking crossly at him.

"Nothing, sweetie. There's no way Lux is going to marry you.

"What the fuck. He could? Are you saying I'm not goc
enough?" She pouted, genuinely hurt.

"Of course you're good enough for him." Roman shook h
head. "I can't believe I'm having this conversation. Never in n
life did I think I would ever have this conversation." He w.
clearly amused.

"So what's the big fucking deal? What's wrong with me? I'
not good enough for your cool friend?"

"If he knew this conversation was taking place I'd never he;
the end of it." Roman continued laughing.

"Stop laughing at me. It's rude," she said, smacking him on tl
foot.

"I'm sorry," he apologized, trying to stop himself. "I'm n
very good at girl talk." He looked up at her apologetically.

"Yeah, so I see. *Jerk.*" She hit him again, this time harder.

Wow, so Violet really did have a thing for Lux? It wasn't ju
some girlie *he's hot* bullshit? Wasn't that just awesome? And
think he nearly, almost, for a second, thought he might be kind (
interested in her? *She likes Lux.* That arrogant asshole.

But of course, that was the story with Lux. How many time
had he watched the guy lead some poor young thing on just t
leave them broken? It was in his nature. And it was happenin
again. Only this time it was with Violet. He would find it hilariou
if it didn't make him want to puke.

"Stop laughing at me. Is it so ridiculous an idea to think he'
find me attractive?"

He looked up at her realizing she was misinterpreting hi
laughter. He could see the hurt in her eyes now and he felt sorr
for having laughed so much. "No, V, not ridiculous on your end.
just know Lux, and believe me, you'd be better off if you'd neve

met the guy. It's not you at all, sweetheart."

Yeah, it probably hadn't been a good idea to laugh at her with her emotions already so tender from the bullshit with her dickhead ex. But it was just so typical that he hadn't been able to stop himself from laughing.

"Well put your shirt on already. And help me or leave," she groused, and walked across the room to her closet pretending to fiddle with something and trying to hide the fact that her ego had been wounded. She had never really felt so small and insignificant. Roman had put her in her place like she'd done a thousand times before to others, and he hadn't even meant to do it. She was way out of her league with him, and Lux too obviously. She shouldn't even be entertaining thoughts of Lux anyway. Roman said he was some sort of drug dealer or something. But so what? Some of her friends sold drugs too and it didn't stop her from being friends with them. Hell, Mark had sold pot and acid occasionally himself.

Violet walked over and sat back down in front of the mound of jewelry. He looked around the floor and found his t-shirt and pulled it on over his head. "What do you need me to help you with?" he asked, standing up and then sitting on the floor beside her. He sat cross-legged and she looked up at him and giggled.

"You look ridiculous." She laughed, checking out his awkward position. His legs seemed too long and his thick arms and chest too bulky to be comfortable sitting like that.

"Thanks," Roman answered, and began looking through the pile of jewelry she'd amassed.

"Seriously, you have to have something better to do with your time than sit here with me sifting through old jewelry," she said, tilting her head to the side.

"Not really." He shrugged. "Sad huh?" he said, as a crooked grin snuck across his face.

"Yes, it really is sad." She shook her head and began sifting again. "So, tell me about Mylori." Violet said casually.

"What do you want to know about her?" Roman asked.

"Is she your girlfriend?"

Roman laughed, completely hit off guard by the question. "Uh, no. No way. What would give you that impression?"

179

"Well, I'm a woman right?"

"As far as I can tell, yes."

She gave him a dirty look then continued. "Well, I see how sh
looks at you. She kissed you and all that."

"Yeah, well, we've had sex, if that's what you're after," Roma
replied matter of factly.

It was Violet's turn to be stunned. She coughed and the
cleared her throat, taken aback momentarily and simultaneousl
intrigued by his bluntness.

"You asked," he said, shrugging his shoulders.

She regained her composure and continued probing. "I figure
that much," she replied coolly. For as hip and cool as she though
she was, she was still somewhat naïve when it came to som
things. As silly as it was, she had hoped he was one of those kin
of guys who didn't sleep around with women who meant nothin
to him.

"You figured, huh?" Roman asked, looking up at her, his eye
quite amused.

"Well, I *assumed*." She shrugged.

"Shouldn't assume, Violet."

"Well I was right, wasn't I?" she said, jutting her chin forwar
and shoving her hands on her hips.

"This time maybe. But she's not, and has never been, m
girlfriend."

"Well she wants to be."

"I think you're wrong."

"I'm soooo not wrong."

"I don't have girlfriends, Violet."

"Why not?"

"I just don't," he said, dismissing the notion with a shrug.

"Well maybe you should? Maybe you should try lovin
someone besides yourself," she said, annoyed by his casual ton
regarding the matter. Her chin was drawn in as it always wa
when she was pouting. It made her mad that he thought the idea o
having a girlfriend was stupid or something. Because if wanting t
be with someone was stupid then what did that make her? Yeah
STUPID. His tone of voice pissed her off. Why the hell did sh
even give a shit what he thought about it anyway?

"You have no say over my life and I don't answer to you. You giving advice on relationships is rather insulting considering your own lack of success in that department."

He looked at her intently now; his eyes were smoldering dark green, the color alive as the anger boiled in them. He had never had a conversation with someone like this in the whole of his life and he was angry at her for prying. There was no one on this planet he had to answer to but himself. It was none of her fucking business who he fucked or loved.

"I didn't mean to insult you," she stammered.

The shocking turn of the conversation really threw her. He was beyond angry at her and she hadn't really expected that. Sure, she knew she was being snotty, and in truth, kind of meant to be cruel, but dang. His words stung her to the core.

"I'm not one of the little morons you surround yourself with that you can manipulate and control. I'm not your puppet and you can't direct me like like you do the others. You have no idea the depths of my emotions, or what I was even doing six months ago. You think I should try having a girlfriend? You don't fucking know me, You think you know what's best for me? You fucking don't."

He glared at her. Emotions roiled inside. Who the fuck was she to tell him anything? No one knew him, let alone her. He was angry with her for assuming anything about him, let alone assuming he had never loved another person. Who was she to even discuss such things with him?

His brain was firing rapidly. Too many warring thoughts and emotions, anger being the predominant. But it was more than anger towards her for what she'd said, he was angry because she was right. It pissed him off to be confronted about it by this *child* who was so out of control of her own life. He didn't like hearing that he'd never loved someone. It sounded so sick and dysfunctional. It had never dawned on him just how fucked up he was until he met this girl, and now she was pointing it out to him.

"I'm sorry, Roman," she said, her voice sincere and worried. Her eyes were wide and sorrowful as she looked up at him. The last thing she had meant to do was hurt him, though she knew the statement was cruel when she'd made it. She wasn't even sure

why she was so mad at him. She was used to cutting people wit
her words, or a glance even, and he was not going to take that sh
from her. He wasn't some teenage sycophant she could fuck wit
and belittle.

Why did she always do this to those she cared about? Her eye
were welling with tears, terrified he would walk out of her life ju
as quickly as he had walked into it. The fear gripped her, she wa
petrified he would leave her... just like her parents had. Sh
couldn't bear the thought of another person she loved being gone.

He wanted to get up and leave. Wanted to leave this who
town. Nothing but weakness had come over him since the night h
met her. He wanted to slap that sad little face and yell at her fo
making him care about someone besides himself. She wasn't
problem he could physically destroy and remove from his life. H
actually cared about her. He wasn't afforded the luxury of lovin
anyone. He'd never had that luxury. A sniffle drew his eyes bac
to her. God, he was so weak and so fucked.

"Why do you do that?" he asked, so aggravated by her an
caving under the weight of those big tearful blue eyes.

"I don't know what you mean?" she asked, pleading with he
eyes. She felt like getting to her knees and begging for forgivenes
but she wasn't really completely sure what she'd done. She hadn
said anything so fucked up that it should be this big of deal, ha
she? Her throat clenched and she closed her eyes. He couldn't g
away. She couldn't lose someone else.

"Why do you think you can say whatever you want to people
Don't you realize how cruel that is? You think I've never love
anyone but myself? Do you know how insulting that is to me
Like I'm some heartless bastard?"

"I'm sorry, Roman. I'm sorry. I don't know what else to say
I'm not a very good person." She looked down at her hands whic
sat in her lap. She couldn't bear the sight of his angry eye
anymore.

"That's such a cop out. Don't pull that self-pity crap with m
Stop using that as an excuse for everything. And look at me when
talk to you." He reached over and pulled her chin up. His hand
were gentle. Even angry he could not and would not be rough wit
her physically.

"I'm sorry," she said again, her bottom lip quivering slightly.

"God," he said and stood up, pacing the room and throwing his hands in the air. "And now I'm just this big asshole who's making you cry. I'm no better than that fucking loser boyfriend of yours."

"That's not true," she whimpered, her voice choking in her throat.

"It *is* true. You *are* crying." He stopped and looked at her. "*I* am making you cry."

"I deserve it. I shouldn't assume you wouldn't love her, Roman," she stuttered shyly.

He looked down at the carpet knowing that he'd gone too far. This was a complete and total overreaction based on way more than anything she'd said. His heart raced. God, he wanted to yell at her more, to tell her that she would once again get away with her behavior by crying and looking so sad and small sitting there with her eyes filled with tears and her lip quivering like a little baby. That she was a spoiled brat that everyone had bowed to and had allowed to get away with being a brat.

But motherfucker, she was right, and that pissed him off even more. He *hadn't* loved Mylori at all the way that he should have. He knew that Mylori cared more about him than he cared about her, and yet he'd allowed their relationship to continue for too long anyway. Relationship? There was no relationship. He used her, she used him. And it pissed him off royally that Violet was calling him out on it. She was correct and he had no right to be angry with her for simply reminding him of what a callous, heartless fucker he was.

"Of course I didn't love her," he said, the anger still seeping from his words. "It's not always about loving someone, Violet. You should know that at your age."

Violet looked up at him. She was silent, completely at a loss for words. She didn't want to anger him further, and she didn't want to hurt him either.

"I didn't love her then and I don't love her now. I've never loved anyone. Not in the way you mean. I have no right screaming at you about any of this. You were right." He walked back over to the bed and sat down. No he didn't care about Mylori at all. The idea was repulsive. And he didn't really even care that

183

he didn't care. What made him angry was that Violet ha
reminded him of just how unbelievably isolated and detached h
was from everyone and everything. It was infuriating to realize h
had never cared about that fact, and now he did. Weakness was
death sentence. Any weakness. And that included giving a fuc
about anyone.

Violet sat there quietly absorbing the words he'd just spoker
She could feel the shift in her emotions and knew that he wa
about to get an earful. Despite being scared he would leave, sh
was not a person to take being yelled at lightly, especially if wha
she'd said was right in the first place.

"So, let's see, you're angry at me for pointing out the obviou
then? You use her for sex and I'm in trouble for pointing that out
Funny how that works, *Mr. Honesty*." She stared at him, her eye
ice blue now and glistening with fury. She had felt so guilty fc
her words and yet she had been right all along.

He looked up at her not knowing how to react to her sudde
turn of emotion. It's not like he ever knew how to deal wit
emotion from anyone, but especially not in this stupid situatior
Mr. Honesty? What the hell was that supposed to mean? H
wanted this conversation over. He was tired of fighting. It wa
never his intention to fight with her in the first place. She'd struc
a guilty nerve and he'd lashed out at her. He didn't have enoug
energy to keep this up, especially considering how confused h
was.

"Look, I'm sorry for yelling at you. I'm sorry for accusing yo
of being insensitive or whatever. Let's just let this go. I'm in th
wrong here, okay? You're right and I'm wrong."

"So it's just that simple is it? You let me off the hook for bein
a bitch and I let you off the hook for being a manwhore?"

He looked up at her briefly and shrugged his shoulders. He wa
tired of arguing. It was an asshole move to get pissed off and the
think she should just drop it, but that's what he wanted to happen.

She stood up and walked to the bed, sitting down beside hir
and taking his hand in hers and squeezing.

"Just know that I expect you to be honest with me just as yo
expect it. You've never allowed me to hide behind my walls an
stupid facades. I'll stop hiding if you do."

She was so perplexed by him. He was just as closed off as she was, more so even, and that surprised her because she hadn't really seen it until now. He was far more charming than she was outwardly, but in terms of deep emotional bonds with others he was probably more scared. Unreal.

He looked over at her and smiled, then shook his head. "I never should have come to this place. You're going to make me human."

"What the fuck are you talking about? Of course you're human, you dumbass."

"Nice." He smiled and shook his head.

"Seriously, Roman, you're the closest thing to a perfect human I've ever known besides my mom. Please don't disappoint me." She leaned into him and rested her head on his shoulder.

"But no pressure, right?"

Her words were like lead weights pressed down on his chest. He couldn't breathe from the weight of what she'd just said. God if she knew how far from perfect he was. He was no ideal by any stretch of the imagination. He was a fuck up, but the strange thing was that he hadn't realized just how fucked he was until now.

"I can't guarantee anything. Remember, I've never loved anyone. I'm not used to having to live up to expectations." He shoved her gently with his shoulder, leaning heavily into her.

"Yeah, well, maybe I haven't really loved anyone either," she said, looking up at him.

He looked at her for a long moment. Her eyes were dry again, her face back to its soft pink cherub-like glory.

"I don't like her anyway," Violet said with a shrug, and stood up then bending over to pick up the jewelry she'd just spent an hour sorting and just tossed it all back in the jewelry box. "So who cares if you don't love her? I'm glad you don't love her. She sucks."

"Why yes, yes she does," he teased, knowing it would make her groan.

"Oh sick. And TMI." The scowl on her face was priceless.

"Okay, so we make a deal? I won't marry Mylori, since I don't love her, and you won't marry Lux."

"And no fucking either," she interjected, as she wagged her finger at him.

185

He laughed. "I haven't fucked her in a long time. And I war you to remember this moment in case it becomes an issue at som point down the line." *Knowing Lux as he did it could.*

"Yeah, yeah, whatever."

"I'm serious. He's not a good guy, Violet."

"So you keep saying, and yet you're friends. You slept with he and I bet she's not any better than he is. How many times anyway?"

Roman groaned. "Enough."

"So, then you have to uphold your end, but don't expect me t uphold mine."

"What? How the hell is that fair?"

"Well, because you've already done her like, what, a hundre times or something? So big deal if you have to refrain now. She' old hat anyway, right?"

You have no idea how old hat she is.

"Well, we'll wait till Lux is old hat for me and then we'll do th not marrying them thing," Violet said, being silly. But really thinking about Lux's kiss the night before, she seriously wouldn mind rolling around with him for a night or two, or three, or...

"I don't see how it's relevant how many times I..."

"What? Are you reneging on the deal so soon?" Violet said interrupting him with a smirk.

"There is no deal. If I have to hold to my end, so do you, c there's no deal."

"Look, you're taking this whole deal thing waaaaay to seriously," Violet said, and smiled mischievously.

"You are such a dork. Lux is so stupid."

"Don't call my future husband stupid, *stupid.*"

Roman shook his head. "By the way, you know that girl yo think sucks and I'm not in love with? She'd be your sister-in-law.

"Well, good. Cuz I thought maybe he was fucking her," Viole said, and sat back down on the floor to sort through a stack c magazines. Roman laughed.

"No, I don't think they've ever fucked," Roman said, th thought was nauseating.

Violet wrinkled her nose in disgust. "No Lannister bullshit."

"Lannister?" Roman asked with a frown.

"Nevermind."

They both sat there quietly trying to digest the conversation they'd just had. Ordinarily when Violet and Mark had fought it had never ended with them being able to joke. He'd fly off the handle and she'd leave or vice versa. It felt strange to her that he was still there and he didn't seem to still be angry with her. And why was he so mad really? She hadn't really said anything too awful had she? How strange.

"So, fifteen kids huh?" he asked, looking at her.

"At least." She grinned

"Wow."

9. BLOOD PROMISE

He walked through the neighborhood. The sky was filled with
million shining stars. The cool air was crisp and sharp in his lungs
He needed to start running again, he had gotten lazy since he'd me
her. He thought back to the prior evening and wondered why thos
few simple words about love, or the lack thereof, had provoke
such a reaction in him. It's not like she hadn't been right, but h
never thought about that shit because it had never been relevan
And he was going to stop thinking about it now because it sti
wasn't relevant.

He needed to keep Lux away from her and her friends. That h
did know. And Roman hoped that he'd just stay away. The realit
was he'd be back, and so would Mylori. Why they felt the need t
come in and out of his life "helping" he had no idea. Well, it wa
their arrangement, but it was still mindboggling. And he knew tha
either of the two could have snapped at any moment, and he had le
them in anyway. He had seen Lux's destruction enough times t
know better than to trust him, and Mylori could be twice as viciou
because she truly cared for no one but herself. No, she cared fc
Lux, but just barely.

And what about the promise he'd made to Violet? Would h
stay away from Mylori? He hadn't really been very successful i
the past. He and Mylori had some kind of agreement between th
two of them. So, how would he keep that promise? Why would h
keep that promise? She had already hinted that she wouldn'
though he would stop anything that could theoretically transpir
for her own safety. He figured Lux feared him enough to behav
at least a little. He had more than proven his own mercilessnes
night after bloody night - enough to instill quite a bit of caution i
Lux and his sister. And wasn't that why they'd stopped what the
had been doing? Fear of him? Wasn't that how they'd turned an

decided it was best to help instead of being destroyed? Yes, it was.

His thoughts were rambling all over the place. He didn't care about Mylori. She'd pushed herself on him, probably to keep him from killing her. What she didn't know is that he wasn't that sentimental, and he'd do what he had to if the time should arise.

Besides, he was kidding himself. Lux and Mylori had no reason for doing any of the things they did. He was just a little plaything to them both, just as everything and everyone else in the world was their plaything. The only difference with him was that he could kill them if he so chose, or at least he'd stand a better chance of killing them than anyone else could.

Roman remembered back to the night they'd explained their vantage point. It had made such utter sense, but there was no use for their philosophy in this age. They needed to change. They needed to rein themselves in. It wasn't okay to go about causing mass panic anymore. In this day and age they'd get caught eventually, and then all hell would break loose. There'd be a war on humans, and Roman couldn't defend them all.

He stopped to look at the three dogs that had gone ballistic the first night he'd met Violet. They watched him walk just on the other side of their fence, looking up silently from the old wooden front porch. Their eyes, green with phosphorescent glow, with a slight whimper in their throat.

"Good boys," he spoke quietly to them and watched as their heads bobbed with interest. But they never left the porch.

He resumed walking. He was anxious for the snow to start falling. His preference was for colder weather. It was still technically summer, but the smell of dusty dead leaves was already beginning to permeate the night. It was a dank and sweet scent. He was reminded of last autumn. That had been a lonelier time than usual for him for some reason. At least now he had Violet to distract him. And he actually enjoyed Amber and Randy as well. They were the closest things to friends he'd ever had.

Lux would be wounded by that, though he knew full well he was no friend to Roman. If Lux were at all convinced that he was completely Roman's superior, Lux would kill him. But as it was, Lux wasn't sure.

It was good to be powerful. It was nice knowing he was good at

something at least. His hands, and the power in them, never faile
him.

But what about Mylori? Had she not been so damned lethal i
black leather he could have resisted her. But who was he kidding
He'd been lonely and she had been willing. More than willing
she'd been aggressive. He would've surely never pursued he
otherwise.

***

Violet lay back in the bed staring at the ceiling. All the poster
were gone now. She had accomplished that at least. Her room wa
starting to look bare in comparison to the way it had been. Sh
would get this task finished eventually. There was no hurr
anyway. Her phone rang so she picked it up and said hello. It wa
silent for a moment and it made her wonder if it was the woma
calling again.

"Violet?" he said softly.

"Hello," she replied, her voice caught in her throat.

"How are you doing?"

"I'm doing alright, how're you?" she asked, rolling onto he
side and staring across the room.

"Okay." He was quiet for several moments.

"What do you want?" she asked tentatively.

"I want to talk to you."

"Mark, I don't think this is a good idea."

"Come on, come and have coffee or something. Just meet me a
the diner. I just want to talk and clear the air about all this." Sh
didn't say anything. "Violet, I promise you I'll behave. I just nee
to know exactly what happened."

"I think it should be obvious to you," she said, her voice
whisper. She felt her heart heaving at the sound of his voice. Sh
felt dreamy and intoxicated by the familiar cadence and tone. Hi
deep, lulling voice had always soothed her when he was being kin
instead of hateful.

"Can't we just talk? And then I promise you I'll go away." Hi
voice had that sad resonance that had convinced her a thousan

times to give in to his wishes like so many other women had before her.

Though she had no intentions of ever getting back with him, the sound of his voice still felt comfortable, and the sadness of his voice still made her feel guilty and petty for wanting to deny him. She sighed, slowly letting a deep breath escape. "I'll meet you in a half an hour."

She hung the phone up, and stood up, looking across the room to the vanity mirror and shaking her head. This was a stupid idea. She would be better off letting this all just go. She walked to the closet and pulled the black hooded sweatshirt out and zipped it up, then sat on the edge of the bed and laced her boots. Hesitating, she took several deep breaths, and then walked downstairs.

Randy was sitting in the kitchen eating a sandwich. "Going to Roman's?" he asked, looking up at her.

"No. I'm going to The Oven. If I'm not back in a while come looking for me, alright?"

Randy looked at her, concerned. "What's going on?"

"I'm meeting Mark," she said, knowing the questions that would follow. "I know, I know, probably stupid, but this is it and then I'm done with him."

"I'm coming with you," he said, standing up and grabbing his shirt that he had spread over the back of the chair.

"That's very gallant of you, Randy, but it's really not necessary. It's a public place, no need to worry. And anyway—like I said—if I'm not back in awhile come and get me."

"Like what's awhile?"

"I don't know… an hour and a half?"

"Let me state for the record that I think this is terrible idea, but whatever," he said, sitting back in the chair and picking his sandwich up.

"I agree." She rolled her eyes and walked outside.

***

Roman decided to run the rest of the way home. Maybe he

could convince her to run with him. She needed exercise
Everyone needed exercise. It would be good for her to know how
to use her body to its full potential, and running taught that more
than any other activity. Well, there were close seconds. A vision
flashed in his head that made his groin jerk.

Not going to go there.

Running was a drug to him. Feeling his body move like
perfect machine was the best feeling. His lungs expanded filling
his chest. His heart beat strongly. It felt good. It felt like old
stale oxygen and blood was being pushed out of his system. He
liked running until his muscles felt numb, his lungs burned, and his
body was completely wet with perspiration. Being this fit had kept
him alive so many times. No one had his stamina, at least no one
he'd ever encountered.

Yes, it would be good for her to get in shape. He tried t
imagine Violet running. The picture didn't seem to paint itself
properly. He couldn't envision her in black velvet and clunk
boots with her long messy hair running around. He also couldn't
picture her in a track suit and tennis shoes. She was enigmatic in
the way Mylori had been to him at first, though a thousand year
younger in every way.

He ran up the metal stairs and unlocked his apartment. It was
dark and quiet just the way it always had been, just like ever
house, apartment, or warehouse had always been. Only now it fel
achingly so. He almost hated how empty it felt. This had been his
sanctuary, not this apartment particularly, but a hundred just like i
for years. And suddenly it felt like nothingness. He could hear the
muffled television set from downstairs and it made him fee
relieved in some strange way. Knowing someone living was near
even if he would never really know him, was a relief somehow
The keys made a loud chinking sound as he tossed them down on
the coffee table. He unlaced his boots and pulled them off the
walked to the bedroom, flipping on lights as he went.

Roman undressed and folded the sweat-soaked clothes and
placed them in the hamper, then peeled his socks off and did the
same. He walked to the bathroom and stopped to look at his face
in the mirror. God, he felt old, though his face hadn't changed
from yesterday or the day before, or in the last five years for the

matter. He reasoned it was from being around Violet and her friends so much that he felt so ancient. He reached into the medicine cabinet and took his toothbrush out and brushed his teeth. The water sounded like it roared against the utter quiet of his apartment. He rinsed his mouth then leaned forward looking into the mirror.

"What is wrong with you?" he asked himself with a scowl.

He stepped into the shower, turning the water on and then stood there beneath the ice cold water letting it spark his nerve endings. He needed something to wake him up.

***

"I'll have hot chocolate," she said softly, and slid into the booth. The waitress rolled her eyes and walked away. It hurt Violet to feel that sting day in and day out. She had never admitted that to anyone, but it was her fault for the most part. The fact that she walked around so self-absorbed and acted so condescending towards just about everyone set her up for shitty treatment. She deserved it. The woman returned with a mug which was half full and walked away.

Violet took a sip of the sweet drink and looked up to see Mark walking toward her. He was handsome, no denying it. His hair was growing in a bit, she reckoned because she hadn't been around to trim it for him, and he hadn't shaved his face in what looked like three or four days. She'd always liked him scruffy.

"Hey sweetie," he said, sliding onto the bench opposite her. They were never the sit on the same side of the booth kind of people. So she was glad he didn't try to start that shit now.

His tone made her wince. Him being nice always meant trouble. His insane personality shifts were enough to drive her crazy. She wished he could just be mean all the time. That would make all this so much easier.

"Hey," she said tentatively. The stab of hearing "sweetie" was probably obvious to him since she cringed like he'd hit her. He wasn't an idiot, just insensitive most of the time.

The waitress walked up with the coffee pot in her hand knowi
what Mark always ordered. She filled the cup and walked awა
not saying a word, or even glancing at either of them.

"Yeah, *thanks*," Mark said sarcastically.

Violet looked down at her lap, used to his abrasiveness but sι
disgusted by it. "So, what did you want to talk about, Mark?" s
asked.

"Jesus, jump right in," he said, taking a sip of the hot coffι
He winced and then blew on the drink having scalded his tongue.

"Sorry, I just don't know what you want to hear? I don't knc
what more I can tell you."

He sat silently studying her. There wasn't going to be any w
he could get her back this time. There'd been more than o
occasion that he'd seen the dead look in her eyes directed at othε
and he knew what it meant. She was done with him. The light s
once had in her eyes when she looked at him was gone. In tl
past, even when she was furious with him, she still had it. But l
could see nothing but emptiness now when he looked at her.
was over. The longer she sat silently, the angrier he got. Η
wanted her to cry about this. He wanted her to feel guilty like sl
always did. Instead he looked at two hollow eyes.

"Tell me anything, make something up, I don't care," he sai
reaching to get a reaction from her.

"I don't know what you want from me?" she askє
despondently. "I don't make you happy, and you don't make n
happy, isn't that all there is?" She was trying to be as gentle aı
diplomatic as possible, but she could see by his twitching fingε
he was agitated.

"You make me happy," he said dryly.

"Mark, obviously I don't, or you wouldn't be so angry aı
frustrated all the time. If I had made you happy you wouldn't hav
had to worry about where I was, and who I was talking to all tľ
time." She pleaded with him to see this for himself. The look є
sadness behind the anger, which she was always able to perceive ı
him, was hard to take. Even knowing how he was, it hurt her to ł
the source of pain to him.

"That's ridiculous. We were happy until a few weeks ago."

"No, we weren't," she said, her words lacking emotion.

194

He looked up at her again, the life in her eyes gone. There was nothing there that indicated she really cared at all about him. "It's that guy," he accused.

Violet was taken by surprise by his comment, though she really shouldn't be. Of course it would be easier for Mark to blame Roman than to take any responsibility himself. She clicked her tongue against the roof of her mouth and crossed her arms over her chest. "This has nothing to do with anyone but you and me."

"Yeah right, Violet, like you aren't banging him." His voice was getting more animated.

She didn't want to dignify his statement with a response. "Why do you have to react this way? You wanted to talk and the first thing you do when you don't hear what you want to hear is lash out. You don't know him, and you sure as fuck don't know me either, obviously."

"I know exactly who you are," he said, looking at her intently.

She felt a shiver run through her as those dark blue, rage-filled eyes bore into her.

"I'm going to go," she said, opening her bag and pulling out her wallet.

"Run and hide, little girl. That's all you ever do."

"I wonder why?" she said, under her breath.

"Yeah, it's my fault entirely," he growled, shoving the silverware across the table at her. It made a loud scraping sound before hitting the seat behind and clanking to the floor. "It's all me."

She stood up and started for the cash register with her keys in her hand and a ten dollar bill. Mark followed closely behind her, barking insults and commands at her. The few guests in the restaurant watched as the two made their way through the restaurant. Violet was embarrassed and starting to get very scared. Mark's rage was growing with every step she took. The waitress met her at the counter, having sensed Violet's desire to exit quickly. Violet looked up at her fearfully and the waitress seemed to understand the look that passed between them. Maybe the woman had never liked her, but something in her related to that look in Violet's eyes.

"It's that guy. It's that *fucking guy*," Mark said behind her.

195

She handed the woman the ten and whispered for her to kee
the change and headed quickly for her car, thankfully parked i
front. Mark followed closely behind her, repeating himself ove
and over. She opened the door, slammed it shut and locked th
doors. Mark stood beside the car looking down at her. Viole
looked back to the restaurant and saw that the waitress and severa
customers were looking out at her. Surely to God they wouldn
let anything happen to her?

"I'll fucking kill you," he said, no longer angry. The stillness o
the cadence drew Violet's eyes. His face was completel
composed and calm, and it was terrifying.

Fear shot straight through her. The dead look of evil and hatre
chilled her to the very marrow of her bones. She started her ca
and quickly backed out and pulled away. Mark stood ther
watching her drive off his eyes never leaving her until she couldn
see him anymore. She reached into her purse and dialed her hous

"I'm going to Roman's," she said, trying not to cry, afraid fo
her life. She didn't think Mark would really kill her, but the pur
evil in his eyes and the calmness that had come over him scare
her to death.

"You okay?" Randy asked, sensing the trepidation in her voic
"Did he freak out on you?"

"Yeah, he did. I'll talk later, Randy. I'm okay, tell Ambe
everything's alright. Okay? I'll be home tomorrow morning. I'1
going to stay with Roman because I just don't trust Mar
anymore."

"I told you it was a bad idea," Randy said with sympathy. "
think it's a good idea to go to Roman. Mark doesn't know wher
he lives and wouldn't try anything with him anyway."

"Thanks Randy. No need to worry. I'm safe. Just let Ambe
know so she doesn't worry. You know how she gets."

"K," Randy said, and then sighed.

She hung up and gripped the steering wheel tighter, looking int
her rearview mirror, expecting to see Mark tailing her. The car fe
like it was driving of its own volition because she was so frazzle
from the ordeal. It felt as if something had taken over for her an
that she was hiding inside the body of another human. She wa
having a total and complete dissaciative disorder moment.

***

Roman toweled himself off, leaving his hair tangled. He reached into the cabinet and found the cotton swabs and cleaned his ears, then put on deodorant. He walked back into the bedroom and grabbed his plaid pajama bottoms off the bed, he pulled them on then flipped the light off. He walked out into the living room turning lights off as he went so that the apartment was dark.

He walked to the kitchen and grabbed a glass from the cupboard turning the faucet on and swallowing two full glasses of water. His stomach growled to be fed, but he'd eat tomorrow. It was too late to bother. He was tired.

He walked over to the couch and slouched down into it grabbing the remote from between the cushions and turned on the television. He flipped through the channels and stopped on *The Andy Griffith Show*. His eyes felt heavy, his body numb. He pulled the blanket she'd given him off the back of the couch and covered his chest with it and closed his eyes.

***

Violet pulled off to the side of the street and looked up at his window. She saw only the faint blue light that would radiate off a television through the kitchen window. It appeared he must still be awake watching something. She felt stupid for running to him all the time. There was no reason she shouldn't be able to take care of herself and her own problems, but she liked being with him. He made her feel safe and okay like no one else had since she was little.

She took a deep breath and looked in the rearview mirror. Her makeup was thick and melted around her eyes. He had seen her looking far worse. It's not like it mattered anyway. She opened the door and walked up his driveway slowly, questioning herself for coming to him again. All the arguments roiled around in he brain, finally deciding to accept the fact that it was okay to com by his house. Roman didn't mind. He had told her he didn't min a million times. Besides, Roman needed this as much as she di He needed a friend, at least she thought he did. But there was n way for her to know his thoughts. He wasn't exactly forthcomin with them. She rapped her knuckles softly on the aluminum doo The sound was tinny and obnoxious. She looked back towards th street as a car drove by slowly. She half expected it to be Mark, s she leaned in closer to the house, hoping to shield herself from view in case it was. But it wasn't him, thank God. She exhaled sigh of relief and she relaxed some.

There was no reason she should be this afraid. It wasn't righ for her to have to live in fear like this. She furrowed her brow hating the fact that she needed her protector, her big brothe Roman, to keep her safe again. She leaned on him too heavy. Thi wasn't his job, but she wanted him to take care of her. She als wanted him to kick the shit out of Mark again. But mostly sh wanted him to make her feel safe and protected like he always di *It isn't his job though.* Her brain was twisting with all thes conflicting thoughts and feelings. She started to turn around an then Roman peered out the door, unsure he'd really heard th knock. He saw her standing there and opened the door.

"Hello," he said, standing aside to let her in.

"Hello," she said, and walked in, sitting her things down besid the door. She walked over to the chair and sat down. Roma followed her, sitting down on the couch.

"What's going on?" he asked, concerned by her manner and th look on her face.

Violet unlaced her boots and set them aside. God, she couldn bear looking at him. "Before you say anything, I know this wa dumb of me, but I met Mark at The Oven, and he got really angry and now I'm afraid he's going to really do something to hurt me."

Roman leaned forward, resting his forearms on his thigh fingers laced. "Tell me what happened."

She explained the meeting she'd had with Mark, and how h had gotten so angry and had threatened her life.

"Nothing is going to happen, Violet. You've got nothing t

worry about." He literally had zero concerns about Mark.

"I've never seen him like that, Roman," she said. Her eyes were wide and glossy, full of fear.

"Trust me on this, you'll be fine. He's just mad he can't manipulate you anymore." The look in her eyes pained him.

"I know, I just never saw him look at me like that. As angry as he's been with me, he never looked that cold. Like he was filled with pure hate."

"Everything will be okay," he reassured.

The calm demeanor and self-assurance of his words made her relax some. She sat quietly admiring him for a moment. His hair was all wet and messy and he looked red with warmth. "Thanks for allowing me to invade your life," she said sincerely.

He smiled and stood up. "Want something to drink?" He walked toward the kitchen, looking back over his shoulder.

"Yes," she answered, and hoisted her legs over the arm of the chair facing the television. "I'm glad you were still awake."

"I wasn't awake," he chuckled.

"Oh man, I'm sorry," she said, turning in the seat so she could see him. He was pouring her a glass of pop from the two liter the pizza guy had delivered the last time they ate pizza together.

"It's fine," he said, walking back to the living room handing her the glass. He felt content to have her here. It was nice. "So you're going to stay?" he asked, sitting back down on the couch.

"If you'll let me, I'm a little nervous about Mark showing up at home." She swallowed a big gulp of the soda.

"Stay as long as you like," he said, laying back down on the couch.

They both watched television, neither of them saying a word. Having each other's company was enough. She finished the glass of soda and walked it to the kitchen.

"I'm gonna go wash my face and stuff," she said, walking towards his bathroom. Her skin felt taut and sticky from the tears she'd shed.

He looked up at her and then back to the television. He was so damn tired. He had definitely been slacking off way too much lately. Usually at this time of night he'd be hunting something, or at least working out.

She turned the faucet on and splashed herself. The cold water felt good as she lathered her hands with the green bar soap and scrubbed her face. She patted her face dry with his red hand towel. There was water all over the counter so she mopped it up with the towel, not wanting to mess up his spotless apartment. Her stomach was in knots from what had transpired earlier. She couldn't believe how much she'd been through in the last several weeks. The stinging returned to her eyes as they welled up with tears again. All this crying and feeling like a nervous wreck was really getting old. She took a deep breath and walked back out to the living room.

"You can sleep in my bed," he said, as she walked back into the living room.

"You don't want to sleep there? It's your bed. I can sleep on the couch," she offered, and walked over to the door and grabbed her bag. It was strange that either one of them was even feeling weird about sharing a bed considering they'd slept together a number of times. Things were starting to feel different for Violet though, even though she tried not to see him as anything but a friend. She didn't think he was interested in her in anything but a friend though. He'd never acted like he was, at least not as far as she could tell. *Stop thinking about this.* She pulled a hair band from one of her pockets and wadded her hair up on top her head.

He looked up at her and then back to the TV. "You sleep in my bed," he said, and leaned his head back onto the blanket he'd balled up into a makeshift pillow.

"If you're sure," she said, not wanting to inconvenience him yet again.

"I'm sure," he answered, barely opening his eyes. "Goodnight V."

"Thanks Roman," she said, and padded off to his room.

She flipped the light switch on and took her clothes off, folding them up and setting them on top of his dresser. His house was so neat it didn't feel right tossing them on the floor like she would at home. She turned the light off and crawled in bed. The sheets were cold against her bare legs. It felt good but the unfamiliarity of his bed, the awkwardness of the situation, and what she'd been through earlier with Mark made her uncomfortable. It was so dark and quiet. The stillness made her feel a little creeped out because she was used to her night light. She felt uncomfortable laying there with her eyes open, unable to see much of anything as she peered into the darkness. He had turned the television off, which made the house so quiet and so black. The only light was peeking through his blinds, and it wasn't much. She really wished Roman was here beside her. At least it wouldn't feel so scary if he was near. She wanted to go out to the living room and curl up on the floor beside the couch just to be near him. How ridiculous was that? She groaned out loud at herself. She hated the darkness. She closed her eyes trying to force sleep to come, the sooner she was asleep, the sooner it would be morning.

***

Music was loud. Drums were pounding. Guitars were screeching.

She could hardly breathe from all the smoke in this place.

Roman stood against the far wall with his arm around Mylori and talking to her. Occasionally the woman would look over at her and smile. Her teeth seemed sharp and too white, something feral about the way she looked. Her breasts spilled over the top of the leather corset she was tied into. Her long legs were lean and muscular. In her thigh high spike heeled boots she was nearly his height. Violet didn't remember her being that tall.

Violet sat back leaning against the bar in disbelief. What was she looking at? Where was this place and why were Roman and Mylori here? TMore importantly, why was she?

The wood felt hard and sharp against her protruding shoulder blades. She looked down at herself. Her own body was too thin and too sickly looking. Her skin was ghastly white and too dry. She looked like she was covered in chalk dust.

"Come with me." The soft breath of his voice brushed against her neck, sending a warm sensation through her body as though he had touched her all over.

She turned to look at him. His crystalline eyes glistened, his

201

pale pink lips were lush, so soft looking, and smiling devilishly.

She took his hand and let him lead her to a table. He helpe
her up onto the stool and then rested his arm on the table , lookin
deeply into her eyes. His gaze followed hers to where Roman an
Mylori rested against the far wall.

"You think he'll save you?" he asked seductively.

"Yes," she answered, closing her eyes and swooning from th
low lull of his voice.

"Hmm.....save you from what?" His voice was a warm
soothing balm that calmed her.

"Myself?" she whispered.

She opened her eyes. Roman was looking at them as Mylor
was busily sucking at his throat.

Lux leaned into her and tilted his head towards the two. "Yo
see, he's not always going to be there for you, little flower."

She closed her eyes again, her blood seemed to tingle as
raced through her veins towards the spots where he'd touched her
She noticed the surface of his skin warmed where it touched her
But his hands were corrupting her.

She forced her eyes open. Roman had his back towards ther
now. Mylori peered over his shoulder and smiled at Violet.

Lux's mouth was pressed against her ear. His whole bod
pressed against her as her legs parted. She wrapped her arm
around him pulling him closer, their bodies joined togethei
melded.

He kissed her. His tongue felt like ice against her hot skin.
was electric as it slid over her tongue, filling her mouth. She fe
his body warming to hers, swelling as he fed from her mouth. H
pulled his head back and looked into her eyes. "He's not alway
going to be here."

The pupils grew and consumed the color of his eyes. His lip
were red and lush, succulent. She looked past him to Roman wh
still had his back to her. A painful twinge of sadness pierced he
languid heart.

Lux tapped her on the chin to get her attention. She wanted hi
mouth again and he smiled, knowing her thoughts. His finger
crawled over her skin, delicately, like soft feathers trailing ove
her, tickling her nerve endings to life. Her breath escape

whispering over the surface of his skin causing him to make a soft groaning sound that drew her attention back to his mouth. All shiny and wet and glistening in the dark red glow of the bar. The pearl teeth were daggers, long slivers of bone china. She felt a jolt of electricity shoot through her brain, tingling like it had fallen asleep. As if a thousand ants crawled across the surface.

"You don't know what you are."

"What am I?"

"You don't know who you are."

"Who am I?"

He smiled, his eyes alight with amusement, and he sank his teeth into her neck. The popping sound of his fangs piercing her flesh was loud in her ear. The searing pain shifted her backwards on the stool. He caught her in his vice-like arms and refused to let her go. Her arms grasped at the air, her eyes darting around the room for someone to help her. She tried to yell for Roman, he was still across the room with Mylori wrapped around him. Mylori looked intently at Violet, smile wide and satisfied. But no sound came out, her vocal chords were severed by his long knife teeth. She felt her eyes closing as Lux took her life, the bliss taking her as he held her to him, sucking at her neck like a starving lion.

"Princess."

***

Violet leapt up sucking in gasps of air. Her heart pounded in her ears, making her feel so dizzy. A peal of thunder and flash of lightning lit the room briefly shocking her system. She looked around confused by the dream she'd had, confused by her surroundings. She was terrified. It had been too realistic.

Her hands went to her throat, feeling for a yawning gash that didn't exist. The feel of Lux's mouth was so fresh in her mind that she could picture it perfectly. The way his body pressed against hers, the feel of his arousal, the sound of his voice tickling against her ear. The smell of the bar, the temperature, the music, all of it was so real. She tried to calm herself, replaying the dream in her mind, the words, and his face.

The apartment was too quiet—too dark and too quiet—save fo
the pounding rain and intermittent thunder and lightning that rage
outside. She repeated to herself that this was only a dream,
product of her subconscious, but the images were too fresh and to
vivid. Did this mean something? Of course it didn't mea
anything. It was a dream and nothing more.

"Violet?" he asked, as he walked out of the bathroom peerin
into his room. He could see her dark silhouette there on the be
sitting upright and moving around.

She was too afraid to even answer.

"Hey?" he asked, walking into the room. "What's wrong?" H
could hear her breath coming too quickly, as though she wer
panicked.

She hid in the thick blankets. The bathroom light behind hir
hid his face from her. He was walking closer.

"Hey," he whispered again, reaching out and touching he
shoulder. She flinched. "What's wrong?" He sat on the edge c
the bed.

"I had another dream," she said, leaning into him. He could fee
her hot tears against his shoulder.

He rubbed her back with his hand trying to comfort her. "It"
okay, sweetie," he said, rocking with her as she moved. "Wha
was it about?"

"Lux," she sniffed.

Roman felt his stomach tighten.

"And you and Mylori." She wiped her eyes with her finger
and pulled away from him. "It was just scary," she said, trying t
calm herself, she was feeling embarrassed. It had only been
dream, no matter how realistic. She lay back on the bed pullin
the blankets up to her chin.

"What happened?" he asked, rubbing her forehead with th
back of his hand.

"Nothing, just weird, and scary. He asked me if I thought yo
would save me and then told me you wouldn't always be there an
then he bit me and I couldn't scream and you had your back to me
It was just really real," she said, starting to cry again.

Roman contemplated her words. He knew both Lux and Mylor

could manipulate dreams, but what would be their purpose in torturing this poor girl after having warned him she was in danger? What game were they playing? Or maybe it was just one of them, but which one? Of course he knew they didn't need a reason for any of the shit they did, but he didn't understand the relevance of the dream or what their rationale would be for fucking with her. He wanted to tell her about Lux and Mylori, but why? All it would do is put her in more danger and he didn't even know what danger she was in yet, apart from Mark and the potential premonition of her dream. Telling her would serve no purpose but to scare her more than she was already scared. Her world had been turned over enough without all of this.

"It's over now, Violet. Just try to sleep." He rubbed her cheek and starting to stand up.

"Stay please." Her hand flew out from under the blanket, clutching his arm.

He hesitated and then stood up, walking around to the other side of the bed, and then lay down beside her. She rolled over and got as close as she could without touching him, just close enough to feel his heat radiating.

"Try not to be afraid." He reached his hand towards her and felt the contour of her soft face with his index finger. He was used to all those images. It didn't frighten him anymore, and hadn't since he was young. What would she be thinking? Would she believe those images were real or not? He couldn't imagine how scary the idea of being attacked by a vampire would be to someone who didn't know anything about them, especially someone who had gone through so much violence recently.

"I know," she said softly. "I know it's just a dream. I feel stupid for getting scared."

"Come here," he said, and lifted his arm. Violet slid against him and rested her face on his shoulder and chest. He wrapped his arm around her and squeezed gently. "You've had a rough day," he said, and placed a kiss to the top of her head. Her hair felt silky against his lips.

"I've had a rough life," she said sadly. She was already drifting back to sleep, feeling the magnitude of his protection. Her mind kept trying to replay the dream, so her tired body forced sleep upon her.

Princess.

***

Her arm was wrapped around his waist. She could feel the so
flannel material of his pajama bottoms on her fingertips. Her fac
was pressed between his shoulder blades. She could feel hii
breathing, her arm lifting, her head gently moving to the rhythm c
his lungs. His body was so large and warm beside her and sh
didn't want to move to break this spell. The cadence of falling rai
thumped against the roof soothingly. Her eyes were heavy an
sleepy. Taking a deep breath, she rolled over onto her back an
rubbed her eyes, and then let her hand flop to the bed.

Roman rolled over. His hands were tucked beneath his face, hi
large shoulders and muscular arms made the position loo
uncomfortable. She wondered if he was able to get trul
comfortable being that bulky. The idea made her smile at him. H
looked peaceful and cute sleeping there, his long dark lashe
resting against his white skin, his mouth slightly parted, so
breaths barely audible. She rolled onto her side again, drawing he
knees up and tucking her hands beneath her cheek.

"Stop staring," he said, the corner of his mouth quirking u
without opening his eyes.

Violet lifted her hand, and let it fall against him, resting again:
the crook of his neck. His eyes slowly opened. He blinked a fe
times, never letting his eyes leave hers. She stared into the sleep
green fields noticing their utter brilliance for the first time. A blac
ring around the outside and golden flecks around the iris. She wa
filled with awe at the way they looked at her now, his expressio
was so open, so unguarded. She took her hand and wiped a stra
eyelash from his cheek, holding the lash up in front of him on he
fingertip.

"Make a wish," she said, looking from the lash to him and bac
again.

"What?"

206

"Make a wish," she said, moving her head on the pillow so that their heads were touching as she looked up at the eyelash that rested on the pad of her index finger. "Make a wish and then blow it away."

Roman's voice rumbled in her chest by proximity. It was so deep and resonant it made her belly warm. "You make one for me," he said, not about to partake in something so childish. Beaten and jaded men didn't make eyelash wishes.

"Oooo… You may live to regret this decision," she said, closing her eyes like she was thinking.

Roman watched her. Her youth so evident as she lay there with pink cheeks and perfectly soft and pore-less skin. With her tiny hand raised in the air and her lips pouted, she blew his eyelash away.

"Well, I'm sure it only landed back on the bed, but it's the thought that counts, right?"

"Sure," he said, taking her hand and holding onto her balled up fist which fit neatly in the palm of his hand. She had kicked the blankets off of herself and was laying there crooked, head on his pillow, feet off the other side of the bed. The pink cotton tank top and matching panties with black hearts on them looked like something a child would wear, or at least a teenager. God, she wasn't far removed from being a teenager. But she was sexy as hell, *so warm, so soft*. The conflicting imagery confused the fuck out of him. It was disturbing in ways he didn't want to admit or even think about. He pushed the thoughts from his head not wanting to visit his feelings on the subject.

"You feeling better?" he asked to distract himself.

A sudden dread came back over her as she remembered the dream she'd had. Then it faded as she turned her head and focused back on his eyes. "I'm okay," she answered.

10. ANOTHER DAY

The smell of citrus cleaner was nice. The chrome and cerami was nice. The green soap was nice. Everything about the way h lived was nice. She liked how clutter-free his place was. Hi minimalistic ways put things into perspective. The less clutter i your life the less junk you have to deal with. It was a *du* realization. She really did need to overhaul her house one of thes days.

She turned the water off and opened the shower curtain reaching for the towel she'd set on the toilet. She dried herself of and then wrapped her hair up, pulled the curtain shut, and walke to the mirror. Reaching into her bag, she grabbed her toothbrusl toothpaste, and deodorant. She was glad she always carried thi stuff with her. It had taken her many years of winding up i strange places to finally convince herself to have the whole arsens in her purse. She went through the ritual then pulled the towel of her head and hung it over the shower rod. Her hair was wicke messy, filled with knots, but that would have to wait until late She twisted it up on top of her head with a hair band again an then walked out into the living room still wearing what she'd slep in.

His eyes unerringly found the skin peeking between the bottor hem of her tank top and the waistband of her panties. He looke back at the bar above his head. "Go put something on," he saic setting the bar down and sitting up.

She looked at him with a disgusted look on her face. "What" the big deal?" she asked, and sat down on the couch.

"Cuz you're half naked," he groused, and reached for the han weights.

"So are you." she laughed, making reference to the fact that h was shirtless.

"Well, so what. I don't have breasts."

"Neither do I," she laughed out loud.

"Shut up," he said dismissively, and rolled his eyes.

"Well what's the big deal? It's not like you haven't seen me naked anyway."

"You know, I *am* still a man—old and decrepit as I may be— I'm still a man."

She gave him a dirty look and stood up. "Yes, you most certainly are," she snapped, and walked back to his bedroom. She wasn't angry at him at all, just being a brat.

She picked her clothes up off the dresser and put them on, zipping her jacket up all the way and pulling the hood up over her head. She tightened the strings and tied them tight at her chin then walked back into the living room and stood before him, hands on hips. "Is this better, horn dog?"

"Much, though I'd like it better if it hid your face too," he teased, and grinned at her.

He was busy lifting weights when she sidled up. A look of awe came over her face. His arms were freaking humongous. The swollen veins had risen to the surface, he was glistening with sweat. She snapped her jaw shut to keep the drool from coming out.

She walked over to the couch and sat down, deciding to watch him as he went through his routine. It was utterly amazing how strong he was. His big, huge arms lifting all that weight again and again was impressive. Mark had been strong, but he never really worked out much. He was one of those guys who was just naturally big from genetics and from doing manual labor. Roman was an absolute machine. He was huge, like giant huge, the biggest man she'd ever seen. The size of his arms was awe-inspiring, and she'd never really been a person who was impressed by something like that.

"You should teach me to do that," she said, sitting up and leaning forward.

"I'll teach you," he said standing up. "Come here."

"Right now?" she whined.

"Well, no time like the present, you slacker."

"I just took a shower."

209

"That's not the last of the water and soap. You can tal another."

"Yeah, but you're all sweaty and you were laying on tha Gross." She grinned and walked over to him releasing a feign exasperated sigh.

"Such a drama queen," he said with a smirk.

"Well, what do I do?"

"You can take that stupid hood off for starters. You look li an idiot."

"Ha ha." She shoved the hood back and stood there waiting f his instructions.

"There's really not that much to learn. You take the weigh and lift them, that's pretty much the extent of things. Though the are several different ways in which you can lift to work vario muscle groups."

"How much weight is on this bar?" she asked, leaning on it.

"Three fifty."

"Three fifty? Three hundred and fifty pounds? You can lift th much weight? That's *insane*, Roman."

"No it's not," he said, slightly embarrassed by her enthusiasr He could actually lift quite a bit more.

"Let's see how much I can lift," she said, sitting down on tl bench. "Sick, it's sweaty," she said, frowning and sliding arour on the bench.

"Yeah, that's what happens when you exercise."

"Gross."

"Whatever. I know you can't lift this much," he sai dismissing her comments and started adjusting the weights. don't want you to get hurt, so we'll start light, fifteen pounds."

"I could lift that with my tongue," she scoffed.

"Oh really? Interesting," he teased, and waggled his eyebrows

"Shut up, perv." She laughed, and leaned back into the benc and arranged her limbs comfortably. He told her where to put h hands, guiding her placement, then she lifted the bar and pressed to her chest and back up to the holder.

"Good." He smiled, and bent over to add more weight.

He continued to add weight, astounded by her natural abilit and the fact that she was lifting so much, considering how sma she was and that he highly doubted she ever lifted much more than a make up brush. She didn't look like this was any effort for her at all, so he kept adding in five pound increments.

"Ugh, that's it. No more," she said, setting the bar down and sitting up. "So where'd we end up?"

"One hundred and twenty five pounds, Violet. I'm stunned," he said, walking over and sitting down on the coffee table.

"That's good? It doesn't sound good. You were lifting three freaking fifty."

"Well, considering you're probably what, like ninety-five pounds soaking wet?"

"Um, try a hundred and five," she said with a grin. It made her feel good that he seemed impressed with her.

"That's unbelievable. It's amazing that you lifted more than you weigh and this is the first time you've ever done this, I assume?"

"Well, yeah, I've never done this before, but, you lift more than you weigh."

"Yes, but I've been doing this for years. And not to be sexist, but I'm a man."

"Whatever, who cares? You sexist," she said, pulling her hood back up and walking over to the couch. "I'm gonna call Amber and let her know I'm alright."

Roman shrugged, and walked back to the weight bench and loaded the weights back on the bar. He lay back onto the bench and started lifting again.

It was strange listening to her recount what had happened the night before to her friend. She went into far more detail with Amber than she had with him. It was sort of surprising to what length she went into detail describing the scenario actually. She told every nuance of the entire exchange from start to finish. He thought it was funny how she was lying on her stomach kicking her feet back and forth like she was Gidget or something. He expected her to be twirling her hair and blowing bubbles too. Was that what teenage girls did? He'd never really been around one. His image was entirely based on *Gidget*, having watched that one with his mother. She loved Sally Field.

He finished his reps and sat up. His body was wet with sweat,

so he gestured that he was going to take a shower and walked o
of the room to his bedroom to get clean clothes. He undressed
the bathroom and started thinking again about the dream she'd h;
the night before. He'd been thinking about it all morning. T
dream had to mean something, but what? He grew more and mo
furious and confused the more he tried to understand the image
and words. Then he thought about the fact that she could lift
much weight. It had been clear she could lift more but had gott
bored of it and stopped. She definitely seemed like the kind
person who quit something once it became uncomfortable
boring. He stepped into the shower relishing the cold water. H
lathered himself up, his mind wandering to the vision of her
those pink undergarments. *Stop.*

He turned the water off and quickly toweled himself, g
dressed, then walked his dirty clothes back to the room ai
performed his usual ritual of folding and placing them in tl
hamper. He walked back to the living room. She was sitting on tl
edge of the couch with her boots on and her keys in her hand.
strange sadness fell over him for a brief moment as he walked
the kitchen to get a drink of water.

"I'm gonna go out and get us something to eat," she sai
walking over to him and leaning against him resting her hea
against his arm.

"Okay," he said, putting his arm around her loosely and guzzle
the last of his water. "Seriously, are you feeling better today?" I
asked, and looked down at her. His lips were wet, a thin mustach
of water adhering to his unshaved upper lip. God, she loved tha
She licked her own lips and looked away from his.

"I guess. I've been avoiding certain subjects in my head.
know I need to talk about things though," she said, and walke
away. "Or at least think about them."

"Well, whenever you want to, I'll be here," he reassured her.

"I know." She turned around to smile at him. "I'll be back in
little bit." She opened the door and walked out then stopped an
turned around. "Am I overextending my welcome?" she aske
concerned by her constant intrusion on his life.

"No." A slight, but warm smile came to his lips, then he dran
the rest of the water in his second glass. He thought she looke

tired. There was no way she was dealing with all the crap that had happened, but he couldn't blame her for avoiding any of it. He was not one to judge where avoidance was concerned. Avoidance was a good thing. He watched as she closed the door, then walked over to the phone and dialed as he pulled up a chair and sat down.

"Yes?" the voice melted on the other end.

"Mylori?" he asked, surprised that she'd answered.

"Yes." Her voice was sultry and low. The way she drew out the sibilant and let the words flow from her tongue was seductive and unnerving because it still caused a reaction in his body that he didn't want or appreciate.

"I'm surprised."

"I've probably used this machine twice since its invention. I'm disappointed you aren't calling for me, Roman." Her voice was so even and deliberate, it was mesmerizing.

"I'm sorry," he answered, having been drawn in by her. He remembered the fight he and Violet had over Mylori a few days prior. It bothered him to think he'd been so almost clinical towards Mylori. She met a need, nothing more. The idea didn't make him feel very good about himself.

"Brother is occupied with something young and cute."

He felt the anger building in him again. His disgust for the way in which Lux operated, and the fact that he was attempting this with Violet, infuriated him. "Maybe you can answer my questions then?" he said impatiently. Remembering what they were took away any sense of guilt he felt for using her.

"Roman, I will try, but I am not my brother."

"What's going on with these dreams?" he said bluntly, getting straight to the point.

"Dreams?"

"Mylori, you know what I'm talking about."

"I do, Roman, but I'm not sure it is my place to speak on such things."

"Why are you singling her out? What's going on?" His voice was growing increasingly more agitated. "What was the point of you telling me she needs help and then harassing her?"

"I have done no such thing, dear. Lux is your perpetrator. I don't particularly even care. She's just another human girl to me."

Roman stopped for a second, gathering his thoughts. She *did*
care, that was an absolute truth. Mylori cared for no human, b
why did Lux? "Well, she's been having these dreams for a whi
since even before I came to this town. So what the fuck is h
game?"

"There aren't any games, dear."

"So there's no real trouble then? Nothing and no one I need
worry about hurting her besides Lux?"

"There is trouble, that is true."

"Why is she being singled out by him, Mylori?" He explode
slamming his hand down onto the kitchen counter.

She laughed seductively, deep in her throat. She knew Roma
so well. He must be so confused and frustrated. It amused he
"He has some affection for the girl," she said flippantly, bored.

"What is this about, Mylori? Tell me." He wanted her
confide in him, to be his confidant now? Even though he ha
rejected her a thousand times. It infuriated him that not only we
they fucking with Violet, but also with him, by proxy. What wa
the point of bringing him to this town under the guise he wa
supposed to protect her, only for them to fuck with her?

"Lux has no affection for anyone," Roman said angrily. "F
only cares about himself. So what the fuck is going on?"

"Tsk Tsk, Roman. Such proletariat argot." She laughed wi
arrogance, entertained by his anger.

"Fuck you, Mylori," Roman growled.

Mylori was snapped out of her amusement then. "Just as yc
have known hundreds of us, we have known thousands of you
Her voice was a controlled hiss.

"What the hell is that even supposed to mean? That's not a
answer. Was he here before I arrived? Did he see her then?"

"Like a billion buzzing bees humming in the hive. I hear the
buzzing and buzzing and buzzing... relentlessly buzzing, buzzin;
buzzing. We are the keeper. You are the bee. We pluck one littl
bee at a time from the honey comb, separate it from the hive, drin
the honey from the belly. Drink the marrow from the bone."

"What are you talking about?" He was tired of her riddles. Sh
always spoke in riddles. It was annoying as fuck.

"We drink the honey, and the buzzing stops."

"Why is he attracted to her? Tell me." He wanted answers, and he was tired of her gibberish.

"Because this little bee can sting. She is a queen." The cadence of her voice was sing songy, rhythmic, sultry.

"Tell me what that means." He pled with her, wanting answers instead of more questions.

"You need to talk to Lux. He is occupied," she said despondently, and hung up.

Roman sat perfectly still listening to the dial tone for several seconds, then heard Violet fumbling with the door. So he hung up the phone and walked over to help her. She was sopping wet, soaked to the bone and looking like a drowned rat. Roman took the bags of food from her and set them on the coffee table as she peeled her soaking sweatshirt off and quickly unlaced her boots, kicking them off beside the door. She had goose bumps from the cold steady rain that had wet her through to her tank top.

"Hey," she said, smiling at him. "Breakfast was over so I got us cheeseburgers and fries. I just love greasy food first thing in the morning."

"Me too," he said, forcing a smile for her to cover his frustration from the phone call. It took all his energy to make his face relax. The last thing he needed was to have to explain his black mood to her when he honestly had no fucking clue what was going on. And besides that, what would he tell her even if he did know? He let out a long, slow breath and sat down on the couch. Violet handed him a large soda, which he took gladly. His throat was parched. Maybe some caffeine would help him focus a little so he could figure this mess out. God, he just wanted to know what the hell was going on, what he needed to do to keep her safe... who the fuck he even needed to protect her from.

He took a sip from the straw. The carbonation burned going down his throat. He looked over at her, tank top soaked through. He had to force his eyes away. "You look cold."

"It's kinda cold outside, but nice. The rain is peaceful, even though it's pouring." She picked up her pop and took a drink, then sat it back down on the coffee table as she slid to the floor across from him. "You know, I love eating. I know that's a silly thing to say, but um, I kind of lost track of that."

"You should eat. It gives you strength. I mean, maybe eatin like this isn't your best option, but at least it's food." He smiled a her. "You can get one of my shirts or something if you're cold."

"You think I look disgusting, don't you?" she asked, completel out of the blue. It wasn't a statement she made because she wa feeling overly negative or anything, she was simply stating th obvious. It was pretty clear that he didn't find her appealing at al There had been a few occasions he'd mentioned her being to skinny, and judging by his lack of interest in her as far a relationships went, it was fairly obvious that he must think she wa ugly or something. Despite her mantra of them *just being friend* realistically, spending so much time with him had caused her t have feelings for him. His rejection hurt.

He stopped chewing his food for a second, and looked at he like she was an idiot. "Don't be stupid."

She shrugged her shoulders, standing up, then trotting off to hi bedroom. Roman's eyes trailed after her, dumbfounded. It wasn' a matter of him not finding her attractive. It was a matter of neve allowing himself to view her that way. Of course she wa attractive, beautiful actually.

Walking over to his closet, she noticed the shirt he'd worn t the Ox Roast was hanging front and center, so she took that on and pulled it on over her wet head. The sleeves hung way past he fingertips and fell to her knees, so she rolled the sleeves up an jogged back to the living room and plunked herself back down o the floor.

"I'm not being stupid, I know I look bad. I need to gain weigh you told me that. Thanks for the shirt." She winked at him an took a big bite of her sandwich and then shoved some fries into he already full mouth.

"Well, I certainly never said that you're disgusting. You're nc disgusting. And you're welcome."

"Well, I'm no Mylori. And remember, I'm *nothing special*, she teased him.

He leaned back into the couch and shook his head. "Wh would you want to be? Mylori I mean—not special—of cours you're special. I told you that was bullshit after I said i remember?"

Hearing his own words thrown back at him made him realize just how big of an asshole he'd been to her that day. He had said some cruel things in haste that had obviously affected her for her to bring it back up.

"She's fucking beautiful, you dolt. Yeah, *special ed*."

"She's alright," he said dismissively, shrugging his shoulders. "No you're not special ed., moron."

"Come on, Roman. You don't be stupid. And you said it yourself."

"Whatever, she's beautiful enough to look at, but who cares? Let's not talk about Mylori." Mylori was truly a subject he wasn't interested in discussing. "And I didn't mean it when I said that you were nothing special. I was angry. How many times do I need to apologize?"

"Let's talk about her brother," Violet said with a grin, completely taking him by surprise. "And it's good to know you don't believe what you said, so stop apologizing. I won't throw it in your face again, okay?"

"You want to talk about him, after that dream you had last night?" He was confused by this girl and was content to drop the other subject.

"It was just a dream, freaky and scary, but just a dream. Anyway, I figured it out."

"The dream?"

"Yeah, it's simple. I depend on you for a lot of support now, so it's natural for me to worry about you not being there to save me."

"That makes sense I guess. What about the Lux part though?" He was interested in finding out how she justified him attacking her.

"Well, the night of Dory and Malinda's party he showed up while they were drinking each other's blood. You and I talked about vampires. I like vampires. There you have it." She seemed calm now, almost lighthearted about the whole thing.

"But you were terrified last night?" It would be easy to dismiss dreams about vampires for someone who didn't know of their existence. The frightening thing was that they did, and Lux was a vampire, and dreams that pointed that out didn't happen without a reason. The truth would come out, one way or the other, and he would do everything in his power to be damn good and ready.

"Well, of course, because vampires are supposed to be scary. Plus, maybe I'm a little afraid of him because I have the hots for him, and the last guy I had the hots for sucked the life out of me?"

"Well, you seem to have the whole thing figured out." He was surprised at how easily she'd explained it all away. But then he supposed that if he had no idea what the reality was, his rational thought would take over too.

"So anyway, have you heard from him?"

"No, *honeybee*, I haven't."

"Honeybee? That's cute."

"Yeah, really cute," he said, as he finished his sandwich.

***

Violet and Roman spent the next few days hanging out. She never ran into Mark, but he had sat outside her house waiting for her. Amber had advised her when it was safe to come home to get some clothes and whatnot. Violet hadn't spent much time at home at all, she just didn't want to deal with him. They were all pretty surprised Mark hadn't figured out where Roman lived, given the proximity to her house and the smallness of the town. It wouldn't take a rocket scientist to figure out where the giant with the long black hair lived, if Mark had truly wanted to find out. Perhaps he did know, it wasn't as if Violet or Roman had sat at the window looking for him. Neither cared.

Roman was never afraid of anyone, certainly not Mark. He'd seen enough death in his life to stop fearing it for himself, but he was concerned for Violet. So he stayed around her as much as possible. He still hadn't been able to finagle an answer from Lux that he really, wholeheartedly, believed. He refused to trust that the man had nothing to do with Violet's dream, or whatever it was that had called him to Mantua in the first place. Lux had to be behind it somehow. Obviously. There was a reason Roman was here that Lux knew but wasn't sharing.

She had finally convinced him to go out and do something

besides their usual late night jaunts into Kent to Taco Bell or their long walks in various locales. He'd been particularly fond of the "Bike and Hike" trails that seemed to run from one town to the next. Miles and miles of endless trails cutting through the Cuyahoga National Forest. Violet's legs were shot from all the walking, but she felt good. She finally had someone in her life who enjoyed walking as much as she did, and he never complained about it. In fact, it was her who usually had to whine about how tired she was to get him to stop.

So, she'd gotten dressed in her usual "going out" clothes and coerced Roman into going to a different bar that she and her friends sometimes frequented in downtown Kent. The crowd was usually comprised of college kids, so they were of the "higher education" ilk and tended to leave her and her weirdo friends alone, for the most part, save for the drunken frat boy on occasion. She'd never worried about it before because she'd had Mark with her for protection. Typically men didn't harass her for being "weird". Attractive girls get away with that shit a little more than men. Sometimes Randy, Mose, and Steve would get messed with, but rarely did her and Amber. So, unless they were trying to fuck her, and that had never happened when Mark was with her, she was mostly just left her alone. Even drunk frat boys had known better than to push his buttons. And tonight she had Roman. What fool in their right mind would fuck with her with him around?

The bar was packed with the usual crowd of college kids and other fellow miscreants. They sat in a booth and picked at a basket of various deep fried goodies. Roman drank beer and Violet her Diet Coke. The reason she and her friends frequented this particular bar was because of the cheap food and drinks coupled with the unlikelihood of being harassed. They got fucked with a lot when they went most places. People always seemed to hate what they didn't get, and people in exurban Ohio didn't get their whole goth/punk vibe.

As soon as Violet left the table to go to the restroom, Roman looked at the two men who had been watching them since he and Violet sat down. He tipped his beer to them and then took a drink, then turned and looked straight ahead again.

He saw them approaching and kept looking forward as they slid into the booth across from him.

"Hello," the man said, some sort of heavy eastern European accent. He was average height, muscular build, with jet black hair and eyes to match. A thick scar ran across his forehead and through one eyebrow to continue down his cheek.

The other man was taller, maybe close to Roman's height. Muscular, stoic with long auburn hair that hung loose. His eyes were piercing amber, penetrating. His nose had been broken many times, and long ago.

"I know what you are," Roman said, casually.

"And you're not afraid?" the man said, a sneer of a smile.

Roman chuffed. "If you knew what I was, you wouldn't ask."

"What are you?" the man asked, his head tipped to the side, eyes honed.

"The fact that you don't know is very telling. Either you are young or just stupid."

The man said something to the other one in Czech. Roman didn't speak Czech, but he recognized the language. "What is she?"

"Mine," Roman answered plainly.

"She smells of old blood."

Roman's brow was drawn for the briefest moment. "What are you doing here?" His words were full of threat.

"We ask the questions," the man said with arrogance.

Roman took another drink from his bottle. "Your friend doesn't speak. Is he mute?"

The man laughed. "He doesn't speak English."

"How unfortunate for him."

"Why unfortunate?"

Roman smirked. "Because if you don't tell me what I want to know, and make it believable, I won't be killing you quickly."

"And what would you need information for, *upir*," the man said, grinning with razor teeth.

Roman leaned forward. "Why are you here?"

"Who are you to ask me anything? Who are you?"

Both men glared at him, eyes glistening, and yet neither of them seemed to understand how close they were to death. The only vampires that ever underestimated him were those who didn't

220

know who he was, or were too young and stupid to realize they could still die at the hands of a human.

The mute vampire shifted, his eyes darkening. "I am going to rip your throat out, and then fuck her until she dies."

Without thought Roman flew across the table, his hand latching onto the man's throat. He could feel his fingers sinking into the flesh, locking onto the windpipe and crushing it as the man flailed in shock. Roman stood and slammed the man to the ground, his head banging against the bar before falling to the floor. The other man leapt onto his back as Roman swung around, hooking him under his arm and slamming his fist into his jaw with a loud crack.

"Roman!" Violet called, rushing forward.

"Get out of here," the bouncers yelled, as they shoved Roman towards the door.

The other two men snarled and growled as they were also shoved towards the doors. The room was a cacophony of shrieks and cheers.

"Take it outside," another bouncer ordered, as he pushed Roman through the door.

Roman turned, his eyes ablaze and almost glowing green. He was breathing heavy, pacing like a stalking animal.

"Roman," Violet called again, shocked, her eyes tearing with concern. She had never seen him look like this. Even when he was fighting Mark he had never looked so feral.

He reached out, taking her hand and pulling her against him.

The other two men circled him as the bouncers stood there waiting to call the police if necessary. The taller man's throat was already turning black from Roman's crushing grip.

"Roman?" the shorter man said, his jaw too loose on its hinge.

"Vrah," the taller man said in comprehension as he looked at his cohort.

Their demeanor's changed. Roman glared, a promise, as the men backed away and then tore off so quickly they were nothing but a blur.

Violet squeaked and gripped Roman's hand. "Roman, who was that?" Violet asked, as he dragged her along behind him towards his car.

He was walking so fast she was having a hard time matching his long strides. The sky had opened up again for the fourth day in a row, crying heavy cold drops of rain. She put her hand to her eye, shielding them from the spattering onslaught.

"Nothing, they pissed me off," he said, slightly out of breath. His knuckles were throbbing and flayed open.

"Just pissed you off? Did they say something or what?" She yanked his arm forcing him to stop.

"I don't know," he answered gruffly, dragging her along again. He'd gotten no answers. Now he would have to track them down later.

"What happened?"

"Nothing."

Violet stopped walking, and Roman nearly yanked her arm from its socket from the stop in momentum. "Ouch," she said, taking her arm back and rotating her shoulder.

He halted immediately, turning to make sure she was okay. He reached out, taking her shoulder in his hand and feeling the joint as he rotated it..

He looked down at her. It was painfully obvious by the look on her face she was concerned by his actions, but there was no way he'd tell her what had transpired. "It's not a big deal, they just said something that pissed me off, so I shut them the fuck up."

"Uh, you more than just shut them up, honey," she said, grinning from ear to ear. She was overwhelmed by what she'd witnessed. He had put two rather large grown men to the ground in a matter of seconds. It had been pretty hot watching him stand over them like some sort of Viking warrior or something.

"Yeah, what can I say?"

"That was, um, hot," she said, laughing to take some of the seriousness away from her statement.

"Oh, shut up," he said, rolling his eyes and shaking his head.

"I'm serious. That was exciting. If I was, you know, into you, I'd be all over you right now."

"Whatever, weirdo." He felt her shoulder again, holding her arm out and feeling the joint.

"I'm okay," she said, laughing slightly. "But seriously, what the hell was all that?"

"I got into a fight," Roman said, and shrugged.

"No shit, Sherlock. What the hell about? And don't tell me they said something that pissed you off."

Roman sniggered and looked around the parking lot. He knew the men were nowhere around, since they finally figured out who he was, but he needed to be safe.

"They were harassing a woman." Not entirely untrue.

"And you crushed his windpipe for that?"

"It shut him up," Roman said, and shrugged again.

"There's blood on your hands," she said, taking his hand and checking it over. "Does it hurt? It looks painful." His knuckles were split open. "Roman, there's blood under your nails?"

He remembered his fingers sinking into the man's neck.

"Holy cow, were you going to rip his throat out?" she asked, still looking over his hands.

"Yes."

Violet looked up at him, her eyes sort of wide and confused. And then he smiled, so she would think he was only kidding.

"That was scary," she said.

"I'm sorry," he said, gripping her hand and guiding her back toward his car. "Come on, we're getting soaked." She had no idea just how scary it could have been under different circumstances. He had a lot to think over tonight.

"Seriously though, that was pretty hot."

"Whatever."

"I'm just sayin'"

He looked down at her out of the corner of his eye and shook his head.

"Well, what did they say to make you so mad?"

"Just some stuff to some girl sitting there at the bar. It's no big deal, V." He was covering up the reality of the situation. More trash to clean up later in a not-so-public place.

"Cool," she said, looking down at the ground and watching her boots shuffle through the muddy gravel.

"Yep, I'm super cool, aren't I?" he said mockingly.

"Well, yeah. I think so." She slapped his back.

Roman shook his head and dropped her hand as they got to his car. He unlocked her door and waited for her to get in, scanning the night around them. She slid onto the seat and he shut the door, then walked around to the other side. Violet reached over unlocking his door for him.

"So, I guess we won't be going back there for a while?" she said, looking over at him with a sly smile as she wiped the rain from her face

"Whatever," he said, returning her smile nervously. It was weird that she found beating the fuck out of people hot, but if she did, then he supposed she was with the right person. Of course she shouldn't be finding anything he did hot, and they really weren't ever going to be with each other. He looked over at her. She was looking at him with a strange twinkle in her eye.

"Strange girl."

"Strange boy."

11. THE DUTCH OVEN

The night was quiet. The picnic table her dad had built made a nice lawn chair in the backyard. She always laid out here at night staring up at the sky, had for years. The fresh coat of gray paint she had applied at the beginning of summer was already peeling from the heavy rains they'd had recently. It peeled like grease when she raked her fingernails across it. For whatever reason it had never dried right. She must've used the wrong kind of paint or something. Her dad would have told her to stop picking at it, but just like nail polish, or fuzz on a blanket, she couldn't help but pick at it.

The damp of the wood felt cool and sticky against her body, the boards nice and hard. A faint, silent breeze kissed her bare arms and face. The trees swayed gently as they danced against the bright stars of the night sky, hiding the moon intermittently with their rustling branches. She could see a thousand stars out here in the dark tonight.

Up and down the street, a few houses were dotted by a sparse few windows that were still aglow with that blue television-in-the-dark glow. People were still awake in some of these houses, and it made her wonder what they did during the day that allowed them to be up this late. Or maybe they were just sleeping with the television on? Maybe they couldn't stand the silence like she couldn't stand it.

She felt him approaching. Well, she assumed it was him by the thud of his heavy feet. Roman always made sure not to sneak up too quietly, knowing she'd freak out if she was startled. Everything had been calm lately, but it still paid to be cautious and it was rather careless of her to be out here in the dark alone.

But she couldn't help it. This was her favorite time of the year, her favorite time of night. She remained still, continuing to soak up every bit of this atmosphere that she could. She would file this away as one of those good moments when the world was right and good and calm. Life had been so chaotic that she was thankful for even a few moments of serenity.

Suddenly, like a full moon, his white face came into view hovering over her. His bright eyes caught the metallic shine of the chain around her neck. It was the chain he'd given her, the long silver necklace with a heavy polished silver heart. He had no idea how much that had meant to her, what it symbolized to her, and how many times it had kept her from crumbling in these last few weeks, in those quiet moments when she was all alone. The weight of his heart around her neck was a constant reminder of something good.

"Hey kitten," he said, and pushed the loose hair that had fallen across her face, his fingers barely touching her.

He'd gotten much more tactile with her since they'd started spending so much time together these last few days. The awkwardness that used to be there between them physically was now mostly gone. *Mostly*. He still tensed up in certain situations like when she sat too close wearing too little, or said something overtly sexual that wasn't just a random statement. He'd even started calling her little pet names, *kitten*, for example. It was her particular favorite because it seemed so unlikely coming from his mouth.

She smiled and sat up moving her legs aside and resting her feet on the bench. "Glad you're here," she said with a yawn and timid smile. Being alone with him had started giving her butterflies, even though she tried not to feel them because she knew he just didn't see her like that. She didn't have any right feeling butterflies around him.

"You're cute, Violet." He sat down on the table beside her leaning back on the heels of his hands and looking up into the night sky.

They'd grown so much more comfortable around each other these last few weeks, and especially since she'd been staying with him. Things with Mark had died down so it had seemed like a good idea to get out of his hair some and come back home, even though she really hadn't wanted to at all.

Roman was getting used to being around her all the time, and spending time with her friends. It wasn't normal for him, being a part of anyone's life. It was still disconcerting for him at times, the reliance on someone, her reliance on him, but it was a comfort he'd never had—at least not since his mom died.

There were still so many secrets between them. It made him feel guilty that he had to hide so much from her, but he also knew it was in her best interest for her not to know the truth. It would serve no purpose for her to know the reality of his existence or the reason he was here. He also still knew he'd leave eventually, once whatever had drawn him here was taken care of, and he knew she'd be safe. But he was enjoying his present company and situation just a little more than he wished. He wasn't looking forward to moving on, because he knew it was going to hurt her, and he had to admit it was going to bother him too.

"It's nice tonight. I don't think there'll be rain," he said, running his hand through her hair and getting it out of her eyes.

"Yeah, I think it'll stay clear all night. I'm so tired of rain," she said, tucking her small hands between her knees. "The moon's so clear tonight. See Debbie Harry?"

"Debbie Harry?"

"Yeah, you know, Blondie? See how the moon looks like Debbie Harry?" she said, pointing up at the bright orb and tilting her head. "Kind of look at it, but not, like when you're looking at the Pleiades."

Roman furrowed his brow and looked up at the brilliant moon. "I never noticed that before." He lay back on the table, placing his hands beneath his head.

The chill of the dead summer was making her feel cold. The change was so slight it was almost intangible. But she noticed, just like she noticed the slightly different sun angle and vague drop in humidity. It wasn't something she perceived with her mind, but her body. It was like one day it was summer, the next fall. Like a switch had been flipped on the seasons.

The end of summer was always a weird time of the year. It signified a little death of sorts, dying leaves, barren, harvested fields, back to school and all that. And everyone was back to school now, kids, college students, some of her friends. And she was doing nothing. She'd be twenty-one in a few months. She could do anything she wanted, or nothing at all. This time last year she'd still had her parents with her. The thought disturbed her. How could so much change in twelve short months?

They sat in silence for long moments, absorbing the lushness of the nighttime. It was just so peaceful, so still besides the rustling of the fading leaves.

"Let's go," he said, leaning forward and tapping her bare arm.

Roman was allowing himself to really look at her, to study her features, her expressions. Before he hadn't truly allowed himself the luxury. Yes, he had always studied her to a degree, because that's what he did in every situation, but he was really *looking* now. He was able to read her fairly easily in some ways. Like everyone he came in contact with, he learned them, their movements, mannerisms, and every little detail about their appearance. That attention to detail had kept him alive for many years. But with her, he just wanted to know her. It felt foreign. still made him uncomfortable that he craved it that much. His father would be so disappointed in him. He'd been taught to stay unattached. *Hypocrite.*

She looked different tonight somehow. Her long black hair was tangled with a few thin braids and the wilted yellow mums she'd picked from her mother's garden earlier. Her dad always bought yellow mums for her mom every year, and she'd continued the tradition. Her bangs were short and choppy, like a four year old had cut them, which was the point, he assumed. Her eyes seemed a little darker blue tonight, and full of some kind of energy. Her eyelashes were long, like thin, wispy spider legs, fanning out from her eyes.

When she smiled, her face was open and satiated with happiness, her lips full and red. When she was sad, a small dimple on her chin appeared, giving her emotion away immediately. She was a walking mirror of emotions. Of course he had noticed that the very first night. He found this captivating from time to time— when he allowed himself to be captivated. It was amazing to him that her face could capture so wholly what she was feeling. He had never known another human so naked.

And yet in other ways she was fathomless. She could shut

herself down so wholly when she wanted to, and he had no understanding of what she must be thinking. It was frustrating, because he found himself yearning to know what she was thinking. Wanting to know how she felt.

"I need my bag," she said, hopping off the table and turning back to look into his deep green eyes.

His face was so perfect. *He* was perfect. His tall, powerfully built body towered over her and made her feel so delicate and protected. She loved feeling so absolutely safe when they were together. Nothing could touch her when he was with her. In the past Mark had made her feel protected, but she had always feared him on some level. There was no fear with Roman, only comfort. She had been forced to be strong for too long. Feeling safe meant everything to her now.

His eyes were dark green with gold flecks. She had noticed that just recently, always being a bit too hesitant to look him so firmly in the eyes. But she had finally done that, and in that split second of really seeing him, her heart had felt like it had exploded inside her chest.

She didn't know why she felt so shy around him sometimes. There had never really been a shy bone in her body. But Roman made her feel insecure sometimes. Certainly she wasn't good enough for him. It wasn't that he had ever made her feel that way on purpose, it was her own insecurities who made that decision for herself.

He was so good. So kind. She had seen him do nothing but treat people with respect. It was enviable. She hadn't always been a very nice person. Though she felt shy sometimes, it was mostly easy for her to talk to him. She could be as open and honest with him as she could Amber, more so even because she never had to worry about hurting his feelings. Amber was always too affected by Violet's pain. And there had been so much of it these last months. Roman let her ramble, let her open herself up. He understood her loneliness and grief.

But sometimes, the way he looked past the surface of what she said and did made her feel so naked and insecure. She knew she couldn't fake anything around him. He saw through all her facades and masks, and he was quick to point them out, though he never tried to change her and was never judgmental. She liked that abou him.

And then other times, he was completely clueless when it cam to reading her. Like now. He had no idea how much she wante him, did he? No idea. It wasn't right of her to feel how she felt, s she hid it. No, he didn't know everything about her. It should b so obvious, shouldn't it? But he didn't get it, because he was mal and somewhat emotionally inept, he had told her that himsel Maybe he could read everyone else in the world but himself? O maybe he just knew and didn't care.

She had never been very bold when it came to pursuin relationships in the past. For all her outward arrogance aroun most of her friends, she was unsure of herself, and felt completel unworthy of being loved in any real capacity. Mark had pursue her relentlessly. And it felt like he was still somewhere out there i the dark. Her lack of confidence had been one of the main reason she had made such poor decisions—or no decisions at all— regarding the men she dated. Avoidance and acquiescence ha fared her well, maybe. If only she'd been able to say no, to n care about hurting feelings or making people mad, then thing could have been different. Being alone is better than being wit the wrong person. She knew that now. But as she looked Roman, the thought of being alone made her sick with fear.

Roman's nose was long and straight. She loved his nose. Hi profile was beautiful and reminded her of the Viking Gods she' read about. She pictured him in leather hides and wolf skins ridin a black horse through deep green fields and lush black forests wit his long horsehair flowing behind him in wavy streams. His ha was thick and coarse and curled slightly when it was humid outsid or wet. His lips were soft looking. She could picture it so clearl She'd had many daydreams about various scenarios late at nigh with him the viking god and he the valkyrie. It made her smil thinking about it. His lips. How would they feel against hers?

She looked at them now. All pink and smooth and lusciou When he smiled at her it made her feel like he cared about her, lik someone truly cared about her. He could kill her with his smile i she let him. She couldn't let him though, he didn't feel for her th way she was feeling towards him. If he had to say it to her o loud, it would destroy her. So she'd keep her feelings to herself. She bit her lip and looked back into his eyes.

What was he thinking as he looked at her, neither of them saying a word? She had announced that she was going to get her bag and hadn't moved, held in place by the magnet that was him. God, he was so beautiful all dressed in black, with his long hair catching the moon's glow.

He always wore the same thing: black pants, black shirt, and black boots. The only time she'd seen him in anything different was the time he was wearing just his plaid pajama bottoms and no shirt at all. *That was a pleasant memory.*

She had felt weird seeing him bare-chested. It had embarrassed her even though she hadn't shown it. It was ironic considering he'd seen her naked, but she put no thought into herself being naked. Skin was skin. Big deal. She ran around in very little all the time. Not because she was a skank or an exhibitionist, she just liked not wearing much. But seeing him half naked? That was difficult to see and be maintain any level of cool on her part.

He had to know how stunning he was? Maybe he was as clueless as she was? It had never really occurred to her that she might be attractive to him. Not really. It didn't matter that others told her so, even on the days she looked in the mirror and thought she looked *okay* she still felt ugly and not good enough.

Finally Violet realized she better move it along. It was already weird that she had just stood there staring. But he hadn't said anything either? Something felt different.

He watched her walk up to the house. She looked so cute in her black pleated skirt and black zip up hoodie. He was disgusted with himself for even knowing what a *hoodie* was, they'd always been sweatshirts to him. He had spent way too much time around her and Amber lately learning things no man like him ought to know. Like the difference between tights and leggings, flat irons and crimping irons. He shuddered remembering those conversations, feeling less masculine having just been a witness.

He would do anything to protect her.

The thought kept coming to the forefront. The ferocity he felt at the idea of her being hurt, like he'd seen so many others hurt throughout his lifetime, was frightening and confusing. He continuously fought the urge to smother her with protection. He wanted her to stay with him all the time. Those last few days of her being with him 24/7 had given him peace of mind, to a degree. If she was always at his side, then he could always protect her. But if she was on her own, anything could happen, at any time, and he might not get to her in time to stop it.

Roman leaned forward, elbows on knees, and cradled his head in his hands. What the fuck was he doing? Something was taking over him. He'd never been around a girl so... cute, it was the only word to come to mind... in his life. He had to fight the urge to crush her to him. To pinch her cheeks and bear hug her. It was hard being so near her and not really touching her.

She looked as adorable to him when she was angry as she did when she smiled and acted silly. It took all his energy not to laugh at her when she pouted. Yes, he wanted to squeeze her mercilessly like she was the cutest stuffed animal on the planet. But instead he resorted to *big brother mode*. He groaned out loud with his own frustration.

He would always protect this girl, always. And his stomach turned over at the thought he'd just been thinking about pinching and squeezing her. *What the hell?* He wouldn't even give the *other* brief thoughts he'd had acknowledgement enough to put them together. Having her so close, pressed against him, had been absolute torture.

He had to find out what was going on with Lux. There had to be answers. It wasn't like him not to know what was going on after this much time. He had never slacked off so much in his life and she was by far the most important person he had ever protected. He needed her safe. Was he subconsciously avoiding the situation because the longer he didn't know what was going on the longer he could stay with her? No, he couldn't allow his thoughts to go there. She was his duty. Nothing more.

Besides the occasional run in with a random vampire here and there, he still knew nothing. Was he slipping? Was having feelings for someone, even just a friend, causing him to lose his edge? This was not the time for that to happen, especially not this time. His job meant more now than it ever had.

She walked upstairs to her bedroom and flipped the light on

The room was still a mess, half-cleaned, it seemed worse than it had before. She shook her head and grabbed her leather bag and slung it over her shoulder, checking for the keys and cell phone, and then walked back downstairs. They wouldn't be gone that long so there was no need to shut down all the lights. She locked the door and jogged over to him.

"God, you're cute," he said involuntarily.

She smiled and looked down at the ground. "Come on, doof." She couldn't help the smile she tucked away before reaching over and squeezing his wrist.

They walked to the Dutch Oven. It was a well-known stop in their town. All the young people hung out there, as there wasn't anything else to do, and the never ending coffee and soda was cheap. All the locals ate at the all-u-can-eat *Friday Fish Frys* and truckers stopped on their way to the "Big City", which was either Cleveland, Youngstown, or Akron. *Pissburg* wasn't far either. Man she hated the Steelers.

The letters were falling off the marquee and it was a joke with all the kids to climb up and rearrange the letters and see how long it took the owner to notice. The last really good one was "all-u-can-eat tuna tacos". Not very funny at all really, but when there's nothing else going on and you're sixteen you'll laugh at anything. The sign lasted all of three hours. Besides the name of the place was joke enough. Had the owners not understood what a Dutch Oven was? Someone needed to look at the Urban Dictionary online.

And this is where she'd met Mark only a few nights back.

The building had been slightly renovated at the beginning of summer. In other words, the peeling gray paint was painted over with tan and the parking lot was re-paved. They had even shampooed the carpet inside. Fine Luxury Dining.

He pulled the heavy glass door open and waved her in. She walked to her usual spot. The crowd was small tonight, only a few of the regular drunks sobering up before going home. Every last one of them had disgusting plates of eggs and sausage and sludge-like coffee. Violet really didn't get how that would sit well in an alcohol soaked stomach. It seemed to her that would guarantee a worshipping session with the Porcelain God.

No one looked up as the two made their way to the back of th
restaurant. It just went to prove how used them the town ha
gotten, because two years prior all hell broke loose when she an
her friends entered this hole. It was a surprise that Roman neve
got fucked with, though it was fairly obvious given his size and th
darkness in his eyes that picking a fight with him would be futile
But drunk assholes often liked to test a tough guy.

Mark had been goaded umpteen times until people finall
learned, via broken teeth and blackened eyes, that he wasn't one t
fuck with. Poor Randy had been threatened with scissors one time
Everyone in the joint had felt like he needed a haircut and th
waitress was only too happy to supply the shears.

What the fuck was wrong with people, seriously? Why woul
anyone get angry that someone looked different? It didn't comput
in her head. At any rate, she was glad they left Roman alone. N
doubt he could handle himself, she'd witnessed that firsthand, bu
it would make her feel like shit if anyone ever tried to sta
something with him because she loved him. Oh wait, what
Where did that thought come from? She shook her thoughts an
brought them back to present.

The floral wallpaper was greasy, and upon further investigatio
contained many food stains and meal remnants. Flecks of drie
food intermingled with the goldish leaves and vines, adding som
nice texture. Gross. The walls were decorated with cheap prints c
tacky forest scenes and country vistas. Still, this place wa
comfortable. It was home.

"Coffee please," she said, pulling herself across the woo
veneer bench.

"Yea, coffee for me too. And a slice of apple pie," he saic
pulling himself in beside her.

They sat in the usual booth back in the corner. Everyone kne
this was the "weirdo spot" and no one dare sit there. Not tha
anyone would want to anyway.

"You should eat something," he said, reaching in his jacket fc
the folded magazine.

"I ate earlier," she said, taking the magazine from him an
opening it, disregarding his suggestion. She knew he was righ
she'd discussed it with him before, but who cared? She wasn

234

hungry.

He grinned, and pulled the magazine back towards him so they could both see it. "What did you eat?" he asked, leaning into her so that he could read the opposite page.

She loved his smell. It was leather and soap and that man smell (whatever that is).

"Um, chocolate cake and ice cream?" she winced, knowing she was about to be scolded.

"Violet, you need to eat real food," he said, leaning back and looking her in the eyes.

"Well, it was left over from when Amber made it the other day. It couldn't go to waste." She smiled, pouring on the charm.

"Hm, you need to eat like vegetables and fruit and meat or something. You can't live off junk."

"Okay, *apple pie*." She pinched his arm.

He snickered and looked back at the magazine he had picked up from the counter up front, trying to ignore her obvious good point. "Yeah, well, I ate something earlier," he said, trying not to grin.

"Yeah, like pizza or something."

"Do as I say and not as I do."

"Yeah, that's what I thought." She grabbed the magazine and took it back to read.

"So, where is everyone?" he said, looking around the room. None of her friends were there, which seemed odd to him considering she'd gone on and on about how "everyone" came here. He expected to see the huge gaggle of misfits he usually saw when he came in.

"I don't know. I think they were going to some club. Some band is playing."

"And we're not there why?" he said, pouring three packets of sugar into his black coffee. He noticed the oily iridescent sheen on the top of the drink and sneered, taking a big sip anyway.

"I don't know, cuz I'm tired of watching stupid pseudo punk bands? I mean, yeah, you don't need much musical talent to play punk, but at least be able to tune your fucking guitar."

"I don't even listen to music and I can recognize how bad some of that crap is. But we could have at least had a drink and had some fun or something."

"Not twenty-one remember? I don't drink. And since when ar
you interested in having fun?"

"Well, *I* could have had a drink," he said with a smirk. Really
he'd just wanted to scope things out and see if anything unusua
was going on.

"You can drink at home," she said, disregarding the notion.

He reached across the table for the silver cream container. H
was sure the cream was likely curdled, but he poured some in hi
coffee anyway and watched the cloud swirl in the dark oily roas
At least it wasn't lumpy.

"So anyway, I guess it's nice to just be here with you." He too
another big gulp of the drink.

A smile spread wide across her face that she tried hiding b
tucking her chin into her chest. She squirmed and looked aroun
the room.

"We look retarded sitting on the same side of the booth. One c
us needs to move," Violet announced, looking up at him.

"Will you please stop saying retarded? And no we don't loo
retarded. We look like one of those obnoxious couples who can
stand being more than five inches apart." Really, he was jus
interested in being a wall between her and anyone who migl
approach.

"Yeah, like I said, *retarded*. Move," she said playfully an
shoved him with her arm.

He reluctantly moved to the other side of the booth, leanin
against the wall and stretching his leg across the bench. "Bette
princess?"

"Much," she said, looking back down at the article she'd bee
attempting to read since she sat down. She hadn't read more tha
five consecutive words. Concentrating on anything but him wa
difficult, especially when he was so close that she could feel th
heat radiating off of him and his scent was all in her head.

"Why are you so grumpy anyway?" he asked, as he tapped th
spoon on the side of his mug.

"My uterus is acting up," she muttered, not looking up from th
paper.

"Uh, uterus?" he asked, as he took another sip of his coffee.

"Yeah, you know, *cramps*?" She looked up with a mischievou

236

grin on her face. She thought it was funny whenever she touched on some sensitive girlie subject that made him antsy. Then again, most guys didn't like hearing about periods. Also funny. And stupid.

"Hm, well sorry to hear that. Take some aspirin?"

"Do you want me to get Reye's Syndrome?" She laughed, knowing he would have no clue what the fuck she was talking about. But any girl who had read an aspirin box would know.

"No?" he said, looking befuddled. It made her laugh harder.

He lifted his mug towards the waitress seated with a customer across the room. She was a heavy woman in her late forties, who looked like she was in her late fifties due to having lived a hard life. When Violet and her friends had first started coming here they were aware this woman despised them because they were "weird", but Roman had apparently instantaneously wrapped her around his finger.

"May as well leave the pot, Kim," he said, reading her name tag and giving her his nice man smile.

Violet looked up at him and watched intently. She loved watching him interact with others. The room seemed to bend towards him. He was a magnet. It wasn't just her that felt his pull.

"Okay, sweetie," the woman said, as she sat the pot down on the table.

"And my pie, Kim?"

"Oh lord, hold on there," the woman said, sauntering back to the glass pie carousel. She returned with a huge warm slice of homemade apple pie with a "complimentary" scoop of vanilla ice cream for her dear friend.

"Thanks, Kim. You're the best," he said, taking a big forkful of the pie.

Kim smiled at him and then at Violet, and walked back to her other customer. *Wow, that was a first.*

"You really know how to work it," she said, kidding him. "That's the first time that woman has ever looked at me kindly since I started coming here."

"You have to know how to make people feel good about themselves."

"To get what you want?"

237

"No, Violet, you make people feel good and you end up getting what you want as a reward for your kindness. Remember that."

"Hmm..."

"What do you mean 'hmm'?"

"I just wonder something."

"What's that?"

"Do you really like making people feel good? Or is it just some ruse you use to manipulate people? Like maybe it's not sincere and it's some sort of act?"

"I'm insulted by that," he said, taking another bite of pie. "I am sincere. Have I ever given you reason to believe I'm not sincere?"

"Well, no, not really, but how is it that you treat strangers with the same kindness you treat your friends? It seems like there'd be a difference. I mean, it makes sense to treat your friends so kindly but why strangers? How could you be sincere when you don't even know them? They could be evil for all you know, and you're being kind to them. Is that being sincere or being fake?"

"It's sincere because I'm a nice person. I was taught to treat people with respect regardless of who they are. Is that a bad thing?" He kept his eyes down, feeling annoyed and uncomfortable.

She realized she'd offended him. Yeah, what she'd said had been rude. "Well, no. I guess I just don't understand is all."

"You don't have to understand. You're just in a different place than I am."

He seemed to want to end this conversation. She looked back down at the magazine but wasn't reading it. What kind of different place was she in? Her parents had taught her to be polite too. But people had been so damned hateful towards her since she'd started dressing different that her attitude had pretty much gone from nice to fuck everyone until they prove themselves. Was that wrong? Why should she be nice to people who could potentially hurt her?

"Hey, Roman," Steve called, making his way to the back of the room.

Violet was happy that Steve finally seemed to accept Roman which was strange, but whatever. The last couple times they'd seen him he'd acted human and actually friendly. But there was still something off. She wasn't sure what it was but there was something.

Roman smiled and pulled his leg off the bench. "Hey, where've you guys been?"

Violet pulled her eyes away from the magazine to look up at Steve. She noticed Amber and Randy walking toward the restrooms.

"Be right back," she said, jumping out of the booth and hopping towards the bathroom.

"Gee, no hello? Okay," Steve said, sitting across from Roman in Violet's seat.

"Girls," Roman said, laughing. "Anyway, where were you guys?"

"We went to Mimi's and saw Randy's new band play."

"Oh, so V was right, some retarded punk band..."

Violet opened the restroom door. The room smelled strongly of toilet sanitizer. So much so that it nearly took her breath away. "What the fuck is that smell?" she asked, covering her nose.

"It wasn't me" Amber laughed from the stall. "That you, Vi?"

"Yeah, hey, how was the club?"

"Boring as ever. But Mark was there."

"Ugh, please tell me he left you alone."

"Well, pretty much. I mean, he asked where you were and stuff, but Randy sort of steered me away from him, thankfully." Amber walked out of the stall to the sink and began washing her hands.

Violet studied her friend as she was talking. Her face was heart shaped, and Violet thought she had the cutest eyebrows. Thin red-brown lines that arched smoothly over dark chestnut eyes. She always thought they looked like upside down smiles.

Amber looked particularly fetching tonight in her club gear, tight black leather pants and corset. Amber had always been like this; tall and hot. She'd never had a problem making friends or getting a guy. Violet had been jealous, but not in a mean way. The weird thing was that Amber had just recently told her that she had always been jealous of Violet for being "tiny and gorgeous". Those were Amber's words. That made no sense to Violet as she had always just felt like a scrawny cat.

"So the band was good?" Violet asked and leaned against the

wall.

"He tries," Amber said, and laughed. "Well, he's my boyfriend so I sort of have to say they were good, right?" She smiled, and leaned against the sink, turning to face Violet.

"Oh, I didn't even know it was Randy's band you were going to see?"

"Well, considering how many damn bands he starts and quits who can keep track? So, what'd you do tonight?"

"Well, I hung out on the picnic table stargazing for two hours then Roman came over. Then we came here. Nothing very thrilling."

"Well, probably better than the club. I mean, it's good you didn't come with Mark being there and all."

"Yes, plus I'd rather be around Roman, ya know?"

"Well, *duh*," Amber said, pulling the door open and walking back into the restaurant.

The girls walked back to the booth. Amber slid in beside Randy and Steve, and Violet took her spot next to Roman, as was customary of late.

"Aw look, here we are, retarded again," Roman teased her quietly, and shoved her with his shoulder.

She smiled and leaned into him, slouching down in the seat and resting her head back against the bench. He lifted his arm and let it fall over her shoulder.

"So, Steve and Randy were telling me that Mark was there tonight, Violet. Good thing you didn't want to go watch the *retarded* punk band," Roman said, grinning at the girl.

"Hey," Randy laughed, kicking her under the booth.

Violet smiled sheepishly and shrugged her shoulders. "Stop saying retarded, Roman." Roman laughed in response to his word being thrown back at him. "So, what about him?"

"Seriously, stop saying that. It's mean," Randy said.

Violet looked at him and furrowed her brow. She'd never meant it in a mean way, but yeah, he was right. "Duly noted," she said, resolving to quit joking like that. "But what about me ex dick of boyfriend?"

"I don't know. He seemed all weird, like he was on something. He just walked around asking everyone if you were going to show

240

up and wanted to know what you'd been up to blah blah blah. You know the typical stalker bullshit," Randy said, taking a sip of his Coke. "He was weird."

"Weirder than usual?" Violet asked stoically.

"Well, yeah, I mean weird like something was different or something."

"Who cares, he can go fuck himself," Violet said, trying to sound indifferent.

They all sort of laughed and changed the subject. Steve fidgeted, not wanting to talk about his friend at all. Roman noticed but thought little of it.

"So, why don't we go back home and watch movies, or bad TV, or something?" Amber said, bored of sitting.

"Sounds good to me," Roman said, sitting up, trying to stir Violet.

They put their money on the table and walked out.

"Thanks for the ice cream," Roman called to Kim, who was chatting up another regular.

They jumped in Randy's car. It was an old Lincoln boat from the seventies. The thing was a huge gray rust bucket. The muffler needed repair, and it was loud as it roared to life. Steve, Violet, and Roman sat in the back. The vinyl seats were cracked, and felt sharp and cold against the back of her legs. Randy and Amber rolled the windows down to avoid the inevitable carbon monoxide fumes and they sped off towards home.

She loved the way the heavy night air stuck to her skin. The wind made her nose stuffed up and her eyes feel heavy. She leaned into Roman, resting her head against him as he wrapped his arm around her and rested his head against the seat. His hair tickled her face. She wouldn't dare move though, she loved it when he held her close like this. His hair smelled like coconut shampoo as it blew its scent with the wind.

She wondered what he looked like when he washed his hair. Did he use a washcloth in the shower or just a bar of soap? She didn't remember seeing a wash cloth in his bathroom, though she hadn't really looked for one either. Did he sing to himself or get in and out as quickly as possible? Her thoughts drifted to all that tall muscle, naked, soaped up, hair trailing down his back. It made her

241

ache in low places just thinking about it.

She didn't fully understand how his personality worked yet. I
was strong, and fierce, and powerful, and yet so gentle ar
nurturing with her. He was kind to every person he came
contact with, and yet so quick to force physical violence if he felt
was necessary. He seemed methodical about every area of his lif
including his emotions—or what he allowed of his emotions
show. He held her like this, so close, and yet he was also so cut o

There was some kind of love between them, but it w
completely undefined and most definitely not discussed. It w
confusing because she wanted to let herself really have feelings f
him, but since he never opened up in that regard she wouldn't l
herself.

***

Re-runs of *Three's Company* were always quite enjoyabl
That show brought back good memories of being little, ar
protected, and happy. She loved falling asleep to these old show
Violet slouched on the couch, staring blankly forward. She wasn
her usual self today. Something about the weight of the air and tl
stillness outside made her uneasy. Not to mention the fact that sl
was having her stupid period. She wanted to shove her face in
tub of chocolate ice cream and bawl her eyes out for any and a
reasons.

Life had been brutal. In some ways it felt like her parents ha
been dead for a year now. She couldn't remember what it was lik
to come home and see her mom in the kitchen, or her dad ridir
the lawn mower out in the yard. She couldn't feel them anymor
In other ways, the pain was as fresh as it had been the day
happened. Roman had told her that's how it would be, and he wa
right.

Every time she stopped to think about them, or saw or fe
something that jarred a memory, she was taken right back to th
second when she got the call and heard the words. She tried ever
effort possible to stop thinking about that.   Kind of har

considering she was living in their house surrounded by their things. It helped having the others here. It also helped that she didn't have to function in the real world because her parents had had a huge life insurance policy, and her grandparents had given her an inheritance that was mind boggling, given the fact that they had been poor. In all reality she'd never have to work again. And considering her lawyer was fighting the fucker that killed her parents and the company he'd worked for in court, she may end up with even more. It wasn't that she wanted the money, she just wanted them to pay for what they'd allowed to happen.

If it hadn't been for Roman and Amber she would have probably been dead by now, too. Mark certainly hadn't helped matters.

"Hey, kitten, what's up?" Roman fell back into the couch beside her with a bowl of popcorn.

"I dunno, watching television?"

"Yes, I see that. Popcorn?"

"Nah, I'm not in the mood for salt," she said, reaching her hand into the bowl.

Roman snickered and sank deeper into the couch. "Where's everyone?"

"Upstairs watching some horror film, I wasn't up for it. I've had enough horror in my life. Where'd you go anyway?"

"I walked home. I had to do something." He'd called Lux, yet again, to no avail.

Violet looked at him suspiciously and grabbed another handful of popcorn.

"Nothing *cloak and dagger*, just had to make sure the trash was out for tomorrow."

"Planning on staying the night?" She raised her eyebrow.

"Well, it does happen from time to time. Tonight felt like a good night to cram myself into your tiny bed. Is that okay?"

"It's fine, Roman. You're always welcome." She leaned into him and pulled the soft afghan over her shoulders. "In fact, why do you even bother with an apartment when you could stay here? There's that whole room in the basement. It's big enough for all your stuff down there. It's clean and everything. My dad just finished working on that before the accident."

"I don't know. I don't know, maybe… it just sounds like i* not a good idea. I don't know, Violet." He couldn't live with h* He was already too ingrained in her life as it was, and he knew was going to really mess her up when he moved on, once he h* taken care of whatever threat was looming.

"Well, like I said, you're always welcome," she said numb* sad but trying not to show it. Her eyes grew heavy and she * them close. The dark room, blue glow of the television, a* Roman, made it feel okay to sleep.

Roman sat the bowl down on the floor and closed his eyes too.

12. CHANGES

The sky was warm, red and blue, the color of the Superman ice cream she always got as a child from the little café beside the convenience store. The sky doesn't make these colors in the real world. She spun in a circle, arms wide, embracing nothing, everything. Alive. Happy. It had been so long since she'd truly been happy. Maybe since she'd had that Superman ice cream all those years prior.

Across the field he came. Tall. A mountain. Striding towards her with determination, purpose.

She stopped and watched. Held in place by his body as he moved towards her. Her breath caught in her throat, the air stilling as he stopped a few yards away. Time stood still. No air. No rustle of green, green grass, or spring baby leaves. Only the babbling water of the stream not far away still sung. Like a heartbeat. The pulse of this place. She smiled.

His head tilted to the side, almost unnaturally. The angle strange, off-putting. His mouth opened, his tongue slipping between his lips, before he straightened his neck and smiled in return. The same old Roman.

He closed the gap between them and wrapped his arms around her lifting her off the ground. He crushed her to him, her body melding to his as her fingers sunk into his hair. He kissed her cheek, skimming along her jawline to her throat.

"Roman." Breathless. Boneless.

She felt his hand sink into her chest. The sucking sound was maddeningly loud as he pulled her heart out and let her drop to the ground. She looked down at her chest, a gaping hole that seeped black and red expanded, dissolved. She looked back at him, mute, as he held up her heart and bit into it like a candy apple. His lips, red and glistening.

"Roman?"

The scene switched. She was above him. The wound in her ches
healed with no sign of there ever being a hole there. He lay ther
so still. So still, with eyes open. The green so green it wa
unnatural. Dulling matte and staring straight through her. An
then the blackness expanded in his chest, the hole dissolving h
chest cavity. And she looked in her hand. A heart. Throbbing
Beating. And then the sounds crashed back in.

***

She was the first to wake up. It had to be around nine by now
The sun was coming through the front window and it always cam
in around nine. The dust flitted about in the diffused sun beams
She exhaled, pursing her lips in the shape of an O and stirred th
particles to dance. She looked down at Roman, who wa
peacefully sleeping in her lap, snuggled beneath the afghan he
mother had crocheted, and she wondered how he had gotten ther
What in his sleep last night provoked him to this position? He wa
perfectly still and his breathing was very shallow. She moved he
hand slowly to his chest, wanting to feel the rise and fall as h
inhaled then slowly exhaled. The thick muscle of his chest wa
firm and strong beneath the black t-shirt and soft yarn of th
blanket. Her fingers gripped him slightly. It felt good to feel soli
flesh. He was so warm.

He looked dead, peacefully dead. She placed her palm over h
heart to ensure it was still beating. It was.

Her bladder was full. It was to the point of becoming painfu
She didn't want to move, though, because she didn't want t
disturb him. She wanted to stay this calm and quiet an
comfortable. This was the only time there would be perfect peac
from the usual chaos in the house, early morning when no one els
was awake. And even her dreams hadn't always been peaceful c
late. A shudder passed through her as she remembered the drear
she'd had. But this moment was peaceful and quiet, and he wa
here and okay.

But her bladder was full and there was nothing comfortable about that. She was actually fairly uncomfortable physically. Her thighs were numb from his body weight, and his head was pressed against her ridiculously full bladder and crampy uterus as she had been slouching when he'd fallen asleep on her. Her knees ached from being propped up on the coffee table and sustaining his weight all night.

She didn't dare break the spell of the moment though.

The house was perfectly noiseless. He was perfectly still.

His long black lashes rested against his cheeks. His skin was so milk white, smooth and poreless. A dark shadow of beard had come through during the night. She loved it when he didn't shave for a few days. He was so masculine, and so damn pretty.

He would kill her if she said that out loud. It was doubtful he'd want to be referred to that way. He was the most masculine man she had ever been around. Even more so than Mark, because Mark was just a loutish jerk who acted more like a spoiled boy than a man. Roman was large, muscular, strong, and very gentlemanly. A lot of his mannerisms were old fashioned. He always held the door, always refrained from the usual macho talk. He always made sure he was taken care of first, kind, compassionate. But at the same time he was brutally masculine, brutally honest, and would be considered sort of sexist to the types of people who didn't like men holding doors and whatnot.

She didn't care. It didn't bother her to be taken care of the way he took care of her. It wasn't in a condescending way. He just genuinely wanted to make sure she was okay, which meant everything to her. She would do anything he wanted if it meant keeping that protection, and she had never been subservient to anyone really, but of course she knew he wouldn't require anything from her in order to give his protection.

It was a moot point, they weren't a couple. She was still every bit as alone as she had been since losing her parents and ending things with Mark. It didn't matter, she wasn't nearly beaten down enough to ever allow anyone to own her anyway.

She thought back to a few nights before when he'd thrashed those two guys at the bar. She had been so filled with desire for him. The fire in his eyes, the burning rage he'd shown, had been enthralling and had elicited a reaction in her she never expected She couldn't imagine another man capable of taking him on in fight and winning. She had once thought Mark that strong, but the was before she knew Roman. Even if she'd never seen Roman in fight, she'd know he was indestructible just because of the way h carried himself. She saw how others reacted to him when h entered a room. Men always sort of backed away, even if it wa just a slight turning on a bar stool, or giving their back to him. was subtle, and sometimes even obvious. She wanted to be lik that. She wanted to be such a force people knew better than t mess with her.

Obviously Roman couldn't really be indestructible, but sh liked to imagine him so. The idea of losing him now left her gu churning. Despite repeating the mantra *we're just friends* she fe herself falling in love with him. It scared her, because she wa certain he didn't feel the same for her. What he did feel she wa unsure, there were mixed signals. Men didn't spend this much tim with a woman they weren't interested in normally, right? But h never made any sort of attempt to kiss her or anything and they' had a lot of moments alone, even in bed together. He mo certainly had never mentioned anything about having those kin of feelings. He so didn't seem like the kind of person wh wouldn't discuss something like that. He never seemed avoidy?

But then, he did seem to get sort of nervous on occasion whe they were alone, or when some topic came up that resemble anything remotely related to the subject of their relationship. Sh imagined it was because he wouldn't want to blatantly hurt h feelings. There was no way someone as worldly as him woul want her. No way. She was surely no Mylori, and that was h type, right?

She hadn't even thought about Lux since the day she'd reall looked into Roman's eyes and saw who he really was looking bac at her. It's strange how a moment like that could complete change a person's perspective, but it had. She'd seen who h really was, not just a guy who was being nice to her, but someon who was full of depth and passion. It was there, brewing an building right behind those green, ocean sized eyes. What lurke there in those depths? What had he seen? Who was he really?

Her heart had felt like an explosion in her chest when all those questions had come bursting open like the first blossoms of spring. It wasn't as though she hadn't been curious already, but something had changed. A switch had been flipped that went from friendship to love. She had to hide her feelings though. He wasn't interested in her in that way, well, probably wasn't... and it would only lead to humiliation and probably the destruction of the openness they shared. How could something like that do anything but lead to walls and awkwardness if he didn't share her feelings? And she knew he didn't. *Why am I so sure?*

She pushed the stray strands of hair away from his face, lightly moving her fingers across the pale softness of his skin. His eyes moved beneath the surface of his thin pink lids, dreaming. She hoped his dreams were pleasant, something involving happiness, or possibly even her. His eyebrows creased then relaxed, his mouth barely tightening and releasing. Then stillness again, his dream had ended.

She tried to shift his weight by adjusting her legs beneath him. He stirred, turned his head towards her stomach, and then went back to rest.

She watched the artery pound in his neck, the rhythmic throbbing beneath the surface. It was hypnotic, lulling. The muscles pulsated as his heart pounded relentlessly. She traced the blue veins that had risen to the surface with her eyes, wanted to touch them so badly.

The veins beneath his pale skin reminded her of seeing him after his workout. Veins all swollen to the surface, skin glistening, and his hair in curling wet coils down his back. He reminded her of some mythical being, some barbarian sent to watch over and protect her. He was a comic book hero, larger than life. The image of him dressed like a Viking came to her mind again, making her smile.

That is what he was to her. It didn't matter that she didn't know anything about his personal life beyond the few things he'd told her, and what she'd personally experienced with him. She didn't know his history; she didn't even know how old he was for sure. The only thing that mattered to her was that he was here right now, protecting her and making her feel okay. That had become increasingly more important these last few weeks.

And then she remembered the last dream she'd had...how inhuman he had looked with the crooked neck, the way his tongue had snaked out. And then he'd pulled her heart straight out of her chest and bitten into it. Was this symbolism? Her stupid brain making up analogies? Or was her subconscious warning her? But in the end it was her who had been holding his heart. What the fuck was up with her subconscious? What did it all mean? It had to mean something.

She had gotten lost in her thoughts, watching him so intently her eyes had blurred and she was almost asleep. She felt her bladder twinge and her pupils dilated as they focused again. He was looking directly at her, his green eyes burning straight through her into some place so hidden even she didn't know what he saw. Like he'd found some secret crevice in the back of her brain behind her eyes, that only he knew about.

Neither of them said anything, or reacted to the other visibly. There was no movement, no smile, or slight variation in the eyes. It was as if they were both still asleep or in some trance. No blinking, no shifting. She wondered if he was even awake. It was almost frightening how still he was, how deeply his eyes bore into hers.

Silence, pure and palpable.

Slowly his mouth curled upwards, his white teeth visible behind the veil of pink lips. She watched the skin around his eyes crease as his mouth smiled.

Violet returned the smile and then shifted beneath him, feeling uneasy at the intimacy of the moment. "I have to go pee," she interrupted the silence awkwardly.

"Oh, okay," he said, sitting up and letting his feet fall to the floor. He watched as she walked from the room towards the stairs nervously, looking back at him and smiling intermittently.

What a strange girl.

***

"So you were sort of snuggly down there," Amber said as she pulled her hair back away from her face. Her red tresses glistened like stained glass.

"What? How do you know?" Violet said, pacing back and forth in the hallway. "Gotta pee, Amber," she said, holding her abdomen.

"Oh, sorry," Amber said, walking out of the bathroom.

Violet closed the door and barely had time to pull her pants down.

"I snuck downstairs about an hour ago for some water and saw you," Amber said, her voice was muffled behind the door.

Violet finished and washed her hands, reaching to open the door.

"Very cute," Amber said, grabbing her toothbrush from the glass vase on the marble vanity.

Violet dried her hands and sat down on the edge of the bathtub. "Yeah, not sure how we ended up like that."

"You're such a dork." Amber laughed, turning to look at her friend with her toothbrush hanging out of her mouth.

Violet looked at her slightly embarrassed. "Tell me something I don't know."

"For God's sake, the boy is hot for you. You have to know that. Why the hell else would he be hanging around, picking fights with random men at bars, etcetera etcetera etcetera."

"I don't know, he feels sorry for me? And he wasn't defending me, douche. He was defending some other girl," Violet said, standing up and grabbing the hand lotion from the shelf over the toilet. She squeezed some of the lavender scented cream onto her hands and began rubbing them together.

"Well, I hardly think he feels sorry for you. Stop being *dumb* already."

"Whatever," Violet said, standing up.

"I meant that in a good way, not in a trying-to-hurt-your-feelings way."

"I know, stop being dumb." Violet grinned, and walked back downstairs.

Roman was standing in the kitchen drinking water from a large plastic cup. He stopped drinking and turned to her, "This water

251

tastes like soap," he said, then continued to drink.

"Drink the bottled water, Roman. Lord knows what's in the tap water."

"Yeah, it's strengthening my immune system though," he said with a smirk, and sat the cup in the sink. He leaned against the counter, folding his arms across his stomach. "So are we going to go out to that club tonight?" he asked, staring at her again.

"Well, I don't know. Are we?" she said, opening the fridge and grabbing a carton of orange juice and taking a swig from it. "Are you allowed in?" She grinned, closing the carton and sticking it back in the fridge.

"Of course, why wouldn't I be allowed in?"

She walked over to him and leaned against the counter beside him. Standing there beside him with him slouching she still only came up to his chest. "Um, thought maybe you'd beaten someone up there too."

"Nope, not yet," he said, flashing a quick grin.

"I guess I'll go."

Amber walked in the room getting ready to take off for her job. She worked at a small boutique in Kent. It wasn't much of a job in terms of an actual career, but it was a cool job. She got discounts and pretty much the whole clientele were people they a considered "cool" by some marginal standard. She got paid to peddle interesting crap and hang out with her friends all day. She grabbed an apple off the table and took a bite, stopping to look at the two slouches who were leaning against the counter.

"My God you would make pretty babies," she said, a devilish smile spreading across her lips, knowing how uncomfortable the comment would make Violet.

Violet squinted her eyes at Amber.

Roman laughed. "Yeah, as long as they look like her and not me."

"Shut up," Violet growled, shoving his arm and walking back into the living room.

"Seriously, what's the deal?" Amber said, pulling out a chair and sitting down.

"What's the deal with what?" Roman asked, shifting his weight onto one leg and crossing one ankle over the other.

"You know what I'm talking about, Roman. What's the deal, you like her right?"

"Of course I like her. Why else would I come around, right?" He smirked.

Amber looked at him somewhat confused. There was no way on earth he'd heard her and Violet's conversation, but he was repeating exactly what she'd said only a few minutes prior. "You know what I mean. Don't be retarded."

"You guys really need to stop saying 'retarded' so much. It's retarded."

"You know I don't meant it like that," she said, rolling her eyes. "I don't know how she stands you." Amber grinned, and grabbed her purse off the table slugging him with it as she walked by on her way out the door. "Later, Vi, stop by the store if you're bored," she said, calling out to the other room.

"Bye," Violet yelled from the couch.

"So, I guess we're going out tonight right?" Amber asked, as she opened the back door. No one used the front door to Violet's house much. Amber and Violet always parked their cars on the street behind the house. Randy and their various guests were the only ones to use the driveway.

"Yeah, the princess says she'll go. So count me in I guess," he said, walking towards the living room. "See you later, Amber."

Roman was more interested in scanning the crowd for threats and clues than actually hanging out at the club. He could give a fuck less about hanging out in any club. It was work. That's why he wanted to go.

"Bye, dork," she teased, opening the door and pulling it shut behind her.

He smiled and walked over to the couch and sat down. Violet was flipping through the channels snuggled beneath the afghan.

"I'm gonna take off in a few minutes," he said quietly.

"Oh, okay," she said, sitting up quickly. "You can hang around here. Nothing's going on today—I guess that goes without saying."

"Thanks but I'm gonna go shower and stuff. I need to work out and run some errands."

"What do you do all day?" she asked, turning to look at him. "I

253

mean, you don't work right?"

"No, I don't work, you know I don't work. I just do stu
Work out, I don't know."

"Well, how do you afford stuff? Are you rich? Do your pare
support you or something?" The questions just started falling fro
her mouth more quickly than she could stop them. It wasn't rea
any of her business how he spent his days and she hadn't ev
cared until the words started coming.

"Wow, look at you with all the questions."

"Well, Roman, you know everything about me, for the mo
part, and I don't know anything about you. I don't even know ho
old you are, or when your birthday is. Where did you come fro
for real?"

He took a deep breath and looked down at his hands. I
figured this would come up eventually. He just wasn't sure ho
much he should or could tell at this point. "Well, I'm thirty thr
years old. My birthday is September thirteenth. And I hail fro
the *Planet of the Apes*."

"Wow," she said hastily.

He looked at her, not changing his facial expression, not rea
getting what would elicit the "wow".

"I mean, not wow like you're old, I just never would ha
guessed that."

"Gee, and I thought you were wowing my *Planet of the Ap*
lineage. I'm old compared to you, Violet."

"Not *that* old, I mean, it's not like gross or anything."

"Well, glad to hear I'm not gross," he said, and laughed.

"I didn't mean it like that," she said, suddenly very embarrass
by her reaction.

"I know what you're saying, V, no need to dig your hole a
deeper," he said, teasing her.

"And where are you from? Where is your family? Why d
you move here?"

"One thing at a time, kitten," he said, standing up and lookii
down at her. "I'm a wealthy man, is that enough for now?" H
eyes were intense and glistening in the diffused light of the room.

"And you ended up here why?"

"I guess something just drew me here." He smiled and starte

walking towards the back door. "Okay, I'm going to leave now. I need to drag my tired old bones home to take my cod liver oil and change my adult diaper."

"Shut up," she said, following him through the kitchen. "I didn't mean anything..."

"I know, I know, it's okay, Violet," he said, patting her on the top of the head. He wrapped his arm around her shoulder and led her to the door. "Be a good girl today."

She frowned at him. "I'm always good."

"Oh, okay," he said, squeezing her shoulder and pulling the door open. "I'll be by around seven tonight, alright?"

"Okay," she said, "You know I didn't mean anything right? I was just surprised cuz you don't look that old."

Roman laughed.

"I didn't mean it like that," she said again with a pout, frustrated with her inability to articulate properly. "I just wanted to know more about you."

"We'll talk about it some other day." He kissed the top of her head and walked down the garden path through her back yard and onto the street behind her house. She watched him until he disappeared from view.

"Thirty three, wow," she said, pulling the door closed behind her. She walked to the refrigerator and opened the freezer drawer. "Score," she said, grabbing the chocolate fudge brownie ice cream.

13. REVELATION OF GHOSTS

"Glad you stopped by," Amber said, stopping the shirt foldin she'd been busying herself with for longer than necessary.

"I was bored. Maybe I should get a job here?" Violet state nonchalantly, leafing through one of the free music newspaper sitting on the counter.

"Why the hell would you want to do that?"

"I don't know, something to do I suppose."

"I know what you should do..."

"What?" Violet asked, looking up from the paper.

"I don't know, just wanted to get you excited."

"Man, don't do that," Violet said, shutting the paper and tossin it aside.

"I know what you want me to tell you to do," Amber said resuming her folding duties and looking at her friend slyly with devilish grin on her lips.

"Oh yeah?" Violet asked, her brow risen warily as she sat on th stool behind the counter. "What do I want you to tell me to do?"

Amber laughed, looking at her friend out of the corner of he eye knowing the reaction she was going to get. "Roman."

Violet shifted uncomfortably on the stool. "No, I wouldn' want you to tell me that. That would be a bad idea," Viole scoffed, her face warming.

"Just do it already for crying out loud."

"Shut up."

"Whatever," Amber said, walking behind the counter and takin a sip of her pop. "You know it's the right thing to do."

"Embarrassing myself horribly is the right thing to do?"

"Shut up. I'm telling you, you're both morons. Make freaking move already."

"Amber, we're not in high school, he's a grown man and ha

made it more than clear he's not interested."

"I don't care what the fuck he's said, Vi. It's so obvious you guys are in love with each other, and have been since day one."

"Okay, I think I'm going to go now," Violet said, hopping down off the stool and picking her bag off the floor. It made her uncomfortable talking about this. Why, she wasn't entirely sure.

"Don't leave, I'm sorry. It just seems ridiculous that you two social inept fools aren't together already."

Violet stopped and turned towards her friend. "Yeah, I'm a social inept fool, I'll give you that, but he's not. I've seen the way he is with other chicks."

"Other chicks? When?"

"Um, I don't know. Around and stuff."

"Riiiight…" Amber said, rolling her eyes.

"Well, whatever," Violet snickered, and sat back down on the stool. "Seriously though, if he was interested he would have let me know by now. I mean, don't you think? Dude, he was with *Mylori*, what the hell do I have to offer compared to her?"

"Mylori? Really? Well, whatever, Violet, prolong your agony then." Amber walked out into the store to help a customer. "Wow, he was with Mylori?" she asked, turning back.

Violet gave her friend a scowl and looked down at the silver heart hanging around her neck. If there was a possibility this meant more to him than she thought it did, he certainly hadn't let her know. There was no way for her to know without blatantly asking, either—and that wasn't something she felt like she could do. He wouldn't really answer any questions about himself, how the fuck could she expect him to talk about their relationship, or lack thereof?

The fact that he was so much older than her alone led her to believe he couldn't be interested in her in *that* way. Plus he always treated her like a child. The way he fawned over her to make sure she was alright, even the way he patted her head and shit. She had watched him on several occasions with other women, and he never seemed shy towards them. He was always pretty upfront and open with everyone for the most part, minus his mysterious hidden life. So it stood to reason that if he was interested in her as more than just a little sister kind of thing then he would have said something by now. Right?

She remembered the time she went to his house and Mylo answered the door. She had been wearing his t-shirt and nothing else. Mylori was her complete opposite: tall, blonde and an actual woman. Not some little elfling type creature like her.

Finding Mylori there had weirded her out more than irritated her. She had been so self-centered, thinking he didn't have a life outside of her, that it had thrown her for a loop. It took all her will power not to snap at him and make rude comments the next time she saw him. She wanted to ask about "the skank" at his house and whether or not she was good in bed, blah blah blah and whatever other inane, bitchy thing she could think of to say. And then her brain kicked in and convinced her it wasn't any of her business, and she had no right to ask, which was absolutely true. Yay for those few intelligent firing synapses. It was only fair, after all, he had never really asked her about Mark. And besides, it had been none of her business.

Oh, and then to find out who Mylori was, there'd be no competing with someone that beautiful and worldly. Besides, she was supposed to be lusting after Lux, right? She had certainly made a big enough deal about that. *How embarrassing.*

Roman wasn't in love with her, it was plain and simple. So there it was. Case closed.

"Hey, are you hungry? Let's order food from next door. We'll make them deliver cuz the delivery boy's a hottie," Amber said, walking back over to the cash register. She rang up the customer and smiled.

"I guess I could eat," Violet said, standing up and looking through the rack of t-shirts. "I want a tuna sandwich. I want this too," she said, holding up a small black baby tee with a blood red star on it.

***

She pulled the shirt over her head. It was tight, but that was okay, it showed off her small breasts and made them look less small. She pulled on the black cargo pants and slipped on her shoes.

Roman sat in the living room talking to Steve and Mosley. Amber was in the kitchen straightening up as Randy told her very loudly about the day he'd had. Randy had a way of filling up the house with his enthusiastic story telling. Amber frequently had to ask him to use his "indoor voice". They all loved his charisma, though.

Violet laughed to herself and walked into the living room and slumped down in the red velvet lounger. She kicked her feet out, making a thump on the hardwood floor and watched Roman as he talked to Steve about some deeply interesting topic she was unable to concentrate on long enough to figure out. Something about inter-dimensional travel, String Theory, something-or-other. Instead of trying to follow she watched him. His face was smooth and semi-emotionless as he spoke, which was different from when he spoke to her. He had more character in his face when he talked to her.

The heavy ridge of bone over his eyes gave his face a stern appearance; though it was contradictory to how he had always treated her. He was always nice to everyone, well, unless he was beating the shit out of them. He looked pretty ferocious (and hot) then. Most people were frightened by him because of his size and intimidating facade. She had been herself that first night, but then something about the smooth rumble of his deep voice had comforted her, even then.

He randomly looked over at her, acknowledging her silently with some extra something in his eyes, and then continued with his dialogue. She could tell by Steve's expression that while he was interested in the conversation, his growing dislike for Roman (due largely in part to his friendship with Mark) was making it difficult for him to take part wholeheartedly in the discussion. Mose hadn't spoken since she had walked in the room. He wasn't much of a talker anyway, but she could tell by his inability to look her in the eyes the last few times she'd seen him that Mark had also tainted his opinion of her. So-fucking-be-it. They could both suck her dick as far as she was concerned. She knew who her real friends were anyway. Sad, she had once considered these guys real friends. Such was life.

She was very close to telling them both to get out of her house. This was *her* house and she didn't need Steve to help he financially, so why put up with his annoying presence now? Sh had just wanted bodies to fill up the place after her parents ha died. No, that wasn't entirely true--they had all had such goo times in the beginning when they'd first met. She looked back ver fondly at those first few months when they had initially becom friends. They would all go out dancing, then for coffee c pancakes. There had been late nights of debauchery and othe nights of innocent fun, just playing at the park, or freakin themselves out in the graveyard down the street. Then her paren died, and it made perfect sense to her to let them all move in.

Times were changing. There was a heaviness that sat over ther all now. She could tell this era was ending. Too much ha happened in the last few months to go back now. Besides, sh knew when someone disliked her. She could always read it in the eyes, no matter what words were falling off their sugary tongues.

And maybe she had given them all reason to dislike her at on time or another? She hadn't been the most cordial or patier person in the world, often spouting off things she knew better tha to say out loud. The truth was, she was an unhappy perso fighting to find the right path in life and lashing out at others whe the frustration level got too high. She needed to learn to be grown up and stop acting like a spoiled brat. In all reality her onl real friends were Amber, Randy, and Roman.

Steve started talking about stuff he knew nothing about, tryin to sound smart to Roman. He did this a lot. He would use "bi words" to try to sound intelligent but used them wrong most of th time. She sighed heavily and rolled her eyes.

"Hey, Violet, is that a new shirt?" Roman asked, leanin forward. He could tell that she was bored or disinterested with th company. She hadn't said anything since coming downstairs, an the way she'd been looking at Mosely and Steve, he knew she wa about to get snotty. He liked it when she acted bratty. He found amusing.

"Yes," she answered looking into his eyes, a devilish smil curling her lips. She knew he could read her instantly.

"It's nice," he said, leaning back into the couch. The way he looked at her was intimate, the kind of look only best friends or lovers could give, saying everything with just a twinkle in the eye or a lift to the lips.

"Yes, I rather like it myself," she said, stretching the bottom of the shirt and looking down at it.

"It's very nice," he repeated.

Steve and Mosley stood up nearly on cue, sensing they better get out of there before Violet started. "We're gonna leave for The Cage now," Steve said, glancing back at Mose.

"What? You don't need a ride?" Violet snarked, looking at the two.

Roman grinned, covering his mouth and tilting his face down. It always cracked him up when she acted like this because they all just let her. He sure as hell wouldn't.

"I brought my car," Mose said, reaching into his pockets.

"You brought *your* car? Since when do you have a car?" she asked with disdain.

"I got it off Mark," he said, dismissing her obvious barb.

"Hm, interesting," she said, looking at Roman. "Is he going to make you pay him back the way he always made me pay him back?" She snickered, her eyes glistered evilly.

"Shut up, Violet. I always liked you so much, but, God, now I see why he dumped you," Steve said, walking out of the room with Mose trailing him.

"He dumped me. That's funny," she said, rolling her eyes and looking over at Roman.

He leaned his head against the back of the couch and looked at her through half closed eyes.

"What?" she asked, tilting her head to the side and grinning at him.

"You're such a snot. Why can't you just let things go?"

"Because I'm a bitch and that's what I do," she said, looking away from him.

"You aren't nearly the bitch you want people to believe you are," he said, smiling at her softly.

"What's that supposed to mean?" she asked, leaning forward in the chair and resting her forearms on her knees. Her voice was soft

261

but agitated.

"Nothing, kitten, you just don't have to put up that front all t time."

"Whatever." She stood up and walked out of the room. "A stop calling me that."

She was embarrassed and wounded by his words. She felt as she'd been scolded to some degree. The truth hurt sometime especially when it came from him. She couldn't hide from hi He saw through all her bullshit. And she was tired of him callir her those cute pet names that made her insides go all squishy. was utterly confusing.

She walked through the kitchen and started for the back door.

"Where ya goin'?" Amber said, looking up from the sink.

"Just outside," she said, pulling the door open and walking ou slamming it behind her.

Roman sat for several seconds, trying to figure out why wh he'd said had pissed her off so badly. He had said things far wor in the past. He stood up and then followed after her, looking Amber and smiling as he grabbed the door handle.

"Put your foot in your mouth?" Amber asked knowingly.

"Apparently," he said, shaking his head and walking outside.

"Good luck with that," Amber said with a giggle.

Violet was sitting on the picnic table beneath the huge map tree. She was leaning back on her elbows, and she looked so sma and fragile sitting there alone in the darkness. He walked over her and sat on the table beside her. She didn't speak or move, ar he just sat there looking at her, wondering what on earth was goir on in her mind.

"*Ugh*, stop staring," she said, shoving him with her hand as sh leaned on her other arm.

"Sorry, it's hard not to stare at you," he said with a smile, ar shoved her back.

"Yeah right," she said, turning red. "Give me a break."

"You really have no clue, do you?"

He sat forward, leaning on his knees, and watching the family i the house across the street as they moved about in their livir room. He knew that Violet sat out here watching them nearly ever night, wishing that her house was still filled with her own famil

He had seen her laying out here a few times, watching them and crying, when she didn't know he was there. God, why did he care so much? He'd seen girls devastated by loss before. He'd simply done his job and moved on. What the hell was different this time?

"Clue? Clue about what? What a moron I am? I'm well aware. Thanks for reminding me."

"For fuck's sake, stop feeling sorry for yourself."

"If I don't who will?" she said, trying not to laugh. She knew she was being a baby.

"You are such a brat," he said, looking back at her. Her eyes almost glowed with the reflection of the street lights. "Am I allowed to call you that?" he teased, shoving her arm.

"Come on, let's go for a walk," she said, pulling herself up and tugging on his sleeve. For all the confusion he caused her, she could never stay mad at him for more than a few minutes. She wasn't mad at him anyway, just annoyed from being put in her place.

She looked at him, all tall and beautiful and perfect with that wavy black hair and pillowy lips and... and she wanted to beat him senseless. She wanted him to go away and never see him again because it hurt so bad not to be able to tell him how she felt. She wanted to find him doing something gawdawful so she could once and for all convince herself what a jerk he was.

And there he stood. Gentle. Kind. Perfect. And the most beautiful man she'd ever seen.

They walked through her yard and onto the street. There was still quite a bit of action in the neighborhood, as it was only about nine o'clock. Cars drove by intermittently, and parents hustled their children inside.

"Shouldn't we let Amber know we're leaving?" Roman asked, looking down at his companion.

"She knows to leave without us. You can drive us later if we even want to go," she said, as she kicked a rock in the street.

"It's getting old isn't it?" he said.

"Yeah, it's been old for a long time."

"You know what I meant earlier, right?"

"Yes, I know exactly what you meant."

"Good. I mean, I know you're a badass, just not in the way you want people to think you are."

"Huh?" she said, looking at him perplexed.

"You aren't *mean*, Violet. You just play one on TV."

She laughed. "You're such a fucking weirdo."

"So how come you can call me a fucking weirdo, and I can't te
you that you aren't a bitch?" he asked, kicking the stone awa
from her.

"Double standards, baby, ever heard of 'em?" She grinnec
pushing him off balance. He nearly fell over and she reached an
grabbed his arm steadying him.

"You're so violent."

"Violent Violet, that's me," she said, slapping his arm.

"You need to put that violence to good use."

"Hmm, is that an offer of some kind?" she asked, stopping an
standing in fighting stance.

"Oh, little girl, you couldn't possibly hurt me," he laughed, an
kept walking.

"Well, I could if I wanted to," she said, and grabbed his han
and laced her fingers through his.

This caught him off guard. He looked down at her somewha
mystified. "Yeah, I suppose you could hurt me if you wanted to,
just hope you never want to."

They walked for several blocks not saying anything. Th
weight of his hand against hers felt like heaven to her. His han
was so strong and warm. It reminded her of when she was littl
and she would hold her dad's pinkie as they walked through th
store, or around the fair. She had always felt so tiny and protecte
with him, and she felt that way now with Roman. *Gross, sto
comparing Roman to your dad, sicko.*

"Come on, let's get some candy or something," she sai
motioning to the convenience store several blocks up the stree
The sign was half lit from burnt out bulbs.

"You don't need sugar," he teased her.

"I always need some sugar, *sugar*." She let go of his hand an
ran towards the store. He reluctantly jogged behind her.

As they entered the shop she noticed that besides their slightl
heavy breathing from the jog, the store was abnormally quiet an
still. She didn't see the clerk behind the counter or any othe

customers milling about.

"Kind of quiet in here?" she said, looking back at Roman, who was walking in the row beside her.

"Yeah, something's not right," he said, looking around the store, his eyebrows heavy over his eyes. He was tall enough to see over the aisles and saw no one. His body tingled, internal alarms going off. He knew something was off, and he had to get her out of here.

"We should go," he said, turning and heading back toward the door, looking around, on alert.

As they walked past the counter they heard gasping. Roman looked at Violet and put his hand out, stopping her from moving forward. He stepped in front of her, peering over the counter. The clerk lay on the floor, bleeding profusely from his neck, a puddle of coagulated blood spilling around his head like a red halo.

"What is it?" Violet said, reaching for Roman.

"Don't look," he said, holding her back.

Suddenly, they heard a commotion in the storage room. Two large men came stumbling out from behind the metal doors.

"Violet, run," he said, pushing her towards the door. She stood frozen, unable to respond to his command. "Go," he demanded, pushing her again.

The men noticed the two and began laughing. "Oh lookie, the main course just arrived," the taller of the two said, walking straight for them. His hair was ratty and long. His eyes burned like black coals.

"And she's purty too," the other laughed, with his southern drawl. His short shaved hair was greasy and spiked. His skin ruddy with blood and moist with perspiration.

Their faces were mangled and inhuman. Large vicious teeth dripped red saliva as their mouths contorted into a grimace. Their eyes seemed larger than normal, and their skin was so white it was almost transparent.

Images flashed in Violet's head of the dreams she'd been having.

"Go, Violet!" Roman demanded, pushing her again.

"Don't go, Violet," the smaller of the men mocked, as he leapt towards them.

Roman stepped in front of her and swung his fist squarely at th man, throwing him onto the floor. The other came in on him fas and Roman caught him with his side, then smoothly looped one le in his, one arm around his neck, bent him over, and starte smashing him in the face repeatedly with his fist.

She was entranced by Roman's sudden burst of kinetic violenc and the insanity of the situation. His movements were so smoot and skilled they looked choreographed, as though he'd acted ou this scene many times.

"Violet, run. Get out of here," he repeated as his fists lande again and again on the man's jaw and body.

"No!" she said, leaping forward and kicking the man on th floor as hard as she could. Her foot landed so soundly the ma gasped. It felt like something gave way in his ribcage.

"Bitch!" he snarled and grabbed her foot knocking her o balance.

She reached for the candy rack and held herself up grabbing packaged flashlight off the shelf and pounding the man on the hea with it. He fell back to the floor rubbing his head with his claw like hand, moaning like a drunk. She struck him again and again a he writhed around, blood spattering her hands with every blow a she shrieked like a banshee.

Roman looked around as fast as he could trying to find weapon as his fists continually pounded into the larger man's flesl He heard bones crack with every strike and saw peripherally tha Violet was taking care of herself.

The smaller man grabbed her ankle with a bellowing shriek. Sh slipped from his grip and ran through the aisles looking around fc something she could better protect herself with. The man wa slowly coming to his feet, stumbling in her direction, cursing wit every step. Suddenly, he didn't look smaller at all, he looked hug to her. There had to be a display of utility knives or something sh could find. She held the flashlight up and swung it as hard as sh could, just missing the man's head.

Just then sirens screamed from the parking lot. They all looke up, startled by the sudden noise and flashing lights. The two me pulled themselves away from Roman and ran toward the door bursting through the glass and shattering them. Violet stood the stunned for several moments. She was terrified and completely confused. Roman ran to her, taking her blood spattered hands in his.

"You okay?" he asked, wiping the tears from her cheeks.

She slapped his hands away. "I'm alright! Stop asking me if I'm alright! Everyone always asks me if I'm alright!" she broke, taken back to one too many violent scenes in her head.

"Police--freeze!" The officers held their guns on the two.

Violet and Roman raised their hands. One of the officers slowly walked toward them with his gun drawn. They stood still, not wanting to provoke fire.

"Down on the ground," the officer ordered.

Roman and Violet complied. Violet's heart was hammering in her chest, she thought she might pass out. Roman turned his head and looked her in the eye. Violet closed her eyes as the officer handcuffed her then dragged her to her knees. She watched as the same was done to Roman by the other officer before he was yanked to his feet.

"What's going on here?" he said, running his hands over Roman, searching him for weapons and eyeing the blood on his hands skeptically. Thank God he didn't have any weapons on him, for once. What had he been thinking leaving the house without a weapon? Lazy. Sloppy.

"We came into the store and no one was here and then two men came out of the back and attacked us." Roman was calm, concise.

The officer lifted Violet next and patted her down. Her knees were weak, her heart still pounding.

"Sarge, Old Joe is back here behind the counter, we need an ambulance ASAP," one of the other officers called from across the room.

"Okay, stay here, don't move," the officer said, backing away from Roman and Violet and heading towards the counter.

"Roman, what were they?" Violet asked, beginning to shake violently.

"Vampires," he said quietly, looking at her, trying to gauge her reaction. She looked like she might fall over but he couldn't move to hold her up. "Don't say anything. You have to trust me."

Vampires? Trust?

Violet felt the darkness cloud her vision as her knees began t
buckle.

"Trust me," Roman whispered again, as she crashed to he
knees.

"She needs help!" Roman barked to the officers.

One of the cops came over and helped her to a seated positior
tapping her cheek to make sure she hadn't blacked out.

"She needs help," Roman said again.

The police officer looked up at him and back at her. H
unlocked the cuffs on her. "Do not move," he said, garnering a no
from her.

Violet's thoughts swam as the lights and voices dimmed aroun
her. Everything was going dark. Everything she had ever know
had been changed by that one word.

Vampires.

It seemed like it took an eternity for the officers to assess
wasn't Roman and Violet responsible for the murder of the stor
clerk and remove their cuffs. Violet rubbed her wrists absentl
looking around in a daze.

"We're going to need to get some statements from you both,
the officer said, as he motioned for the two to follow him to hi
squad car.

Violet was in shock. She was numb all over, her body tinglin
from the crush of it all. She hadn't blinked in what seemed lik
minutes. Roman kept looking at her trying to measure her reactio
to it all, trying to snap her back into reality, but he knew it wa
pointless. She needed to reevaluate what she'd seen, and wha
he'd said, before she could react.

Had they really just been attacked by vampires? *Vampires*
Everything had happened so fast. A nonsensical blur of motion. I
an instant everything she knew was upside down. Or maybe rigt
side up? There was no time right now to weigh her emotions. N
time to try to understand what she'd seen or what Roman had tol
her. She would have to just function without reasoning. Trus
Roman. *Trust Roman.*

The officer spoke to her first. She explained what she'd seen i
whatever vague detail she could remember, never seeming to tak
her eyes from the cop's eyes. It was as though she was pleadin

with him to give her answers that made logical sense. Maybe they had been escapees from some nut house who believed they were vampires? Wouldn't that explain it all nice and logically. Logic? There was no logic in any of this, or maybe it made perfect sense?

Roman spoke to them next. He gave a detailed description as well, leaving out the most important detail that they weren't looking for humans.

"We may need to contact you both again. We have your information. You're free to go," the man said, and walked back in the store.

"Come on," Roman said, taking her by the arm gently.

She didn't want him to touch her. She felt betrayed for some reason, like she couldn't trust him. She felt like the giant secret of *who he was* had erupted in front of her in those fleeting moments of whirring violence. She wanted answers! And right now she wanted his hand off of her arm.

His words pounded in her ears painfully, her skin cold and numb, like her body was about to shut down. As much as his words were ridiculous, she knew with all her heart that they were true, and that something had died in her the moment they'd passed through his perfect, restrained lips. This was why he'd been so secretive? Why he never spoke of himself and never told her anything about his past, his life, or what he did. Nothing. Their whole relationship had been about her. It made sense in some abstract and still mysterious way. The world was clearer the moment that word--vampire--passed through his lips. The shock and fear of it had stunned her, and yet at the same time she felt awake or maybe complete somehow, for the first time.

Her body was buzzing with some incarnate knowledge that she had known her whole life, and had been buried since she was a child. Like the invisible friend she'd played with alone in the garden now suddenly had flesh and was holding her elbow, leading her through the dark streets towards his home.

"You okay?" he asked cautiously, sensing her revulsion. She had shut herself off from him like she had the night he'd found her stoned on painkillers. She didn't answer for a long moment, deciding instead to jerk her arm free from his grip.

"I'm not your enemy, remember?" he said abruptly.

"You've hidden things from me, Roman. I've shown yo everything, all my skeletons, and you've hidden every last deta from me." She looked up at him, her eyes icy blue flames burnin a hole straight through him.

"Yes, I hide my life from everyone. It's necessary, requirement." Who was she to judge him anyway? She had n idea the sacrifice his entire life had been. And she was going t get her feelings hurt because he didn't spill his guts to her? Th fact that he was even *walking* with her now was far more than mo: people had ever gotten from him.

"Requirement? Stop being melodramatic. I told you I neede for you to be honest with me. This is not honest." She looke away from him and back at the black pavement.

"You know, I was worried about how you were going to tak what you just saw. I was trying to be as delicate with the situatio as I could be, and yet here you are throwing your spoiled rotte brat routine. I just saved your fucking life and you're angry wit me? What was I supposed to say to you, Violet? *Hello, my nam is Roman, I kill vampires.*" He was furious, disgusted by h neediness, and angry with her for making him even bother to car in the first place.

"You kill vampires?" she asked, confused by his statement. Sh looked at him again, eyes searching.

"Yes, princess," he said, looking back at her. "What the fuc did you think was going on?"

"I don't know. How would I know? You sure as hell neve explained anything to me! All you've done since we've met is li and hide everything." What had she thought was going on Random acts of weird fucking violence? She'd certainly neve suspected he was some sort of real life equivalent to a movie hero.

"I have never lied to you," Roman seethed.

"There is such a thing as lying by omission, Roman." Violet' tone was equally toxic.

Roman shook his head in exasperation, raking his hand roughl through his hair. "Well, you know the reality now, so why th fuck are you angry?"

"Why am I angry? You would have never told me any of th had tonight never happened. So, shut up and leave me alone."

"No, Violet, you shut up and listen to me. You can't condescend to me like you do everyone else. You want to know my history and the bullshit I've had to deal with since the day I was born? I will tell you, because now there's no other way to keep you alive, short of shipping you off to the sun or turning you into a fucking vampire. Leave you alone? You better hope to fuck I don't leave you alone."

He grabbed her by the arm, and pulled her towards his apartment. She struggled against him, making sure he knew she was still angry with him. They walked up the stairs to the apartment and stopped at the top while he unlocked the door. She stared out into the street still anesthetized from all that had happened, still reeling inside from all he'd said.

"Coming? Or do I have to drag you?" he asked from inside the dark apartment.

She blinked her eyes defiantly and followed him. He flipped the light on in the kitchen and went to the sink, then took his jacket off and threw it across the room onto the small dinette in an explosion of sound and movement. The heavy leather slid across the table and hit the wall with a loud slap and landed on the floor. He turned the water on and rinsed the blood from his hands. His knuckles were broken open and he suspected he may have a broken bone in his hand. It would heal. He always healed.

She jumped as the jacket flew through the air. It made her nervous to see him this angry. Visions of past violence in her life flashed making her shrink into herself. She sat down on the couch, her arms crossed tightly over her belly as she kicked the coffee table, her boot thudding over and over. Then she noticed the blood on her hands. *The vampire's blood.* She almost threw up remembering the feel of the flashlight crashing into the skull over and over while he looked at her with inhuman eyes, snarled at her through razor teeth. She gagged.

He looked over at her, wanting to complain about her attitude. But even though he was annoyed, the look on her face still got to him and that pissed him off. He had every right to be angry with her, but he also shouldn't allow his anger to scare the shit out of her. Tonight had been bad enough without him becoming another monster for her to deal with. He noticed how she was holding her hands, fingers curled and outstretched, stained and sticky wit blood.

"Come here," he said sharply, trying to contain his aggravatio and only half successful.

She looked up at him, mouth drawn down and eyes glaring. Sh stood up abruptly and walked over to him, looking up at him a though she'd love to hit him as she had the vampire.

He grabbed her wrists and held her hands under the water. Hi own knuckles still dripped blood as he rinsed her hands, lathere them with dish soap, and rinsed them. As soon as the soap wa rinsed, she jerked her hands back and stomped back to the couch throwing herself down into it.

"Don't worry, Violet, I'm alright," he said sarcastically, turnin briefly to look at her.

She felt the sharp sting of guilt. Yes, she should have asked i he was okay, considering he had saved her life, and he was he friend, even if she didn't really know him, apparently. Everythin was so damn confusing. She didn't know how she should b feeling about anything. She reached forward and picked up th remote control and turned the television on and began flippin through the channels blindly. She didn't hear or see anything bu the events replaying themselves in her head. As the scene from th store and the images of her dreams merged it started to make a b of sense to her. She had been having these premonitions fc weeks, before Roman had ever come to town. In truth, she'd ha dreams on and off since she was a child. It was one of the reason she'd always slept with the light on.

He wrapped a dish towel around his bleeding fist and walke towards her, snatching the remote from her hand and turning o1 the television. "No," he said sternly. "You're not going to hid from this now."

He sat down in the chair and leaned back into it lookin absolutely enormous and frightening to her. "So, why are you s angry with me over the vampires? Explain it to me, princess."

She cocked her head to the side, wounded by his tone of voice "Because you kept the truth from me. Roman, I thought we were, don't know, friends. Friends don't lie to each other. I have bee naked in front of you in every way possible and you can't b

272

honest with me about anything."

He felt on the verge of erupting again. No, he hadn't told her anything about his life, but he had not been dishonest. He had always been an honorable person in his life. Everything he had done since coming to this stupid town was for her protection. He had gone above and beyond to protect her, including allowing her into his life at all. Of course he wasn't going to share his history with her, or any knowledge of vampires. To do so was dangerous.

"You're right," he answered, barely able to contain his anger. "I have kept the truth from you."

"No shit, of course I'm right. *Liar.*"

"Let me get this straight, you aren't freaked out by the fact that you were just attacked by vampires? You're angry I didn't tell you they existed before you were attacked by them?"

"It's not just that, Roman. Don't be stupid."

He stood up, pacing behind the chair, then leaned forward, resting his hands on the back, glaring at her. The way his eyes bore into her was unnerving. "I've done everything in my power to protect you from this since the day we fucking met. I saved your life that night by the way. But of course you didn't know that. Those dogs weren't barking at you. They were barking at the vampire that was following you. I wasn't walking you home to be a gentleman, I was keeping you alive."

Her face turned gray. She looked away from him to the floor, not able to bear the weight of his eyes anymore as the reality of what he'd just told her hit her like a ton of bricks. She remembered that night... the feeling of dread and terror that had overtaken her as she ran from the barking dogs that were safely held behind a fence. The dogs that she'd walked by for years, that had never once frightened her previously.

"The last thing I want is for anyone to have to deal with this shit. I saved your life that night, Violet. Not because I really even wanted to, but because I'm supposed to save people from vampires. It's my job. It's the reason I was sent here."

She looked up at him again confused and wounded by what he was telling her. "So, why have you continued to hang around if you don't care? Surely being my friend isn't part of your job requirement?" *Sent here? What the fuck was that about?*

He laughed contemptuously and leaned on the back of the chair "That's a good question. Why do I continue to hang around you I could protect you from afar the way I've always done with other humans. I don't need to be around you to keep you safe. could've watched over you without you ever knowing I exist Why do I hang out with you? You've gotten mad at me before for not having a good enough answer to that question. It's my job."

"So, you really are this detached and hateful? I truly mean absolutely nothing to you?" she asked, hurt by his seeming lack of regard for her and the fact that what she had perceived to be kindness and genuine friendship was really just nothing but bother and some sick sense of duty. She felt her insides collapse She really might throw up now. She covered her mouth and looked down swallowing the bile that rose in her throat.

"Hateful?" That was a new one. He'd never thought of himse as hateful before. "I'm not hateful, Violet, but yes, I really am this detached." He walked back around the chair and sat down. "The truth is I've never had a friend. Period. I've spent the vast majority of my life alone traveling from one place to another, or one random hunt after another, and this is the first time I've ever stopped and cared about another person since the last of my family died. And I have no idea why or how or what purpose this a serves. So, what was I supposed to say to you? Was I supposed to tell you about how my whole family has been dead since I was fifteen years old? And that I've been on this quest to kill vampire since the day I was born, and that it is the main purpose for my existence? Why would I tell you that? Why would I burden you with all of this, after all the other things you've gone through in the short time we've known each other, not to mention all that you suffered prior to my arrival? There was no rational reason to share all of this with you and further put you in danger when once I'm gone none of it will matter anyway."

"Because it's the truth," she answered softly. Her eyes were lost and filled with such grief again, like they'd been that first night when she'd told him about her parents. Hearing him say he was leaving made her feel so sick with the fear of losing him she could barely stand it. She wanted to run away and hide, to leave him before he had a chance to leave her.

He looked down at his feet and drew in a deep breath. He had wanted to tell her a thousand times. For the first time he had wanted someone to share all of this with, to know who he was for just once, and to take some of his burden. How could he have justified adding yet more chaos to her life though? "I wanted to tell you, Violet. For the first time in my life I wanted to tell someone. But how could I?"

"You could've just told me. All I ever wanted from you was honesty. I want to know you, not some illusion. Roman, I knew as soon as I saw those, *monsters*, that every dream I'd ever had was true. I'm not as weak as I seem. I can handle the truth." She couldn't feel weaker at the moment, but it didn't matter. If she didn't really know him, what was the point of living some delusion?

He looked at her finally. Her body was drawn in, her arms wrapping around herself. He felt sick for causing this. "You're going to have to know the whole truth now. I wish you didn't have to, but you've seen too much not to know all of it." He stood up and reached his hand out to her, wanting to feel her hand in his. Maybe there would be some comfort there for both of them.

She stood up and took his hand as he led her to his bedroom. He turned the light on, and gestured for her to sit down on the bed, then he opened the closet door and reached up onto the shelf for a box.

She watched him reaching into the closet. Her head began to swim, heavy, like someone was pressing her temples. She couldn't swallow, couldn't move. The air was sucked from her lungs, held in by some invisible force. What was happening? Panic swept over her.

Roman turned around with a photo album in his hands and stopped when he saw her face. Eyes so wide, mouth open.

"Violet, are you okay?" he asked, setting the book on the bed and kneeling before her.

Her eyes shifted towards his. They were glassy, too wide. "Roman, I'm scared."

He lifted her hands and gripped onto them as her eyes rolled into the back of her head.

"Violet! Violet!" He shook her, trying to bring her back from

whatever spell had taken her over. But she just sat there, perfectl
still, gone.

***

*I am walking down a dirty street. Beggars at my feet, whore
along the buildings. I follow the scent of her. I want her. Where a*
I? A movie I once saw? The one with the gladiator. I look ahead t
where the beauty lies. Tall Cyprus trees in glorious column.
Standing black against the night sky. Not my memories, someon
else's. Who?

I know him. I have always known him.

We walk through the garden, citrus filling the air with suc
sweetness. Such sweetness I have never known. And we slip int
the door. Walk through beautifully muraled rooms. Elegan
Opulent.

She is sleeping. The most beautiful women we have ever seer
He takes me around the bed, admiring the curve of her lush h
rising naked from her slender waist, her back exposed and bathe
in moonlight. We walk around the bed and our breath is stolen t
the swell of her plump breasts. His eyes linger at the junctio
between her thighs, soft dark curls he wants to feel against h
face. Our mouth waters, our tongue wetting our bottom lip. I mal
him look at her face, which he does gladly. Lovingly. I want i
wake her. This is an invasion.

"Shh..." he tells me. "We're going to be one tonight."

My brow furrows. If I could look into his eyes I would kno
him. Who is he? Yes, I know him. He caresses our cheek. His har
is beautiful. Long slender fingers, perfectly manicured nails. I fe
our face and I can tell he is handsome, with long thick hair th
falls down our back...or is it mine?

I can't speak. But he hears me. He knows me, as I know hir
But he doesn't know why I am with him now. Or when I will con
again.

He leans forward, his fingers pushing the thick lustrous wave
back from her face. She is truly beautiful.

"Your twin," he says. "Your sister."

Somehow he turns to look back at me. And yet I don't see his face. But I know he loves me. He knows me. I am his somehow. But not now. Later.

"You better go. I don't want you to see this."

I don't want to go. I want to know what he's going to do to her. My sister. I want to know who he is, how I know him, why I'm here.

"In two thousand years we will find you."

We bend over and kiss her. Her skin so warm, so fragrant. I feel heat coursing through my veins. Pleasure so intense I can barely contain myself. As though my skin is going burst open, my blood molten and burning straight through my flesh.

"Will you stay and watch then?"

I feel the teeth slicing through my gums. I touch my tongue to the tip and blood fills my mouth. We look back at her breasts, her neck. The artery sings. The most beautiful song I have ever heard. And I imagine the sirens calling us to our death.

"No, we are calling her."

She opens her eyes, shocked to see us. And she speaks, but I cannot hear her voice. She is confused, concerned, afraid.

We smile and try to reassure her. He bites into her. His teeth piercing her skin like the flesh of a nectarine, her body writhing against us in ecstasy.

"Go home and wait, little one."

***

Violet's eyes rolled down, her arms pulling Roman against her, crushing him to her. Her breath coming in hard pants as she tried not to break down.

"What happened?" he whispered against her ear. He stroked her hair, holding her head against his shoulder.

"He's coming for me."

"Who is coming for you, Violet?"

"The vampire."

VIOLENT VIOLET

Be sober, be vigilant; because your adversary the devil walks about like a roaring lion, seeking whom he may devour.

1 Peter 5:8 (NKJV)

Please visit the following links and help if you can!

Humane Society
http://www.humanesociety.org/

Juvenile Diabetes Research Fund International
http://www.jdrf.org/

Visit Daniele Serra:
http://www.multigrade.it/

Tara Vanflower/Lycia
amazon.com/author/taravanflower
https://www.facebook.com/LyciaBand/
https://twitter.com/taravanflower
https://www.facebook.com/tara.vanflower
https://myspace.com/taravanflowermusic

ABOUT THE AUTHOR

Tara Vanflower is best known for her work with the darkwave band Lycia. She is currently living in Arizona with her husband Mike and their son Dirk Alrik. She also has two insane little pugapoos and an old cat named Daisy who meows incessantly. Find her online and say hello.

ABOUT THE COVER ARTIST

Daniele Serra is a professional illustrator. His work has been published in Europe, Australia, United States and Japan, and displayed at various exhibits across the U.S. and Europe. He has worked for DC Comics, Image Comics, Cemetery Dance, Weird Tales magazine, PS Publishing and other publications. Winner of the British Fantasy Award.

If you enjoyed this book please share it.

Made in the USA
San Bernardino, CA
04 September 2019